supervisor. With her love of everything medical and
romance, writing for Mills & Boon Medical Romance
is a dream come true.

UNLOCKING THE REBEL'S HEART

ALISON ROBERTS

THE NEUROSURGEON'S UNEXPECTED FAMILY

DEANNE ANDERS

MILLS & BOON

First Published in Great Britain 2021
by Mills & Boon, an imprint of HarperCollins*Publishers*
1 London Bridge Street, London, SE1 9GF

Unlocking the Rebel's Heart © 2021 by Alison Roberts

The Neurosurgeon's Unexpected Family © 2021 by Denise Chavers

ISBN: 978-0-263-29761-4

MIX
Paper from
responsible sources
FSC® C007454

This book is produced from independently certified FSC™ paper
to ensure responsible forest management.
For more information visit www.harpercollins.co.uk/green.

Printed and bound in Spain
by CPI, Barcelona

UNLOCKING THE REBEL'S HEART

ALISON ROBERTS

MILLS & BOON

CHAPTER ONE

THERE WAS NO way to avoid the collision.

Paramedic Benjamin Marshall might have had quite a few years' experience speeding around the rural roads of Central Otago in New Zealand, sometimes pushing his ambulance to the limits on sharp bends, steep hills or even gravel surfaces if he was on the way to an emergency but this time, there was nothing he could do but slam on his brakes and hope for the best when he came around a blind bend to find a car barely off the road, with its driver's door wide open.

Far worse than the horrible thud and screech of metal being mangled as the front bumper of the ambulance tore the door off the car and shunted the whole vehicle forward was the sight of a pair of flailing arms from a person who'd been standing directly in front of the car. Ben got a blurred impression of a slim body, a rope of long, dark hair and arms that were looking oddly graceful as they swam through the air. Arms that vanished at alarming speed as the body disappeared into the deep ditch of a water race that ran along the side of the road as part of the local farm irrigation system.

The shocking thought that he might have just killed someone was foremost in Ben's mind but he couldn't simply jump out of the ambulance to go and find out. He knew, all too well, what could happen if he didn't take the few seconds needed to do something to protect others. He'd seen it happen before. One accident on top of another that had caused totally avoidable fatalities. Slamming his vehicle into reverse, he hit the switch for the beacons before he began moving, to provide a visual warning for anyone else that might be approaching that blind corner. At least any vehicles coming around the bend from the other direction had more than enough room on the other side of the road. Fortunately, the road on this side was still clear and he was able to stop the ambulance, fast enough to skid in the loose gravel on the verge, in a position that could be seen from a distance and would prevent another accident. Ben was already running at the same instant his feet hit the ground as he jumped from the driver's seat. Pushing the car further off the road was an urgent task as well, he noted as he ran past it, but that was nowhere near as imperative as finding out if there was someone drowning in that ditch.

'Hey,' he called loudly. 'Where are you? Are you hurt?'

The silence was ominous. The kind of silence you only got on a road like this, surrounded by farmland for endless miles in every direction, framed by an impressive mountain range in the distance that still had heavily snow-covered peaks in this first month of spring. Ben could hear the tremulous bleating of a newborn lamb that was somewhere close. He could also hear what sounded like a loud sniff of someone who...was crying? Or trying not to, perhaps.

Two more strides and he was on the edge of the water race. The water at the bottom wasn't deep enough to completely cover the sheep that was lying in the ditch but its head was certainly under water and probably had been for some time.

'It's *dead*...' The woman hunched on the edge of the bank rubbed at her nose. 'It was my fault. I killed it.'

'It happens.' Ben crouched in the long grass of the verge beside her. 'The sheep shouldn't have been on the road and it's lucky that you didn't try and swerve which could have put your car into the ditch and killed *you*.' He was looking at her carefully, trying to assess how badly she might have been hurt when she'd been hit by her own car. Or was he making an assumption, here?

'Were you alone in your car?'

She nodded. 'Of course I was.'

Oh? Why was it something that should have been obvious? Was she *always* alone in her car? In her life? Ben blinked away the blip of curiosity.

'Where were you headed?'

It was good to keep her talking. He could see that she wasn't having any trouble breathing. Her colour looked okay and a quick body scan didn't reveal any sign of major blood loss happening. The bottom of her jeans and the ankle boots she was wearing looked soaked, however—as if she'd already been in the ditch to try and help the sheep before climbing out to go back to her car.

Maybe if he'd been a few seconds later, she would

have already driven away from the scene. But he hadn't been later and he couldn't leave this woman to wait until any other help arrived. He still needed assurance that she wasn't injured and that wet clothing meant she was going to need some shelter very soon. The sleeves of the neat fitting jumper were also wet but at least that was woollen and would offer some protection against a breeze that still carried the bite of winter temperatures.

'Cutler's Creek,' she responded. 'I don't think it's that far away.' She turned to look over her shoulder at the crumpled bonnet of the car. At the driver's door that was almost completely detached and was twisted enough to be mostly lying on the grass. She screwed her eyes shut as if she rather not see the evidence of what had just happened. She also let out her breath in an unhappy sigh.

'You're right,' Ben said. 'You're not far away. Not that you'll be going anywhere in that car. Let me check you out and then I'll call for some help.' The relief that he hadn't caused a major injury was wearing off and Ben was starting to feel seriously annoyed that this woman had done something as stupid as creating an obstacle on the road that could have killed someone else. 'Our local cop, Bruce, is a dab hand at sorting stuff like this,' he told her. 'You'd be surprised at how often this kind of thing happens. Especially to tourists.'

'I'm not a tourist.' She had the nerve to sound offended.

'Then maybe you should've known better than to leave your car in the middle of the road.' Ben was quite used to keeping his tone calm no matter how much someone annoyed him. He needed that ability when you couldn't know what else might be going with a patient—like a head injury, perhaps. Or low blood sugar. But this woman didn't look as if her brain function was compromised in any way. She was looking at him as if he was the culprit when it came to doing something stupid. He sucked in a measured breath. 'Nobody coming round that bend had a hope of seeing your car in time to stop safely.'

'I tried to get off the road but I could see there was a ditch. And I had to stop—I'd just *hit* something...'

'And you needed to leave your door wide open as well?'

She looked startled. Ben could see the moment that she realised she'd done something dangerous because she hadn't even thought about any potential repercussions. She looked more than startled, actually. The way her eyes widened and her lips parted made her look horrified.'

'So... Are you injured? Do you have any pain anywhere?'

It only took a blink for her to refocus. 'I'm fine,' she said. 'I don't need checking out.'

'You just got hit by a vehicle.' Ben couldn't resist a verbal nudge. 'Like that sheep.'

'Shunted is a more accurate description. It barely touched me. I just lost my balance and fell into that ditch.' She was looking at the unfortunate sheep again. 'I landed on my feet. I'm fine.'

'I'm a paramedic. It's my job to make sure you're really fine.'

'I'm a doctor,' she flashed back. 'And if I *was* hurt, I could take care of myself.' She was struggling to get to her feet as she spoke and Ben could see her wince in pain as she put weight on her left foot even though she was clearly doing her best not to let it show.

He could also see her face much better now that she had turned. Her eyes were almost as dark as that long braid hanging over her shoulder. So dark, they were making her face look paler. Or maybe that was due to the pain she was obviously in.

'Where's it hurting?'

'It's nothing. Just a bit of a sprain, I expect.'

'You've got X-ray vision, then, Dr…?'

'Hamilton.' The polite response to his query about her name was almost reluctant. 'Joy Hamilton. And you are…?'

'Ben Marshall. Station manager for the local ambulance service.'

She was looking almost disconcerted now which was a bit odd but maybe it was embarrassment instead, as the realisation that she'd done something so stupid was sinking in. Why was she heading for Cutler's Creek anyway? Ben wondered. Was she a friend of one of their local hospital's medical staff?

'You a friend of Liv's?' he asked.

'Who's Liv?'

'Wife of the head of our local hospital, Isaac Cameron. Daughter of the local legend who'd been running the place for decades until Zac arrived. Plastic surgeon. She came from Auckland but if you're on the way to visit her, you're out of luck. She's in Dunedin, what with the baby still being in NICU.'

Dr Hamilton was looking bemused. 'I've never met Liv. Never heard of her.'

'Oh…sorry.' Ben shrugged. 'Guess you look like you belong in a big city.'

She did. Those were obviously designer jeans and expensive boots. She had the points of a white collar sitting neatly on either side of the neckline of her bright red jumper. She looked very neat all over, Ben decided, especially with her hair so tightly plaited. It gave the impression that she belonged somewhere like a library rather than anywhere in a busy hospital. Maybe her doctorate was in something like archaeology. Or philosophy? Not that it was any of his business and besides, he was aware of something else now. He could still hear the bleating of that lamb and the sound was getting louder. Distressed, even.

'I do know Isaac Cameron,' Joy Hamilton said. 'I spoke to him on the phone before I decided to take…' She stopped speaking as she noticed Ben tilting his head, looking for the direction the bleating was coming from. He had to give her credit for the speed with which she cottoned onto exactly what he was thinking.

'Oh…that must have been why that sheep was on the road.' Her brow was suddenly furrowed with deep concern. 'There's a baby here somewhere.'

She turned to start walking along the edge of the ditch. Or rather, limping heavily. It was Ben's turn to frown as he tried to assess how bad that injury to her

lower leg might be but then she turned her head to
glare at him.

'Why are you just standing there?' she demanded.
'Help me look for it.'

There was a sharp pain in her ankle every time she
tried to put weight on it but Joy Hamilton wasn't about
to admit it. Not when Ben the paramedic would probably give her another one of those looks that told her
she was too stupid to be allowed out of a city.

And maybe she was. She'd murdered a sheep. She
hadn't given a thought to any blind bend in the road
behind her as she'd slammed on her brakes after that
horrible thud and…how could she have been thought-
less enough not to make sure her door was shut properly
after she'd jumped out of the car? She *never* did anything without thinking about potential consequences.
She was the most careful person on earth, in fact.

How could she not be when she'd been brought up
having to atone for the fact that her mother had been
the complete opposite? She knew how to tick every
box and to never miss any important details, which
was exactly what made her so good at her job in emergency medicine.

So far, the only real risk Joy Hamilton had ever taken
was to apply for the locum position at a hospital in the
middle of nowhere, here in the South Island. She might
not come from the country's largest city of Auckland
but her hometown was the vibrant capital of the country and, right now, Joy would feel a lot more comfortable walking on an inner city Wellington footpath than

pushing through almost knee high grass on the edge of this isolated road.

That pain in her ankle was getting worse every time she stepped on it so it was quite possible that she did have a fracture but she'd been humiliated enough by the expression in this paramedic's eyes when he'd asked whether she had X-ray vision. A patient kind of expression, with just a hint of amusement, as if he was dealing with a naughty child. Or someone with very limited intelligence.

Very blue eyes, she remembered now. So blue, in fact, that she turned her head as if she wanted to check that her memory wasn't playing tricks on her. He was too far behind her to see properly but she took in the spiky brown hair with its streaks of blond that made him look like he spent a lot of time outdoors in the sunshine. If they weren't hundreds of miles away from a beach, she wouldn't be surprised to learn that he was into surfing. Not that she should be remotely interested in what this man's hobbies might be. The realisation that the station manager for the local ambulance service, who already knew she didn't belong here, was an undeniably gorgeous looking man only made this situation worse.

No…what really made it worse was the way he smiled at her as she looked back.

She knew that kind of smile. The gleam she would have seen in his eyes if she'd been any closer. This was the kind of man who revelled in anything unconventional. Created chaos, even, by an inability or lack of desire to follow rules. The kind of man her grandfather had had absolutely no sympathy for when their exploits resulted in damage to property or loss of life or limbs.

'Should've followed the rules, shouldn't they? They're there for a good reason...'

The kind of man Joy had known to steer very well clear of for her entire life.

A bad boy...

She was definitely getting closer to the lamb, because the bleating was louder, but she couldn't see where it was in this long grass. Then she heard Ben's voice behind her.

'It's in the ditch. Looks like it's stuck in the mud.'

Sure enough, when Joy stepped closer, she could see the small, woolly creature with its legs sunk into the muddy edge of the shallow creek at the bottom of this ditch. It was looking back at her, with black, button eyes and ears that were far too big for it that stuck out sideways and something just melted inside Joy's chest.

'Oh...you poor wee thing.' She slid down the edge of the bank, taking no notice of the way her new Italian boots were disappearing into the mud. She got hold of the lamb and pulled it clear, holding it in her arms as she turned to get back up the bank.

It was then that she realised her injured ankle was highly unlikely to be able to support her weight enough to climb out of the ditch when she couldn't use her hands to help.

'Here...' She held the lamb up. 'You take it.'

Ben's eyebrows rose enough to let Joy know that he was more than a little surprised by her bossy tone.

'Please...' she muttered as an afterthought.

He was grinning broadly as he took the lamb from her arms. He started to turn away but his head swerved as he heard the cry of pain Joy was unable to stifle as she took her first step to climb the bank. He tucked the lamb under one arm and leaned down to offer her his hand.

She had no choice but to take it because the bank was too steep to try and get out on her hands and knees. They both had muddy hands now, thanks to the lamb, which made their skin slippery so Joy had to hold onto Ben's hand with both of hers even as she felt his fingers curl into a firm grip. It was a big hand. Warm. And strong. So strong, she had the impression he could have hauled her out of that ditch in the blink of an eye but he was taking his time and his movements were considered enough to feel oddly gentle.

She had to stand on one leg when she reached level ground. How embarrassing was this? She was covered in mud and her clothes were damp enough to make her shiver in the cold gusts of wind. Far worse than that, however, was that she was going to have to admit that she hadn't been completely honest earlier. She *was* injured and she was going to have to ask for help.

Except she didn't have to ask for anything. Ben put the lamb down on the ground where it promptly collapsed into the long grass.

'Stay there,' he ordered. 'I'll be back soon.'

Stepping forward, as Joy could feel herself wobbling enough that she was about to lose her balance completely, Ben simply scooped her up into his arms and strode back along the road to where he'd parked his ambulance. If his handhold had felt strong and capable, it was nothing to how it felt being in his arms. Joy was fairly slim but she was tall enough to have never felt petite. Until now...

She'd never been swept off her feet and carried like a child by any man. Ever. Her grandfather had had a bad back and hadn't picked up anything heavy. Her boyfriends would have never considered a move like that because she would never have dated them if they had. She was hating this feeling of being helpless, of course, but Joy had to admit there was a rather different reaction beneath the current of what felt like humiliation. A frisson of...what was it?

Pleasure...?

No. That would be unacceptable. It was probably more like relief, perhaps, in that she could temporarily relinquish responsibility and let someone else make decisions and look after her?

Fortunately, the journey was over before such an unwelcome notion could make itself any more pronounced. Ben opened the back doors of the ambulance and flipped the steps down with one hand, climbed inside and put Joy down on a stretcher that had a pristine, white sheet over it.

'Where's it hurting?'

'My ankle.'

'I need to get that boot off. Might need to cut it.'

'*No*...it's brand new.' A hint of something like panic was enough to make her not think about what she was saying. 'You'll ruin the luck.' She ignored his raised eyebrows. 'It's got a zip on the side. Somewhere under that mud. Here… I'll find it.'

'Uh-uh…' Ben pointed to the pillow at the top of the stretcher. 'Lie down. I've got this.' As Joy hesitated he gave her a stern look. 'My truck, my rules,' he said.

And there it was again. An invitation to let someone else look after her and…it was irresistible this time. Joy sank back against the pillow with a shiver, pulled the blanket Ben draped over her up to her shoulders and let him open the zips and ease the boots free from her feet. Her uninjured foot first but she knew he was doing that because it was important, whenever possible, to compare any injured body part with a normal side. It was ridiculous to know that her cheeks were going red because it felt as if she was being undressed for something other than a medical examination.

At least the pain of her injured ankle, especially as he peeled off the damp sock, put this experience firmly back into a professional realm. She could even ignore the extraordinary warmth of his hands against her chilled skin.

'I can't see any obvious deformity,' he told her. 'You've got a good pedal pulse and capillary refill. Can you wiggle your toes?'

She could.

He held her leg with one hand and her foot with the other, putting pressure on in different directions.

'Does this hurt?'

'Yes.'

'How about this?'

'Ouch…'

'Sorry. You've got some bruising coming out already there. I don't think you've broken anything but we won't know until you have an X-ray.' A twitch of his lips suggested that he was tempted but had decided against making a comment about her visual abilities again. 'I'll put a compression bandage on this, elevate it and then take you into Cutler's Creek emergency department.'

With a groan of defeat, Joy closed her eyes. This *so* wasn't the way she had intended arriving at her new position. Then her eyes snapped open again.

'You're not just going to leave that lamb all by itself, are you? With its dead mother in the ditch?'

Ben shook his head. 'Don't worry,' he said. He had ripped off the plastic covering of a crepe bandage and he held the end of it against her ankle as he started unrolling. 'It's all under control. I sent Bruce a message before we went on that lamb hunt.'

'Bruce the…policeman?'

'That's the one.' The bandaging that was happening was well practised and swift. It was also firm enough to already be reducing the pain Joy was aware of.

'What did you mean before?' Ben's tone was casual, as if he was just trying to make conversation while he worked. 'About ruining the luck if I'd cut your boot off?'

Okay…this was embarrassing but he was going to find out before long anyway.

'I always get new shoes for a new job. For luck…'

There was a sharp focus in those blue eyes as they flicked up to meet hers.

'You're heading to Cutler's Creek for a new job? As in…the locum that Zac's been trying to find?'

'That's the one.' It was only after she'd spoken that Joy realised she was echoing both the words and tone of what Ben had just said about Bruce the policeman.

He was silent now, however, as he hooked the crocodile clips in place to fasten the bandage and then ease a pillow under her foot and ankle. It felt as if he didn't know quite what to say about the fact that they would quite possibly be working together in the very near future. Because he wasn't exactly thrilled by the idea?

'Wonder what's holding Bruce up…?' Ben straightened and then turned to peer through one of the small, square windows in the back doors. 'Ah…about time.' He opened the door and raised his voice as he jumped out. 'What took you so long, mate?'

Joy could hear the response.

'I was trying to find someone at home with a tractor who could tow this car off the road. Greg'll be here in a minute but he's not exactly thrilled about cleaning up after another tourist.'

'Ah…' Ben poked his head through the door before pulling it closed and Joy could swear he actually winked at her. 'Be back in a minute,' he told her cheerfully. 'Don't go anywhere.'

As if she could. Joy closed her eyes again and tried to remember why it had seemed a good idea to apply for this new job. Oh, yeah…she'd been fed up, hadn't she? Sick of herself and bemused by yet another relationship disaster which had to win the prize for being the most humiliating.

She was the one who ended relationships—usually because they had become so predictable and unexciting they could only be described as boring—but this time *she* was the one who'd been dumped. By Ian, one of the radiologists in her emergency department, in favour of a ditzy, blonde nurse who was probably ten years younger than Joy. He'd been apologetic when he'd ended things. Kind, even, but his words still rankled.

'You're a lovely woman, Joy. Gorgeous and smart and damn good at your job. But...you've got zero spontaneity. I don't think you've ever taken a risk in your entire life, have you? I'm sorry, but do you even have any idea how...how boring that can get?'

Watching the two of them making eyes at each other when they had all been on the same shift had sparked the disturbing thought that there were aspects of life that were passing Joy by. That, perhaps, she might never actually experience?

Her colleagues had been so astonished when she'd announced she was taking leave because she needed a change of scene that Joy had to wonder if they all thought the same as Ian—that *she* was the most boring person on earth. Had Ian been right? Was she the reason her relationships had always fizzled out?

Well...they wouldn't think she was that boring now, would they? She was creating havoc even before she'd stepped through the door of her new job. So much for those lucky new boots. Her car was written off, she might have broken her ankle, there was a dead sheep that someone would have to deal with and...

And she didn't need to recall that cute little face of an orphaned lamb because the back doors of the ambulance opened again and there it was, peeping out from the crook of Ben's elbow, with its long, skinny legs trailing below.

'Can't leave him for Greg to take back to the farmhouse.' Ben used his free hand to scratch the lamb between those ridiculously large ears. 'Poor little guy seems to have broken its leg.'

The lamb bleated loudly as if to agree. There was something about this tall, capable man holding a vulnerable baby creature that was doing something odd to Joy's gut. Something she wasn't sure she particularly liked because it was rather too distracting but it was impossible to look away.

'X-ray vision, huh?'

Oh, yeah…his eyes were an extraordinary kind of blue. And there was a gleam in their depths that suggested that, even if he might think she was somewhat stupid, he didn't think she was the most boring person on earth. Deep down, Joy had to admit she kind of liked that. It even occurred to her that, seeing as nobody here knew anything about her, she could choose to become a totally different person. And create a completely new, exciting kind of life to go along with that new personality?

'Here, hold onto him.' Ben shoved the lamb at her so Joy had no choice but to take hold of it in her arms. 'I need to find something to use as a splint.'

He was bandaging some folded cardboard around the lamb's front leg a minute or two later when the ambulance doors were opened again. A large man leaned in and put something on the floor.

'Here's the doc's handbag,' he told Ben. 'Thought she

might need her phone and whatnot. I'll get her suitcases out before the car gets towed and bring them in to the hospital.' He caught Joy's gaze then, and smiled at her.

'Welcome to Cutler's Creek,' he said.

Ben's gaze flicked up to meet hers and she could see that he was very well aware of just how much she thought her lucky new footwear had failed to do its job.

'Yeah…' He seemed to be trying not to laugh. 'Welcome to Cutler's Creek, Dr Hamilton. You're going to love it here.'

CHAPTER TWO

'SO...HERE IT IS.' Joy's new boss, Zac Cameron, was smiling as he pulled off the road to park in front of an ancient barn. He gestured towards the small cottage to one side. 'I have very fond memories of living here myself, so I really hope you like it.'

Joy took in the cute weatherboard house with a red, corrugated iron roof and a chimney that meant it had a fireplace. There was a garden bordered by a tall, green hedge between the cottage and barn, an uninterrupted view of those spectacular mountains that were still well snow-capped at the tail end of winter and she'd already noted the lack of any close neighbours.

'I was looking for a change of scene,' she told Zac. 'And this certainly couldn't be more different than my central city apartment in Wellington.'

Joy was aware of a frisson of something like nervousness as she wondered what it would be like in the middle of the night, knowing that there wasn't a single soul nearby. How was she going to cope with that when she'd often felt so lonely living in a crowded apartment block?

Zac came round the car to open the passenger door. 'Come on in. I'll give you a quick guided tour and then leave you to settle in. How's the ankle feeling?'

'It's actually feeling a lot better. Probably because I know it's not fractured.'

The firm bandage was a help as well, as Joy followed Zac to the back door of the cottage. 'See—I'm not even limping that much now.'

'That's great. Back in the day, we'd probably have given you crutches for a while but it's been proven that a low grade sprain will heal faster with early weight bearing. As long as you don't overdo it, of course.'

He lifted a small garden gnome beside the step to reveal a key. 'Not that there's any need to lock up here but you might feel safer at night.'

Zac opened the door that appeared to lead straight into the kitchen. 'Betty, who runs our hospital kitchen and laundry, got the bed made up and she's stocked your fridge with a few essentials.'

'That's very kind of her.'

'And Jill, who's one of our receptionists and is also Doc Donaldson's wife, has been on the phone and found someone who can lend you a car until you get your insurance sorted and a replacement delivered. They'll drop it off tomorrow morning.'

'Wow...' Joy blinked in surprise. 'If I was doing a locum in a city, I expect I'd be lucky to get a hotel recommendation.'

'Small communities have an amazing ability to come together to deal with a crisis of any kind. On the downside, everybody knows everybody else's business but I wouldn't live anywhere else.'

'It's a bonus having accommodation provided. I think that was what persuaded me to take the job.'

'That was the plan.' Zac's nod was satisfied. 'It's hard enough to get anyone to come to a rural hospital for a locum position, let alone consider it as a permanent proposition. We'll have trouble persuading my father-in-law to retire if I don't find someone else.'

'Oh...'

Joy caught her bottom lip between her teeth and took a moment to look around as Zac opened the fridge, perhaps checking on the supplies Betty had provided? There was a black, pot belly stove inside a brick chimney at the end of the room with what was presumably a rack for drying washing hanging above it, a window above the kitchen sink that framed the view of the mountains, well-used-looking pots hanging under a high shelf and an old wooden table and chairs. Realising that this was the absolute opposite of the sleek, modern kitchen in her apartment made it look even more homely. Welcoming, even, but she had to be honest with her new employer.

'I'm not really thinking in terms of a permanent position,' she confessed. 'As I said—I'm just looking for a change of scene, a bit of time out from both where I live and work. I can't commit to longer than the three months we agreed on last week.'

Zac nodded. 'I understand completely.' He pushed the fridge door closed. 'It's not as if Don has any plans to retire any time soon, anyway. I think he's loving going back to full time, to be honest. But you never know. You might just fall in love with—'

He stopped mid-sentence as the back door opened to reveal a large cardboard box being carried inside. Even though the box was hiding the face of whoever was carrying it at that moment, Joy knew who it was as soon as she saw those arms. Ben might have disappeared as soon as he'd delivered her into the care of the Cutler's Creek Hospital staff but he'd left a lasting impression. It was, in fact, disturbingly easy to conjure up the feeling of what it had been like being held in those arms as she'd been carried back to the ambulance. Of having those damp socks peeled off her feet with such care…

Zac was laughing. '…with country life,' he added, quickly to finish his interrupted sentence. 'Hey, Ben. What's in the box? A housewarming present for our new staff member?'

'Something like that.'

The kitchen felt a whole lot smaller all of a sudden. Ben put the box down beside the pot belly stove and it was then that Joy could see what was inside. Curled up on a bed of straw, with its front leg wrapped in one of those sticky firm elastic bandages, was the orphaned lamb she'd pulled out of that muddy ditch.

'Thought you might like some company,' Ben said. 'And that you might like to be the one to look after it seeing as…well…'

'Seeing as I'm the one who murdered its mother?'

Ben's grin widened. 'Let me get this fire going for you. Feels like it could be a frosty night.'

Was he referring to the weather or her tone of voice?

And how on earth was she supposed to know how to look after a newborn lamb? For heaven's sake, Ben knew she was a city girl. Was he doing this to wind her up? Maybe coming here had been a big mistake. And maybe it was that negative thought that made her aware that her ankle was aching again. She pulled out one of the chairs and sat down slowly, all too aware that both men were watching her.

'You should put that foot up,' Ben told her, as he struck a match and held it to the kindling already stacked in the stove. 'Be a good idea to ice it a couple of times a day, too, until the swelling is well down.'

Zac was nodding. 'And remember not to overdo the weight bearing. Avoid any strenuous exercise like running or jumping, even if it is just a mild sprain.'

'No problem there.' Joy's huff of sound was intended to be amused but she didn't dare catch Ben's gaze. 'Jumping isn't something I'm generally known for.'

There was a moment's awkward silence. Perhaps both these men were considering how unsuited Joy was to country life. It was Zac who broke the silence.

'Don't feel bad about any of this.' His smile was sympathetic. 'It's almost a tradition around here to start out with a bit of a bang.'

'What do you mean?'

'The day my wife, Liv, first came to Cutler's Creek, she had a plane crash in a field right beside her. On the same road you had your accident, in fact.'

'Good grief...' Maybe running into a sheep and writing off her car wasn't so bad, after all. 'How many people were involved?'

'Just the pilot.' It was Ben who answered her. 'It was a small plane but it was a pretty exciting case.' He blew into the stove to encourage the flames. 'I still use it as a training exercise for our first responders. Not that I got to do much more than watch the doc and Liv in action.'

'Not true,' Zac put in. 'You were just as much a part of saving his life as we were. It *was* a great job, though, wasn't it?'

'It had everything.' Ben stayed crouched by the stove but turned to grin at Joy. 'A trapped victim, open fracture with significant blood loss, exploding wreckage, intubation needed and the rescue helicopter called in to land right beside us.' He sighed happily. 'Yeah…it was a *great* job.' He turned back to his job of building the fire, reaching for a larger piece of wood in the basket beside the stove.

It was only then that Joy realised she'd been holding her breath as he'd been speaking—caught up in a story she could read between the lines of with that succinct summary. It occurred to her that the survival of the victim had been a bonus. The real satisfaction had been the excitement and adrenaline rush of what sounded like an astonishingly dangerous situation to have been working in. Exploding wreckage? A chopper coming in to land right beside you? Joy had never dealt with anything like that and she didn't want to, either.

Revelling in danger was another 'bad boy' trait, wasn't it? Along with the better-known ones of breaking rules and breaking hearts and not giving a damn because they were just incurably reckless and overconfident, as well.

Joy had to force herself to drag her gaze away from watching what Ben was doing. What was it about men like this that was so inappropriately attractive to women like herself, who would never dream of breaking anything like hearts or rules? Was it because another one of those traits was being passionate? A lover like no other? Joy blew out a breath, soft enough not to attract attention. Okay…maybe they'd *dream* about it. Just occasionally…

She had a horrible feeling that that was exactly what she might be doing later on tonight. Joy closed her eyes for a long blink, just to make sure that neither of these men could see the slightest hint of what she needed to stop thinking about. Right now.

Helpfully, the lamb bleated loudly at that point. Zac started talking at exactly the same time.

'Speaking of Liv, I need to get going,' he said. 'I'm taking Milly and driving up to Dunedin so she can have a couple of hours with Mummy tonight and I can get a cuddle with the mighty Hugo.'

'The mighty Hugo?' Joy was more than willing to talk about something completely unrelated to the man she was having to fight the urge to stare at again.

'Milly's little brother that decided to arrive too early at twenty-nine weeks.' Zac's smile was such a mixture of happiness and worry and pride that Joy could feel the prickle of tears at the back of her eyes. 'He's a wee fighter and he's doing great but he's pretty much the reason you're here. Life's been chaos with the travelling between here and Dunedin and trying to keep the hospital adequately staffed. Thank goodness Liv's dad has been able to increase his part time hours and fill the gaps.'

He turned to Ben. 'Don will be at the hospital to cover any inpatient concerns and I should be back by midnight. I'm hoping you'll be in town for anything out of hospital—or is it date night tonight?'

Date night? It certainly wasn't a surprise to learn that Ben Marshall was not single. It shouldn't have been a disappointment, either, and…it wasn't, Joy told herself firmly. It just meant that she might have to step up to her new responsibilities a little earlier than planned.

But Ben was shaking his head. 'Ingrid's gone back to Germany,' he said. 'I think she got bored with shoving tourists off a bridge.' He caught Joy's expression and he did that ghost of a wink thing, like he had when he'd tried to convey the message that Bruce's comment about tourists wasn't anything to worry about. 'She worked in the bungy jumping business,' he added. 'Great fun and I'd suggest you give it go but you said that jumping isn't your thing, didn't you?'

Unlike his recently departed girlfriend, apparently. Joy ignored the implied unfavourable comparison and focused on Zac.

'I could go back to the hospital,' she offered. 'And be on call?'

Zac shook his head. 'You need to rest,' he told her firmly. 'We can get you up to speed tomorrow and plan a new routine that will take a lot of pressure off all of us.'

The lamb was still bleating. It had managed to get up on its feet and was peering over the edge of the box.

'Yeah, yeah,' Ben said. 'I know.' He was following Zac towards the door. 'I've got the milk powder and bottle stuff from the vet in the truck.' He threw a smile over his shoulder. 'I just wanted to check that you were happy to look after the little guy before I brought in all his luggage.'

He didn't wait for any response from Joy because Zac was calling back to him.

'Can you get hold of Bruce and see what's happened to Joy's bags? She'll need them tonight.'

'I've got them in the truck.' Ben's voice grew fainter. 'Anyone would think I'm a delivery service, not an ambo.'

Joy didn't move from her chair. She couldn't. Not due to any pain in her ankle because that had subsided as soon as she'd taken her weight off it. No...she sat unmoving because she was feeling like a stunned mullet. A fish completely out of water. Here she was, in a tiny, isolated old house, with an orphaned lamb that she had apparently just agreed to look after. And possibly the sexiest man in the world was about to walk back through her door in a matter of seconds and they would be alone. Together. In the middle of nowhere.

If she was that way inclined—which she *wasn't*—it could be the perfect opening scene for a sexual fantasy, couldn't it?

Oh, help... Action of some kind was necessary here. Maybe checking for breaking news would provide some kind of global disaster that would be enough of a distraction. A volcano going off, perhaps. Or an avalanche that had buried dozens of people or an earthquake that was expected to cause a tsunami somewhere. Come to think of it, though, she hadn't heard any 'breaking news' notification signals coming from her phone and a quick glance into her handbag didn't reveal its whereabouts. This was disturbing. Joy never lost anything but was it possible that Bruce the policeman had left something important in her car that was now who knew where?

Another rapid search past packets of tissues, sticking plasters, throat lozenges and a dozen other potentially useful items was fruitless. It was also creating enough anxiety to make Joy upend her bag to spill the contents onto the table. She *needed* her phone. If nothing else, it gave her a sense of connection to the rest of the world and that, in turn, would give her a sense of safety when she was alone in the middle of nowhere with Ben the bad boy paramedic.

The new locum doctor was looking rattled.

Ben raised an eyebrow at the mess on the kitchen table. Who would have thought that someone who looked like she could well be a neat freak would just empty her bag like that? Not that she was looking so neat right now, mind you. There were streaks of dried mud all over those fancy jeans and that expensively soft looking jumper and even on the collar of her shirt. Wisps of shorter hair had come loose from that long braid, too, to curl around the sides of her face and she had bright, pink spots on her cheeks.

Kind of cute, really, despite the fact that she was nothing like the type of women that Ben was attracted to. No… Ingrid had been a perfect example of his type.

Tall, blonde and as much of an adrenaline junkie as he was himself. The trouble with the gorgeous European girls who came to work in the adventure tourism industry here was that they were never around for long. They got homesick or their visas ran out and they went back to the other side of the world. But then again, if he was really honest, that was probably a big part of the attraction in the first place. He knew he had an extremely low boredom threshold.

'Too hot in here?' He put the sack of milk powder on the floor and a plastic jug, stirrer, bottle and teats on the bench.

'No, it's lovely. Unless it's too warm for the lamb?'

'He'll be loving it. When he's a bit bigger you can put him out in the barn.'

'How often does he need to be fed?'

'The vet reckons he's a couple of days old, judging by how dry the umbilical cord is so that's a good thing. He's had some colostrum from his mum so you shouldn't have to be up every two hours during the night or take him into work with you tomorrow to keep up with the feeds.'

Oh…he liked that he could shock her so easily and the way her eyes widened like that. He wasn't sure why he was deliberately making this out to be a bigger deal than it really was. Maybe because she was so obviously out of her comfort zone being in the country? Feeling guilty, he relented.

'Every four to five hours should be fine.' Ben ripped open the bag of milk powder and found the scoop. 'Use this to measure the powder. Let's see…' He read the instructions on the side of the bag. 'It's two hundred grams per litre of water so that's twenty grams to a hundred mils, which is pretty much what this little guy needs at the moment.' He poured a scoop of powder into the bottle. 'That should do the job. Use a bit of hot water to mix it and then dilute with cold so it's about body temperature.'

'Whose body temperature? Mine or the lamb's? And is that a level scoop or a heaped one?'

'Bit over a level scoop, I guess, but that's okay because I'll put in a bit more water. He might drink a hundred and fifty mils.'

'So it's not an exact science, then.' Joy's brow was furrowed, as if this was an alien concept.

'The instructions are on the pack. You need to be careful not to make the milk too rich or you'll end up with a sick lamb.'

The look she was giving him told him that he was not setting the best example in following instructions but even that was kind of cute. It went with that librarian/school teacher vibe she'd given off right from the start. Ben screwed on a teat, shook the bottle to make sure the powder was all dissolved and then led the way to where the lamb was trying to climb out of the cardboard box. He handed the bottle to Joy.

'Give it a go,' he instructed.

She knelt down and offered the bottle to the lamb. Milk dribbled from the teat and the lamb headbutted the bottle, which she dropped instantly.

'Okay…' Ben crouched beside her, leaned over and scooped the lamb up in one hand. 'You behave,' he said. He held the lamb still and, this time, when Joy put the teat near its mouth, it latched on and began sucking greedily.

'Oh...'

The wide eyes this time weren't from shock. It was more like delight and it made Ben smile. He could remember feeding lambs when he was a kid and getting that kind of pleasure out of it.

'Reckon he needs a name,' he said. 'How 'bout Lamb Chops? Or Christmas Dinner?'

The new look he received was withering but it was impressive just how expressive those dark eyes were.

'Shaun,' he offered next. 'As in, you know, the sheep got shorn?'

He hadn't needed to explain. He'd seen the spark of amusement in her eyes as soon as he'd suggested the name. What was entirely unexpected, however, was the soft peal of laughter. And it was a sound that created a not unfamiliar shaft of sensation deep in his gut.

Good grief...he was *attracted* to this woman?

Nah...it was easy to dismiss the thought as completely ridiculous. Even her name was old-fashioned enough to be unappealing. Hadn't his grandmother had a friend called Joy? Oh, yeah...not a friend exactly but an old woman who'd lived down the road and been the biggest gossip in town. She'd had a bad word to say about everyone, that Joy, and a permanent frown on her face that had made the name a bit of a joke.

'See if you can hold the lamb and feed it at the same time,' he said. 'That way you'll know you'll able to cope on your own. Seeing as...you know... I'm not going to be here in the middle of the night.' He couldn't help giving her a bit of a wink, just to tease her. Or maybe he was trying to antagonise her just enough to prove that he wasn't attracted to her in the least. She didn't give him another look, she just took the lamb from his hands, pulled it against the side of her body and continued the feed without missing a beat.

So there... the action said. *You're not needed...*

Fine. 'I'll get your bags out of the truck.' Ben got to his feet. 'It's time I got back to the station.'

He carried the suitcases into the cottage a minute or so later. 'Where would you like these?'

'Just leave them there. I'll sort them later.'

Shaun the lamb had almost finished his feed, his tummy as round as a drum, but Joy was focused on tipping the bottle so he could get the last drops. Ben put the suitcases down beside the table and, as he did so, his gaze landed on the pile of items on the table. There was the usual sort of female stuff, like a lipstick and tissues but a whole lot of foil blister packs, as well.

'You carry a pharmacy in your handbag?'

'I'm supposed to be taking some anti-inflammatories for my ankle. Not that it's any of your business.'

'Fair enough.' But Ben couldn't resist picking up another item. 'Wow...do you need a passport to go between the north and south islands of New Zealand now?'

The wide-eyed look he was getting now was nothing short of alarmed. 'Put that down,' Joy commanded. 'It's private...'

But it was too late. Ben had flipped it open. 'I'm always hoping to see that someone else's passport photo is worse than mine,' he told her. 'It never is, of course, but…'

Joy was on her feet now. She practically dumped Shaun back into his box and moved swiftly across the kitchen, despite her injured ankle, to snatch her passport out of his hands. Ben knew why she was so anxious to get it away from him and it didn't have anything to do with a bad photo.

'Journey?'

She was silent.

'Journey Joy Hamilton.' Ben shook his head. 'I'm not surprised that you go by your middle name, mate. What were your parents thinking? You're far too young to have been conceived at Woodstock. Was it Glastonbury?' He was laughing aloud now. 'Or were they on a retro road trip around Europe in an old VW Kombi?'

'Something like that,' Joy muttered. 'That's how they got killed—driving off the side of a cliff in Italy. I only survived because I was strapped into the baby seat in the back.'

Ben's laughter died instantly. 'Oh, God… I'm so sorry. I…um…really put my foot in it there, didn't I?'

Joy had dropped her passport back into her handbag and now she was scooping up the other items, apart from a phone, and shoving them in, as well.

'Doesn't matter,' she told him. 'It's my fault I've never got round to changing my name by deed poll. I don't even remember them. I was brought up by my father's parents.'

'Really? Well, there you go—we've got something

in common.' Ben was desperate to make up for being what felt like a real jerk. 'I got brought up by my grandmother, too. Along with my mother, when she visited. Never knew my dad.'

Joy didn't seem to be impressed by the connection. 'I'd appreciate you not broadcasting my first name around the district.'

'It will be our little secret,' Ben promised. He headed for the door, needing to escape, but then he turned. 'You know what? I'm not even going to call you by your middle name.'

Hopefully, his smile was another apology. 'See you around, JJ.'

CHAPTER THREE

'You busy, Joy?'

'Not at all. I've just finished the ward round of all three of our current inpatients and I'm writing up my notes. I think Hannah and the twins are ready for discharge later today. Do you want to see them all again first?'

'I'll drop in to say goodbye and wish them luck but not just yet. We've got a patient coming in by ambulance.' Zac smiled at Joy. 'Thought you might like to test out our newly reorganised emergency department?'

'Oh, absolutely...'

Joy returned the smile, abandoning her notes to follow Zac away from the offices that were in the outpatient department, through Reception and into the more clinical areas of the small hospital. It was pleasing to note that, only a few days since her mishap in the ditch, her still-bandaged ankle was taking her weight safely with no more than moderate discomfort.

It was less pleasing to notice a level of anticipation that she couldn't attribute to testing the major reorganisation in the space they used to treat emergency cases that had taken most of a quiet day yesterday. It wasn't that she would be receiving her first patient who was unwell enough to be coming in by ambulance, either. No...while she might not want to admit it, Joy was really hoping that the paramedic bringing this patient in would be Ben Marshall because she hadn't seen him since he'd left her alone with Shaun the lamb.

Only because she wanted to tell him how well the lamb was doing, of course. Joy was proud of herself for how well she was coping with not only getting used to the strange isolation of living in the country but with the added pressure that went with the responsibility of raising an orphaned lamb and keeping up with the feeding schedule. Shaun was clearly thriving, according to the local vet who'd dropped in to introduce himself a couple of days ago and check on how she was doing. What she was a lot less likely to admit, however, was how the small, woolly creature had surprisingly sneaked into a corner of her heart. Maybe it was the anxious bleating that greeted her as soon as Shaun spotted her arrival beside his box, or the pleasure of holding that bottle until the enthusiastic sucking had emptied it. Or perhaps it was the way that the lamb followed her everywhere, as if she was the most important person in the world, until she put it back in its box.

Still in a reorganising mode after work yesterday, she'd cleaned out one of the stalls in the old barn beside her cottage, covering the cobbled floor with a deep layer of clean straw so that Shaun could move out of her tiny kitchen. This morning, heading to work, she'd noticed a stack of old gates behind the barn and wondered if she could make some sort of pen so that the lamb could have time on the grass, as well. She knew she might need a hand to put that together and who better to ask than the person who'd dumped the lamb in her lap in the first place?

It wasn't just an excuse to spend some more time with Ben.

Or was it?

Oh, my... To her consternation, Joy could actually feel her cheeks warming up enough that they would be noticeably pink for some time. Hopefully, the colour would be attributed to her focus on performing well in her new job and not embarrassment that she might have been having some rather explicit and totally inappropriate thoughts about Ben Marshall late at night when a little distraction was needed to prevent the quietness of her solitude dialling itself up from strange to scary.

It would be a good thing if it *was* Ben bringing this patient in. Seeing the real man instead of the fantasy version would probably clear her head instantly. And remind her of why someone like him was absolutely the last kind of man she would want anything to do with in real life. A reality that Joy was not about to let herself get distracted from, especially when she was about to deal with her first emergency case in Cutler's Creek.

They had time to put disposable gowns over their clothes and pull on some gloves before that patient arrived and Joy took pleasure in scanning a room that had been...well...a bit on the chaotic side yesterday. Now there was a logical order and clear labelling to the supplies and equipment and she had to admit she was proud of this, too.

It was a bit of a stretch calling the minor procedures room an emergency department but it was all that Cutler's Creek community hospital had to deal with serious medical or trauma cases and they had everything they needed, including ultrasound, X-ray, ECG and ventilation equipment. Patients that needed more intensive management could be stabilised and then flown by helicopter or taken by ambulance to a larger centre that had the kind of ED Joy was more familiar with.

Two men came in with an elderly man sitting up on the stretcher and, oh, help… Joy could feel the thump in her chest as her heart skipped a beat and then sped up when she recognised Ben. Seeing those blond streaks in that slightly disreputably tousled hair and, worse, having her gaze met by those astonishingly blue eyes made it actually impossible *not* to think about those small but oddly satisfying fantasies she'd been toying with in the last couple of nights.

Fortunately, the temptation lasted no more than a nanosecond but squashing it so relentlessly probably contributed to her ultra-professional expression that made Ben raise an eyebrow. He turned to his partner.

'Mike…you won't have met our new locum doctor, JJ Hamilton, yet.'

'G'day, JJ,' Mike said. 'I'm one of the firies around here but I help out with ambulance shifts on my days off sometimes.'

'And this is Albert Flewellan, eighty-six years old.' Ben was standing at the head of the stretcher and he had a clipboard, with what looked like a patient report form attached to it, in one hand. 'One of our frequent flyers. A neighbour called us because they hadn't seen him out in his veggie garden for a few days and he didn't answer his door when they knocked. He's got acute exacerbation of his COPD due to a chest infection.' A corner of Ben's mouth quirked. 'He's also forgotten where he put his hearing aids.'

He leaned down and raised his voice. 'You've been feeling a bit short of puff for a few days now, haven't you, Albie?'

Albie lifted the nebuliser mask covering his mouth and nose. 'It's Wednesday today, lad... I think... Could be Thursday, mind...'

This casual handover of a patient was like nothing Joy had ever experienced before. Acute exacerbation of COPD could be serious. If oxygen saturation dropped too low, the patient could need to be intubated and put on a ventilator. He might require a bed in an intensive care unit. Although Albert didn't look in any danger of an immediate respiratory arrest, Joy was still going to follow her normal protocol. To do that, she needed more information.

'What was the oxygen saturation on arrival?' she queried. 'And other vital signs?'

Ben glanced at Mike. 'JJ's down from the big smoke so we'll have to be on our game, here, mate.' He didn't bother looking at the clipboard as he cleared his throat. 'On arrival, we found our patient sitting up in bed.' His tone was formal. 'He had a productive cough and was noticeably short of breath with accessory muscle use and an audible wheeze. Temperature was thirty-eight point one, respiratory rate of thirty-six, blood pressure elevated at one-eighty over one-fifteen, in sinus rhythm but tachycardic at one-ten, two to three words per breath and an oxygen saturation of eighty-eight, which is a bit low, even for Albie.'

The summary was succinct and clear. Joy suspected that, if she asked for the next set of vital signs that should have been taken en route, Ben would be able to recite those from memory, as well.

'Thank you,' was all she said, however, as she unhooked her stethoscope from around her neck. 'Let me just have a listen to your chest before we move you onto the bed, Mr Flewellan.'

'Howdy,' Albie said, pulling his mask clear of his face again. 'Are you new around here…?'

'He's responded well to a short-acting bronchodilator and oxygen,' Ben added. 'His oxygen saturation came up to over ninety within five minutes but we transported him because he usually needs a few days' monitoring until the antibiotics and a course of corticosteroids kick in.'

Zac wasn't looking too concerned that a paramedic was outlining a treatment plan for a potential inpatient. He was, in fact, looking rather intently at Joy.

'JJ?' He asked. 'Is that what you prefer to be called, Joy?'

Listening to the wheeze and crackle in the elderly man's lungs gave Joy a perfect excuse not to respond. She didn't want to respond because…actually, yes…she rather liked this new idea of being called by her initials.

It seemed kind of cool. Not something a boring sort of person would prefer. She could also feel her heart sinking. Would Ben remember his promise not to broadcast her unusual first name?

'I suspect it was my idea,' Ben told Zac. 'I've got history with someone called Joy and you know how you can be put off a name? Long story. I'll bore you with it some other time.'

Zac just gave his head a small shake, dismissing the distraction as he saw Joy finish her initial assessment of their patient's breathing. 'Want him on the bed now, JJ?'

A nod was all it took. For both her patient to be transferred and apparently for her new name to be established. Which was fine. New life, new name. Why not? At least all personal distractions were now over and done with and she could focus completely on the job at hand.

She watched as Ben and Mike settled Albie on the bed. Ben raised the end and used an extra pillow as more support to make the task of breathing easier. His movements were swift and efficient as he changed the ECG monitor leads and blood pressure cuff.

'We'll need a chest X-ray to rule out pneumonia, pneumothorax or a pleural effusion,' JJ said crisply. 'Is there any history of congestive heart failure or cardiac arrhythmia?'

'He's on an ACE inhibitor and a diuretic to manage a bit of right heart failure and hypertension,' Zac responded. 'I'll dig out his file for you but, generally, Albie keeps pretty well between episodes like this. Last one was right at the start of winter so it's a few months ago now.'

'You don't need us to hang around any longer, do you?' Ben handed Zac the patient report form but it was Joy he smiled at. 'Unless there's something I can do to help?'

Oh…that smile… For another nanosecond, it was all JJ could think about. Instant warmth, that's what it was. Like sunshine… Fortunately, it only took a single blink to dismiss the distraction. She didn't do distraction when she had a patient to focus on. And she certainly wasn't going to smile back.

'For future reference, I can recommend Ben as a physician's assistant any time you find yourself short-staffed,' Zac told her. 'As far as any emergency intervention goes, you'll find his skills are as good as any colleagues you've had in an ED.'

That was some recommendation and JJ acknowledged it with a nod and just the briefest flick of eye contact. God forbid that it might be taken as encouragement to smile at her again. She could feel herself straightening her spine at the same time. She needed to assert her own place here as well and she was more than comfortable being in charge of a situation such as this.

'I think we could change Mr Flewellan to nasal cannula until he needs another dose of a bronchodilator. He'll be more comfortable breathing that way with a flow of two to four litres per minute.'

'Sure…' Ben turned and walked towards the bench at the side of the room. Then he stopped abruptly. 'Where's the box gone?'

'You'll find them in the Airway cupboard right in front of you. Top shelf, along with other types of masks. You'll also find they're all labelled.' JJ felt another flash of that pride in her achievement of making this area so much more streamlined. In another moment or so, Ben would probably send an admiring glance in her direction. She could actually feel her response to the expected glance starting already—an even more intense glow of pride because it was Ben Marshall she was impressing?

But Ben's jaw actually dropped as he opened the cupboard and scanned the shelves. He looked up to exchange an incredulous glance with Mike, who was folding blankets to put back on the stretcher, and then one with Zac, who simply shrugged and then smiled.

'We'll get used to it,' he said. 'And, I have to say, it all looks a lot more efficient. Almost like a small version of a real ED instead of a minor procedures room trying to be one.'

'Won't be efficient if you can't find something you need in a hurry,' Ben muttered. 'What if we need a cricothyroidotomy kit urgently after a failed intubation?'

'You'll find it in the next cupboard.' JJ's calm tone gave no hint of the disappointment of her not inconsiderable efforts being unappreciated. But then again, this was a good thing. Her hope that replacing a fantasy version of the man with the real one would spell the end of this slightly awkward tension between them was going better than she'd hoped. Clearly, he was not only the sort of man she would never go near on a personal basis, he had a few shortcomings in the professional department, as well.

'The one labelled "Breathing",' she added. 'Middle shelf, along with the chest drain and tracheostomy kits. Circulation supplies like IV kits, syringes, IV fluids are in the next cupboard. It's all organised along the ABC guidelines for primary and secondary surveys that I'm sure you're very familiar with.' JJ knew that the comment was a little condescending but…okay…she was a little annoyed. 'Take a few minutes sometime and you'll see it should be intuitive and easy to find whatever you're looking for.'

'Right…' The syllable was drawn out, which gave it a distinctly dubious note that was even more annoying but Ben found a set of nasal cannula and put them on Albie, gently inserting the prongs into his nose and adjusting the loop to fit securely around his ears. 'You're in expert hands, Albie,' he told him loudly. 'But you'd better make sure you behave yourself.'

Albie seemed to have heard that because he gave Ben a thumbs up signal as he went to help Mike with the stretcher. But then he started coughing and by the time JJ had checked that the figures on the monitor weren't showing a sudden deterioration in his condition and glanced towards the door, Ben had gone. Without any kind of farewell and leaving the unmistakable impression in his wake that he wasn't too thrilled with the changes she'd made here. Or her personality?

Not that she was bothered. It was, in fact, a bonus to add a low level of rudeness to the faults Ben Marshall had already revealed. That she had a mental list of these faults she was only too happy to add to was a bit concerning but she could deal with that without letting it interfere with her new life.

She wasn't going to let anything about the local head paramedic—or possibly the only qualified paramedic in the district—bother her at all.

He had to admit it was bothering him.

For some inexplicable reason, Ben was finding himself thinking about the new doctor in Cutler's Creek far more often than he could find a reason for. Like right now, when he was speeding towards an emergency callout.

She was annoying, that's what it was. A little too neat and tidy, Too organised. Good grief…who labelled spaces on shelves for different types of oxygen masks when you could see what they were through their clear plastic wrapping? Or maybe, if Ben was really honest, the most annoying thing about JJ Hamilton was that she found *him* annoying but she was so determined not to let him get under her skin. She hadn't batted an eyelash at him refusing to use her real name and she'd taken on the challenge of raising that orphaned lamb even though it had to have been a considerable extra stress on top of getting to know a new town and hospital and sorting out a new car.

According to Greg, the local vet Ben and Mike had met at the pub last night, JJ was doing a great job with that lamb that was now living happily in her barn and putting weight on fast. She'd sorted out the insurance on her car in record time and had even made a good choice for a rural vehicle of an SUV with four-wheel drive capabilities. She'd sorted out old Albie Flewellan, as well, and he'd been discharged from hospital with his medications altered and a home oxygen supply available.

Albie, who'd also been back on his favourite bar stool at the pub last night, thought the new doc was the best thing since sliced bread but, for Ben, she gave him the sensation of an itchy patch that you couldn't quite reach and, what was most annoying was that she popped into his head at the strangest moments, like when he saw some new lambs in a paddock as he drove by, or—like now—when he was nearing the scene of an MVA and considering where to stop his ambulance so that it would protect the emergency service personnel as they assessed, treated and transported any victims.

It was only to be expected that he'd be thinking about one of the local doctors, of course, because he was almost surprised not to find Zac or Doc Donaldson or perhaps even JJ there already. This was a priority one callout, which implied that it could be a critical traumatic or medical incident, and the scene was a little closer to the hospital than the ambulance and fire station. The information about the call and its designation as critical would have been sent through to the doctors' phones at the same time he'd been paged.

Not that it mattered that they weren't here. There would soon be more than just himself and his volunteer, first responder colleague, Chris. Bruce was on his way from the police station and they knew Mike was not far behind them, bringing the fire engine and extra volunteers. The initial call about this accident had given them the information that there was someone trapped in the wreckage so the equipment carried on the fire truck that could cut a car into pieces and release the victim could well be vital. Whether additional resources, such as a rescue helicopter, were required was something Ben knew he needed to assess as soon as possible after arrival so it was disturbing to have something else trying to grab some of his attention.

There was another—just as valid—reason that JJ had crossed his mind, however, so the fact that Ben could see her in his mind's eye so damned clearly really wasn't something to be too disturbed about. Like the accident that had written off her car, this was a single vehicle incident, but instead of being on the side of the road, the driver had clearly caught the gravel edge at high speed, gone out of control and flipped, taking out the barbed wire fence and a couple of posts before continuing to roll more than once, by the look of it, to end up on its roof well inside the paddock's boundary.

The only car on the roadside was the person who'd stopped and made the call to the emergency services and, sensibly, had their hazard lights flashing. Rolling down his window, Ben thanked the middle-aged woman and asked if she could stay long enough to be confirmation for the next vehicles that they were on scene. Then he glanced at Chris.

'There should be a gate further down this road. I'd rather drive in so that we've got all our gear handy.'

'I can see it. At the end of that macrocarpa shelter belt between the paddocks.' Chris reached for the radio. 'I'll let Mike know where we are.'

Ben could hear Chris confirming that they'd located the scene but his mind was racing in another direction. Not yet on what he might find in the overturned vehicle but he knew that focus would come the moment he got through the gate and into the paddock.

No...dammit, it was JJ Hamilton he was thinking about. Again. She could have hit the gravel like the driver who'd crashed here if she'd swerved too hard to avoid that sheep. Her car could have been flipped if he'd come round that bend and hit the back of it full on instead of just collecting the door and ripping it off. Ben could see that moment of impact in his mind's eye, like a movie flashback. He could see JJ's body fully airborne and the relief of finding her conscious and relatively unhurt only seconds later.

Oddly, he could also remember that blip of curiosity that went beyond a normal assessment of a potentially injured person. Like how he'd wondered why she'd made it sound as if she was always alone. He could also remember the surprise of his eyes meeting hers that very first time. Because they were so dark? Or was it something more significant, like recognising that she was about to become an annoying presence in his life?

He had a few more seconds as Chris got out of the ambulance and wrestled to pull an old, wire gate through long grass far enough for the ambulance to get into the paddock. His brain was determined to use that tiny amount of time to let one more thought morph with a new one with lightning fast speed—as if it was determined to solve an irritating puzzle by joining the dots in a mental image.

JJ's eyes. How dark they were. The way they'd lit up with delight when she'd been feeding Shaun the lamb that first time. The way it had made him smile. And tease her about a name for the lamb.

The shock of thinking it was possible he was attracted to her.

It felt good to put his foot on the accelerator and bump the ambulance over old tractor ruts in the ground. He was shaking off unwelcome thoughts at the same time.

Of course he wasn't attracted to JJ. Or, if he had been for a nanosecond or two, their last encounter had been more than enough to make any attraction sink as fast as a lead balloon. He liked his women to embrace adventure and the adrenaline rush of the unexpected—just like he did himself. It was obvious that Dr Hamilton compartmentalised her entire life and then probably put labels on the boxes.

And, if that wasn't enough in itself, her real name was Joy, and that reminded him of his grandmother's patience with the old gossip down the road. And that only made him remember his grandmother and feel the ache of loss that the only person who had ever truly loved him was long gone.

It was always best not to think about anything that could pull you down like that and Ben had learned just how to banish thoughts effectively enough to make sure they weren't going to reappear in a hurry. You just needed to keep busy. Keep moving. To embrace any new adventure and that included women, of course. Maybe that annoying niggle he was so aware of was there because he hadn't done anything to fill the gap that Ingrid's departure had left in his life?

Bit of a shame the locum doctor was so not his type. And that she found him so annoying. No chance to get bored or have someone wanting more than he was prepared to offer when they were only in town for a month or three.

He stopped the ambulance just long enough for Chris to clamber back in and then they were off across the paddock. Heading for the unexpected and a potentially challenging job. Ben could feel his adrenaline levels climbing as he prepared for that challenge and he was now completely focused on the only thing that mattered. Throwing himself into a new challenge.

Finding out whether the unfortunate driver of this car was still alive. And then doing whatever it took to keep him that way.

CHAPTER FOUR

AMAZINGLY, THE DRIVER was more than simply alive. He was conscious and alert.

'What's your name?' Ben asked, after introducing himself through the shattered window. While he could see that the young man was upside down and clearly uncomfortable with his head pressed onto the back of a mangled seat, amongst deflated airbags, he was breathing reasonably well and looked alert enough for Ben to think there might be no need to summon backup with extra skills and equipment to deal with critical injuries.

'Nathan.'

'Does it hurt when you breathe?' Reaching through the window, Ben put his fingers on Nathan's wrist, to feel for his heart rate and rhythm.

'Nah…it's all good…'

'Were you knocked out?'

'Dunno…'

'Can you remember what happened?'

'Guess so…it was all a bit quick.'

'Anything else hurting?'

'My leg, man… I can't move it.'

Ben shone his torch up into the interior of the vehicle, to the floor that was currently the roof. 'That's because it's caught under the dash.' The light caught a blood stain on Nathan's jeans but, again, it didn't look enough of an ongoing blood loss to be alarming. 'We're going to need some help from the firies to get you out of here, mate.' He looked over his shoulder to see the fire truck currently negotiating its way past the larger rocks in this paddock.

Nathan groaned. 'I've wrecked my car, haven't I? And I've only…had it for…a week or two.'

The increasing effort of breathing upside down was obvious. So was something else that Ben could smell on the young man's breath.

'You've been drinking, mate?'

'Nah…not since last night. Never…drink and drive…'

Ben caught his Mike's gaze as the older man walked around the car, assessing how they were going to get their patient out. The erroneous notion that you could party hard until the early hours and then get up and be sober enough to drive safely wasn't uncommon.

'You weren't wearing your safety belt, either, were you?'

Nathan closed his eyes. 'I forgot… You're not going to…give me a hard time, are you?'

'Let's get you out of here. You can talk to Bruce about that one later.' Ben unzipped the pack of gear he had beside him. 'We're going to see if we can get a collar on you to protect your neck and then Chris, here, is going to give you an oxygen mask, because it's a bit difficult breathing upside down, isn't it?'

Nathan was groaning again. 'My leg…it's *really* hurting…'

'On a scale of zero to ten, zero being no pain at all and ten being the worst you can imagine, what score would you give it?'

'Eleven…no…*ahh*…make that a twelve.'

'That bad, huh? I'm going to put a line in your arm as soon as I can,' Ben told him. 'And then I can give you something for the pain, okay?'

'Yeah…that'd be good…'

The car jerked as Mike wrenched a door on the other side of the car. 'I've got this one open enough,' he told Ben. 'Can you work on him from this side while we get that other door off so we can roll that dash back?'

'Sure thing.'

'Right.' Mike turned to the volunteer fire officers he had with him. 'Let's get some chocks in to stabilise the car and then I'll need the spreaders.'

It was more than awkward to squeeze far enough into the car's interior to get a cervical collar onto Nathan and there wasn't enough space to make it simple to get an IV line inserted into his arm. Ben's first attempt to find a vein was unsuccessful. The second failed because, as he started to push the cannula into place, the screech of metal being prised open made Nathan jerk his arm clear.

'Try and hold still for me, mate,' Ben said calmly. 'It's going to be a bit noisy because we have to cut the car up to get you out. Chris, can you give me a dot to cover this and another cannula, please?'

He had to make a third attempt. IV access wasn't

important just for the pain relief that Nathan needed. Ben wanted a line available and fluid to keep it open in case his condition deteriorated. He could see the blood stain on the jeans spreading and he had no idea what was happening to the lower part of Nathan's leg that was hidden behind the squashed dashboard. How long it would take to get him clear was also unknown and if there was significant, ongoing blood loss, the longer it took to get venous access the harder it would get as blood pressure dropped and veins shrank.

The team around him might be mostly volunteers rather than paid employees like himself and Mike but these men—and women—were passionate about the contribution they made to their community by keeping the emergency services viable. They took on as much training as they were offered to learn and practise techniques and protocols and Ben was proud of their skills and commitment. The door of this wrecked car was cut free, the crushed dashboard rolled back enough to release Nathan's leg and then as many sets of leather gloved hands that could get close enough got him onto a hard backboard and gently slid him clear of the car and onto the waiting stretcher.

'Hang on...' Ben warned. 'Watch out for the tubing.'

His warning came too late. While he was holding the bag of IV fluid well out of the way as Nathan was being lifted out, the tubing snagged on a rough piece of metal. While he'd taped the tubing in place, he hadn't had time to put a bandage over it as well and it didn't take much of a jerk to pull the tape off Nathan's arm and then the cannula out of his vein. But the amount of blood that was being lost from that puncture wound was not as much of a concern as the bleeding from their patient's leg that had increased dramatically having been freed from beneath the dashboard. The sheet on the stretcher was getting rapidly soaked and Ben's white shirt had blood smears in several places.

'Put a pressure dot on that arm,' Ben instructed Chris. 'I'll deal with his leg.'

'Can I help?' Mike was right beside him.

Ben was using his shears to cut away what was left of Nathan's jeans on this side. 'I need a large gauze pad,' he told Mike. 'And then a couple of bandages. I'll have to try and control this bleeding with pressure.'

It was just as well he'd had time to give Nathan some IV pain relief because he could feel the crunch of a broken bone as he put enough pressure on the deep cut to stop the blood loss. It was still painful enough to make his patient cry out, however, and there was no quick way to top up the analgesic.

'Do you want the IV roll?' Chris asked, as he put another round, sticky dot over the puncture wound on Nathan's arm. 'To get a new line in?'

Ben wrapped a bandage as tightly as he could to keep pressure on the leg wound.

'No,' he responded. 'Grab a splint. I'll stay in the back and keep an eye out for breakthrough bleeding but we're close enough to the hospital and it'll be easier to sort everything there.' Ben had to shake away the thought that it would give JJ a chance to show off her newly organised emergency department again.

'Let's load and go,' he told Chris, as soon as he'd secured the splint as well as his pressure bandage.

'I feel sick…' Nathan was looking pale.

It was Mike who reached for a container and a towel but he was too late. He gave Ben a sympathetic glance as they loaded and secured the stretcher in the ambulance.

'Don't breathe too deeply,' he murmured. 'It might put you over the limit.'

Slamming the doors shut as they took off only intensified the smell in the back of the ambulance but it wasn't anything Ben hadn't already dealt with too many times to count. JJ might find it a bit more confronting, he thought as they got closer to Cutler's Creek Hospital. It wasn't as if they had a team of nursing and ancillary staff to deal with messy stuff like this.

To her credit, however, JJ did not appear fazed by either the smell or the appearance of her new patient when they arrived a few minutes later. She watched intently as Ben and Chris transferred Nathan to the bed and listened, just as carefully, to their handover.

'Nathan Brown, twenty-one years old. His car came off the road at speed, rolled and ended up on its roof with Nathan trapped. He had a GCS of fifteen on arrival, probably wasn't KO'd and doesn't appear to have a head injury.' Ben had to pause and take a breath before he listed vital signs that had all, surprisingly, been within normal limits. 'It took approximately twenty-five minutes to get him out,' he finished, as he tucked a pillow beneath Nathan's head. 'He's had five milligrams of morphine for the pain from that fractured tib/fib.'

'How's the pain level now?' JJ asked, stepping closer to Nathan. 'On a scale of zero to ten?'

'Ten,' Nathan told her.

The look Ben received suggested that he hadn't provided enough pain relief for his patient.

'To be fair,' he said, 'Nathan did say it was twelve initially, so it's improved.'

He noticed that JJ was checking the monitor and knew that she would be thinking that the heart rate and general appearance of this patient did not back up his claim that he was in severe pain and, if anything, his blood pressure was lower than might be expected. He also noticed the way her nose wrinkled, just a little, as she took in a new breath.

It was a very subtle admission of how bad Nathan smelled with that combination of stale alcohol and vomit. A tiny, rabbit-like twitch. Cute, Ben found himself thinking instantly, until he realised that this might be another impression of this woman that would pop into his head at unexpected moments and add to that background level of annoyance she was causing. Not that she noticed his frown, because she had turned to the nurse in the room with them, Debbie, who had shears in her hand, ready to cut away the remnants of Nathan's jeans.

'Maybe you could find a gown for Nathan soon? That way we could…ah…dispose of his clothing?'

Her attention was on the monitor again. 'Blood pressure's a bit on the low side of normal,' she murmured. Her next glance was back at the stained sheet of the stretcher but quickly shifted to Ben. 'Estimated blood loss?'

'Hard to say.' Even a small amount of blood could look like a lot when it was spread around and wicked into fabric. 'Less than five hundred mils, I'd guess.'

But Ben was getting another look that he could read only too easily. Strike two for his patient care? Was she thinking she might want to see their SOPS—standard operating procedures—with reference to controlling haemorrhage on scene? Maybe she had no real understanding of how difficult it could be to control external blood loss when you couldn't actually reach the body part that was bleeding? Or when it took time to remove a victim from wreckage so that you could get close enough to do something like put pressure on a laceration?

That look was no more than a brief glance but it also made Ben suddenly aware of how scruffy he must look, as well, with his bloodstained shirt and it was quite likely he didn't smell so great himself. But it went with the job, didn't it? And he knew he did his job damned well. He certainly didn't need someone giving him a school teacherish look that suggested he could have done better. Ben was officially annoyed now but there were no surprises there, were there? This was Dr Journey Joy Hamilton, after all. Big city girl with a dose of prim and proper and an addiction to protocols.

'We did have a patent IV line and fluids up,' he said, keeping his tone perfectly even. 'Unfortunately the line got caught as we were extricating Nathan from the car. I didn't want to hang around to put another one in.'

He didn't need to add that it had taken more than one attempt to get an IV in in the first place. He could see JJ noting the sticky spots covering the puncture sites before she wrapped a tourniquet around his other arm. Her slick insertion of a cannula, the snap of the tourniquet being released and the tape being torn off to secure the new line was impressively efficient but it felt like another judgement of his skills. Even attaching the tubing and the bag of IV fluid was swift and professional. Of course it was. They were in a controlled environment and everything was far simpler—including the availability of the two-way stopcock in the tubing as a painless way to remove a blood sample or inject medications when needed. The way JJ's gaze grazed his as she moved on was really an unnecessary confirmation of that judgement.

See? It seemed to say. *This is how it should be done. Easy-peasy...*

'There we go, Nathan. I'm going to top up your pain relief a bit while we have a good look at your leg. If it's anything more than a simple fracture, though, we'll have to transfer you to a bigger hospital.'

She'd have to ask Ben what the protocol was for a transfer like that, JJ realised, because it wasn't something she'd talked about in any detail to Zac yet and he wasn't here today. Ben didn't seem that happy to be here today, either, for some reason. He'd been almost glaring at her as she'd finished setting up the bag of IV fluid. Was he bothered that she was replacing the IV line that had been pulled out?

If so, he needed to get over himself. It wasn't a criticism of his work, she was just getting on with what needed to be done. And one of those things was collecting a blood sample. It was quite obvious that this young man had been drinking heavily and, no doubt, Bruce the local cop would want to know the level of intoxication.

Was he annoyed because he was just standing there and watching her work when he could have been more usefully employed by replacing that IV line himself? His colleague was almost finished tidying up the stretcher so it was quite possible that he would head out the door any moment, perhaps without even saying goodbye again? JJ didn't want that to happen. She was the only doctor in the hospital at the moment and, while she could manage on her own if she had to, she'd would much prefer to have Ben's assistance to take X-rays and organise a patient transfer if it was needed.

At least she could give credit where it was due when she took the pressure bandage off Nathan's leg.

'Great haemorrhage control,' she told him. 'That's a deep laceration and it's not even oozing now.'

'You going to suture it?'

'That'll depend on the X-rays. If surgery's needed, there's no point. We can just get another clean dressing on and make sure it's splinted well enough for transport.' She offered Ben a bit of a smile. 'I'll rely on your expertise for that.'

The quirk of Ben's eyebrow suggested that her attempt to defuse that hint of background tension between them had failed. Maybe a direct appeal would work better.

'Can you stay to help with the X-rays?'

There was no hesitation on Ben's part. If anything, JJ could see a flash of concern in his expression. 'Are you and Debbie on your own at the moment?'

'Yes… I persuaded Don to go with Zac to Dunedin to see Liv and the baby. I assured them both I'd be able to cope with anything.'

'Ah…so that's why you didn't respond to the message about this accident?'

JJ blinked. 'I thought it was just alerting me to an incoming patient. Was I expected to turn up at the scene?'

'Zac always does, if he's not in the middle of something here. Doc Donaldson, too. Especially if I'm not on duty or it's a priority one callout where there's the possibility of critical injuries or illness.'

It felt like Ben was criticising her now, which seemed unfair. 'I *was* in the middle of something, actually. A bit of minor surgery.'

Debbie looked up from her recording of a new set of vital signs for Nathan and grinned at Ben. 'A nail trephination,' she told him. 'Old Harvey White's really got to stop carrying bricks around. He dropped another one on his toe yesterday and he couldn't even walk because of the pain today.'

'No way…' The way Ben smiled back at Debbie and the feeling that they both knew far more than she did about her patient made JJ feel distinctly left out and she felt a pang of something she didn't like. Envy, perhaps, of feeling like she really belonged somewhere like these two seemed to have? Or that connection when things could be said without actually saying anything aloud?

Ben's smile was fading as he turned back to JJ but she could see a gleam of amusement still in his eyes. Was he mocking her because she chosen not to respond to a potentially life-threatening situation outside the hospital in order to drill a hole in a toenail to relieve pain?

'What did you use?' he asked. 'A needle or a paperclip?'

Ignoring the query made her tone a lot crisper than she might have intended. 'Let's get on with these X-rays, shall we?'

The images of the complicated fracture involving both the bones of Nathan's lower leg made it obvious an expert orthopaedic opinion would be needed.

'What's the normal protocol for transferring a patient?' JJ asked, a short time later, as she and Ben both stood looking at the illuminated images with Nathan drowsing on the bed behind them.

'If the patient is status one or two, we call in the air rescue service,' Ben responded. 'The helicopter can land in the hospital grounds. If it's not critical, we transfer by road. Usually we can get an ambulance dispatched from either Dunedin or Invercargill and meet them halfway.' He paused for a moment, his gaze level—as if he was about to impart significant information. 'They're both around three hours' drive from Cutler's Creek so that means our ambulance is unavailable locally for at least ninety minutes.'

JJ nodded. It was obvious that calling a helicopter in to transport Nathan would be a waste of valuable resources but…oh…was he was warning her that she would be responsible for any out-of-hospital emergencies while he was gone?

She was about to tell him that wouldn't be a problem. Zac had showed her where the emergency kit was kept so she could put it into her car now, just in case. She could take the defibrillator from the procedures room when or if she got a call. But it was Ben who spoke again before she had a chance to say anything.

'We've got a backup transport vehicle—our old ambulance. I can call on a volunteer to do the driving. Nathan's stable enough not to need a medical escort.'

JJ stared at him. 'Because you don't think I could cope?'

'Have you ever been out with an ambulance crew?'

'Why should that make a difference? I am an emergency trauma specialist. I'm trained to deal with anything.'

'In a big city ED, sure. Where it's relatively easy to work your way through a flow chart protocol and follow every rule. Or even in a minor procedures set-up like this one that's got everything available and *labelled*.'

Okay…that was a direct jab. But he wasn't finished yet. 'You might find things a bit more challenging if you're trying to put IV lines into upside down people and working in conditions like crawling around inside a wrecked car,' he told her. 'Especially in a rural environment when specialised backup might be too far away to rely on. You might even find that it's not easy to control haemorrhage and your patient might lose a bit more blood than you're happy with.'

Had Ben felt he was being criticised when she'd

asked for an estimation of blood loss? Was he also trying to tell her that he didn't think she belonged in Cutler's Creek? Or was he throwing another challenge at her—like leaving her with an orphaned lamb and a sack of milk powder? Not that it mattered, it was just a bit weird how strongly JJ felt she needed to prove herself to this man.

No…maybe it was just that she needed to prove herself, full stop. To demonstrate that she was capable of embracing new challenges. That she didn't fit neatly into some labelled box, perhaps, which could always come across as being unimaginative or dull. Boring, even…

'That's exactly what you *should* do,' Ben concluded.

'What is?'

'Find out. Get out of your comfort zone. Come out on the road with us for the next priority one call or you could just join one of our training sessions in the meantime. If you're up for it, that is.'

Yep. This was a challenge being issued, all right. And JJ was definitely up for it.

'I'm in,' she said. 'For whatever comes first. As long as I'm available, of course.'

He didn't have to say anything. She could see the warning that dealing with something as minor as a painful toenail would not be a legitimate excuse. But there was humour in the look as well and JJ was quite sure he could read her silent acceptance of the message that was also an apology. For a heartbeat, it felt like there was a level of the kind of understanding that formed a palpable connection. That they were about to share a smile. To place the foundation stones of a genuine friendship, even?

Maybe that was disconcerting for them both, which might explain why they both turned away at exactly the same moment.

'Just be prepared for anything,' Ben said. 'You might have to use every bit of that training of yours.'

CHAPTER FIVE

HER TRAINING CLEARLY hadn't included anything like this.

And perhaps climbing the foothills of mountains wasn't something JJ Hamilton had ever chosen as something she wanted to do in her time away from work. She looked like she was struggling with this steep ascent, that's for sure. She'd been out of breath even before they'd reached this rugged part of the track that required some clambering over large rocks and Ben could see how much effort it was taking to cling onto a smooth boulder and haul herself up to the next foothold.

She also looked as if she was going to push herself as hard as it took, despite the fact she was still recovering from that sprained ankle and Ben didn't want to end up with two patients to carry back down the slope. He held out his hand as she reached further up the rock, sliding it beneath and curling it around hers before she had the chance to refuse his offer of assistance.

Her grip was surprisingly strong as she returned the pressure and it was no hardship to pull her up to his level. She felt as light as a feather, in fact, probably because she was also pushing hard herself with her legs.

The ease and speed with which she arrived beside him was enough to put her unexpectedly close to Ben. So close that he could feel the puff of her trying to catch her breath on his own face and he could clearly read the surprise in dark eyes that were only inches from his. It had also been so fast that he hadn't quite let go of her hand yet and, despite the fact that they were both wearing protective gloves, he could feel the shape of her hand and even the warmth of it, as if they both had bare skin.

It wasn't just warmth. There was a heat there that had absolutely nothing to do with body temperature. Shocked, Ben released his grip on her hand. He had to resist the urge to rub his own hand on something to try and get rid of the sensation that now seemed to be racing up his arm and into the rest of his body. He was also finding it hard to break that eye contact.

'You good down there?' Mike and other members of the Cutler's Creek mountain search and rescue team were already out of sight above the rocks on this well-known track.

How long had they been standing here like this? Surely not more than a few seconds, but JJ's breathing was a lot less ragged so maybe it had been longer.

Too long…

'Come on…' There was relief to be found in breaking that eye contact. 'We don't want to get left too far behind.' He knew he could speed up now that they'd negotiated the scramble over boulders and there was a good trail to follow. 'I use this Twin Rocks track as both training and a fitness test for anyone who wants to come onboard as an emergency services volunteer,' he explained, as they picked up their pace. 'I've found that the people who get fit enough to do this track easily have what it takes to cope with just about anything that gets thrown at them unexpectedly. Not a good look if I'm last.'

He couldn't help just another quick glance over his shoulder but that was only professional concern. He had to make sure JJ was going to safely manage this last section of the challenging track.

That look of sheer determination in the face of a task that had to be pushing her to her physical limits was actually quite impressive. It didn't really matter if he came in last, did it? The other members of his team would know he was just taking care of the new doctor who'd put her hand up to join this training session.

Ben slowed his steps. Not enough to make it obvious he was trying to make it a bit easier for JJ. He was just adjusting the pace to make sure she didn't collapse or something. He didn't want to break that determination, either, because he knew how important it could be. He also knew that a city girl's level of fitness was unlikely to be honed for an outdoor challenge like this so he turned his head just far enough to offer a half-smile.

'You're doing great,' he muttered.

Doing great?

JJ was dying here. Her face felt like it was on fire, which could explain why her lungs were burning so painfully. Her heart was thumping and she had trickles of perspiration making her back itch. The muscles in her legs were about to give up completely and her ankle, although it was well strapped, was aching more than it had in the week since she'd made that pact to either go on a priority one callout or join one of Ben Marshall's training sessions that Zac had warned her were legendary.

'You'll certainly see how fit you are,' he'd said with a grin. *'Unless you die first.'*

And…to add insult to injury, Ben had just done it again—acted like he really, *really* didn't like her. He'd offered her his hand and helped her over a boulder that would probably have been too much for her aching body but then it had been like he'd suddenly noticed it was her hand he was holding and he'd dropped it like it was burning him. He'd been looking at her, too, kind of like after they'd been talking about transferring Nathan with his badly broken leg. When she'd almost believed that there was a real connection between them and that they could end up being good friends.

Ha… That wasn't going to happen, was it? The best JJ could hope for was that she could prove she was good enough for these Cutler's Creek locals to give her a chance to feel like she was accepted here. That she could belong. If she wanted to, that is. And maybe that was the crux of this challenge. JJ wanted to prove that she could be whoever she wanted to be. She was only thirty-five years old. Surely she wasn't too old or set in her ways to choose a path that could change her life for the better?

'Hey…' It was Mike the firie who started the applause as JJ and Ben finally caught up with the small group standing under what appeared to be a rather dramatic cliff as they busied themselves getting into harnesses and sorting ropes. 'Go you, Doc. First time is always the hardest.'

JJ had no breath to respond but she couldn't help a smile that felt like the widest she'd ever had. Ear to ear, that's what it was.

Pride…

'So, this is Twin Rocks.' Ben wasn't looking at JJ as he waved an arm towards the cliff but it was clear that she was the only one who needed this information.

'It's really one rock face but it looks like two separate cliffs because of that deep gap in the middle. A hundred and fifty metres of rock wall that's been well set up with permanent bolts to rappel from and varying degrees of difficulty depending on which section you choose.' He still wasn't looking at JJ. 'People come from all over the country to abseil here so it's not that uncommon to get a call to someone who's injured themselves and they may well be stuck on the wall somewhere. That's why just getting here might not be enough to save them.'

He turned to JJ and she could see he was perfectly serious. The huge effort she'd just put into getting this far up the mountain wasn't all that was expected of her.

'Abseiling is a skill we use quite a lot. It might be a climber up here or a car that's gone off the road in the gorge that leads into Cutler's Creek. Sometimes it's not possible to get a chopper in to winch someone down in time so it's up to us. We've got to get to a patient, stabilise them and then carry them out somehow.'

JJ nodded. It made sense. Her respect for what

Ben did in his line of work had just gone up too many notches to count. That there were members of the community here prepared to train and then risk their lives to help in difficult rescues was also impressive enough to take her breath away.

'This is just one of our regular training sessions to keep our skill sets sharp,' Ben continued. 'All these guys have done their basic abseiling training so you've got a bit of catching up to do. Let's take the track that gets us up to the top and then I'll throw a harness on you and you can give it a go.'

This training session for the mountain search and rescue group had been astonishingly challenging so far but it hadn't been terrifying. Until now. Not that she was going to let Ben see how much she wanted to turn around and get back down that track as fast as possible. There had to be an inspirational saying she could benefit from right now. 'No guts, no glory' perhaps? Or 'Feel the fear and do it anyway'?

She could do that.

Maybe…

It was like a point of no return and she was ready to take that step but then she saw the quirk of Ben's lips. A beat later, there was a ripple of laughter through the group.

'That's Ben's little joke,' Mike told her. 'Don't worry. You'll do your abseiling training somewhere else.'

Ben was nodding. 'And it won't be when you're already stuffed from walking five kilometres up a steep hill.'

'I would have given it a go,' JJ said quietly.

'I know.'

Good grief, was that a flash of something like admiration she could see in his eyes?

'What I will ask you to do, if you're up for it, is to be a patient for us. See that ledge up there?' Ben pointed towards an overhang that was only a few metres off ground level. 'We'll set you up with a helmet and a harness and just get you to sit on the ledge. The rest of us will pretend you're actually further up the cliff, go to the top and plan how we're going to get you off the ledge safely, assess your injuries and then get you down the track to where the ambulance will be waiting in that roadside parking area.'

It sounded like JJ could actually be a useful participant in the training session, despite being tired and sore and having probably slowed the session down already, and she was more than willing to play her part.

'What are my injuries going to be?'

'Oh…let's see…' There was another smile hovering around Ben's mouth. 'How 'bout we make it an injured ankle? A bad sprain? No…a fracture.'

'Am I conscious?'

'Yep. You're in a lot a lot of pain and you're cold. You've been sitting on that ledge for a few hours waiting for help, and the weather's closing in, which is why they couldn't send a chopper to rescue you.'

'Past medical history?'

'You're young,' Ben told her. 'And perfectly healthy.'

'Okay. One more question…'

'Shoot.'

'How do I get up onto that ledge without *really* breaking my ankle?'

'Come with me.' Ben started moving closer to the cliff, turning to speak to Mike as he passed the group. 'Take everybody up the track,' he said, 'and get sorted with your ropes and knots. I'll be there in a couple of minutes. This will be more authentic if you don't see exactly where JJ's going to be.'

By the time JJ reached the almost vertical wall of rock, the rest of the group had already vanished up another steep track to one side of the cliff. It felt like she was completely alone with Ben, who had pulled some items from what was left of the pile of equipment the team had carried to the scene.

'One harness.' He held it up to show JJ. 'This is so your rescuer can clip you to his or her harness to make sure you're kept safe.'

JJ nodded. 'Safe is good.'

Being safe while being lifted from a rock ledge was the least of her immediate worries, however, because Ben was standing close enough to her to be causing some odd ripples of sensation in her gut.

'Three loops. One for your waist and one for each leg.' Ben gave the harness a shake. 'We don't want anything twisted.' He was crouching as he spoke. 'Put your left leg in this loop.'

It was easy enough to put all her weight on her un-injured ankle to poke her foot through the loop but JJ had no choice but to hold onto Ben's shoulder when she needed to lift the other foot. She could feel her cheeks reddening even before he began to slide the loops up her thighs.

'I can do that.'

'Take them right up. High as you can. They're elasticised so they shouldn't be either too tight or too loose.' Ben straightened up to take the ends of the waist band and thread a strap through the central buckle. He pulled it tight but then put a fingertip beneath the belt and ran it across her belly.

Dear Lord…that sensation in JJ's gut felt like a trail of small flames.

'Most important thing is to make sure that this band sits over the top of your hip bones,' Ben said. 'That way, you'll still be safe even if you get tipped upside down.'

JJ already felt as if something was being tipped upside down. She didn't dare look directly at Ben as he secured the strap by threading it through a second part of the buckle and then ducked to find her a helmet. She jammed it onto her head but then fumbled with the fastening beneath her chin.

'Here…let me.'

JJ closed her eyes as she lifted her chin. She could feel the brush of Ben's fingers on the delicate area of skin beneath her jaw bones that she'd never thought of as an erogenous zone. Until now…

She opened her eyes when she heard the buckle click shut, knowing that Ben had finished his task. The last thing she expected was that he wasn't moving away. He was staring at her and, for a moment that seemed long enough for time to have stopped, JJ was convinced he could read her thoughts.

That he knew all too well that the only thing she was thinking about was being kissed. By *him*... That, for a split second, it was possibly something she wanted more than she'd ever wanted anything else in her life.

It might have happened, too, if a two-way radio Ben had clipped to his belt hadn't crackled into life.

'We're all set, boss.' It sounded like Mike's voice. 'You planning on coming up any time soon?'

Ben didn't break his eye contact with JJ until he had the radio in his hand when it seemed like pressing the talk button flicked another switch at the same time.

'Just need to position our patient,' he radioed back. 'Do a check on everybody's harness and the Prusik loops they've used to attach their ropes. Don't let anybody go over the edge till I get up there, though.'

'Roger that.'

'Come on.' Ben jerked his head but didn't look back at JJ as he led her to where she needed to scramble up onto the ledge.

Those flames in her belly were becoming something rather more solid now, she realised as she followed Ben. Fear, perhaps?

Or was it the knowledge that an inappropriate attraction that she'd thought had been confined to the odd, hidden, middle-of-the-night type of fantasy had just exploded into something that was about to break out of that very private part of her life?

Which wouldn't be a problem, except...

Except that, in that weird moment when time had done something strange and elastic, she could have sworn that Ben had been doing more than reading her mind. He had been thinking about kissing her.

And he'd wanted it as much as she had.

CHAPTER SIX

QUEENSTOWN.

The small, South Island town that nestled on the shores of Lake Wakatipu, in the shadows of New Zealand's dramatic Southern Alps, was widely regarded as the adventure tourism capital of the world and it was Ben Marshall's favourite place. Not simply because of the great bars and restaurants or the stunning scenery or even the lively crowd of young, mostly foreign travellers who came looking for work where an income was either a bonus or a means to an adrenaline rush. Queenstown had been the closest thing to a big town when Ben had been growing up nearby and it still felt like home. His first holiday jobs had included driving jet boats through the rapids on the Shotover River and as a coach on the ski fields in the Remarkables and the thrill of discovering adult freedom in such a vibrant atmosphere was a memory he would always treasure.

It was still the focus of his social life away from Cutler's Creek and it had been too long since he'd enjoyed this particular tapas bar on the lakefront that was also known for its great range of boutique beer. Ben took another appreciative sip of the only drink he intended having on his night off. It wasn't until he was wiping a bit of foam from the corner of his mouth with his thumb that he noticed his companion was mirroring his action—with her tongue. He looked away as he cleared his throat.

'Great idea, this, Heidi. Thanks for texting me.'

'No problem.' Coming from the French speaking part of Switzerland, Heidi's accent was as sexy as her long, platinum blonde hair, blue eyes and legs that went on for ever. 'I've been missing having Ingrid as my housemate so I thought you were probably feeling lonely like me. It seems like too long since you were in town.'

Ben was tracing drops of moisture on the outside of his beer glass with his fingertip. 'Life's been busy, I guess.'

'Really? You have a lot of exciting accidents in your little village?'

'Not often,' Ben had to admit. 'In fact, the most exciting thing in the last week or so wasn't even real. We had a practice rescue of someone stuck on a cliff with a broken ankle after an abseiling accident.'

'So you used a…what do you call them…the pretend people?'

'A mannequin? No, we used a real person only she didn't have a real broken ankle. She had sprained it not so long ago, though, so that helped her acting.'

Maybe it hadn't been purely acting. JJ's ankle was probably pretty sore after the way she'd tackled that tough track like a champion. She hadn't flinched at the prospect of being deposited on a narrow ledge, either, and putting her safety totally in the hands of a team that was still learning about difficult rescue situations—not just for being taken off that ledge but being strapped onto a stretcher and carried down the track, including that gnarly section with those big boulders in the way.

She might come across as being someone who was overly cautious and liked her environment to be organised to the nth degree but it wasn't because she lacked courage, was it? Far from it...

'So...the next time, yes?'

'Sorry?' Ben realised he hadn't heard a word of what Heidi had just said.

'The next time. I can be your patient? I can come and play with you?'

Oh, man...the invitation in those blue eyes was something any red-blooded man would probably give at least an eye tooth to be the recipient of.

'Have you eaten enough?' Heidi was sliding off the bar stool beside him. She was also sliding her hand into his. 'Shall we go for a walk?'

A walk back to her place?

Ben was perfectly happy to accept the invitation. It was, after all, the reason he'd come into town for his night off, wasn't it? Heidi was right, it had been too long and...he knew he needed this. A reminder of an important part of his life.

There was enough moonlight to be gilding the soft ripples of the lake as they walked along the beachfront, away from the busy town centre. Ben knew that Heidi's apartment was not far away but, for some strange reason, his steps were slowing. Heidi thought he needed a moment to savour the view and the tug on his hand made him stop completely.

'It's funny, isn't it?' Heidi smiled. 'I come right across the world and I love it because I find mountains that remind me of home.'

She was still holding Ben's hand as she turned to catch his gaze and it was blindingly obvious that she wanted him to kiss her but, instead of being exactly how he'd wanted this evening to progress, Ben was aware of a sinking sensation in his gut. He'd seen a look very much like this only days ago, hadn't he?

In JJ's eyes...

Dammit...this wasn't working. He still wanted to kiss JJ, which made absolutely no sense at all.

Perhaps kissing Heidi would do the trick. Desire should inevitably kick in because Heidi was exactly his type—and the total opposite of JJ Hamilton.

Except it didn't change anything. It only made it even more painfully clear that this wasn't going to work.

'I'm sorry,' he murmured, breaking what was possibly the most unsatisfying kiss he'd ever experienced. 'My head's not in the right space.'

'No worries...' Heidi shrugged. 'Next time, maybe?'

'Maybe...' Ben offered an apologetic smile as he let go of Heidi's hand.

He gave her a wave a minute later, after he'd said goodnight and was heading for where he'd parked his car.

That sinking sensation had settled into a weight inside his chest that didn't feel like it was going anywhere in a hurry. It was kind of a sad feeling.

As if he knew there wasn't going to be a next time?

'Queenstown?'

'Yes. My favourite spot in the world. I've had a holiday house there for twenty years now. And a mooring for my boat right on the waterfront. Ah...' Visiting specialist Nigel Shaw was clearly familiar with his destination as he pushed open the doors of Cutler's Creek Hospital's kitchen. 'Betty... I hope that's some of your famous vegetable soup I can smell?'

'And your favourite toasties, Dr Shaw. With cheese and mustard.'

'You know me so well, Betty.'

'Come and sit down. You, too, Dr Hamilton.'

'Thanks, Betty. Don't mind if I do.' JJ put the books she was carrying to one side as she sat down at the table. 'There's a couple of patients you saw in your cardiology clinic this morning that I should catch up with.'

'Of course. I'll do a full report for their medical records and email it through by this evening but is there someone in particular you're concerned about?'

There was a container full of cutlery in the middle of the table and another one with paper serviettes beside it. It didn't matter how many people turned up here at mealtimes because Betty always had food and a warm welcome available. In the few weeks JJ had been working here, she'd had lunch with the other doctors—Zac and Don, Bruce the policeman, various local firies and other volunteers and, of course, Ben.

JJ closed her eyes in a determined blink, as if that could stop her thoughts going in an unwanted direction. She'd put a plan into place immediately after that unfortunate moment during that training session on Twin Rocks track and she wasn't about to deviate from the programme.

'Yes. Shirley Keen. She was very anxious when I saw her last week about the palpitations she seems to still be experiencing.'

'Mmm. Her ECG was normal—apart from the changes you'd expect from someone with a BMI of thirty-five. I've ordered blood tests to rule out something like a potassium or magnesium imbalance. Hypomagnesaemia is surprisingly common.'

'Did she bring her diary in? I encouraged her to make a note of any possible triggers, like caffeine, exercise, alcohol, etcetera.'

'She said she'd forgotten.'

'To bring it or fill it in? Never mind...' JJ shook her head. 'I'll follow that up. It's not your problem.' She sniffed appreciatively as Betty put a steaming bowl of soup in front of her. 'That looks amazing.'

'Toasties are on the way. And there's plenty more soup where that came from.'

Nigel Shaw was happy to eat and discuss patients at the same time. 'We can think about doing a twenty-four-hour Holter monitor test for Shirley if you think she could cope with that. It would be helpful if you could catch any episodes of dysrhythmia on a rhythm strip and send them through to me in Dunedin. Is your ambulance service up to covering that?'

'Oh…absolutely. We've got an extremely competent paramedic in charge here.'

'Ben?' Nigel nodded his thanks to Betty as she added a platter of toasted sandwiches to the table. 'I've met him. He came up to Dunedin to do a training course we ran on thrombolytic administration in rural settings. You're lucky he's still here. I seem to remember he was talking about switching to a job with the helicopter rescue crew.'

'Oh?' The thought of Ben not being here came as a shock. Which was crazy because JJ was doing her best to convince herself that she wasn't going to let him mess with her head any longer and she had her plan in action already. Thanks to that training session, she'd realised not only how unfit she was when it came to climbing hills but how little she knew about the kinds of outdoor skills she might need in an area like Cutler's Creek so she'd embarked on an ambitious programme to improve both her fitness and knowledge.

'So…' Nigel reached for a sandwich. 'Anyone else you're worried about?'

'Thomas Sefton? I know he's got a lot more going on than his angina. I'd really like to help him with the peripheral neuropathy that's contributing to his inability to exercise. He's worried about dependency if he goes onto an opioid based analgesic.'

Nigel smiled. 'He's ninety-three. It's really not an issue. I can have another chat with him, if you like. I'm not heading back to Dunedin until Monday. I fancied a long weekend in Queenstown. I imagine you're enjoying discovering all the local delights?'

'I'm ashamed to say I haven't explored much in the area yet. I got a bit caught up as soon as I arrived here.' JJ made a face. 'I've been bottle-raising a lamb but I've got him down to two feeds a day now so I could get away for a day.'

'Come this weekend, then. I could show you around. A vineyard tour, perhaps. Or a cruise on the lake?'

Oh, help…was this visiting cardiologist *flirting* with her? Asking her for a date, even?

'That is, if you've got free time. I haven't seen Zac around this morning, come to think of it. Or Don.'

'Don's here.' It was a relief to be able to dodge that invitation. 'He's probably in his office and hasn't re-alised it's lunchtime. Zac's in Dunedin, which is a trip he's making a couple of times a week at the moment. He and Liv have a baby that arrived a bit too early.'

'I heard.'

The concern on Nigel's face made it apparent that he really cared. He was a nice man, JJ realised. And he wasn't bad looking, either. That moustache of his was impressively well trimmed. He was, in fact, just the kind of man she'd always been attracted to. Exactly her type. So why wasn't she feeling remotely interested by the attention he was giving her?

'I'm…ah…not sure exactly when Zac's due back so I can't really make plans for the weekend. Covering his gaps is the reason I'm here in the first place.'

'I understand completely. I'll console myself with my favourite pastimes of fishing and bush walks.'

Nice, safe pleasures, JJ noted. He probably loved reading interesting, non-fiction books, as well. Or watching classic movies. He should be becoming more attractive by the minute.

'I'm doing a bit of walking myself,' she found herself saying. 'With Shaun.'

Nigel blinked. 'A friend of yours?'

'The lamb I was telling you about. He follows me everywhere and is surprisingly good company for a walk. I'm trying to improve my level of fitness.'

She was walking further and faster every day, in fact, and when the challenge of flat ground and smaller hills became too easy, JJ was planning to leave Shaun at home so that she could have another go at that Twin Rocks track. How embarrassing had it been to get so out of breath in front of Ben and to need his assistance in climbing over rocks?

'Always a good thing.' Nigel nodded. Then he smiled. 'Though, in my professional opinion, I have to say you look in perfect shape already.'

Yep. This was flirting. JJ averted her gaze instantly. 'I'm learning some bushcraft, too,' she said, hoping to change the subject completely. She shifted her diary to expose the cover of the other small book she had been carrying. 'This is full of all sorts of stuff. I'm reading the chapter on how to cross rivers safely.'

Nigel reached for a serviette to wipe his mouth and fingers, turning away from JJ. 'That was delicious, as always, Betty.' Then he smiled at JJ. 'I'll head off, unless there's anyone else you want me to see or discuss? It's such a lovely afternoon, if I finish those patient reports soon, I might even get out on the lake for an hour or two.'

'Enjoy,' JJ responded, as she shook her head in response to his query. 'I've got your email address and I'll contact you if there's anything to discuss.'

'Please do.' The warmth of Nigel's smile made it crystal clear that he would welcome the contact even if it had nothing to do with a patient. Especially if it didn't...

Betty collected the plates from the table as soon as the visiting specialist had gone.

'You could do worse,' she murmured, giving JJ a wink. 'He likes you.'

'*Betty*... I don't even know if he's single.'

'He is. I believe his wife ran off with her yoga instructor a year or so ago.'

'Hmm... I wonder why?' JJ grinned. She shouldn't say anything else but she felt a sudden need to dispatch an image of how pleased her grandmother would look if she knew that JJ was dating a good looking, respected cardiologist. Someone safe. The absolute opposite of a bad boy who took risks and wasn't about to follow all the rules if he could get away with it. And there it was...she could see the look in Ben's eyes again. The one that she was sure had told her that he'd been thinking about kissing her.

Any embryonic interest in a new male acquaintance evaporated instantly. 'Maybe his wife got bored with fishing,' she muttered.

Betty headed for her sink with a snort. 'If you're going anywhere near Doc Donaldson's office, tell him the soup won't stay hot for much longer.'

'No need.' It was Don Donaldson who spoke, as he

entered the kitchen. 'I caught Nigel as he left and he told me I was late for lunch.'

He wasn't alone.

'I'm just gatecrashing.' Ben's wide smile was aimed at Betty. 'Your soup is as irresistible as you are, Betty.'

JJ was scrambling to her feet. Sitting around chatting with Ben Marshall was not part of the new plan. It was high time she got back to work, anyway. She was a little too quick in grabbing her books, however, and one of them slid from her hands to land on the floor. Ben swooped to pick it up.

'Bushcraft?' His eyes widened as he flipped it open to where JJ's bookmark was. 'River crossing, huh?'

JJ shrugged. 'It was in the cottage. Maybe Zac left it behind. I just thought that you never know when information like that could come in handy.'

'What are you doing tomorrow?'

'What? Why?'

'Because I can teach you more about crossing a river safely than you'll ever learn by reading about it.'

'She's not doing anything,' Don put in. 'Not around here, anyway. I'm on duty.'

'You're doing a training session? On river crossings?'

'Am now.' Ben's eyebrow lifted. 'It was shaping up to be a boring afternoon given that I had nothing exciting planned and I can't stand getting bored, so how 'bout it? As you said, you never know—it could save your life one day. I'll pick you up. One p.m.?' He didn't wait for an answer because he was moving to where Betty was ladling more soup into bowls. 'I'd marry you, Betty,' he said, 'if you weren't already taken.'

She was laughing. 'Thirty years ago, lad,' she said, 'you wouldn't have stood a chance.'

It was the sound of that laughter that was making JJ smile as she slipped out of the kitchen. Such a happy sound, it was no wonder that her day had just acquired a new glow.

'So where's everybody else?'

Good question... But the only response Ben offered was to raise his eyebrows because he didn't really have the answer. Maybe that's what he'd decided he needed to find out himself when he'd discarded the list of other potential volunteers who might appreciate some bush-craft training.

JJ's deep frown was making a furrow on her brow 'You said you were running a river crossing training course but there's nobody here except us. Are we going to wait for them?'

'I never said it was a team training session. Did I?'

'Um...no...'

Was that simply wariness in those dark eyes now? Or something more? Surprise? Pleasure, even...? The thought that JJ might like the idea they were going to spend some time alone together in the mountains created a flicker of anticipation in Ben's gut and he knew that was the key to why he'd engineered this situation even as he'd tried to talk himself out of it last night. There was something about this woman that was messing with his head. His *life*, even, given that disastrous date with Heidi the other evening. He needed to identify what that something was and deal with it.

JJ was eyeing the backpack as he eased his arms through the straps. 'You planning to stay in the high country for a week?'

He flicked a glance at the small hiker's day pack she was holding. 'You got a complete change of clothes in that? Pack liner? First aid kit? A torch, fire-lighting gear, toilet paper and a pocket knife?'

Her eyes widened, as if she hadn't realised how big a deal river crossings could be. As if she was more than a little nervous all of a sudden. But, instead of being annoying, Ben found he rather liked that idea. He could look after her. Keep her safe at the same time as teaching her something important.

'It's all good,' he added. 'That's why I've got everything we might need.'

'I've got food.' JJ's smile was hopeful. 'I made some cheese and mustard sandwiches because Betty's were so good yesterday. And I've got a Thermos of soup because I thought we might get a bit cold with wet feet. It's only tomato soup out of a can, though. My gran would be appalled.'

'My childhood favourite,' Ben told her. 'And something that *my* nan always kept in her pantry.'

Her smile faltered and he could see it was because she'd picked up on his use of the past tense.

'She died when I was fifteen.'

'Oh... I'm sorry...'

He shrugged as he turned away. 'It's a long time ago. It's not uncommon, is it, to lose your grandparents?'

'I'm lucky I've still got mine. Gran, that is. Grandad died a few years ago.'

Ben acknowledged the information with a nod but he didn't want to talk about it. He didn't talk to anyone about his nan, for that matter. Or even think about her much. He'd actually forgotten that he and JJ had something quite unusual in common, having both been raised by grandparents. Because he'd preferred to push that particular moment when he'd felt that connection with her from his mind? In the same way he'd been trying so hard to dismiss the desire to kiss this woman?

'Come on...' He knew he sounded too abrupt but he was starting to think this whole idea might be a big mistake. 'Let's go.'

It was easy enough to steer clear of anything he didn't want to think about as they tramped upriver to find the section that Ben always used to train newbies. A typical, New Zealand braided river, Cutler's 'Creek' offered several different channels that meandered and crossed each other as they headed towards the sea. They offered varying degrees of difficulty, from easy and shallow to a stretch of white water further upstream that could challenge even experienced participants.

JJ seemed happy to listen as he explained how to choose the best place to cross a river, or even whether it was safe to cross at all.

'Look at the river from as high a place on the bank as you can find. You want to try and judge the depth and speed of the flow, whether it's over shingle or boulders and any dangers like rapids, submerged tree branches and side streams that will be adding to the water volume.' He stopped several times as they walked upstream to encourage JJ to select what she thought would be a good spot.

'There. No...that's not good, is it? Steep banks mean deep water, don't they? And they can make it impossible to get out on the other side. And what happens if you get swept off your feet further up from banks like that?'

'I'm not intending to let you get swept off your feet,' Ben told her. 'This is River Crossing for Beginners and I'll be hanging onto you.' He could start teaching her the techniques to keep herself safe, floating with the current, when they got to a more difficult crossing.

There were two variations of the mutual support method that Ben taught. They both involved putting an arm around each other's backs and getting a good grip on either a pack strap or clothing. Even teaching JJ to take small, shuffling steps, not to lift her feet too high in the water and to watch the far bank as much as possible so as not to get disoriented by the flow of the river wasn't enough to distract him from the awareness that his hands were touching her body.

And maybe that was why he wasn't holding quite tightly enough when JJ slipped on a small boulder when they were in the middle of their second crossing—this time in knee-level water with a faster current. He kept his promise to hang onto her but, try as he might, he couldn't keep them both upright and the current was strong enough to sweep them downstream just far enough for them both to be soaked from head to foot by the time he found his footing again and managed to pull JJ onto the safety of a shingle island between two channels.

Just far enough for JJ to have swallowed a bit of water that was making her cough, for her to have become cold enough to be shivering badly already and to have scared her so much she looked a great deal younger than she actually was.

So vulnerable that Ben could feel something melting inside his chest. A liquid kind of feeling that matched the external river water that was streaming from his clothes and hair, except that the internal sensation was a lot more powerful and it was spreading throughout his entire body.

Good grief, it even seemed to be reaching his eyes.

'It's okay,' he heard himself saying aloud as he pulled JJ into his arms. 'It's okay…you're safe now… I've got you…'

CHAPTER SEVEN

HOW TERRIFYING HAD that been?

The fear hadn't kicked in in that first moment when she'd felt her foot lose contact with the boulder beneath it because that had happened too fast. The shock of being plunged into water that felt like barely melted ice was so great that JJ didn't have the brain space to feel frightened then, either. It was when she felt the power in that current tipping her so that she couldn't get her face out of the water, the brush of a large rock beneath her that she'd probably just missed hitting her head on and she realised how easy it could be to drown that fear not only kicked in but instantly ramped up to terror.

Not that the intensity of that terror had lasted for more than a heartbeat. Or maybe two. Because she'd known that Ben still had a grip on her. She was trusting him with her life but she had no choice and, at some level, she knew that trust wasn't misplaced. And she'd been right. Here she was, out of the water. Safe. Shaking like a leaf, of course, but she was safe. Ben was holding her in his arms and, to be honest, JJ had never felt so safe in her life. How crazy was that?

Crazy enough to make her laugh, anyway, as she pulled back to look up at Ben.

'River C-Crossing for Beginners, huh?' Her teeth were chattering hard enough to make her stutter. 'I'd h-hate to do one of y-your advanced classes.'

'You're the first person I've dropped in a river,' Ben told her. 'Sorry about that.'

'I wasn't h-holding on tightly enough,' JJ confessed. 'And I was l-looking d-down…'

'And you're freezing. Come on. Hopefully the extra clothing in my pack will have stayed dry enough.'

The channels they needed to negotiate to get back to the riverbank where they'd started this training session got progressively easier and Ben was certainly keeping a tight grip on JJ but she was so cold ten minutes later that her fingers refused to co-operate by holding onto the strap of Ben's backpack. Even her legs didn't seem to want to hold her up.

'How f-far?' she asked. 'To the car?'

'We're not going to the car,' Ben responded. 'Not yet. With this wind picking up, you'll be hypothermic in no time. There's a hut a lot closer. Just basic but we can get a fire going and some dry clothes on.' He grinned at JJ. 'Think of it as your survival training session.'

The hut was small. Just a single room with a couple of old, wooden chairs, a tiny table and a pot-bellied stove but it was a huge relief to be out of the wind.

'Get those clothes off,' Ben ordered, as he opened his pack. 'Yes…that dunk wasn't enough to get right into the sealed bags in here. I've got a pair of trackpants and a sweatshirt that you can put on. There's a foil sheet in here if they're not enough.'

'What about you?'

'There's an extra pair of trackpants but I'll be fine for the moment while I get this fire going. I've got merino thermals on.' He handed her the bag. 'Take everything wet off,' he instructed. 'It won't take long to get your undies dry and, by the time we've got warm and had something to eat, everything else will be at least wearable for the trek back to the car.'

But JJ barely heard the last of his words. He wanted her to take her *underwear* off? She should be horrified at the thought. So why was there suddenly a heat in parts of her body that couldn't possibly be explained by simply having shelter from the wind? This didn't make sense. Any more than her reaction had, when she'd discovered that there weren't going to be any other people joining them on this training session. She should have been annoyed by that. Feeling manipulated, perhaps. Instead, she'd been secretly pleased because it made her feel...special?

Ben let his breath out in an amused huff at her expression. 'Don't worry, I won't be looking.' He peeled his anorak off, leaving it to hang and drip from a large hook on the wall. 'I've got enough to do making a fire, here. If you hurry up, I can show you how to shave kindling off pieces of wood that are too big—like those logs in the corner, there.'

He was crouched in front of the stove by the time he finished speaking, a pocket knife in one hand and a piece of wood in the other. He had his back to JJ so he couldn't possibly see what she was doing and she turned her own back on him as she began to peel sodden clothing away from her body but this still felt incredibly… wrong, somehow. Naughty, even? Certainly something that rule-following people shouldn't be doing.

Something a *boring* person would never dream of doing, that's for sure, but JJ was in the middle of an adventure, here, wasn't she? She'd just been washed down a river, for heaven's sake. Saved from drowning by the kind of hero any woman would dream of being rescued by—someone who was even giving up his own, spare clothing so that she could be warm and dry.

No wonder she was feeling a very different appreciation of life right now. Or that rules she had lived by her entire life seemed suddenly irrelevant.

She'd known from when she was old enough to start asking questions that it had been her mother's fault that her grandparents had lost their beloved only son. She'd been driving the van that day. Touring around Europe had been her idea—something their sensible boy would never have considered doing if he hadn't fallen in love with someone as wild as JJ's mother. It didn't mean that JJ had been any less loved, of course. It just meant that they'd made sure she understood what she needed to do to stay safe, for her own sake and for the people who loved her.

She'd always known that she had to fight any inclination to be anything like her mother.

JJ had done that literally by accident today. But, instead of being consumed by guilt, she was feeling more alive than she ever had and there was no way she was going to fight this kind of exhilaration. For perhaps the first time ever, she could understand why her mother had chosen to live her life like that. Maybe it was also no wonder that JJ had to bite back a smile as her cold fingers fumbled with the catch on her bra strap.

He couldn't see what JJ was doing.

But he *knew* what she was doing and he could imagine that wet clothing being peeled from her skin to leave it exposed. He could even imagine the goose bumps that would give it a texture that could only be smoothed by warmth—like the fire he was building, or the warmth from the touch of another person, perhaps?

Oh…man… Even being thoroughly chilled himself and making sure he was distracted by a physical activity that he needed to focus on if he didn't want to slice a good part of this thumb off wasn't stopping the heat of his body's reaction to what was going on behind him.

This was what the problem was with JJ Hamilton, wasn't it?

Despite the fact that she was so unlike any other woman he'd ever been attracted to before—or perhaps *because* of that—this attraction was off the scale. It was far more than attraction. More than desire, even. This was lust, pure and simple but that was okay. He could control it. Hide it, in fact, given that he was a very long way from being some inexperienced teenager.

Ben gave JJ plenty of time to get out of her clothes and into the dry ones. He had the fire crackling by then and had taken off his own outer shirt to leave just the short-sleeved, close-fitting merino thermal against his skin. He moved to shift the wooden chairs close to the stove to use as a clothes rack to speed up the drying process and, even then, he avoided looking directly at JJ but he caught what was happening from the corner of his eye. He saw the most perfect, naked butt disappearing beneath the trackpants she was pulling up and he had to close his eyes as he let his breath out very, very slowly. He needed to clear his throat, too, before he could hope that his voice would sound normal.

'We'll hang all the wet stuff over these chairs by the fire.'

'Okay.' JJ wasn't about to notice anything odd in his expression. She was looking down at the old, soft sweatshirt of his. 'I really like this. Red is my favourite colour.'

'Keep it,' Ben told her. 'It suits you.'

JJ handed back the bag he'd used for the spare clothing. 'Here…you can get this other pair of dry pants on now.'

'I'll help you wring as much water as we can from your clothes first.'

JJ's hair was still soaked and the end of her long braid was making a damp patch on the front of the red sweatshirt. Ben tried very hard not to look at it. Or think about what was underneath that damp patch. JJ didn't seem bothered. She worked briskly, wringing out the smaller items of clothing and then draping them over the rungs on the back of her chairs.

Good grief…who knew that someone that came across as being so uptight would wear underwear that was so lacy it had to be pretty much see-through?

Ben finally stripped off his wet trousers, leaving his merino long johns on as he reached for the other pair of dry trackpants that JJ had left on the table. She didn't even look in his direction. She was busy pulling something from her small pack.

'Oh...no...'

'What?' She had something in her hand. Something that was dripping through her fingers and Ben found himself grinning broadly. 'Yeah...sandwiches don't usually like getting wet.'

Her face lit up as she returned his smile and for a long, long moment they held eye contact that made the room seem an awful lot smaller than it had a minute or two ago.

It was JJ who finally broke that gaze as her smile faded.

'Yuk...' she murmured, dropping the bulk of what she was holding back into the wrapping. 'At least the soup should be okay.'

Her hand was still covered in a sticky mess. Without thinking, Ben reached out to wipe it clean with the soft fabric in his hands.

Startled, she looked up at him again and, this time, he could actually feel the flash of something igniting. Maybe it was because they were skin to skin where he was holding her hand. Or maybe it was because he could see her eyes darken even more than they were naturally—as if her pupils were dilating. Or...maybe this had just been waiting to happen ever since he'd first laid eyes on this woman.

Whatever caused the spark, it wasn't going to fizzle out any time soon. It had, in fact, found some real fuel—like that match Ben had been holding against wood shavings in what suddenly felt like a very long time ago. He knew that JJ wasn't about to break this gaze. He could feel a solid wave of exactly the same level of desire that was currently taking over every cell in his own body.

Ben wasn't going to break the gaze, either. He held it as he dropped the fabric he was holding and lifted his hand to touch her face. With one finger, he traced the outline of her temple and cheekbone and then down the side of her nose. He watched as JJ's eyes drifted shut as his finger touched the corner of her mouth and then tracked along her lower lip, so gently he could feel only the tingle of that incredibly soft skin. When her lips parted and he felt the tip of her tongue touch his finger, Ben knew he was completely lost.

So, apparently, was JJ, judging by the way she came up on her tiptoes as he cupped the back of her head and tilted back to offer her mouth to his. And this was no gentle, exploratory first kiss. He'd been right to think that this had been waiting to happen. There was a sense that an unbearable tension was being finally released, here. That this was something they'd both wanted for too long and it couldn't happen fast enough. Dear Lord, he already had his hands beneath the oversized sweatshirt JJ was wearing. Was it that damp patch that was making her nipple as hard as a pebble from the creek, or was it the touch of his hand that was arousing her so much? And, if it was, he could only dream of how she might react to the slippery warmth of his tongue.

This was happening too fast but it felt like neither of them wanted it to slow down. Or stop it going a whole lot further except…this was breaking a rule that Ben had never broken in his adult life. How could he, when his own mother had told him that her unplanned pregnancy had ruined her life?

'We can't do this…' It was the hardest thing he'd ever done, pulling back from that kiss. That touch. But it had to be done. 'It's not safe…'

Of course it wasn't safe.

This was the most reckless thing JJ had ever done in her life. She was about to have sex with a real-life bad boy. The kind of man she'd wouldn't have gone near in a million years in her previous life because she'd known better than to do something wild and be accused of 'being just like her mother'. She might very well never do it again so she knew that if she didn't do it now, she would lose a once-in-a-lifetime opportunity to see whether real life was anything like the kind of fantasies she'd been playing with.

And it wasn't *un*safe. Not in the way Ben was worried about, anyway.

'I'm on the Pill,' she told him.

She could feel his breath on her face as he closed his eyes, leaning in to touch her nose with his. She could feel his hands on her waist, his fingers closing in to shape the hollows just above her hip bones.

'You want this?' His voice was so deep it was like the crunch of gravel beneath feet. 'As much as I do…?'

The shaft of sensation his fingers were creating was

moving diagonally from her hips, nosediving to pool in the place she most needed him to touch her.

'Yes…' JJ's voice was as raw as Ben's. She couldn't bear it if he stopped. He mustn't stop. *'Please…'*

They didn't make it to the dusty floorboards of that hut. JJ felt the rough wood of the wall behind her back by the time the second most astonishing kiss of her life had ended. Somehow, they shifted their clothing enough to get their skin touching exactly where it was needed and JJ was oblivious to the danger of splinters in her back as Ben finally cupped her buttocks and lifted her feet from the floor to perfect their alignment. She wrapped her arms around his neck and her legs around his waist—a move she'd only ever read about before but it felt astonishingly natural. Easy.

And safe…as safe as she had been in Ben's arms when he'd pulled her from the river. Only this time she could let go and float with the current of a building pleasure like nothing she'd ever known existed.

The cry of ecstasy that came from her throat a short time later was also like no sound she'd ever heard herself make. But, then, she'd never experienced anything like this before, had she? She'd just been taken by a bad boy. In a way that made it feel like she'd just lost her virginity all over again.

Nothing was ever going to be the same.

'Wow…' As post-coital conversation, this wasn't impressive but Ben was still having trouble finding any words in an almost awkward space of time when they had finally recovered enough to pull themselves apart.

He had to lean in to kiss JJ again, though. Softly, this time, because passion that exploded that ferociously couldn't possibly happen again.

Or maybe it could... The touch—and taste—of JJ's lips felt familiar now but it was just as exciting. Ben closed his eyes.

'What just happened there?' he murmured.

'I'm not sure.' JJ's voice was no more than a whisper but he could hear the smile in it. 'But...it was... um...really good.'

Ben groaned. 'I know...and it shouldn't have been.'

'Why not?' There was a wary note in her voice now. 'Because it was...boring?'

His breath came out in an incredulous huff. 'Are you *kidding* me? Boring is the last word on earth I'd use to describe what we just did.'

'But you thought it shouldn't have been good?'

'Yeah...' He wasn't about to admit that he'd hadn't believed a real sexual encounter with JJ would be anything like as good as any fantasy he might or might not have considered. 'Because...no offence, JJ, but you're so not my type.'

This time there was a hint of laughter in her voice. 'And you couldn't be further from my type. You're right, it shouldn't have worked at all.'

Ben opened his eyes to catch her gaze. 'But it did, didn't it?' He kissed her again. 'Okay...if I'm honest, I've been wanting to do this for a long time.'

'Mmm...'

That sound was pretty much an admission of the same thing, wasn't it?

'So…' Ben knew they both needed to move closer to the fire and start getting properly warm but JJ wasn't shivering any more and he could feel the warmth of her skin against his own. 'Did we get it out of our systems, do you think? Enough to go back to our usual "types"?'

There was a flicker in JJ's eyes that could have been amusement. Or possible a desire to do it all over again?

'I'm not sure,' she said. 'What do you think?'

Ben could feel his mouth curling on one side. 'I'm not sure, either. But I do think we should pick somewhere more comfortable for next time.'

Oh, yeah…that was definitely desire he could see in her eyes. But she broke her gaze, as if she didn't want him to see how much she wanted a 'next time'.

'It's not as though it's going to last,' she said, slipping away and pulling that sweatshirt down to cover herself properly. 'I'm only here until things settle down for Zac and he's back on deck full time but, even if I was here for ever, it wouldn't last, would it? Not when we're so completely incompatible.'

'True. I'm not even going to be around that much longer. I've been thinking of moving on for a long time now. I'm determined to get some helicopter rescue training in at some point in my career.'

Ben knew that the extraordinary physical pleasure they'd just discovered with each other was purely down to lust and would burn itself out in no time but it was a relief to hear that JJ recognised that, as well. He'd been curious about an unexpected attraction and, while it had been infinitely better than he might have imagined, of course it wasn't going to last.

It never did. Even with the women who were a hundred percent his 'type'.

But who wouldn't want to enjoy it for as long as it *did* last?

How weird was this?

JJ was acting as though nothing momentous had just happened. Like she had casual sex with bad boys all the time. She was even getting that Thermos of very ordinary tomato soup out of her pack like they were about to have a picnic or something but maybe she just needed to do something with her hands.

Other than touching Ben Marshall.

Maybe she needed a distraction from the words that were echoing in her head but that she could feel deep down in her belly.

Next time…

It wasn't as though she was behaving totally irresponsibly here. She was just doing something she'd never considered doing before so maybe it was simply a delayed teenage rebellion. Something everybody needed to do before they really knew what they wanted from their life?

Finding that out had been the reason she'd come here in the first place, wasn't it?

And maybe this was it, in a nutshell?

Passion.

Something she'd never dared to play around with. A glimpse into what life could be like if she wasn't so bound by the rules and expectations she clung to. A glimpse into the kind of person her mother had apparently been and…maybe that *wasn't* as bad as she'd grown up believing? Being adventurous, spontaneous, passionate wasn't necessarily a recipe for the destruction of lives, was it? She'd seen other people not only get away with it but experience a joy in life she was unfamiliar with. It wasn't as if she'd want to spend her future with someone like Ben, of course, because they both knew that could never work.

But, oh, boy…it could be fun for a while.

JJ had worked so hard and diligently all her life. Followed every rule and made sure that nobody thought she was anything like as irresponsible as the mother she knew only from faded photographs. She deserved a bit of fun, didn't she? She and Ben were both adults and it wasn't as if anyone was going to get hurt.

She turned her head to smile at Ben, who was rearranging their wet clothing over the chairs by the stove.

'Soup? It's still nice and hot and I reckon it's probably just as good as your nan used to make.'

The smile she was getting in return as Ben walked towards her felt like it was reaching right inside her body. Lighting it up.

Oh, yeah…who wouldn't want to make the most of this kind of fun while it lasted? And if 'next time' was even half as good as the first time, how could she possibly resist?

She couldn't, of course.

For the simple reason that she didn't want to.

CHAPTER EIGHT

FOR SOMETHING THAT should never have worked in the first place, it was quite remarkable how it could not only continue to work but to get better.

Every single time.

Right from that first day when they'd only stayed in the hut long enough to have a hot drink and get properly warm because an hour's hike back to Ben's vehicle wasn't a big problem, even wearing still-damp clothes. There was a long, hot shower waiting for them back at JJ's cottage, after all, not to mention a chance to deal with the astonishing level of desire that had apparently already rebuilt—on both sides. That 'next time' wasn't half as good as the first time.

It had been twice as good.

The final discovery that day had been that even the comfort of a soft mattress and warm duvet—the only kind of environment JJ had considered appropriate for this kind of activity in her previous life—didn't make the sex any less exciting. If anything, it revealed that her partners in the past had been either sadly lacking in expertise or she simply hadn't been attracted enough to flick a switch she'd never known existed. A switch that seemed to open a connection that encouraged her to be more adventurous than she could have believed and enabled her to not only receive unimaginable pleasure but to give it, as well.

JJ had expected the novelty to wear off, of course. Or for Ben to get bored and move on—probably to another one of those gorgeous blonde adrenaline junkie visitors to this part of the world—but it didn't happen. Maybe that was because Ben crammed so much into his life he was almost always busy and that meant he could only find a night or two a week to visit JJ at her cottage and he never stayed the whole night, not just because they wanted to keep their connection as private as possible but because Ben always seemed to have an early start the next day for a shift or a meeting or a fitness session.

A week sped past and then another and another. Until neither of them were counting. Until Shaun had become a small sheep rather than a lamb. He didn't need bottle-feeding any longer and was earning his treats of sheep nuts by wearing a collar and chain and being a lawn-mower around the cottage.

Locals were getting used to seeing him trotting behind JJ when she went for a run along the road and they weren't surprised when Ben began to be seen regularly in her company. It was common knowledge that he was helping her with her fitness levels, after all, but Cutler's Creek's ambulance station manager was working hard to get everybody who was involved in the emergency services around here up to speed in both fitness and bushcraft skills. He had even inspired others to jump in and help.

Everyone had splinter skills, it seemed. Bruce was an expert in creating shelters by using whatever materials might be at hand and the group that his training day attracted included people from as far away as Queenstown and the West Coast—a surprising number of whom were already becoming familiar faces to JJ. When Bruce produced a map of the huts that were available on public land and she and Ben exchanged a very private glance, she felt even more a part of this group.

It turned out to be one of the best days ever, learning how to use fly sheets or natural features like big rocks and overhangs and gather dead tussock grass, fern fronds or moss to create a surprisingly comfortable and warm mattress. You could even pull some of the dry material over your head, apparently, to trap air and retain body warmth.

Bruce also had an old school mate who'd worked in the Meteorological Service before retiring back to Central Otago and he gave a fascinating lecture in the town's school hall about how to read weather maps or the clouds and spot an approaching front that could develop into a potentially dangerous storm. Wispy clouds that were called 'mares' tails' were a sign of high-level winds and were often the first sign of bad weather. Fluffy, cumulus clouds could develop ominously dark bases and go on to signal the imminent arrival of a low-pressure system that could bring high winds, heavy rain and even snow at almost any time of the year.

JJ herself had given a talk about first aid kits—what

to put in them and how to use the contents—that had also attracted interest from all over the area and, on that occasion, she not only felt a part of the group but that she was making a real contribution to this community.

Each new training session, in addition to every new or returning patient treated at the hospital, made local faces more familiar and personalities better known. JJ could look back at her arrival here and be amused by how she'd felt like a fish out of water and that she'd worried about how isolated and potentially lonely a sparsely populated area could be for a city girl like herself. She'd been far lonelier in that crowded apartment building in Wellington. Cutler's Creek was beginning to feel very much like a real home and creating a sensation of belonging that was something very new for JJ.

It felt like she was putting down tendrils of roots that could ground her for ever if they were allowed to keep growing. She was coming to love being near the mountains and the feeling of freedom that came from the open farmland. She liked these people and she admired their spirit of adventure, ingenuity and their generosity in spending so much time and effort on things that were designed to let them help others who might get into trouble in the great outdoors.

Not that she could stay *here* for ever, given that Don Donaldson wasn't showing any signs of wanting to retire yet, but maybe she could find something similar. New Zealand was a big enough country to need lots of doctors in rural areas. She might need to make the move before those roots got any deeper, mind you, because it was only going to get harder to pull them out.

'What's that face all about?' Ben was in the kitchen of Cutler's Creek Hospital as JJ walked in for a cup of coffee mid-afternoon, after the outpatient maternity clinic that she'd and midwife Debbie had been running had finished.

'Just thinking.' But JJ's heart had lifted as soon as she'd seen him and she could feel her frown evaporating.

'Hard work, was it?'

Oh…that cheeky grin. It was something else she was going to miss about this place, that was for sure.

'I'm just wondering if I'll be able to take Shaun with me when I leave Cutler's Creek, that's all.'

Betty dropped the pan she was scrubbing in the sink with a clatter. 'You're not planning on leaving us, are you?'

'I was only ever here on a locum basis, Betty.' JJ poured herself a cup of coffee and then sat down at the table. There was a basket, lined with a tea towel, full of freshly made date scones and a big pat of butter on a plate beside them. 'Doc Donaldson tells me that the mighty Hugo is doing so well he's going to come home in the next week or so and that means that Zac will be back onboard full time very soon.' JJ reached for a scone and tried to keep her tone cheerful. 'I might have to start looking for a new job sooner rather than later.'

'Don't think Shaun would be very impressed with living in your apartment in Wellington,' Ben said.

'I might not be going back to Wellington.'

'Where might you go?' The quirk of Ben's eyebrow was a sure sign he was interested in her plans.

What would his expression reveal, JJ wondered, if she told him she might like to find another rural position, maybe even close to Cutler's Creek? That it might be possible for them to continue seeing each other every so often? As friends, of course.

Really close friends.

The kind that could pick up where they'd left off— even when it included the kind of intimacy that JJ would never have considered enjoying on a casual basis. She didn't want to consider it now, actually, but it would be better than knowing it was gone for ever, wouldn't it?

'The world is my oyster.' JJ tried to sound nonchalant. 'Coming here has taught me I can start a completely new life and…do anything I want, really…' She grinned at Ben as she caught his gaze. 'Maybe I don't want that to stop.'

She held his gaze for a heartbeat longer. Hopefully just long enough for him to get the message that their unexpected friendship was one of the things she didn't want to stop.

'Hmph.' Betty wasn't sounding impressed. 'Don't hold with things changing so fast,' she muttered. 'Not when we've just got used to the way they are.'

'Everything changes, Betty.' The scone Ben was pulling apart was still steaming. 'Except how good your cooking is. You never know, I might head off myself one of these days.' Judging by the subtle wink he gave JJ, he was quite aware of the way Betty was glaring at his back. 'I reckon JJ's right about doing what you want to do and maybe it's about time I did something about what *I've* always wanted to do and got myself a job on one of those choppers. Hey…' He turned to offer the older woman one of his most charming smiles. 'I'd still see you, Betty. Look how often the helicopter gets called in here. I could…you know…send you a text so that you could have some soup and toasties ready…'

Betty looked as though she was about to tell him that he wouldn't necessarily be welcome in her kitchen simply for free food but she didn't get the chance to say anything because Ben's pager sounded and he immediately reached for his phone.

'What's happening?'

JJ could hear the town's civil defence warning sounding as Ben was listening to the information. She could imagine Mike and Chris and Bruce, amongst others, dropping whatever they were doing right now to rush to their stations. Within minutes Bruce would be on the road in his police car, Mike would have the fire truck ready to go as soon as any volunteers arrived and Chris would be outside the ambulance station ready to jump in as Ben went past. Others would be waiting for news, as well. JJ could see Betty glancing towards the pantry, as if she was wondering what stocks were like in case something big was happening and she might need to feed some hungry crews.

'Roger that,' Ben said, ending the call as he got to his feet. 'I'm on my way.'

'What is it?' JJ asked.

'Camper van's gone over the edge in the gorge. It's wedged in rocks halfway down the cliff by Goat's Corner. No indication of how many passengers or what condition they're in.' Ben was already halfway out the door but JJ was right behind him.

'I'll come with you. Just let me grab the pack and my overalls.'

He stopped so abruptly that JJ would have banged into him if he hadn't put his hands out to catch her arms.

'No.' He was shaking his head. 'I don't want you to come this time.'

JJ's jaw dropped. She'd been out with him often enough in the last few weeks that it was becoming a normal part of her work routine. Possibly her favourite part.

Ben must have seen her bewilderment at his decision. That she was hurt, even? She knew he was poised to move fast but he wasn't going to leave her looking like that.

'It's a camper van,' he said softly. 'Down a cliff. There could be fatalities and...' His eyes were as dark as she'd ever seen them. '...and that's the way your parents died, isn't it?'

He'd remembered something she'd told him what seemed a long time ago now. A muttered comment that had been part of her trying to get past the embarrassment of him finding out her real first name. She'd said that she didn't remember anything about the accident but he still didn't want her to see something similar. Did he think it might spark some kind of flashback that could be emotionally traumatic? Was he trying to protect her?

Because he cared...?

It only took a split second for JJ's world to change.

To shift on its axis as much as it had that first time Ben had kissed her. More, in fact. Because, this time, her reaction wasn't simply physical. The idea that this man cared enough to try and protect her went so deep it felt like her soul had just captured that emotion and recognised it as a missing piece.

It only took that tiny fraction of time for JJ to understand just how much *she* cared about Ben.

A blip of time so fast that Ben only had time to turn away from her while she realised that she might actually be falling in love with him.

So fast that it was easy to pretend it had never happened. Okay, so she might have to think about it later but not right now. There was something far more urgent happening. Something that many people in this community were a part of. And JJ was part of this community now and wanted to remain a part of it for as long as possible.

'It's really not a problem,' she called, picking up speed. She caught up with Ben as he entered the hospital foyer. 'I can do this,' she told him. 'I want to come. Please…?'

It was a good thing that JJ was in the front passenger seat of the ambulance because Chris was nowhere to be seen in front of the station as Ben drove past, despite him being on call as a volunteer responder today. Maybe he was out of cell phone range somewhere on the back of the family farm or he'd had a problem with his car. Ben could call in another volunteer but he'd much rather have JJ with him, despite the likelihood that this callout would prove to be far more challenging than anything she'd had to face so far when she'd been out on the road with him. He could only hope that her own confidence in being able to deal with it—emotionally, as well as professionally—was not misplaced.

He hit the switch to activate his beacons and siren as he put his foot down to get through the township and onto the open road that led to the gorge. There was no additional information on what they were heading for yet. Bruce was almost on scene, had set up a road block at this end of the gorge and would be able to position himself to stop any traffic coming in the opposite direction but, even with the road clear, nobody would be able to get near the camper van until Mike had the fire truck in position to provide any necessary stabilisation of the crashed vehicle. A rescue helicopter crew from Dunedin was on its way because winching someone down the sides of the steep gorge might be the only way to reach any victims.

Even at the speeds Ben was pushing his ambulance, it was going to take some time to get to Goat's Corner, which was a notorious bend about halfway into the dramatic gorge with the river far below the level of the road. Between the radio messages updating him on the activity of everybody being scrambled to deal with this emergency and the automatic thought processes of running through any likely protocols for dealing with critically injured patients, Ben was aware of snatches of thoughts about the woman on the passenger seat beside him.

Of just how wrong his first impressions of JJ Hamilton had been.

That impression of her total neatness in her designer jeans and pricey boots was only a faded memory now. Kind of amusing, when a sideways glance showed her wearing a pair of steel-capped boots and that ugly, orange, long-sleeved pair of overalls that were thick enough to protect skin from superficial injuries.

Had he really pegged her as unbearably prim and proper as well?

Ha! Even Ben's total focus on the road in front of him and the upcoming corners leading into the gorge couldn't stop the flash of remembering that what he'd experienced in that high country hut totally blew that impression out of the water.

And as for sticking religiously to protocols and rules, she wasn't saying anything about the way he was pushing the ambulance to the edge of safety as the wheels clung to the road around the tight curves of this narrow road. He was breaking all the normal road rules, the way he was crossing the centre line at times. How far he was breaking the speed limit. A glance at JJ's face, in fact, revealed a gleam in her eyes that he recognised all too easily and any doubts about her being on this callout evaporated.

He knew that she didn't lack courage. She'd taught him that when she'd been up for anything he'd thrown her way that day she'd pushed herself up Twin Rocks track and agreed to be their patient for cliff rescue training. There was more than bravery in her eyes right now, however. Ben could see what he knew was a potent mix

of professional concern about what they might have
to treat and the adrenaline rush of potentially putting
one's own life in jeopardy to save the lives of others.
A balancing act of tempering risk factors with a determination to succeed.

He wouldn't have believed this version of JJ Hamilton had even existed that first day he'd met her. And it
occurred to Ben that maybe she wouldn't have believed
it either but that was the last, fleeting thought he had
on the subject because as he rounded another corner
he could see the flashing lights of Bruce's police car
blocking any oncoming traffic.

They were on scene.

CHAPTER NINE

JJ HAD ASSURED Ben that this callout would not be a problem but, as she stood on the roadside, looking down an almost sheer cliff to where the camper van was lying on the driver's side, wedged onto a ledge between the cliff and a huge, protruding lump of rock, she had a moment of serious doubt that she'd been telling the truth.

This was…shocking.

At first glance, it looked very unlikely that anybody had survived this crash but who knew? This wasn't an old VW Kombi, it was a modern, square white box and it probably had airbags and other safety features everywhere. Was it a young couple in there who had just had their love of life and dreams of adventure come to a crashing halt? Did they have a baby in a car seat, perhaps?

And how were they even going to find out? How could they get down to that crumpled vehicle and, if they could, how on earth could you treat a badly injured patient in a space like that? JJ was experienced enough and had confidence in her own skills to deal with any level of trauma but maybe that only applied when she was in her nice, safe environment of an emergency department with medics and equipment and all manner of other resources that she could summon. Where were the protocols for dealing with something like this?

What rules needed to be followed in a situation that looked so dangerous that the only direction that might have been sensible would be to stay as far away as possible?

Ben was the one who really wasn't bothered, here. He was pulling big coils of rope and other climbing gear from a compartment on the side of the fire truck and having a conversation with Mike between the directions he was shouting for his team. There were steel cables being rolled out from the back of the fire truck. Someone was laying out the pneumatic cutting gear on a tarpaulin and another crew member was lowering a long ladder over the edge of the cliff. Bruce knew exactly what he was doing as well and there was a long line of traffic already held up behind where his police car was parked sideways, its beacons flashing, to block both sides of the road.

It was a relief when Ben came towards JJ.

'You okay?'

JJ nodded. She was better than she had been a moment ago, at least, when she'd been standing here alone. Just having Ben by her side was enough to make her feel considerably braver.

'Put this harness on. And a hard hat.'

'We're going to abseil down?' JJ tried to stamp on her fear but her training sessions hadn't yet got as far as learning the skills she would need to be able to do that safely.

'No. Mike's got a ladder in place to cover the first twenty metres or so. Someone's going down to get steel cables hooked onto the vehicle to stabilise it and there'll be other ropes to use. The harness is so you can have a line attached for safety at any time. It might also be useful if we need to get winched out for any reason when the chopper gets here.'

Safety… That one word stood out enough for JJ to find the courage she needed.

Ben was helping her into the harness. 'You could also wait up here until we can extract any patients but it could take a while. We don't know yet whether we'll need to get cutting gear down the hill to get them out.' He caught her gaze and held it. 'It's your choice, JJ.'

'I came here to help. Not much point in standing back and just watching, is there?'

'That's my girl…'

There was a gleam in Ben's eyes that could be interpreted as pride. Definitely approval, anyway, and his words gave JJ more than courage. There was determination there as well now. She might not know what she should be doing but she could trust that Ben did. And she wasn't about to let him down. More than anything, she wanted to be the person Ben thought she was. Someone he had reason to be proud of. *His* girl…?

There was limited room on the rocks around the van so they had to wait until some of the fire service crew came back up, having secured the ladder, cables and ropes.

'Vehicle's stable. It's well caught in the rocks but we've got cables on, as well. You're good to go.'

'Occupants?'

'Two people. Older. The driver's not responsive. There's a woman in the passenger seat and she doesn't seem too bad. Terrified, though. We've left Jack talking to her until you guys get down. Her name's Glenys.'

'Access?'

'Front door's jammed but the side door is partially open. We'll get some gear sorted and should be able to get access that way.'

Ben nodded. 'I'll go first,' he told JJ. 'And have the pack lowered at the same time.' One corner of his mouth lifted. 'That way I'll be at the bottom and ready to catch you if you're not good with ladders or ropes.'

The worst part for JJ was having to push past the fear of lowering herself over the edge of the cliff and getting onto the ladder in the first place. This had to be the most dangerous thing she'd ever done but nothing was going to stop her. Because Ben was waiting for her at the bottom? Thank goodness she'd been working on her fitness level for weeks now. She needed the strength she had gained in her muscles, especially when it came to hanging onto ropes to get over sharp edges of rock above the ledge.

Ben had swapped places with Jack the firie as JJ climbed more rock to get high enough to see into the passenger side of the camper van. A white-haired woman had a laceration in the middle of a lump on her forehead and several trickles of blood down her face.

'Hello...' Ben leaned closer to the broken window.

'You're Glenys, aren't you? I'm Ben. I'm a paramedic. And this is my partner JJ, who's a doctor.'

His partner. JJ liked the sound of that. She managed to edge a little closer.

'We're going to look after you until we can get you out. Can you remember what happened?'

'It was all so fast... I think Derek fainted. I tried to hold the steering wheel but he fell towards me and pushed me away...'

'Were you knocked out?'

'I... No, I don't think so...'

'Headache?'

'A bit...'

'Are you feeling sick or dizzy at all?'

'I'm...just really scared...'

JJ's heart went out to the woman who had to be close to her own grandmother's age, yet she was adventurous enough to have been on the road for a camping trip. She listened as Ben sped through an initial survey to try and find out how badly injured Glenys was.

She was talking well, which meant her airway was clear and her breathing adequate. She also seemed alert enough to suggest that the bump on her head wasn't severe enough to have caused a brain injury. She might have injured her neck, however. Elderly patients could have significant C-spine trauma and show few or no neurological symptoms.

'Please...' Glenys was pleading with Ben. 'Don't worry about me. Can't you check on Derek first? He's... not moving and...' Her face crumpled in distress. 'I think he might be...it might be...too late...'

If her husband had collapsed at the wheel it was very likely that a medical event, such as a heart attack or a stroke, had been responsible for this crash. It took no more than a glance at the slumped figure on the other side of the van to see unmistakeable signs, like the colour of Derek's skin and the total absence of any visible respiratory effort or other movement, that Glenys's fears were correct.

Even if Derek had initially survived the crash, the position he was in now, with his chin on his chest, would have occluded his airway completely when he'd been unconscious. They still needed confirmation, however, and JJ could see Ben's glance go to a narrow gap where the crumpled side door of the van had been pushed in. It was probably fortunate that he was far too big to try and enter the vehicle, JJ thought. Surely that would be against any protocol for dealing with a situation like this, anyway? What if the van slid further, with someone inside? That idea was enough to send a chill down her spine.

'Ow...' Glenys cried out as she tried to turn her head to look at her husband.

'What's hurting?' JJ reached through the window to support the woman's head. 'Is it your neck?'

'Yes... But only when I move.'

JJ palpated her neck carefully. 'Does this hurt? Or this?'

'Ow...yes...that's really sore.'

'C six/seven,' JJ told Ben.

'Try and stay very still,' Ben told her. 'We're going

to put a collar on you to help look after your neck. Is anything else hurting?'

'My...my arm...' Glenys groaned again. 'I can't move it...'

She was trying to move her head again to look at her arm this time and JJ wasn't in a good position to keep it steady. She found herself eyeing up that gap in the side door. She was a lot smaller than Ben.

'Would it be safe?' she asked quietly. 'To get inside?'

'Jack seemed to think things are stable,' Ben responded. 'It might move a bit with extra weight inside but it's not going to fall. It's got steel cables that will prevent that happening.'

JJ nodded. 'I'll see if I can get inside, then. I want to get that neck stabilised. And check on Derek.'

'Wait a bit. Someone will be down to help with that any minute,' Ben said. 'I think cutting that door clear and tipping the seat flat back will be the best way to get them out.'

But with every extra minute that passed, there was a chance that Glenys could try and move her neck again and, if she had a cervical fracture, it could make a huge difference to her outcome. It might even make the difference between life and death. And JJ could see that Ben was still trying to protect her and she didn't need to be taken care of right now.

She could do this.

A month or two ago the very idea of being confident to do something like this would have been a joke but, since then, she had created a new life for herself and she had become a new person along with that. She had a new name, even. Thanks to Cutler's Creek.

Thanks to Ben Marshall.

JJ edged sideways to reach the gap in the door. Because the van was tilted, she had to climb to get a foot through into the space.

'Watch out for sharp metal,' Ben warned. 'Take your time.'

Very slowly, JJ turned sideways and eased herself cautiously through the gap, freezing for a moment at the creak and screech of metal moving slightly against rock. The rope attached to her harness went tight, preventing her going further, so she unclipped it. She could hear Ben on his radio telling Mike what was going on. Then, as she steadied herself against an inbuilt table in the back of the van to move towards the front seats, she could hear the reassurance in Ben's voice as he spoke to Glenys.

'You've broken your arm, love,' he told her. 'That's why it's so sore. Can you feel me touching your hand here?'

'No.'

'What about here?'

'No... I can't feel anything except where it hurts.'

'We're going to give you something for that pain. I just need to put a little needle in your other arm, okay?'

'But...but what about Derek? I can wait...' Glenys was breathing faster between groans and her level of distress was clearly increasing.

JJ was right behind the front seats now. She could lean forward to tilt Derek's head and open his airway.

To feel his neck for a carotid pulse. The only thing she could feel, however, was Ben's intense gaze on her. She met his eyes and gave her head a tiny shake. There was nothing they could do for Derek.

Confirming such a huge loss for Glenys was not something JJ wanted to add to an already terrifying experience. A flash of memory came and went, leaving just a shadow of how hard it had been for her own grandmother to lose her life partner and how distressing those first shocking moments of realisation had been. She could see an echoing flash of understanding in Ben's gaze, as if he could read that thought and agreed that the awful news could wait, if possible. If Glenys didn't ask, either because she wasn't ready to know herself, or because she was distracted by her own situation?

'Okay, Glenys…' he said. 'I'm going to slide this collar around your neck. Stay very still for me, okay?'

JJ held her head steady as Ben slipped the collar in place. She kept up a constant stream of reassurance for their patient but Glenys was crying now. Staying exactly where she was to hold Glenys's head still would have been a priority in any normal patient management but there were other things that needed to be done here. Like trying to get some vital signs.

'I've got a radial pulse on this side,' JJ told Ben. It wasn't possible to use a cuff and get a blood pressure reading but the fact that she could feel the pulse in the wrist meant that it wasn't low enough to be a concern. 'Heart rate's a hundred and four. Respirations twenty-two.'

'I can't get IV access on this arm,' Ben told her. 'Glenys has a displaced fracture of her radius and ulna and a dislocated elbow. Limb baselines absent in her hand so…we need some pain relief on board.'

JJ heard a lot more to that message. An absence of limb baselines meant that circulation was cut off to that hand and Glenys could lose it completely if the fracture wasn't realigned and the elbow joint relocated to prevent permanent damage to the brachial artery or nerves. This was an emergency and it would need more than simply pain relief. They were going to need some of the strongest medications they carried, like IV fentanyl and ketamine and midazolam that would pretty much knock Glenys out.

It also meant that IV access was essential and, if the arm that Ben could reach through the broken window was the injured one, access would have to be gained in the other arm. The one that JJ could reach through the gap in the front seats. Just as she was wondering how to prevent Glenys moving her neck, which could still cause damage even with the collar on, Ben leaned in to pass her a roll of tape.

'I'll put a dressing on that forehead laceration. Tape over it and round the headrest and that will keep everything still. We'll have to cut this safety belt but I don't want to do that until we're ready to get her out.' The seat belt was helping to hold Glenys still against the tilt of the van. 'I'm going to pass you the IV gear so you can get access on your side. You good with that?'

JJ nodded. She was more than good with that. She was in a space she excelled in now—with an urgent medical task to focus on. And, okay, this was an incredibly awkward space to be doing it in, compared with a nice, safe emergency department but that only made it an even more satisfying challenge to succeed in.

With a cannula safely in place and fluids running, JJ checked each ampoule that Ben had taped to the syringes he was passing her and, within only minutes, Glenys's level of distress had eased amazingly and she was sedated deeply enough to not be trying to move. It would still be painful to manipulate her broken arm and dislocated elbow but she wouldn't remember the procedure.

The awareness that her husband had probably died in this crash had also been temporarily paused and Glenys seemed to be totally unaware of the increased drama that was happening around her. A helicopter was hovering overhead and two firies were using cutting gear and a crowbar to remove the side door. At times the van was rocking enough to terrify JJ but she got through that by focusing completely on what she and Ben were doing. The awkwardness of this confined space made it very difficult for JJ to provide the counter-traction above the elbow so that Ben could pull the deformed bones and joint of Glenys's arm back into an alignment that would allow blood flow to resume and reduce ongoing nerve damage. By the time they had the arm splinted enough to keep it aligned, the back door of the van was gone. A paramedic with a stretcher was being winched down to join the rescue effort and the ledge around the crash site was becoming crowded.

'Come out, JJ. We've got this.'

'But what about getting some oxygen on? I want to

check her breathing. And we need to have someone with a bag mask available.'

'I'm monitoring her. We can't get her out with you in there. It'll be very quick to winch the stretcher up.'

'We'll take her up to the road first.' The air rescue paramedic raised his voice to be heard over the sound of the helicopter rotors. 'We'll make sure she's stable before we transport her.' He was grinning at JJ. 'See you up there, Doc.'

There were several sets of hands to help JJ climb out of the van. A rope was clipped to her harness again and someone went with her as she climbed up to road level. She was only halfway up the long ladder as the stretcher carrying Glenys was lifted, with the paramedic holding it steady. The helicopter was so close JJ could feel the beat of the rotors right through to her bones. It was terrifying but exhilarating at the same time. She could understand completely the attraction that working with a team like this had for Ben. Every day would be an adrenaline rush. Every job serious enough to provide the kind of challenges that someone like Ben thrived on.

And he was certainly at his best right now, working with the air rescue team to make sure they hadn't missed any other injuries that Glenys had and that she was stable and as comfortable as possible for transport to a major hospital. The flight paramedics clearly knew Ben well and respected his skills and, although JJ had the medical seniority here, there was nothing she would have suggested be done any differently. She was proud of the confidence and competence that Ben was displaying. Still proud that he had referred to her as his 'partner' when he'd introduced her to Glenys.

Was it true that people came into your life for a reason? Standing back to watch what was happening gave JJ a moment to feel incredibly lucky to have met Ben Marshall. Privileged to have been allowed as close as she was to this man, even if it was only for a brief time.

Because of the level of sedation she was still under, Glenys was going to need careful monitoring.

'Want to come with us, Ben? Follow up on what happens in the ED?'

He wanted to. Everyone could see just how much he wanted to.

'Go,' Mike told him. 'Bruce and I can deal with everything else that needs doing here. We'll get the driver out and the road open again. There's plenty of people who can get the ambulance back to town and JJ will be around for any emergencies, isn't that right, Doc?'

JJ nodded. Firmly. Ben had given her something amazing by including her in this callout—a confidence in herself and her ability to tackle anything in life that she would never, ever forget. She wanted to give something back.

Something that she knew could be just as life changing for him—an opportunity to live a dream of his, even if only for a brief time.

'Go,' she echoed Mike.

He didn't need telling again. They were already loading the stretcher into the helicopter down the road and Ben ran to catch up, ducking to keep well clear of the spinning rotors. He turned his head just before the clamshell doors cut off JJ's view and she saw his 'thumbs up' sign. She could almost feel the same thrill he was probably experiencing as the aircraft lifted and then swooped into the gorge to head off towards the city.

JJ could feel something else, as well. As if a part of her heart was in that helicopter with Ben and something was stretching tighter and tighter until it snapped.

And, suddenly, she felt very much alone even though she was still amongst a crowd of emergency service responders. It was only then that it really hit her. That she knew it was far more than just a suspicion that she was falling in love with Ben.

The helicopter was no more than a speck in the far distance now and it would vanish in a blink. That feeling was still there, however, and it wasn't just a part of her heart that was with Ben, was it? Without even realising it was happening, she seemed to have gifted him far too much of it.

It was a problem that would have to be dealt with at some point.

But not yet.

Please…not just yet.

CHAPTER TEN

IF YOU LOOKED through the kitchen window of the small cottage that had become JJ's home in Cutler's Creek, you could see a rather overgrown vegetable garden between the house and barn on one side and a patch of grass on the other side, where Shaun the young sheep was creating a perfect circle around the post that anchored his long chain.

Just under the kitchen window was a rustic garden bench that was in a direct line with a wooden gate beneath an archway in the dense hedge that provided excellent protection for the cottage from any wind. Right now, it was also providing a very picturesque frame for the background of the spectacular mountain range and a sunset that was beginning to make both the sky and any last remaining winter snow on the peaks look as if they had just caught fire.

'How glorious is that?'

JJ let her breath out in a contented sigh. She was also letting go of a new sense of something poignant that came with being close to Ben. A feeling that time was running out? That she needed to make the most of every single moment?

'And how good is this?' She took a sip from the glass of white wine she was holding. 'Zac told me not to even think of doing any work tonight.'

'He told me the same thing.' Ben held up his bottle of lager in a toast. 'He's going to cover any callouts. He said we were local legends after that job last night and the least he could do was give us a proper night off.'

The lingering glance he gave JJ told her exactly what he thought a 'proper' night off should include and it was enough to take a curl of desire in her belly and make it explode into a heat as glorious as the deepening flames in the evening sky. It made it even easier to forget about that disturbing wobble she'd had when she'd seen Ben flying off into the distance yesterday.

Maybe the tensions of such a dramatic callout had led to her overly emotional reaction. She'd been able to get her head around it later. To remind herself that what they had between them had only ever been meant to be a temporary thing. Something fun. Something to make the most of. If she wanted to make it last just a little longer, she needed to remember that and that delicious curl of desire was more than enough to let her push aside any anxiety about any heartache the future might bring.

It would only take the tiniest encouragement—like running her tongue along her bottom lip, perhaps—and JJ knew that Ben would sweep her into his arms and carry her off to bed. And that would be heaven but she wanted to savour this moment, too. To stretch it out and revel in a connection with someone that went so much further than something that was only physical. They'd be able to stay friends, wouldn't they? Even if life pulled them in different directions?

'Local legends, huh?' JJ smiled. 'That might explain why so many people were tooting at me and waving when they drove past while I was out for a run with Shaun. Bruce even blipped his siren behind me, which nearly made me jump out of my skin.'

She had assumed it was just that she was becoming a local curiosity—the woman that went running with her pet lamb—but the idea that she had gained respect for her part in that dramatic cliff rescue yesterday felt... really good. As if her place in this community now had a solid foundation.

'I'm surprised you had the energy to go running. I was so tired I slept for the whole bus trip back from Dunedin.'

'It was more of a jog,' JJ admitted. 'Pretty much a walk on the way back. I felt a bit wrecked myself.'

'It was full on, all right.' It was Ben's turn to sigh and the sound was so satisfied that JJ knew he was smiling without looking. 'Possibly the best job ever.'

'Was it your first time in a helicopter?'

'Yep.' Ben wiped his mouth after taking a swig of his beer. 'Won't be the last, though, that's for sure. It was way better than anything I'd imagined. And I even got invited to go into Theatre and watch the surgery.'

'Zac told me. He said that Glenys did have a cervical fracture and it was a good thing we'd immobilised her neck early on.'

'The neurosurgeons did a posterior joint fusion with screws. Orthopaedics sorted her arm fracture and the elbow dislocation. She was in Theatre for hours. I had time to visit her this morning, though, before I got the bus back and she was doing well. She made me promise to say thank you for your help. Not that she remembered very much.'

'She must be devastated, knowing that the crash killed her husband.'

'Yes and no.' For a long moment Ben tilted his head back to look up at the sky where the colours were getting even more intense. JJ was caught by the poignant lines of his profile. And that the movement had exposed that soft, vulnerable skin just below his jawline. If she touched it with her fingers, or her lips, she would feel his pulse beating against her own skin. She was on the point of moving to do just that when Ben cleared his throat and spoke again.

'She said that she was going to miss him more than anyone could imagine but she was glad it had happened the way it did.'

'Really?'

'They both knew he had a bad heart and they'd wanted to make the most of whatever time they had left. A road trip around the South Island had been a dream of his for a very long time. It was a sudden death and he wouldn't have known anything about it, and he died living his dream. Glenys said she couldn't have wished for a better way for him to go.'

He was silent for another, long moment. 'Are we living our dreams, JJ?' he asked softly.

It was on the tip of her tongue to tell Ben what she was really thinking. That this was a dream for her. She was living in the most beautiful place she'd ever known. She had a job that allowed her to not only use all her skills but provided the challenge of learning many more. She was close enough to feel the warmth of a man she could very easily fall totally in love with if she let herself and she knew that, very soon, he would be taking her into his arms and stirring a passion that she just knew she would never find again in her lifetime.

Yes…she was living her dream. But it was one she would have to wake up from, wasn't it? Because Ben wasn't living his? He'd had a taste of what he really wanted to be doing with his life yesterday when he'd been working with the air rescue crew. But, then again, there was the way he'd looked at her only minutes ago. As if there was nothing more in the world he could want. Was she brave enough to try and find out whether he might have changed his mind about his 'type'? About *her*?

'Zac offered to sell me this cottage today,' she told Ben. 'Doc Donaldson is going to finally retire and he says there'll be a permanent job for me here if I want it.'

'Don's retiring?'

'He's excited about being a full-time grandpa. Liv came home today with baby Hugo and she's going to need lots of support, with Milly to look after, as well. She popped into the hospital on her way and you should have seen Betty. She was having to dry her eyes with her apron.'

'Do you think you'll stay?'

'I'm certainly going to give it a lot of thought.' JJ looked up at where the dramatic colour in the sky was fading into a much fainter pink. 'I'm happier here than I ever thought I would be. I actually feel like a completely different person than I was when I arrived.'

'I was just thinking that myself not so long ago.'

Ben's smile was so tender it almost hurt. JJ had to drop her gaze because it felt as if she might reveal far too much. There was something else she wanted to tell him, though.

'I rang my gran last night. Treating someone like Glenys who's the same sort of age always makes me think of her, of course, but I was also thinking about what I'd told you—that my parents' accident didn't bother me because I was too young to remember it.'

She could feel Ben's steady gaze on her. 'But it did?'

'Not in the way you might think. But I did start to wonder later how different my life might have been if they hadn't died. How different *I* might have been. I think my grandparents wrapped me up in cotton wool because they'd been so devastated that they'd lost their only child. I learned to be scared of anything that might hurt me and make them unhappy. In a different life, I might have been a lot braver.'

'You are brave.' Ben's voice was little more than a whisper. 'The woman that followed me down that ladder yesterday and climbed inside the back of a van that was being held up by rocks and a couple of steel cables is one of the bravest people I've ever met.'

There was a lump in JJ's throat as she finally met Ben's gaze, which threatened to stop her being able to breathe properly. Oh, dear Lord…she wasn't in danger of falling in love with this man, was she? The fall had already happened but the landing had been so painless she hadn't even noticed. She had to look away before Ben saw something that might make him run. Had to change the direction this conversation was going.

'My gran was so horrified when I told her about doing that.' JJ even managed a chuckle. 'She didn't quite say, "You're as bad as your mother," but I could hear her thinking it.'

Ben was smiling as he pulled her into his arms. 'I'd like to have met your mother,' he said. 'And I'm quite sure your dad adored her. But you do realise you might have grown up being called Journey, don't you?'

JJ was laughing now as he kissed her. 'You'd better make sure you don't break your promise.'

'What promise?'

'That my real name is our secret.'

'Why would I break it?'

'Because my gran has decided to come and see where I'm living. She's arriving next week. I suspect she wants to persuade me to go home to a place where camper vans don't drive off cliffs. She was the one who decided I had to be called by my middle name because my first name was so appalling so you'll have something in common. You just can't talk about it, that's all.'

But Ben was clearly thinking about something else as he kissed her again, his lips soft against hers, issuing an invitation JJ knew she had no hope of resisting any longer.

'Next week?' he murmured as he finally broke the kiss. 'That's only a few days away.'

'Mmm...'

JJ could still taste that kiss but she wanted more. She ran her tongue slowly over her bottom lip to capture the memory and, because she hadn't broken the eye contact with Ben, she could see the moment that passion ignited. She wrapped her arms around his neck as he got to his feet with her in his arms.

'We'd better make the most of having this place to ourselves, then, hadn't we?'

It wasn't that Ben was deliberately avoiding meeting JJ's grandmother when she came to Cutler's Creek the following week.

He was just busy, that was all.

As always, if he wasn't already up because of an emergency callout, he was out of bed the moment his alarm sounded, and he started several days a week with a workout that had evolved over the last year or two to become a fitness session for quite a few locals because there was no gym or instructors in town. He would meet Bruce and Mike and others in the local rugby field for a vigorous warmup and then a run, and by the time he'd showered and had his breakfast it was time to start work.

Normally, some days were very quiet compared to others but Ben preferred to be cruising around if that was the case, rather than sitting on station and twiddling his thumbs. He had a few regulars in town that he could check on, like Albert Flewellan, who was still getting used to having a home oxygen supply and monitoring his lung function, and Bert, who was almost as old as Albie and had angina that had been stable for years but he still needed reminding to use his GTN spray before he started mowing his lawns or digging the vegetable garden to avoid a frightening episode of chest pain that required an emergency ambulance call. If Mike or some of the other guys were at the fire station, it was good to call in there as well to have a yarn and plan some new training sessions.

This week, however, Ben didn't have to employ his usual strategies to stave off the slightest hint of boredom because there seemed to be a sudden spike in callouts. An eight-year-old boy had fallen out of a tree in the school playground and given himself concussion. Two girls came off their ponies when they were out for a ride and one of them had broken her wrist. He had a hypoglycaemic episode of a young diabetic man and a long trip to a farm on the edge of the area he covered to a nasty accident where a farm bike had rolled on a hill. The helicopter had had to be called in for that job and Ben had been away from town for the whole afternoon.

He'd almost forgotten that JJ's mother was *in* town, in fact, when he spotted an elderly woman on the other side of the road from the ambulance station when he drove in after a cruising session on Friday afternoon. He knew she wasn't local, of course, but Cutler's Creek was a picturesque enough country town to persuade tourists to stop for a while. They liked to take pictures of the old, stone church, read the names on the war memorial in the main street or have lunch in the beer garden at the pub. Not many of them wandered as far as the ambulance station, though, or stopped to sit on the bench seat that happened to be there because it had once been a bus stop.

Ben parked the ambulance in the garage and wandered across the road. 'Are you all right, love?' he asked. 'Not lost, are you?'

'No... I'm just out for a walk. I thought I'd go and have a look at that gift shop I went past the other day.'

'The Crafty Corner?' Ben smiled. 'It's well worth a visit. People around these parts still knit tea cosies.'

'It's a bit further than I thought it would be.' The woman sighed. 'I just stopped to give my feet a bit of a rest.'

'How far have you come?'

'From the hospital.'

'That's quite a walk.' Ben was looking at the woman more carefully now. 'You weren't there because you were sick, were you?'

'Oh, no... I went out to lunch with Dr Donaldson and I was just filling in time until my granddaughter finished her work and we could go home.'

Finally, Ben clicked. 'You're JJ's grandmother, aren't you? Pleased to meet you. I'm Ben.' Would JJ have said anything to her grandmother about him? About *them*? No. Ben brushed the thought away. Why would she? It wasn't as if they were in the kind of relationship where you got introduced to family members.

'I'm Shona Hamilton.' The look Ben was getting made him feel as if he'd misbehaved in some way.

'Why on earth does everyone here call her "JJ"? What's wrong with being called "Joy"?'

'Nothing at all.' Ben couldn't help his grin as he lowered his voice to a conspiratorial whisper. 'It's a lot better than being called "Journey", though, isn't it?'

Shona Hamilton's eyes widened and then narrowed into a sharp gaze.

'Joy never tells anybody her real name. How did you find out?'

'Can't say,' Ben said. 'I'm sworn to secrecy and I'm an extremely trustworthy person.'

Shona's face softened into the kind of creases only a woman in their eighties can collect and her smile was slow and genuine.

'I think I like you, Ben Marshall,' she said. 'We'll keep this our little secret, too, shall we?'

'No worries. Now, would you like me to get you a glass of water? Or take you into town in my ambulance to save your feet?'

'No, no… I'll just sit here for a moment longer and I'll be absolutely fine. It's not exactly a hardship, is it, with that amazing view of the mountains? I'm starting to understand why Joy loves this place so much. Did you know she's thinking of staying here for ever?'

'I did hear that she was thinking about it.'

'That charming Dr Donaldson told me at lunch that they're very much hoping to persuade her to stay. He even suggested me moving here myself. Can you imagine that?'

Actually, Ben could imagine that. Shona Hamilton would fit right in amongst the older characters in this community and it would be the perfect place to spend the last years of one's life. He would probably drift back here to live himself, sometime in the future, when he'd had his fill of adventures. Who wouldn't want to sit on a bench like this, on a quiet street, soaking up the sheer pleasure of looking at mountain peaks like theirs?

He and his nan used to sit like this, at the top of the steps on the edge of their veranda, and they'd gaze at a very similar mountain view. His earliest memories were of being cuddled in her lap as she'd sat and watched a sunset but, as he'd got older, they would sit side by side. They wouldn't say much, if anything at all. He'd lean his head on her shoulder, even when he'd got to be a teenager and would have died of embarrassment if any of his mates had seen him, because that had been his happy place. His refuge. The place where he'd known he was loved the most by the person *he* loved the most. His nan. The one person who had ever really wanted him.

He'd missed sitting with her, so, so much. He'd only been fifteen when she'd died suddenly but his mother had been living in Australia for years by then. She'd sold his nan's house and used the money to pack him off to a boarding school and then university so that she could finally abdicate a responsibility she'd never wanted in the first place.

And here he was, with someone who was about the same age as his nan would have been, and she wasn't someone familiar enough to have been slotted somewhere safe, like into the compartment of a patient he could focus on treating or someone who had a clearly defined role, like Betty at the hospital. To him, Shona was JJ's grandma. Someone who'd raised a child of *her* child.

Just like his nan.

And…and Ben could feel a lump in his throat that he'd never sat still long enough to feel since…for ever ago. Since he'd been about fifteen, in fact. He couldn't sit still any longer, either. He was on his feet before he'd even processed the thought.

'I'll have to go,' he said. 'There's a patient I forgot to check on when I was out and about before. Are you sure I can't drop you into town? Or back at the hospital, maybe?'

'No, thanks, love. I can manage the rest of the walk into town and Joy will come and pick me up when she's finished work.' She got to her feet, picking up an old-fashioned handbag from the seat beside her and Ben realised she was just about as short as his nan had been. The white curls on Shona's head barely reached above his elbow. She was smiling up at him. 'Don't forget…' she warned.

'Forget what?' Ben was already moving—the need to find something to distract himself almost overwhelming.

'Our little secret.' Shona tapped her nose. 'About Joy…?' Her smile widened as Ben turned back. 'Or perhaps I should remember to say JJ? I get the feeling she likes her new name as much as this place and all her new friends.' Already faded blue eyes were looking distinctly misty now. 'I worry about her. I always have and always will. But she's happy and that's all you ever want for someone you love, isn't it?'

* * *

'So… I hear you met my gran the other day?'

'It was supposed to be our little secret.' Ben put the newspaper wrapped parcel of fish and chips he had picked up from Cutler's Creek's only takeaway on the kitchen bench of JJ's cottage. 'It's a thing I have with Hamilton women.'

JJ laughed. 'You certainly made an impression. She only told me about meeting you when we were on our way to Queenstown this afternoon so she could get her flight home. She said you were a very "charming young man".'

'And did you agree with her?' Ben was smiling down at JJ, loving the way she held his glance, her eyes dancing with amusement—or perhaps just the pleasure of seeing him again.

'I didn't dare say anything. I think she guessed that there was something going on between us. I don't think she would have believed me if I'd told her we were just good friends, so it was safer not to say anything.'

The shaft of disappointment that JJ would describe their connection as simply a friendship came from nowhere. Or maybe it went deeper than that and it was a fear that he might be missing out on something important in life but, whatever it was, it had no right to appear at all. It wasn't as if Ben wanted anything more than a good friendship with JJ. Heaven forbid…he had always run a mile when any woman had got 'serious'. The beat of silence between them made him think he was expected to say something himself but JJ was still smiling up at him and she was the one who broke the silence.

'She liked you a lot. Which is possibly why she warned me off.'

'What?' Ben's eyebrows shot up. 'And there I was thinking we'd bonded for life, your gran and me.'

JJ was laughing. 'She said she suspected you were a "bit wild".'

'A bit wild, huh?' Ben pulled JJ closer.

It had been too long since he'd kissed this woman, what with her having a visitor in the cottage all week. And what better way to dismiss that odd feeling that he might be missing out on anything. This was everything that any man could possibly want—a gorgeous woman and the best sex ever with no strings attached.

An almost desperate desire to sink into that delicious distraction didn't mean he couldn't take his time, though, with a gentle, teasing touch of his lips on hers. A tiny flick of his tongue on her lower lip as she pressed closer, her body melting against his as she wrapped her arms around his neck. He loved the way she did that. And the way her eyes drifted shut as she tilted her head back, as though all she wanted to focus on was this moment.

This kiss...

If he turned up the heat, they would be in her bed in no time flat. How was it that he'd completely lost track of how many times they'd made love over the last weeks but it still felt just as thrilling as that very first time in that mountain hut? No, that wasn't quite true, was it? It felt *better*. Just as exciting but there was a different dimension to it that he couldn't quite name. Safety, perhaps? Because they knew each other's bodies so intimately now but, instead of creating boundaries, it provided a foundation that was safe enough to keep exploring. To find a new touch or rhythm or level of closeness that seemed to suggest being with JJ could never, ever get boring.

Maybe *trust* was the word he was looking for?

Not that an accurate analysis was needed. Ben just knew how to play the heat level like a well-tuned instrument now and a crescendo would be all the more satisfying if they waited a while to enjoy the anticipation. Besides, he'd missed lunch today.

'I'm starving,' he confessed, breaking the kiss before desire could obliterate anything other physical need. 'And I'd hate for Cutler's Creek's best battered cod and chips to go soggy.'

JJ's hand slid from his neck to the front of his chest and pushed gently as if she needed a boost to move away from him. 'Make some space on the table,' she told him. 'I'll get the bread and butter so you can have your chippie sandwiches.'

The pile of stuff on the table suggested that JJ had had trouble finding something in her shoulder bag. It reminded Ben of that first day he'd met her and how he'd known how rattled she'd been because she was a neat freak but she'd just emptied the contents of her bag onto the table. He'd also known that he had been the one to help push her well out of any comfort zone by arriving with that lamb in the box.

He would have taken it away again if he'd thought she couldn't cope—he'd just wanted to tease her a bit. In retrospect, however, he knew that he'd liked being the reason she'd been rattled. He'd teased her because it had been a safe way to play with what was a totally inappropriate attraction. He might have believed he didn't want anything to do with the new locum doctor on a personal level but, deep down, his body—or soul—had recognised something very different.

There was an old, lumpy envelope amongst the collection of things like hand cream and tissue packs and a lipstick or two. It wasn't sealed so he could see that it was stuffed full of photographs as he picked it up. JJ reached past him to put down the board with a mound of freshly sliced bread.

'Gran gave me those. At the airport. She said she thought I might need some family stuff around if I'm wondering whether to stay here for ever.'

'May I look?'

JJ's eyebrows rose. 'You're asking permission?'

'It's a private sort of thing.'

'Oh…yeah…like a passport?'

So he wasn't the only one to get flashbacks of the first time they'd met? Interesting… There was no reprimand in JJ's tone, however. It was more like a private joke about what had led to a pact to keep a secret. That first baby step they'd taken towards a connection, and a friendship that might not be 'serious' but it was certainly more significant than anything Ben had ever experienced before in his life.

Because…yes…*trust* was the word he'd been searching for.

They trusted each other. They were on the same page about enjoying what they had together with no expectations of anything permanent. Quite the opposite, in fact, and maybe that was why it was always so good to be together, because they were both making the most of every moment while it lasted.

It was a rare night off for both of them at the same time so they opened a bottle of wine. Ben flattened chunky pieces of fried potato between his slices of buttered bread and they broke off generous servings of delicious fish fillets in crispy batter to eat with their fingers. They had to wipe their hands as they spread the photographs from the envelope over the table in front of them.

'Most of these I've never seen,' JJ told Ben. 'They were part of the only belongings that got packed up and taken back to New Zealand when my grandparents came to get me—and my father's body. Gran said she was sorry. She should have given them to me long ago.'

'What happened to your mother's body?'

'She's buried somewhere in the south of France. I got the impression that her family blamed my father for the accident as much as my family blamed her.'

'So you've never met your mother's family?'

JJ shook her head. 'I've always wanted to go but… well, I knew how much it would upset my grandparents. Even falling off my pony when I was seven frightened Gran so much I stopped my riding lessons and that was my favourite thing to be doing.' She shook her head. 'And, yeah… I know it's a bit pathetic but I was so focused on med school and then life just got so busy and… I just haven't made it to the other side of the world yet. One day…'

Ben stilled for a moment, his heart giving a peculiar squeeze. The words were on the tip of his tongue but something stopped him from saying them aloud.

We could do that one day... I'll come with you... It'd be fun, wouldn't it?

Maybe it was that squeeze tightening a notch or two that squashed the words so they didn't emerge. He couldn't make a promise he might not be able to keep because he would hate himself if he hurt someone who was such a genuinely *nice* person. He could imagine JJ as a small girl, taking on the responsibility of trying to keep her grandmother happy because she cared that much. Enough to make sure she followed all the rules and kept herself and the people she loved as safe as she possibly could.

But there was another part of the real JJ, wasn't there? And maybe Ben was the first person to have seen the brave, adventurous side of her. Looking at these old snapshots of a young couple making the most of life—plastered with tomatoes in La Tomitina festival in Spain, dancing in the rain at Glastonbury, walking in a lavender field in Provence—he could see who she'd probably inherited her adventurous streak from. She was definitely her mother's daughter.

'Your gran would have said your mum was a "bit wild", too, I guess?'

'Oh, absolutely. It was the biggest reprimand I could get as a kid. Nobody had to say it. They'd just look at me—sort of surprised and disappointed at the same time—and I'd know they were thinking that I was just like my mother and that it wasn't a good thing to be.'

'You look so like her.' Ben wiped his fingers again and then picked up the photograph of her parents dancing in the rain. With drooping flowers in her waist-length dark hair that was loose and totally soaked, wearing denim dungarees with nothing but a bra beneath them, she must have been frozen but he'd never seen such a look of joy on someone's face as she looked up at the tall, young man whose hands she was holding. And he was looking just as happy. Just as utterly in love with life and the person he'd found to share it with.

'I probably *was* conceived at that festival.' JJ was grinning. 'You were spot on when you guessed but I didn't want to give you the satisfaction of being right.'

'Is that where they met?'

'Yes. My father had gone to a conference in London. He'd just finished his double degree with honours—in law and accountancy—and my grandfather had already changed the letterhead for his legal firm to be Hamilton and Hamilton but some people he met at the conference were going to the festival for the weekend and he got invited to tag along. My mum, Celine, was singing there and they somehow met each other and that was that. My dad…never came back. I'm sure he meant to. Eventually.'

'I'm not surprised they wanted time to just be together,' Ben said softly. 'They look so much in love.'

'They do, don't they? I like to think that they were that happy. It's not something everyone finds in life, is it?'

There was an odd note in JJ's voice. Something so poignant it brought a lump to Ben's throat and made him want to offer comfort. To tell her that she would find that kind of love one day herself. Why wouldn't she? Who wouldn't want to be with someone as beautiful and intelligent and courageous as JJ?

She was gathering up the photographs now. Stuffing them back into that old envelope. And then she started clearing the table and Ben could recognise that need to be busy to stop thinking about something that caused some kind of pain and he knew he could help.

He knew exactly how to distract JJ. And, as a bonus, it was exactly what he wanted most in the world himself right now. He got to his feet and went to where she was standing in front of the sink. He turned off the tap and took the dish brush out of her hands. Without saying anything, he smoothed tiny, stray tresses of hair away from her face and then held her head between his hands as he bent to kiss her.

And, this time, the gentle teasing with his lips and tongue swiftly morphed into something that both offered and demanded complete focus. He meant business, and, when he slid his hands down the length of JJ's body a minute or two later to pull her hips closer to his own, she would be in no doubt what that business was all about. It seemed like she more than welcomed the distraction and the task of tidying up and washing plates was abandoned without a second thought for either of them. It could wait. Until the morning, even, because Ben couldn't imagine wanting to leave JJ's bed any time soon.

There was only so long that even the most passionate lovemaking could last, mind you, and at some point considerably later Ben found himself with JJ in his arms, feeling her heart rate slowly decrease and hearing her breathing return to a resting soft sigh. Her skin was warm against his. His lips were being tickled by her hair as he pressed a kiss to her head and the scent of her was filling his nostrils. She was so quiet that Ben wondered if she was falling asleep but her muscle tone told him that she was still awake. She was just... being with him...

Slowly—so slowly that Ben hardly noticed it happening—he could feel himself slipping into a space that he'd been reminded of very recently thanks to that encounter with JJ's grandmother.

That space of just being with someone that you loved and that you were loved *by*. A sense that all was right with the world. That pure joy could be as simple as just sitting still with that person. Being *with* them...body and soul...

It was why Ben had never let himself sit still ever since his nan had died, wasn't it? Because, if he did, he would remember how it felt to love and be loved like that. And he would have to remember the devastation of losing that kind of love. He'd never let himself get close enough to anyone to be in danger of facing that kind of loss ever again but...

But he was in very real danger of falling in love with JJ Hamilton.

He could feel it hovering. A force that had the power to push him over that particular cliff and create the fall. And he couldn't let it happen because he would lose before he'd even attempted to win. This had never been meant to happen. Part of that trust he had with JJ was because he'd felt safe. Had that feeling of safety meant that he'd let down his guard and that closeness had grown without him even noticing it?

But neither of them were anything like each other's 'type' and they'd both agreed they were incompatible and it could never work long term. JJ had made it crystal clear that this connection was only temporary and he'd been totally on board. He just had to live up to his end of the bargain, now. For both their sakes. And, for the sake of a friendship that they might be able to keep for ever, if he didn't ruin it by suggesting it could be something more.

So much more, it felt like it could be everything—more than he'd ever had before, and that was a terrifying thought because he already knew what it was like to lose something huge. How hard it had been to build a new life and to find something that he could be passionate about but still keep himself safe. He'd found that in his work. Never in a person because he knew when he was stepping into dangerous territory and he knew so well how to retreat or change direction, it had become automatic. How had he ventured further than ever before into that forbidden space without an alarm sounding?

It was sounding now, however, loudly enough to scare Ben into action despite it feeling oddly hard to breathe suddenly and that it was taking an astonishing amount of effort to force his body to move.

He pressed another kiss to JJ's hair. Took another breath just to drink in what he knew was going to be the last intimate scent of this amazing woman.

'Gotta go,' he whispered. 'Early start tomorrow.'

'Okay...'

He knew JJ was watching him as he pulled his clothes back on but he didn't turn back. Not until he was at her bedroom door and even then it was only for a heartbeat.

''Night, JJ... Sleep well...'

CHAPTER ELEVEN

IT HAD BEEN the most perfect night of JJ's life.

She had woken up the next morning knowing that something had changed. Something amazing. Something that had the promise of making the rest of her life as perfect as it could possibly be?

She was still thinking about it when she went to give Shaun his container full of sheep nuts for breakfast, just as the sun was rising and the first light was kissing the mountaintops in the distance with a promise of it becoming a glorious spring morning. How could it not be a gorgeous day when it felt like JJ was floating an inch or two off the ground? Happier than she'd ever felt in her life?

That moment, when Ben had tried to protect her from dealing with the camper van crash and she'd felt that touch on her soul that had warned her that she was falling in love with him had been one-sided. Last night had made her feel as if there was more to it than simply a touch. That there was a kind of filament attached to that place that had been touched and it was being held on the other end by Ben. She could believe that what she was feeling wasn't one-sided any longer. He might not be ready to accept it, but it was there.

Maybe it had been something in his eyes when she'd told him that her grandmother was suspicious there was something more than friendship going on between them—as if he wanted that to be true but was afraid of admitting it? It had been her turn to feel protective then, and it had been no hardship to respond to that… oh, so distracting kiss.

Or perhaps it had happened when he'd been looking at that photo. That note in his voice when he'd commented on how much in love her parents looked had almost brought her to tears. She could hear a poignancy that suggested he was looking at perfection in a relationship that he never expected to find for himself.

Maybe JJ hadn't expected it, either. She most certainly hadn't expected to find it with someone like Ben Marshall—the kind of rule-bending, charismatic, maverick bad boy that she'd been brought up to believe that getting too close to would only lead to trouble. Or worse…

But wasn't that exactly how she'd found what she'd been searching for?

This chapter of JJ's life had all begun because her relationship with Ian had died a natural death. Because he'd let her know that she was possibly the most boring person on earth. Because she'd been left wondering if was doing something wrong in the way she was living her life and that she might be missing out on something that was very, very important. As crucial as the real meaning of life, even?

Coming to Cutler's Creek had indeed changed her life. Changed *her*. Or, rather, meeting Ben Marshall had.

He'd given her a new name right from the start which, with the benefit of hindsight, JJ could see as pretty much an invitation to discover who she really was. Joy, the good girl? Or JJ, who might actually be a bit wild and adventurous, just like her mother had been?

He'd challenged her, physically and emotionally, to get fitter and to learn new things that she'd never considered relevant before. To become at least a more interesting person, if not a markedly better version of herself.

And he'd shown her what passion was all about. More than ever before in her life, JJ was missing having a mother. No, not 'a' mother. *Her* mother. So that she could have talked about how she was feeling right now with someone who had, apparently, lived life in a way that gave her the kind of joy—and love—that was precisely what JJ had feared she'd was never going to experience.

Talking to Shaun the sheep wasn't going to be helpful in any way at all but JJ found herself doing it anyway. Perhaps it made how she was feeling more real by hearing the words spoken aloud?

'I'm in love with him,' she told Shaun, as she moved his post so that he could enjoy fresh grass for the day. 'Yeah… I know he's a bad boy but, you know what?'

Shaun nudged her hand, looking for more food, but JJ pretended it was because he wanted the answer to that question. She was smiling as she leaned closer, checking that his collar was comfortable.

'I reckon I've got a bit of bad girl in me. Deep down and you know what *that* means?'

Shaun had started eating grass. He wasn't interested, but JJ was going to tell him anyway. Because she had to tell someone.

'It means we're soul mates. And I think that Ben knows that, too. He just needs a bit of time to get used to the idea.'

Yes…it had been the most perfect night. Or *almost* the most perfect night because it would have been even better if she'd fallen asleep in Ben's arms and they'd woken up together this morning. That didn't really bother her because he'd never stayed a whole night. Yet. He probably thought he was protecting her reputation in Cutler's Creek or that he didn't want to disturb her sleep with the kind of pre-dawn start that let him have a workout with his fitness group before starting a shift at the ambulance station at seven a.m.

Maybe that was why JJ didn't see it coming. And why what happened only a couple of days later was so shocking.

He hadn't intended to tell her like this, in front of a whole bunch of people.

It just happened.

Because he'd only had the phone call the evening before and all the people who needed to know what was about to happen were all in the same place at the same time.

Cutler's Creek Hospital's kitchen.

Betty had outdone herself making a morning tea

to welcome Zac Cameron back to work full time and to celebrate his family being together again. His gorgeous wife, Liv, had baby Hugo in her arms and the adorable two-year-old Milly was being held up by her grandfather so that she could choose a treat from the laden table.

'What about a lamington, Milly? Or a sausage roll?'

'No. *That* one…' A small finger was pointing to a platter right in front of Ben.

'A girl after my own heart.' Ben picked up two warm triangles of cheese toastie. 'Here you go, sweetheart. One for you and one for me.'

The staff on duty, including nurses, cleaners and the receptionist, were balancing cups of tea and paper serviettes laden with food but there were lots of other people as well, like Bruce and Mike and many of the volunteers that gave their time to both the ambulance and fire services. Don Donaldson, the man who'd followed in his father's footsteps as the local doctor and who'd kept Cutler's Creek Hospital going despite threats of closure, had just given a speech to welcome Zac back and to express his profound relief that their family was reunited.

'I never dreamed my life could be this wonderful,' he told everyone. 'All those years ago I thought I'd hit the jackpot, just getting a locum to come to Cutler's Creek for a while, when Zac arrived here. I never thought he'd bring my daughter back into my life, let alone start a whole new chapter of the Donaldson family's story. I nearly didn't get to live to see it, mind you, with that bit of drama that put me out of action for a while but that only makes it all the more precious. All I need now is to find my replacement so that the next party we have will be to celebrate a *real* retirement. None of this part-time nonsense, no matter how much I enjoy working with you all.'

He was looking at JJ as he spoke, his smile teasing, but everybody knew there was a genuine plea there. They all knew that the offer had been made and that JJ had promised to think about it and they were all hoping she would choose to stay. Ben agreed with the consensus. JJ was perfect for Cutler's Creek. Dedicated, clever and courageous. A brilliant doctor who would only become more and more of a vital part of this community in general and the emergency services branch of it in particular. It was just a damn shame he wouldn't be here to watch that happen.

This was the first time Ben had seen her since the night he'd taken the fish and chip dinner to her cottage. The place he'd ended up being oddly desperate to escape from. It had been a lot more difficult to escape from that background need to keep moving and stay well clear of that disturbing kind of stillness that had prompted him to leave her bed that night but the perfect opportunity to prevent him possibly ever being that still again had presented itself only last night.

The chance to live his dream.

JJ's head turned, as if she could feel Ben watching her as Don Donaldson was finishing his speech, and the instant her gaze met his, Ben knew she could see something in his expression—or perhaps even read his mind—and she was suddenly confused. Bewildered, even? Had she been seeking encouragement to commit to the job here and being a part of Cutler's Creek permanently but she had picked up the vibe that he wasn't going to be here himself?

Everybody was waiting for JJ to respond in some way and Ben could sense her hesitation. He could understand it, too. She was standing at a rather significant crossroad in her life at this moment and it was a huge decision. One that he didn't think she should be forced to make in public, like this, which gave him an urge to protect her. To deflect the attention and give her some time to collect herself.

He did realise that it might not be the kindest way to tell her his news but it was certainly the easiest. Possibly the only way, because if he was alone with JJ and close enough to touch her, he might have changed his mind and taken a chance on a very different direction in his own life.

'I have a bit of an announcement myself,' he said aloud.

Every head turned in his direction. Except for JJ, who dropped her gaze, as if she knew she might need a moment of relative privacy.

'I had a call last night,' Ben told them. 'One of the guys on the helicopter crew in Dunedin had an accident on his motorbike and he'll be out of action for some time. I've been offered a spot to train and work with the crew.'

He'd certainly made himself the centre of attention instead of JJ. Mike was beaming.

'Wow…you've had your heart set on that for a long time, mate. Congratulations.'

But Zac was looking dismayed. 'You're going to be missed around here. What will we do without you?'

'There's a locum paramedic from Invercargill who'll fill in until a permanent station manager can be found but, hey, you guys—and the volunteers on the team—can manage anything yourselves, you know. I can just drop in and do the transport.'

Betty was scowling. 'When?' she demanded. 'When are you leaving?'

'Um…it's short notice. I'm sorry. I'm hoping to head out of town by the day after tomorrow.'

The silence that followed his admission was broken only by whimpers from baby Hugo. People were exchanging glances and Ben was taken aback by the wave of emotion he could feel in this room.

Had he become a more integral part of this community than he'd realised? In his need to keep moving and his instant acceptance of the job offer, he hadn't really factored in that he was going to hurt people that he cared about. A lot. He was going to miss them as much, if not more than they would miss him.

He was giving up the place that had been his home for several years.

He was giving up friends. The kind of friends that would have always had his back, no matter what, just as he would have had theirs.

He was giving up JJ.

The silence grew. So did the lump in Ben's throat. But then someone spoke. Clearly enough that perhaps it was only Ben who could pick the note of courage beneath the words.

'Seeing as it's the morning for announcements,' JJ said, 'I'd like you all to know that I'm going to accept the permanent position that I've been offered here at Cutler's Creek. You can be as much of a full-time grandpa as you want, Don, and enjoy more time with Jill. And, Zac? Let's talk about that cottage later. I think Shaun and I will be very happy to make it our home for the foreseeable future.'

The atmosphere in the kitchen did a rollercoaster swoop and any upset about Ben's departure seemed to have been forgotten in the very real delight that JJ had decided to stay. He was as delighted as anybody. He was also proud of her. She'd come a very long way since he'd knocked her off her feet on the side of the road. She'd not only made herself a part of this community, she seemed to have found her feet and a confidence in what she wanted in her life.

JJ Hamilton was going to be fine, even if he wasn't going to be around to look after her, and knowing that was probably going to make it a little easier to leave. Ben was still relieved that he wasn't going to have too much time to think about it, though. No time at all, really, given the amount of packing and organisation he had to have done by tomorrow.

He needed to get on with that, in fact, so he shouldn't be standing around here drinking coffee and eating Betty's cheese toasties. The noise level in the kitchen was increasing rapidly with people gathering around JJ, eager to tell her and each other how happy they were that she wasn't going anywhere.

Nobody noticed when Ben slipped quietly from the room.

He'd told her that she was one of the bravest people he'd ever met.

She was certainly a very different person from the one who'd arrived in Cutler's Creek, looking for time out from a life that she hadn't been sure she'd been happy with, and JJ knew she had Ben to thank for the new version of herself that she'd grown into.

However hard it was going to be to get used to not having Ben Marshall in her life, she would always be thankful that she'd met this amazing person and perhaps the best way she could show him how much he meant to her was to give all the encouragement she could so that he could find exactly what he wanted from life.

Maybe that was why she found more courage than ever at that moment and had made a choice that was a public confirmation of the new person she had become. Someone who recognised what the most important things in her life were and that was…belonging. Caring about something to the point of passion, and that didn't necessarily have to be a particular person, did it? It could be a profession with new facets to her work—like a qualification in mountain rescue. A community that had more than its share of warm-hearted, generous people. A small, rural hospital, even, that offered such a variety of work and skill levels required that it would never get boring.

It took even more courage, however, to keep smiling when she'd seen Ben walking out of those kitchen doors—out of the perfect life that she'd been dreaming about only in the last day or two—and JJ knew that it might take a long time for her to be able to remember that moment without a pain that was sharp enough to make her catch her breath every single time.

She wasn't wrong.

In some ways, it actually got worse. For the first few days, that included saying goodbye to Ben, wishing him all the best and exchanging promises to keep in touch. Pushing that pain to one side was necessary to simply keep functioning. That the first couple of weeks without him were so busy also helped keep it at bay. Having negotiated the purchase price of Zac's cottage, a few visits to Queenstown had to be slotted into her timetable to talk to her bank manager and arrange for a solicitor to draw up the sales agreement and there were plenty of other things to think about, too.

'That big paddock through the gate in the hedge is yours,' Zac warned JJ. 'It needs a bit of managing. I've been getting Greg to mow it for hay every summer and he runs a mob of sheep on it occasionally to keep it down but you might want to use it for something else. There used to be a Clydesdale horse there, called Chloe, who kind of came with the property. Greg's looking after her on his farm at the moment but I'm sure she'd love to come back to her old paddock. She'd be great company for that pet sheep of yours.'

'I'll think about it,' JJ promised. 'I need the contact details for the septic tank company, too. And that hedge cutting firm. Oh…and I'll need to get some firewood in so that it's dry for next winter, too, won't I?'

Cutler's Creek's temporary ambulance station manager, Trevor, was doing his part to keep JJ busier than usual. A perfectly pleasant man in his late fifties, Trevor was an EMT rather than a paramedic but he was keen to provide the best service he could at his lower skill level. JJ was determined to do *her* best as well and not to make negative comparisons to Ben but it wasn't easy, especially after she noticed on his first visit to the hospital that Trevor carried a notebook version of ambulance protocols in a pocket of his uniform and referred to them frequently.

It made JJ realise how she must have seemed to Ben when he'd come into the hospital that day and found she'd labelled practically every single item and cupboard in their treatment room/emergency department. It seemed like a lifetime ago that she'd needed to follow rules so rigidly to feel safe but, at the same time, it was so patently obvious that they were such different people. How had she been so sure she'd found the person who was her soul mate? And why was she now living with an emptiness that made her so sure she was never going to meet anyone else she felt like that about?

With Zac's family responsibilities including a very precious, tiny baby, it had been easy to persuade him to let JJ be first on call—day or night—for any ambulance callouts for potential medical or trauma emergencies that might need a doctor attending. With Trevor's skill level combined with his determination to follow every guideline and to err on the side of caution those calls for backup were coming in often enough to add noticeably to her workload.

There was a dislocated finger on the rugby field on a Saturday morning and an urgent call to a suspected heart attack later the same day, but it turned out that Bert had, once again, forgotten to use his GTN spray before doing something a bit more energetic. The call to a woman in labour a couple of days after that had both JJ and Debbie responding to meet the ambulance at a farm well out of town, but that also turned out to be a false alarm. The woman, who was visiting her aunt, was most likely experiencing her first Braxton-Hicks contractions and they had both panicked.

'I miss Ben,' Debbie said as they drove back to the hospital, now well behind in everything else that needed to be done that afternoon. 'Even if she'd been well into second stage labour, he would have probably just delivered the baby and turned up at the hospital with them both.'

JJ simply nodded her agreement. She and Debbie had become good friends but she couldn't admit just how deeply she was missing Ben. Because talking about it not only wouldn't help, it could, quite easily, make it a whole lot worse.

'Do you think he made the right decision? To leave?'

'I think we all have to do what's best for us. You only get one life, don't you, and you have to follow your dreams.'

'And you think you've made the right decision? To stay here?'

'I love it here.' JJ nodded again, more enthusiastically this time. 'I'm still getting surprised by how much. D'you know, I told Zac the other day that I needed to know where to order firewood from so I can get a supply in before next winter and I got home from work yesterday to find that someone had dumped a trailer load of cut wood in front of the barn. I have no idea who. That's not something that would have ever happened anywhere else I've lived.'

Debbie had turned to watch the countryside rolling past from the side window. 'I'm glad you're happy here. I hope Ben's happy in his new job, too. No... I take that back.' Her sideways smile was mischievous. 'I hope he *hates* his new job and comes back here before anyone permanent gets appointed to our station.'

'I suspect he's very happy,' JJ said quietly. 'One of these days, he'll drop in wearing his flight suit and helmet with the biggest smile on his face we've ever seen.'

When she had reason to summon the rescue helicopter only a week or so later, she watched it land on the road close to where she was stabilising a young man who'd come off his motorcycle at high speed and her heart was pounding. Was that Ben at one end of the stretcher, stooping to move beneath rotors that would keep spinning so they could take off within minutes to get this critically injured patient to a major trauma centre?

Any disappointment that Ben wasn't part of the crew was easily dismissed until the handover of her patient was complete and the air rescue crew was ready to load the stretcher back into the helicopter. It was only then that JJ couldn't stop herself asking.

'How's Ben? I… I thought I might see him today…'

'He's up in Christchurch for a couple of days. Doing a HUET course.'

'HUET?'

'Helicopter Underwater Escape Training.'

JJ's eyes widened. She could only imagine how much of an adrenaline rush learning to deal with a time-critical emergency like that would be. 'Wow…he must be loving that.'

The crew was already moving now but the paramedic turned to grin at JJ. 'If anybody was born to do this job, it's Ben. You'll see him soon.'

In a way, knowing that she was very likely to see him soon made JJ miss him even more. How hard was it going to be, that first time, to see that he had made totally the right decision and that he was loving his new life away from Cutler's Creek?

Away from her…

She wasn't the only person missing Ben, of course. Mike was looking downcast when JJ met him in the supermarket early on Sunday afternoon.

'We're all losing our fitness,' he told JJ. 'And getting rusty on important stuff like our abseiling skills. We've decided to do something about that. I might hike up Twin Rocks track later today and make sure it's not blocked by any trees or a slip or something.'

'Good for you.'

'So you're in, then? For a full session on Twin Rocks with the whole group next Saturday?'

'Oh, help…' JJ hadn't even been jogging with Shaun in the last few weeks and she could remember only too well the pain of struggling up that track that first time. She had a whole week to get her body moving again before Saturday, though, and she couldn't encourage others without showing she was willing herself. The skills the guys in this community had when it came to difficult rescues were part of the legacy Ben had left a community he'd been passionate about. And it was a legacy more than well worth preserving. 'Okay... I'm in. Next Saturday.'

She would take Shaun out as soon as she got home, she decided. And, in the spirit of honouring Ben's legacy, she was also going to wear that old red, sweatshirt of his that he'd given her that day of the river crossing incident.

The day they'd first made love...

As a means of distracting herself, JJ couldn't wait to get started but it seemed that her pet sheep wasn't so enthusiastic and he was big enough now for it to be impossible for JJ to drag him into co-operating when he had no desire to go running.

'Oh, fine... I'll go by myself.' But, on the point of heading out to the roadside to start running, JJ changed her mind. If she was by herself, there was nothing stopping her from jumping into her car, driving to the start of the Twin Rocks track and giving that a go—just to find out whether she had, indeed, lost every bit of that fitness Ben had helped her achieve. The keys were still in her car, because Cutler's Creek was the kind of place where you didn't need to lock your car or house, so she didn't even need to take the time to go back into the cottage.

And it didn't matter that a quick glance at the sky revealed the slightly ominously dark bases to the huge, fluffy clouds. She wouldn't have to go all the way to the top to test her fitness level so she'd probably be home in an hour and back before Mike got started, which might be a good thing if she was out of breath and stopping too often. And, even if it did start raining before she got back home, it was no big deal. She wasn't going to melt, was she?

Halfway up the Twin Rocks track, JJ realised just how much harder this was after a few weeks of not pushing herself. She could even feel discomfort in that sprained ankle that had healed months ago. Instead of turning back, however, she pushed herself harder. Because she could imagine that Ben was watching her and, even if he couldn't possibly know about it, she still wanted to feel that he would be proud of her. The extra motivation worked well until she got to that point in the track where she had to scramble over those huge boulders. The ones that Ben had helped her negotiate that first time. How could she not remember what had happened only a little later that day. That moment when he'd been helping her into that harness. When the world had stopped turning for a heartbeat because they'd both been thinking about kissing each other.

And how much they'd wanted to…

The curl of desire was more like the stab of a knife in her belly and JJ knew she had tears streaming down her face. But she didn't stop. Or even slow down. She couldn't, because if she did, she might sit there sobbing, and how pathetic would that be? Ben had given her the gift of believing in herself and she was damned well going to make the most of it.

Maybe it was a burst of too much enthusiasm that did it. Perhaps it was because she was half-blinded by tears. It could have been that the first drops of rain had made the boulders more slippery than she remembered or, more likely, that she still had a residual weakness in the tendons of that ankle she'd sprained. Whatever the cause, the result was just as catastrophic. As she put every ounce of effort into boosting herself over the last obstacle, JJ lost her footing. She not only fell hard towards the downhill side of the track, she found herself rolling down the edge of the steep gully, through ferns and bracken and over hard lumps of rock.

It wasn't until she was caught by a larger rock nestled in the roots of a tree that the fall came to a crunching halt. She felt, rather than heard the snap of the bone in her ankle but she couldn't miss hearing the distant rumble of thunder that came in the next few seconds as she lay there, desperately trying to make sense of what had just happened and working out how badly injured she might be. The good news was that, apart from bumps and bruises, she didn't seem to have broken any other bones. The bad news was that JJ was realising just how many rules she had broken.

She wasn't dressed for bad weather.

She had no emergency supplies with her. She hadn't even brought her phone because she hadn't needed to go back into the cottage for her car keys.

She also hadn't told anyone where she was going or when she might return.

At the same time she was cataloguing her stupid errors, JJ had two other thoughts vying for prominence in the back of her mind.

One was how disappointed Ben would be in her.

The other was that she might well be in trouble, here. Big trouble.

CHAPTER TWELVE

'BIT OF BAD weather brewing down south. We might get grounded later on this afternoon.'

'Fine by me.' Ben waved at a stack of books on the table beside him. 'I've got a lot of revision to do. I've stuffed so much into my head in the last few weeks, some of it's in real danger of falling out.'

'Doubt that.' Phil, one of the air rescue base crew, grinned at him. 'You've aced your winch training. Your turn to dangle next time.'

'Maybe not today.' Ben looked through the windows of the rescue base's staffroom. 'I can see how fast those clouds are moving from here.'

A quieter spell on shift was welcome enough to make Ben wonder if the thrill of joining this crew might be wearing off just a little. Not that it wasn't as exciting as he'd dreamed it would be, it was just that you got used to anything, didn't you? He loved knowing that there was almost always a critically ill or injured patient waiting for them with every call and that the speed with which they could respond and the expertise they could bring to stabilising their patients made it very clear that lives were being saved.

But he did miss Cutler's Creek. He even missed having a callout to an old man who was a bit 'short of puff' due to his chronic lung disease rather than a severe asthma attack that had someone on the edge of a respiratory arrest. Because a case like Alfie was someone he knew? Part of a community that he'd also been a part of? He was missing Mike and Zac and all his other mates that he'd spent so much time training with. He was missing being near the mountains. And he was missing JJ a lot more than he'd expected, but wasn't that a warning signal that he'd left just in time? He'd never wanted an attachment that couldn't be broken voluntarily because that way, even if it got taken away from you, it wouldn't mean that you had to rebuild your whole life.

He was deep into a chapter of a manual covering winch techniques in difficult conditions and terrain when a call came in. The revision was forgotten as he listened to Phil on the radio. A mountain search and rescue team was asking for backup. Someone was missing in rugged country. A member of the team had found a car but its owner couldn't be located on the only track accessed from that parking area. With the weather closing in fast, they only had a small window of time to try and find the missing person before night fall and they needed help.

'Co-ordinates?'

Phil had their pilot beside him as he circled the area on the huge map behind glass on the wall. Ben was on his feet, as well. His mouth had gone dry as he saw the target area.

'That's Twin Rocks,' he said. 'Near Cutler's Creek.'

'You know it?'

'Like the back of my hand.'

Their pilot looked up from the screen where he was checking the latest weather information. He shared a rapid glance with Phil and the decision was made with a nod.

'Responding,' Phil told the control centre. 'Keep us informed. Any further details on who we're looking for would be helpful.'

'All we know so far is that it's one of the local doctors. A woman in her thirties. Name of Hamilton.'

'JJ...'

The name came from Ben's lips in a horrified whisper but nobody else heard. They were all moving fast towards the helipad. In less than a minute they were airborne and on their way and they couldn't get there soon enough as far as Ben was concerned.

JJ could be hurt. Or worse...

And it made no difference that Ben had taken himself away. It wasn't going to make that particular loss any easier to live with. He'd thought he'd been in danger of falling in love with JJ. How blind had he been? It felt like his heart was already being ripped out here.

Because he already loved her.

He'd thought he could have lived his life knowing that she was safe and happy and with the type of person she would prefer to be with but he'd been wrong about that, too. He didn't want JJ to be with anyone else and…and he didn't believe that he could feel *so* sure of something if it was one-sided. If it was, he had to find out because living without JJ was always going to feel like living only half a life and, if it wasn't too late, he had to tell her that.

Please… he found himself repeating silently, with every air pocket that buffeted the aircraft as they sped towards the centre of the South Island. *Please don't let it be too late.*

They told her later that it was only thanks to that bright red sweatshirt she'd been wearing that they'd managed to spot her huddled between the rock and the tree on the side of that gully. And it had only been possible because they'd been circling Twin Rocks track with someone on board the aircraft who knew the area so well. Due to the distance she was from the track, the rain, the sound of wind in the trees and then the noise of the helicopter overhead, she hadn't heard any calls from the people on the ground who'd been searching for her and, even if she had, they wouldn't have heard her calling back.

They also told her she was lucky she hadn't been far more seriously injured or become more severely hypothermic given the amount of time she'd been missing, but it was all a bit of a blur for JJ. The fall had happened so fast and then she'd become cold very quickly and all she could really remember was the pain in her ankle that had made it impossible for her to move and try and save herself and how very, very scared that had made her feel. She'd huddled into that soft, red sweatshirt as it had begun raining harder and it had been another reminder of the last time she'd felt this scared—when she'd fallen in that river and the current had been threatening to sweep her away.

Perhaps that was why it had seemed like only a fantasy, through the blast of icy air and the roar of sound from the rotors above her, that the person inside that flight suit and hidden beneath the helmet and visor could be Ben Marshall. It wasn't until he'd unclipped himself and his equipment from the winch lines and had crouched right beside her that JJ had realised that she wasn't crazy. She really was about to be rescued and it really was Ben who was there to save her.

It didn't matter that he'd had to shout to make himself heard. He might as well have been whispering the words for her ears alone.

'You're safe now,' he'd told her. *'I've got you.'*

The pain relief Ben gave her before rapidly splinting her fractured ankle so that she could be moved without making the injury worse created a dreamlike edge to the drama unfolding around her that contributed to the blur that would come later. JJ had heard those words before, when she'd been pulled from that river and she had still been cold and shaking and frightened and yet she'd never felt so safe in her life—because she'd been in Ben's arms.

Another thought came from nowhere as he helped her into a harness. She'd known that somewhere along the line she'd fallen completely and utterly in love with Ben. Long before he'd told her how brave he thought she was. Had it been then—when he'd told her she was safe? When she'd *felt* so safe with him?

Like the way she did now?

When they were both clipped to that steel cable and JJ felt the moment they were in the air and being lifted towards the hovering helicopter, she knew that she'd never been in a situation quite this terrifying. There was still trust that she could cling to, however. She had Ben's arms around her again after all. He was with her as they flew to the large hospital in Dunedin. He stayed with her while she was assessed in the emergency department and his face was the last thing she saw before they put her to sleep in Theatre so they could operate on her ankle.

Ben's face was also the first thing she saw when she woke up and, despite everything—or perhaps because of everything—this felt like the happiest moment in her life. This was the face she wanted to see every time she woke up for the rest of her life, with that look in his eyes that told her how precious she was.

That she was loved *that* much...

He saw the instant her eyelashes flickered.

He saw the moment her eyes focused and she recognised who was sitting beside her bed. Holding her hand.

And he saw the way her whole face softened with an emotion that could only come from joy. Or love?

Hopefully both. A bucket of both.

'The surgery went really well,' he told JJ. 'You're doing really well. You just need to rest and recover now.'

'You're still here.' There was note of surprise in her whisper but Ben could see something else in her eyes. Hope...? He could feel his heart squeezing so hard and he just knew he'd been right. What he was feeling wasn't one-sided at all, was it?

'Why would I be anywhere else?' He tried to smile but this was too huge and he could hear the crack in his voice. 'I love you, JJ. Even if you do stupid things and break all the rules and nearly get yourself killed.'

Her eyes were trying to drift shut again but she was clearly determined to hold his gaze.

'I love you, too,' she murmured. Then her lips curved on one side. 'But I thought I wasn't your type.'

'I have a new type,' Ben said.

Her smile widened. 'Me, too.' One eye opened a crack. 'What's yours?'

'It's very exclusive.' Ben leaned closer. So close he could lean his head to touch hers. 'There's only one person in the world who could ever fill all the criteria.'

He could see the tiny wobble in JJ's lips. 'Sounds kind of like my new type.'

Ben had a bit of a lump in his own throat. 'Well…it does work, even if it shouldn't, doesn't it?'

'Mmm…' JJ's eyes were shut again. 'Okay…you'd better kiss me now. Before I fall asleep again.'

'Soon…' Ben had closed his own eyes. 'Very soon. I just want…*this* a little bit longer.'

Not that he needed any confirmation, but the fact that JJ didn't ask him what 'this' meant was proof that he'd found the person he was meant to be with. The way her hand tightened on his and kept holding it told him that she was feeling the same thing he was.

But he wanted to tell her anyway. Maybe he wanted to tell himself so that it became real. Soft words that were only intended for the two of them. JJ might think she'd dreamt them later but he could always tell her again.

'This is one of those moments, isn't it? When the world stops and there's this…stillness. When all you can feel is how much someone loves you. And how much you love them. *Where* you are doesn't matter. It's *who* you're with that's important.'

The soft sound JJ made was no more than a sigh but it was a sound of agreement. Of happiness.

'I had it when I was a little kid. With my Nana. When she hugged me. Or when we were together. Just us, and the rest of the world didn't matter. The fact that my mum never really wanted me didn't even matter. It was…home. When she died, the bottom of my world fell out because I thought I'd never find that still place again. I didn't *want* to find it because I couldn't face how awful it was to lose it and so I keep moving, to make sure I *didn't* find it again.' Ben had to stop for a heartbeat, to swallow the lump in his throat. 'But there it was. When I was with you. In that time and that place that's just us. You and me.'

'Like this…?' JJ's head turned beneath his. She was still sleepy but she was listening to every word he was saying. Fighting to stay awake because she wanted to hear it all.

'Like this,' he agreed. 'But it scared me. Until something else scared me even more and that happened today, when I thought I might have lost you for ever. When I realised that living without you would only ever be living half a life.'

A single tear escaped JJ's eye and trickled down the side of her nose. 'I've missed you *so* much,' she murmured. 'I feel a lot braver when I know you're there.'

'And I need to know that I can go home,' Ben said. 'The world doesn't have to stop. I just need to know, deep down, that that stillness is there. That I can go back to it as often as possible. Because it's where I need to be. The only place I ever want to be. It's…'

'Home,' JJ finished for him. 'It will always be there, Ben. For both of us. For as long as I'm alive, I promise.'

'And that will be for a lot longer if you can just learn to follow a few rules.'

JJ's lips were curling into a smile as he kissed her gently. And then he kissed her again. There would be plenty of time to talk about other things later. To plan the rest of their lives. Right now, he just needed to stay by the side of the woman he loved *this* much.

'Sleep now,' he whispered. 'You're safe. I'm not going anywhere.'

EPILOGUE

A few months later...

THERE WAS ANOTHER one of Betty's legendary morning teas happening in Cutler's Creek Hospital's kitchen. It was becoming a bit of a local tradition that this was the place to make important community announcements and she was more than happy about that. It meant that she was always one of the first people to hear any news.

'This is absolutely going to be my last retirement speech,' Don Donaldson told everybody. 'And that's all I have to say on the matter.'

There was a ripple of laughter in the room.

'We'll see,' Bruce said. 'We all know you'll be back through that door in a heartbeat, Doc, as soon as you're needed.'

'And we wouldn't have it any other way.' Betty put another platter of savouries on the table—tiny potato-topped pies this time, which were one of her specialties. 'Babies, broken ankles, shortage of volunteers for the fire service or ambulance...whatever the problem, we've got it covered.' The solutions were often found during discussions that took place around this very table, a fact that Betty was rather proud of.

'My ankle's as good as new,' JJ said. She bounced on her toes to prove it. 'I got up Twin Rocks track the other day like it had never happened.'

'And there are no more babies on the way,' Liv added. 'Not from me, anyway. I've got more than enough on my hands as it is. Can someone please catch Hugo before he crawls out that door?'

It was Ben who swooped on the baby and then held him up high so that he shrieked with laughter.

'We shouldn't have any more shortages of volunteers for the ambulance either,' he assured the group. 'I'm starting a new training course next week now that I'm back here full time.'

'You're really giving up on the choppers?' Mike looked astonished. 'I thought you loved it.'

'I did. And I'm really grateful for all the extra skills I've picked up in the last few months but...you know... there are things I love even more than the excitement of that job.'

'Like Cutler's Creek.' Zac grinned. 'And all your frequent flyers like Albie and Bert.'

'Too right.' Ben nodded. But he had tucked baby Hugo against his hip and his gaze was on JJ. 'But that's not the only reason I'm back.'

A few knowing looks flashed around the kitchen but, for Betty, the feeling was one of relief. She didn't have to bite her lip any longer.

'Well...it's about time,' she said, with satisfaction. 'It's not as if we really believed that Dr Hamilton needed all those trips to Dunedin for physiotherapy on that ankle.' She was beaming as she peered over her glasses at Ben. 'Home is where the heart is, isn't that right, lad?'

'Oh, you have no idea how right you are, Betty.' Ben handed Hugo back to his mother and went to stand beside JJ. He put his arm around her shoulders and, as she looked up to meet his gaze, there was a soft sound in the room, like a collective, happy sigh. Betty was certainly a contributor.

'Seeing as you're all here and you've probably guessed anyway, we may as well tell you that we're engaged.' Ben hadn't broken that gaze yet. 'JJ accepted my proposal and we're going to get married next month.'

'Here? In Cutler's Creek?' Betty had her hands against her cheeks.

'Where else?' JJ was laughing. 'This is where we met. Ben proposed to me up on the top of Twin Rocks and we're not planning on living anywhere else. This is home.'

A delighted Liv turned to Don Donaldson. 'You never know, Dad. It might be a good thing you've had some practice filling in for people on parental leave.'

It was Ben and JJ's turn to exchange a significant glance but, if there was a secret there, they weren't ready to share it.

Not that it mattered. Betty was quite confident she'd be one of the very first to know officially. Unofficially, she was quite confident she knew already.

These were two young people who obviously adored each other enough that being together was all they needed but there was something in that glance that suggested there was even more happiness to come.

It was contagious, that kind of happiness. Enough to make your heart melt, that's for sure. Betty had to reach for the corner of her apron to dry her eyes but she was already thinking of something else. Something important.

She had a wedding breakfast to plan...

* * * * *

THE NEUROSURGEON'S UNEXPECTED FAMILY

DEANNE ANDERS

MILLS & BOON

To Barry.

While you never could handle the dirty diapers,
you handled all the bloody noses and broken bones
much better than me.

Together, we made a great team.

CHAPTER ONE

HANNAH REEVES SPOTTED THE man she wanted the moment she stepped out of her patient's room. Standing not five feet from her, Dr. William Cooper's tall frame was propped against the wall. The neurosurgery department's Ice Prince was on duty today, which meant her patient, Mrs. Nabors, would be in the best of hands.

Only, this wasn't the same doctor whose frosty control had made him a legend in the operating room. His pale blue eyes were ringed with dark shadows and his mouth was drawn into a tired line, so she knew something was wrong. Was this about Mrs. Nabors's CT? Hannah had known the news wouldn't be good given the look the CT tech had sent her when they'd transferred the woman back to her bed.

"Shelley, I'm sorry. It's an emergency." He ran his hand through his thick brown hair, causing it to stick out in all directions. "I know… I'll make some calls. Just give me a few minutes, okay?"

Hannah was about to interrupt him when he finally ended the call. Trying not to look like she had been eavesdropping, she stepped closer and found herself even more worried about the man when she noted his wrinkled shirt and lab jacket. And what was that stain on his shirt? Something was definitely wrong here, but whatever it was, it would have to wait until her patient was taken care of.

"Did you get the radiology report on Mrs. Nabors's CT?" Hannah asked, hoping to get both her and the doctor's mind back on what was really important. While she had assured her patient's daughter that her mother would be okay, the older woman's recent onset of confusion and the CT techs reaction had Hannah worried.

"I spoke with the radiologist before I came up. Her stroke has converted to a bleed, as you suspected. I'll have to take her to the OR. I'm going to go talk to her family now. Can you ready her consent?" he asked.

"Sure, I'll be right back." Hannah headed to the unit coordinator's desk to retrieve the proper form. Fifteen minutes later, she watched as the orderlies transported Mrs. Nabors to the OR.

Finally, she could start her end-of-shift notes. She'd already finished her patient rounds, but wanted to double-check the chart records to make sure there weren't any new orders to pass on when she reported to the incoming night shift.

For a few minutes, she let herself relax in the cushioned office chair as she reviewed her patients' charts. Her feet had been screaming for mercy for the last hour, so she kicked her shoes off under the computer table and wiggled her toes. She stifled a moan of pleasure. Satisfied with her charting, she closed her files. Just another half hour and she would be done.

Her mind began to tick off all the things that had to be done tonight. There was dinner to cook, Lindsey's homework to check, and then her own schoolwork to do—lately it had turned into a contest between them to see who had the most homework each night. And then there was yesterday's email from her college instructor reminding her that she still hadn't lined up a preceptor for this semester. Had she taken on too much?

At least the dreaded history project had been completed the night before. The memory of Lindsey carrying in her papier-mâché model of the Alamo this morning brought tears to Hannah's eyes. She'd come so close to losing her... She said a silent prayer for Lindsey's heart donor family, then mentally added the cardiologist's appointment to her list of things to do this week.

Hannah looked back at the clock. She had just enough time to make one quick round on her patients before the night nurse arrived and took over. Apologizing to her poor feet, she forced them back into her shoes, promising a long rest as soon as her life slowed down.

"Yes, I understand it's late, but if you could possibly find someone... She's just a baby, she can't be that much trouble... But I'll pay double...triple? I know it's last minute. That's how emergency surgery works. It's not scheduled... No, I'm not trying to be rude... Okay, I understand. Can you at least tell me if you've had any luck finding someone full-time for the position...? Sure. I'll call back tomorrow during office hours. Thank you."

Hannah paused at the entrance to the doctor's lounge

where her favorite neurosurgeon now sat. Had she heard him right? A baby?

Coupled with the few hints from the side of the conversation she'd heard earlier, she now had a good idea of what had upset the doctor. Hadn't she found herself panicking over the same thing many times before? Only, it didn't make sense that the single doctor would be having issues with childcare. She knew for a fact the man didn't have any children. If he had, he certainly would have mentioned them before now.

She thought of the big stack of books waiting for her at home. She should pretend she hadn't overheard his conversation and walk away, but she'd been there herself too many times.

"Hey, Dr. Cooper, we missed you at Marjorie's retirement party last night," Hannah said as she stepped into the room, grappling for a way to approach him about what she'd overheard. She really didn't want to appear to have been listening in on his conversation, but there wasn't really any way around it.

"That was last night?" he asked.

"The flyer's been on the door of the breakroom for the last two weeks," she said. Marjorie had been one of his favorite nurses; it had been surprising when he hadn't showed up.

He leaned back in his chair and shook his head. He had the look of a man that had suddenly woken up and didn't quite know where he was. It was plain to see that he needed help.

"I'm sorry, Dr. Cooper, but I couldn't help overhear

your conversation on the phone. Is there something I can do to help?" Hannah asked.

"You've dealt with all this childcare stuff with your daughter, Lindsey, right? Trying to find someone to watch her while you're working?" he asked.

"Sure, every parent has to at some point," she said. "Is there a problem?"

"Yes, I have a really big problem right now. I need someone to watch a baby for me. I thought the person I hired understood that I needed someone flexible with their hours. They're only temporary, but it was all I could arrange at the time. Now I've got Mrs. Nabors being prepped for surgery and I don't have anyone to take care of this baby. Do you know any childcare services that do after-hours?"

Hannah couldn't help but feel for the man. She'd had her own trials with child-minding while she'd been working and going to school, even though Lindsey had spent what seemed like half her life in the hospital before she'd received her transplant. Hannah remembered those days all too well, especially when she and Lindsey had first moved to Houston.

It was impossible for her not to offer to help him.

Don't do it! Getting involved in other people's lives is just asking for trouble, a voice deep inside her intoned.

As usual, Hannah ignored the declaration she recognized as her mother's—an ingrained voice from which she feared she'd never escape, no matter how hard she tried.

"Look, I've been where you are before. It sucks," she said. "There have been lots of times when I've had a friend save me by volunteering to watch Lindsey. Most of the time, they're single moms like me and I can repay the favor."

Maybe this is a mistake, but what else can I do? The man had to do the surgery and didn't need to be worried about anything before he opened up poor Mrs. Nabors's skull.

"I'd be glad to help," she told him. "It's almost shift change, and I have to go pick up Lindsey at her after-school program, but that's only five minutes away from here."

"Really, you wouldn't mind?" he asked.

Was her offer such a shock? Of course, he was a world-renowned neurosurgeon. He probably never found himself in the position of needing someone else's help.

"Like I said, I've been there. What's her name?" Hannah asked. When he looked at her blankly, she prompted, "The baby? Her name? Her age? The address where I need to go?"

His face froze for a second before it seemed his brain kicked in and took over. There was definitely something more than just a childcare issue bothering him.

"Her name is Avery. She's eleven months—no, I think she's still ten months. I'm honestly not sure. I should know that, shouldn't I?" he said, though Hannah wasn't sure if he was talking to her or to himself.

"I take it she's at your house?" she asked, tearing a sticky note from the pad closest to her and sliding it across to him as his phone rang.

Glancing up at her, he scribbled an address as he took

the call. Picking up the sticky note, she recognized it as one of the more affluent areas of Houston.

"I'll be right there," he said to the caller before hitting the end button. "That was the OR. They're ready for me. Look, Hannah, I don't know how to tell you how much I appreciate this."

"It's not a problem, Dr. Cooper. Like I said earlier, I've been there. How long are you expecting to be in surgery?" she asked, thinking she'd need to make plans for supper if he was going to be late. She would have also liked to ask about the child's diet, whether she was still on baby food or eating table food, but Hannah knew he didn't have the time to answer all her questions. She'd just have to wait till she could question the babysitter.

"I shouldn't be too late. Hopefully no longer than two hours, but I won't know till I get in there and see the size of the bleed," he said as he stood to leave.

She saw the hesitation in his eyes. "Don't worry about Avery. I'll take good care of her. We'll be at your house whenever you get there," she said in the same calm tone she used with her patients when they were anxious.

"Okay. I'll be there as soon as possible," he said before exiting the lounge and heading down the hall to the elevator that would take him to the OR.

Hannah had always found the man to be a bit of a mystery and now she was even more curious about him. He had a ten-month-old baby girl staying at his house. Where was the child's mother? Was he the father? Maybe they were having some type of custody issue…

She heard that voice again telling her to mind her own business and stay out of other people's troubles, and this time she had to admit that it was good advice. But Hannah had been living her life her way for a long time now. She made her own decisions and helping out a coworker was the right thing to do.

"Wow!" Lindsey breathed as they pulled up to the large house clad in stone and dark wood. Two wrought-iron balconies jutted out from the second story, giving it the look of a long-ago castle.

"Yeah. Wow!" Hannah said as she parked at the front entrance.

As Lindsey raced to the front door, Hannah slowly climbed out of the car. The large yard, she noted, was manicured to perfection, azaleas bursting from their buds in pink and purple blooms and shrubs trimmed into precise angles. It was the perfect complement for the impressive mansion.

Hannah planned to buy her and Lindsey their own home as soon as her education was done and she had secured a permanent job with one of the neurosurgeons. But even in her wildest of dreams, she had known that a small suburban home on a postage-stamp-size yard was all she would ever be able to afford in the Houston real estate market.

Following her daughter up to the door, she ran a calming hand over Lindsey's hair as the girl hopped excitedly from foot to foot. The eleven-year old had spent so much of her life waiting for a heart transplant to allow her to experience everything other children took for granted, that now she seemed to race head-long into every situation—something Hannah herself had done today.

The heavy wood door and wrought-iron chandelier that hung above the front porch screamed money. Feeling like the country mouse that had come to town, Hannah rang the doorbell and waited.

"Who are you?" asked the girl who finally opened the door, giving the two of them the once-over.

This was Shelley? The girl couldn't be much older than eighteen.

"I'm Hannah and this is my daughter, Lindsey," she said as she moved closer to her daughter. "Dr. Cooper sent me to watch over Avery until he gets out of surgery."

"Hi, I'm Shelley. Are you Dr. Cooper's girlfriend or something?" The girl gave her another top-to-bottom look.

"No, just a friend and coworker," Hannah said, pointing to the hospital badge hanging from her scrub top.

"Well, I'm just glad someone showed up. I should have been out of here—" the girl pulled her phone from her back pocket "—thirty minutes ago. I'm going to be late for my study group. I tried to explain to Dr. Cooper that I had to be there. College exams are coming up, you know?"

"Dr. Cooper had an emergent surgery or I'm sure he would have been here," Hannah said.

"Hey, I'm premed, so I get it. I thought we could

make it work since it was only a temporary thing, you know, until he can get someone full time," the girl said, still standing in the open doorway. "He's a good guy and all that, so I really wanted to help him out."

"Can we come in please?" Hannah asked.

"Sorry." Shelley stepped aside and then closed the heavy wooden door behind them.

Cooler air welcomed them in out of the Texas heat. Above them, wide beams lined the cathedral ceiling of the entranceway, where a majestic staircase occupied one complete side. On the other side there was a large open-concept great room from where Hannah could glimpse a spacious kitchen and dining room.

The sound of a baby's whimpering led her to a small playpen that had been set up in the middle of the great room. Unable to help herself, Hannah picked up the child and held her close. Pushing damp curls from the baby's face, she was greeted with large brown eyes rimmed in red.

"It's okay, sweetheart," Hannah said as she instinctively began rocking the child in her arms as she checked her forehead for fever. "How long has she been crying like this?"

"She's teething. I've tried to give her that teething ring thing, but she just throws it down. I put some ointment on her gums about an hour ago," Shelley said.

"Poor baby." Hannah checked the baby's diaper.

"I know, it's so sad, isn't it?" Shelley said as she grabbed her book bag from the side of a chair.

"Sad?" Hannah asked as she lay Avery down on a nearby couch and peeled off her diaper. She took the clean one Lindsey handed her, along with wipes and a tube of diaper rash cream laid out on a side table. This really wasn't any of her business. Wasn't she involved enough, already?

"I mean, losing both her parents that way. My momma said it was a shock for Dr. Cooper, too. Losing his dad and stepmom like that and then finding out they'd named him as guardian of their baby if something happened to them. Major life change, right?"

"What?" Hannah paused for a moment. How had she not known that Dr. Cooper had recently lost his father and stepmother? Of course, the man had always been a bit quiet about his personal life. But still, he should have known that his coworkers would be there to support him.

And again, she reminded herself, this wasn't any of her business. If he didn't want anyone to know he had lost his father, she needed to respect his privacy.

She picked Avery up and hugged her close. This poor baby had lost her mother and father. The pain of her estrangement from her own parents still clung to Hannah after twelve years. Except, Avery's parents hadn't turned their backs on her like Hannah's had done the first time she'd gone against their wishes. They'd been taken away. Luckily for this child, she had a stepbrother who was there for her.

"Yeah, he went from Avery's half brother to pretty much her daddy in just a few days." Shelley glanced down at the phone in her hand then swore. "I've really got to go. I'm going to be so late." She started for the door then stopped and turned back. "I really appreciate this. I was feeling really bad because I knew Dr. Cooper didn't have anybody else to help with Avery."

"I'm sure there are a lot of people at work who would've been happy to help out if they'd known about Avery. The staff on my unit are always there to support each other. We just didn't know."

"That's good, because I was really dreading telling him that I couldn't help out anymore. He's a really nice guy and my mother loves working for him, but I have to put my classes first. I'm sure he'll understand. I feel so much better now that I know you'll be here," Shelley said.

Hannah watched as the girl hurried out, trying to understand what Shelley had meant. Surely she couldn't have thought that Hannah was going to…

"Shelley, wait!" Hannah called out as she heard the front door slam.

She set the baby inside the playpen and turned to Lindsey. "Stay here with Avery," she said as she ran from the room.

"Shelley," Hannah called again, rushing out the door. Stopping in the driveway, she watched the bright red Mini Cooper drive away.

That girl was as fast as a Texas jackrabbit.

So many things had just happened that it took a few minutes for Hannah's brain to catch up. Dr. Cooper had recently lost his father and stepmother. Little Avery, who was Dr. Cooper's half sister, was now his responsibility. That had certainly been a surprise, though it helped to explain a lot of the man's behavior earlier that day. And then last, but in no way the least important,

Dr. Cooper's babysitter, the only one he had been able to find, had somehow gotten it into her head that she wouldn't be needed any longer.

Walking back into the house, baby giggles and the laughter of her daughter echoed throughout the great room and soothed away the stress that had filled Hannah just moments earlier. It was going to be all right. In a city as big as Houston, there had to be someone Dr. Cooper could hire to take care of his little sister.

Looking around the rooms, she noticed the pile of dirty dishes in the kitchen sink and the trash can overflowing with diapers.

"Come on, you two, let's go explore this house and find this little one's room so we can get her cleaned up. We have a lot to do before Dr. Cooper gets home."

And she would have a lot of explaining to do if Shelley had really meant she wasn't coming back.

CHAPTER TWO

THE GARAGE DOOR slowly opened as William ran his hand through his hair. It had been a long day that had started with Avery waking him up before five in the morning, had continued through hospital rounds and office exams, ending with an emergent surgery that had proved he was clearly not prepared for all the changes Avery was bringing into his life.

He pulled the car into the garage, put it in Park and shut the engine off. Resting his head on the steering wheel, he took a minute to collect himself. Closing his eyes, he dragged in a deep breath and let it out slowly on a sigh derived from all the challenges of his day and the comfort he felt now that he was home.

A twinge of guilt worked its way into his subconscious as he tried to clear his mind. He'd been overwhelmed when Hannah had offered to rescue him. It was because of her that he had been able to save Mrs. Nabors from permanent neuro damage. He should get out of the car, go inside and thank her. Then she could get back to whatever she had planned for the night. But instead, he sat there, enjoying the first moment of peace he'd had all day. He needed this one moment before he could deal with whatever would be waiting for him in what had once been his quiet refuge.

It had only been a week since he'd received the call that both his father and his father's latest wife had been killed in a car accident. Three days since he'd learned that his father and stepmother had named him guardian of his half sister. Three days since his whole life had turned into a disorganized nightmare. What could his father have been thinking? Maybe, like him, he'd thought he would live forever?

William had no idea what it was he was supposed to do with the little girl. His only thought had been to call his housekeeper, who had six children and several grandchildren. Luckily, Angela's daughter had been happy to help him out for a few days while he looked for some permanent care. But Shelley was a busy pre-med student who was simply doing him a favor, not a professional nanny. Thank goodness, Angela would be here tomorrow to clean and do the laundry—and hopefully help him sort out the mess Avery's sudden arrival had brought into his life.

He glanced down at the crushed banana stain on his shirt. Avery had left it that morning when he'd tried to hand her over to Shelley. For some reason, the child had become attached to him the moment the former nanny had put her in his arms. It was like somehow, instinctively, she knew the two of them were in this together. Sink or swim, they were all each of them had now.

Of course, William had done more sinking than swimming in the last three days. And today, having

Shelley say she couldn't stay while the OR was calling on the other line telling him his patient was ready
for surgery, he'd almost gone under for the last time.
He'd been afraid of just losing it in the middle of the
lounge—something he had never done before—only
to be saved when Hannah had offered a helping hand.

What would he have done if she hadn't been there?
He couldn't depend on others for last-minute help. He
needed a better plan. He'd call all the agencies in the
morning to at least assign him someone for emergency
coverage until they found him some full-time help. It
was impossible for him to believe that the top agencies
in town couldn't recommend someone. Or maybe he
should consider hiring a live-in caregiver. That would
be the smart thing to do. That was what his own father
had done when he'd found himself alone and responsible for a nine-year-old.

And look how well that turned out for you.

He pushed the gibe at his lonely childhood away.

This wasn't about him. It was about his half sister.
He had to do the right thing for Avery. Only, he found
himself floundering with every decision he needed to
make. And the call he'd received from his lawyer today
regarding Avery's great-aunt's inquiry wasn't making
things any easier. What if, as the woman had claimed,
the best place for Avery was with her mother's aunt?
How was he supposed to know?

William had to come out from under the fog he'd
been in since his father's funeral. It had been a week
and it still didn't seem real to him. While he and his
father had not been close, it was still hard to believe

that the man he had grown up thinking was larger than life…was gone. Maybe it was the fact that his father's death had been just as sudden as William's mother's. It didn't seem fair, but he knew from experience that life never was.

What William really needed was to take some time off, but with one of the neurosurgeons out on maternity leave, that was not an option. Somehow, some way, he would make it through another night. Eventually he'd find the right person to care for Avery. He couldn't give up now. It had been what his father and stepmother had wanted. He had to make this work.

Hannah stood in the kitchen of her dreams as she browned the meat to add to the sauce she eyed as it bubbled on the chef-quality stove. She also kept trying to glance at the open pharmacy book she'd laid off to the side, trying to review classes of antibiotics. If she was lucky, she'd make it home in time to give the subject a good hour of study before she went to bed. Of course, given the day she'd put in, she'd probably fall asleep at her kitchen table again.

After taking care of Avery, she'd called everyone she could think of who might be able to help with Dr. Cooper's childcare issue. Not one person had been available for tomorrow. Stopping the search, she'd started dinner. Now, with Lindsey doing her homework at the marble-topped island that spanned almost the length of the large kitchen, she found herself worrying about what the doctor would do if Shelley didn't show up the next day.

Maybe if he called Shelley's mom, he could arrange things. That voice in her head had been right. She should have stayed out of Dr. Cooper's business. She had enough on her plate without worrying about other people's problems. But still, Hannah had been where he was and the only thing that had saved her from losing her job or missing a class was someone giving up their time to help her. She might even have missed being with her daughter for her transplant surgery if it hadn't been for Sarah, the nurse practitioner on the floor, coming to get her.

The sound of the garage door opening sent her thoughts back to the meal she was preparing. Somehow, she didn't think that her offering of pasta and sauce was going to help when he learned there wouldn't be anyone arriving to take care of Avery in the morning.

Hannah tried to make herself smile before the door that led to the garage opened, but it was impossible. There was no way this could go well. She'd be lucky if he ever talked to her again. And she'd miss that. He was one of the few doctors happy to let her pick his brain—pun intended—when something new came up at work.

He walked in and any bravado she had managed to collect disappeared. He stood a head taller than Hannah and what had earlier felt like a spacious room now seemed to shrink with his presence. She hadn't ever noticed how tall he was or the width of his shoulders. It was one thing to see him at work where he blended in with all the other staff members, it was another to be standing in his kitchen. *His* kitchen, which she had pretty much taken over.

"I'm sorry, Dr. Cooper. I hope you don't mind that I

went ahead and started something for dinner. I wasn't sure how long you'd be in surgery," she said, busying herself stirring the sauce while fighting the awkward feeling of being somewhere she didn't belong.

"You're standing barefoot in my kitchen, cooking something that smells delicious, and you saved my life by coming here to take care of Avery. I think you can call me William," he said as he looked over her shoulder, his nearness setting off warning bells. Whether it was the heat from the stove or the heat of his body, she wasn't sure, but something had sent the temperature rising in the room.

"I wouldn't say I saved your life," Hannah said. The man saved lives daily with his surgery skills. All she had done was help out a coworker.

"You did me a big favor. Thank you," he said. "I owe you one."

"You don't owe me anything. I was glad to do it," Hannah said, though she did let the idea of the neurosurgeon owing her a favor roll around in her head. She really did need to find a good doctor to precept with. Maybe later, when he didn't have so much to deal with, she would ask him to be her teacher.

"Avery?" he asked as he bent over the pan of sauce.

"Fed, bathed, and down for the night. Her bottom's a little red, but I covered it with some salve," she said. Standing close to him, she couldn't help but notice his body relax. It must be hard for him to go through all the changes in his life all alone. Now, she was going to make it harder when she reported that his babysitter likely wasn't coming back.

"You got her into bed?" he asked.

"Yes. She was worn out, poor thing. Shelley said she'd been fussy all day. I found some teething medication for her gums in her room and it seemed to help," Hannah told him.

"I owe you again, then. I haven't been able to get her to sleep unless I hold her. As soon as I put her down, her eyes pop open and I have to pick her up. I'd finally given up on putting her in her own bed. I just started sleeping in the recliner with her," William said.

"Hey, Dr. Cooper. So your real name is William?" Lindsey asked, looking up from her book.

"Good evening, Lindsey. And yes, my name is William. Why?" he said as he stepped away from Hannah.

"Does anyone ever call you Bill or Billy?"

Though they had met at several of the department gatherings, Hannah had noticed that Lindsey had seemed very interested in the doctor today. She had been full of questions about him during Avery's bath time.

"No. Just William. Why?" He moved to the fridge and pulled out a bottle of water.

"I just think Billy the Brain Surgeon has a great sound to it. Don't you?" Lindsey quipped before returning her eyes to her book.

"How much to keep that moniker quiet around the hospital?" he asked Hannah, pinning her with a stare before a smile broke over his face.

He really was a handsome man with those startling pale blue eyes and thick brown hair curling at his neck.

Put him in a pair of shorts and a T-shirt and he'd look like one of those California surfers.

"I think we can work something out," she said. "I do need to talk to you after I get supper finished."

"My momma was going to be a brain surgeon, too," Lindsey said, never looking up. "But then I was born with a bad heart and she had to quit college to take care of me. Now she has to be a nurse instead."

"Lindsey, why would you say that? I'm very proud to be a nurse." Hannah was shocked that her daughter would think such a thing.

Lindsay shrugged her shoulders as if it was no big deal, but they would definitely be having a conversation later.

No matter how the birth of her daughter had changed her life, Hannah would never let her child bear that burden. Interestingly enough, it sounded exactly like something her parents would tell their granddaughter. Perhaps it was also time for Hannah to have another talk with them.

Hannah had finally allowed her parents contact with Lindsey after years of their ignoring their daughter and granddaughter. At the time, their insistence that Hannah go to medical school had almost separated her from her daughter when Lindsey was born. She wouldn't allow them to put that type of pressure or guilt on Lindsey. She certainly wasn't about to let them start playing games with her daughter's mind. She would have no problem cutting them out of her life, just as they'd had no problem cutting a nineteen-year-old single mom and a newborn baby out of theirs.

"Well, I'm sure your mother would have made a great brain surgeon, but being a nurse is just as important as being a doctor. Just this afternoon, she noted a change in one of our patients that was a sign something really bad was happening inside her head. If she hadn't observed the patient as well as she did, the woman might have had a very disastrous outcome," William said.

"That's awesome, Mom." Lindsey smiled at Hannah over her schoolbook.

"You are still young enough to go back to school, you know," William said, returning his attention to Hannah. "I had a professor who didn't finish college till he was in his late fifties. You're definitely smart enough and you have excellent instincts."

Hannah felt her face flush with his praise. She didn't know what to say. Being a nurse practitioner in a neurosurgeon's practice might not be the dream she'd had when she was younger, but it was close. And whether her parents agreed with her choices or not, she'd rather be a nurse and have her daughter than be the most sought-after neurosurgeon in the world.

"Maybe someday," Hannah said, not wanting to go into all the reasons why she couldn't make full-time schooling a reality right now. With a mountain of hospital bills from Lindsey's transplant operation and the student loans she had taken out for nursing school, it would be years before she could drag herself out of debt.

"But she's going to become a nurse practitioner instead," Lindsey said. "Grandmother doesn't think that's as good, but I do."

Hannah had known it was her mother who'd been

filling her daughter's ears with rubbish. Definitely time for that talk.

"A nurse practitioner sounds like a great job for your mother," William said before turning back to Hannah. "Are you going to continue on the neuro unit at the hospital?"

Could she tell him that her biggest dream was to assist the best neurosurgeon in Houston? Him.

The *Star Wars* theme suddenly filled the kitchen and William reached into his pocket and pulled out his phone. "Excuse me," he said as he pushed the talk button and moved toward the stairs.

Finding a set of dishes in the cabinet, Hannah took a few minutes to fix Lindsey a plate of pasta and meat sauce. Setting it in front of her, she turned and was surprised to see William had returned. He'd changed into a pair of khaki pants and a clean button-up shirt of light blue that almost matched the soft blue of his eyes.

"That was my housekeeper, Angela, who wanted to make sure I knew her daughter wouldn't be here in the morning. She says Shelley told her that I'd found a friend to help out with Avery, so I wouldn't be needing her anymore."

"Yeah, about that Dr—I mean William…" Hannah set the dishrag down beside the sink. If there was a contest for someone screwing things up for themselves, she'd be a top contender. All hope of asking the man to help her get the clinical hours necessary for graduation disappeared. "Maybe we should step into another room," she suggested, looking over at Lindsey.

With a raised eyebrow, William motioned for her

to follow him along the short hallway beside the front staircase. Opening a door, he stepped back so that Hannah could enter what appeared to be his home office. A large chair sat behind an even larger oak desk in the center of the room. In front of the desk sat two leather chairs, which looked very inviting after spending the last fifteen hours on her feet.

Hannah took a seat and waited. She knew that he couldn't really be angry with her. It had simply been a misunderstanding that had caused the girl to quit. That could be fixed. Right?

Shutting the door behind him, William leaned against it as he looked over at Hannah. From what Angela had said, he could tell something had happened to give Shelley the idea that she wouldn't be needed anymore. Thank goodness her mother had called to confirm the information. The last thing he needed was to get ready for work in the morning only to find he had no one to watch Avery. Now he just needed to find out what had really happened.

"Hannah, relax. I don't know what gave Shelley the idea that I didn't need her anymore, but I'm sure it was some misunderstanding," he said, trying to keep the stress out of his voice. He was exhausted. Between long hours at work and even longer hours at home with Avery, he was running on empty. Three days and his whole life had been totally uprooted by one child who hadn't even had her first birthday. What would the next seventeen years be like? His heart rate shot up.

"Well…" Hannah said.

William watched as she rose and stepped closer to his desk, her back to him. His highest priority right now should be finding a live-in caregiver, but the thought of someone he didn't know being in his house didn't appeal to him. It wasn't that he didn't like people. He just liked his own space and privacy—something he would never have again.

No, that wasn't true or fair to Avery. He couldn't blame the child for interrupting his life after her own life had changed forever with the death of her parents. She was so young to have to go through this. Was she better off without the memories of what she had lost, though? He knew the pain of memories of someone close to him being taken away. He didn't want that for his half sister. Neither did he want her raised by nannies and stepmothers—people paid to care for her. But what was the alternative?

Not moving from the door, he returned his attention to the woman in front of him. He'd always liked Hannah. She was known throughout the neuro unit as not only a talented nurse, but also a compassionate one. She was a pretty, bright, responsible woman and, from what he had seen of her spunky daughter, an excellent mother. But today Hannah had been more than that. She'd been a friend who'd stopped everything in her life to help him. After tonight, it would be hard to think of her as just a nurse he worked with. He found himself wanting to listen to her explanation of what had transpired with Shelley.

"Can I ask you a question?" Hannah said as she turned to face him.

"Of, course." He leaned further back against the door and crossed his ankles.

"When you hired Shelley, did you interview her?" Hannah asked. She'd apparently worked off whatever nerves that had been driving her and had come to lean comfortably against his desk.

"I'm afraid I wasn't given the type of warning that would allow me that luxury. I called the only person I thought might know someone who could help me," he said.

"But you didn't actually talk to her yourself before you left her with Avery?" she asked in a voice that didn't hide her disapproval.

"Like I said, there wasn't time. Angela has been my housekeeper for over two years now. She has kids. She knows what kids need. I don't," he said. A bit of unease settled in his stomach. Had he left Avery with someone who had put her in danger? "Did something happen to Avery?"

"No, of course not. Shelley is a bright young girl who would be great as a fill-in babysitter for date night, but her life is too busy with her classes right now and that's her priority." Hannah added, "I'm pretty sure taking care of Avery was the last thing she was interested in."

"It's okay, Hannah. I know Shelley wouldn't work out in the long run. Her classes do have to come first. I understand that. I just don't understand why she thought I didn't need her anymore."

"Well, that's kind of my fault…" Hannah hedged. "When she told me about your parents passing—"

"My father and stepmother," he amended.

"Yes, and I am so sorry to hear that, William." Hannah's eyes shone with a genuine sympathy that he had seen in only a few of the people attending his father's funeral service.

"Thank you," he said, raw pain eating at him, though he couldn't understand where it came from. It had been years since he'd been close to his father. Why was he feeling so much now?

"So…" Hannah continued, "I told her that I wasn't aware of that or that you had a baby sister to take care of. I explained to her that if we, the staff at the hospital, had known, we would have offered to help. I think she took that to mean her help wasn't necessary any longer." She paused. "I really didn't mean to mess things up for you and Avery."

"I know you didn't. This is all just so new to me that I panic sometimes. I'm afraid I'll mess things up myself. I really don't know what I'm doing." Saying the words out loud, admitting to someone else his fear, seemed to quiet the angst that always seemed to lie right below the surface.

If he could just get one thing taken care of as far as Avery's childcare was concerned, he knew he'd feel better. Just having someone who knew what they were doing, someone with experience with a child Avery's age, would give him some small amount of comfort. At least then he would have someone to ask all the things he needed to know to be able to take care of the little girl. He didn't want to mess this up. He didn't want to mess Avery up the way his father had messed up with him. His father's answer had been to find a wife and a nanny and to leave William's care to them. That wasn't what William wanted for his sister. There had to be another way.

"Tell me something. Who takes care of Lindsey while you're at work? Or is she too old for a babysitter?" William asked.

"She thinks she is, but she's got another year before I'll be comfortable with her staying by herself," Hannah said. "She goes to after-school care provided at the school, and most of the time it works well with my schedule. I do have another mom who picks her up if I'm working late. Also, there's a group of mothers with children who have had heart transplants, or who are waiting for transplants, that's very supportive. We share childcare when needed."

"She's doing okay now?" William asked. With the energy and spunk Lindsey had displayed earlier, it was hard to imagine her before the transplant. He felt a guilty punch to his stomach. Hannah had taken care of a child with a heart defect and had gone through the processes of transplant surgery, all, apparently, while studying and working. And here he was wallowing in feelings of incompetence? It was time for him to man up. He could do this.

"Oh, she's doing well now. It's a miracle the difference the surgery has made. I never would have dreamed that she could be as healthy as she is today," Hannah said, wiping at her cheek.

"I'm glad to hear that. It sounds like it's been hard on both of you," William said. He should say more, but what? He wasn't good at all this sharing of emotions.

He cleared his throat. "So what is it you look for when you have to hire a babysitter?"

"Well, the first thing I look for is someone I can trust with Lindsey medically. She's old enough now that she understands how important it is to take her meds on time, and she's been taught the signs of early rejection, but I still want someone who knows what to do if there was an emergency.

"A lot of the teenage babysitting classes teach CPR now, which is wonderful and I know that there are day cares that require it." Hannah took a quick breath before continuing.

"Second, I check references. I need to know the person is responsible and has taken care of a child of Lindsey's age before. It's a lot different taking care of an infant versus an older child. Someone caring for a child Avery's age certainly needs to make sure that she's fed and clean, but Avery also needs playtime. It's very important for her development. And last, but still very important, I usually let Lindsey meet them before I hire them so I know it's a good fit."

"A good fit?" he asked. "Would that be a good fit with both you and Lindsey?"

"For a good working relationship, I think both the parent and the child should be comfortable with the caregiver. Of course, your needs are a bit different," she admitted. "What you really need is someone to help you become comfortable taking care of Avery. If you'd had other children, this wouldn't be a problem, but getting hit with all of this at once has to be challenging— N-not that you're doing anything wrong," she stammered. "I didn't mean that."

"It's okay. I'm the first person to admit that I'm struggling," he said.

He'd tried to explain to Avery's former nanny that he didn't know anything about babies, but the woman had refused to listen. It had only taken Mrs. Adams five minutes to inform him that his sister was his responsibility and that since he was a brain surgeon, he certainly should be able to figure it out. She'd then handed him Avery and stomped back to her car. How the woman had thought being a neurosurgeon was going to help him with caring for his sister, he didn't know. Was he supposed to suddenly understand childcare because he had a doctorate?

Hannah didn't seem to expect that from him. She understood. She'd said exactly what he'd been thinking all day.

He needed someone to walk him through this whole process of taking care of a child, and he now had a good idea who that person should be. He needed a teacher, and Hannah had all the qualifications. Not only did she understand how demanding work in healthcare could be, she also understood the inherent challenges. Plus, there was the added bonus that he was comfortable around Hannah. She didn't make him feel self-conscious. And if Maria, Avery's great-aunt decided to protest his custody, he needed to be able to show the courts and children's services that he knew what he was doing. Hannah could help him prepare for that. There couldn't be anyone better to help him with Avery than

Hannah. But how could he ask her to help him when she already had more than anyone else could handle between her job and caring for Lindsey? Was there some way that he could help her?

"I know the perfect person for the job," he said as he pushed away from the door. He'd find some way to make things easier on her if she agreed to help him.

"You do?" Hannah asked, relief in her voice.

This woman who had only spent a few hours with Avery really was worried about the child's care. More proof that he was making the right decision.

"I do. She meets all the qualifications," he said. "It's been proved that we work well together, and she would be a great help in teaching me all the things I need to know about taking care of Avery."

"That's wonderful. I'm so relieved. I've checked with all the moms I know and no one knew of anyone that was available," Hannah said. "Who is it? Do you think she could start tomorrow?"

"There's only one person I know who would be the perfect person," William said. "And that person, Hannah, is you."

CHAPTER THREE

"I CAN SEE the wheels turning in your head," he said then took a bite of pasta.

"And exactly what part of the brain would you call the wheels, Billy the Brain Surgeon?" Hannah asked. She watched him flinch as he washed the pasta down with some wine from the bottle he had insisted on opening. The man was apparently not used to being teased.

After William had shown Lindsey where she could watch her favorite sitcom and she'd assured herself that Avery was still sleeping, she'd listened to his sales pitch for fifteen minutes before she'd gotten tired of shaking her head and had decided that what they both needed was to eat. Thinking that, maybe with a break, she could get him to understand just how wrong she was for the job. Oh, she'd definitely been impressed by the figure he had quoted her. If she had known that taking care of rich people's kids paid so well, she could have done that instead of waiting tables before she became a nurse. She wondered about William's background that he could fling numbers like that out without wincing at least a bit.

But that wasn't what had her "wheels turning" right now. He wasn't the only one who could come up with a great plan. Her mind was quickly formulating one of her own. What was really giving her pause, though, was the fact that his suggestion could be a way for her to clock those necessary clinical hours. She was so close to finishing her college courses and she had always dreamed of working in the neurosurgical field. She just needed hands-on preceptor hours, and it would be a bonus for her to work with someone with his reputation.

"Let's say I do agree to this. What would be my hours?" she asked.

William picked up his napkin—one of the cloth ones he'd pulled from a drawer before opening the wine— and wiped at his mouth, bringing her attention to lips that were turning up in a slight smile.

She was amazed at the difference she could see in the man now. It was like he was a different person here in his home. In just the few moments they had talked alone in his office, something had changed between them. They'd had many discussions at work, and even on the occasional outings with their peers, but there had never been a personal connection. Hannah could easily see now that the two of them would work well together.

But still, she needed to consider every aspect of William's plan—a plan that depended on her. There was some pressure knowing that he and Avery truly did need some help, but she could only make the decision that was best for her and her daughter right now. Lindsey would always be her first priority.

"I need someone to take care of Avery while I'm at

work, but I wouldn't expect you to do that. What I really need is someone who could live here and teach me what I need to know to take care of my sister. My stepmother's aunt, who raised her, is making noises about protesting my custody of Avery. My lawyer doesn't think it will ever make it into court, but I need to be prepared," William said as he pushed his plate away.

"Why would she do that? You're Avery's half brother. That makes you her next of kin," Hannah said. Anyone who had just been handed a child to care for would be in the same situation. He just needed some time, a little education, and hands-on experience.

"It's still a possibility," William said, "and if it comes to that, I want to be ready."

"But you want someone to live here? That would mean leaving my apartment and moving Lindsey in here with me," she said as she saw the hope for the plan circle the drain.

How was she supposed to ask Lindsey to move again? They'd moved four times since coming to Houston. Sometimes the moves had been a step up in living arrangements. Sometimes a step down. This would definitely be a step up, even though the apartment they lived in now was the best place they had ever lived. Besides, living off someone else was not the kind of thing Hannah wanted to teach her daughter. She'd fought hard for her independence and she wasn't about to give it up.

"Of course, I would cover the expense of the housing that you would still have to pay and, of course, as I told you earlier, I'd pay for your time." He rose from the table and took his plate to the dishwasher before returning for hers.

"I can't make a decision like this without talking to Lindsey, but I have a proposal of my own," she said, rising and moving to the cupboards to put things away as she went.

Was she crazy to even consider his offer? It would definitely make finishing school this semester easier. She might have to take an educational leave of absence from work, but she had enough saved to cover her expenses. It would be worth it to get to work with him. Being able to put that she trained under Dr. William Cooper would help her get into any neurology practice in the state.

"Whatever it is, I know we can make it work," he said as he wet a dish rag and began to wipe the counters. At least he didn't seem like one of those men that would expect her to wait on him. There was no way that would go over well.

"I'm about to finish up my nurse practitioner program at school, but I still need a lot of clinical hours before I can graduate. How would you feel about me working with you to get them? In exchange, I would be happy to help you become comfortable taking care of Avery on your own," she said, then held her breath.

If he agreed, her life would be so much easier. She could finish her semester strong and still be able to pay the bills and spend the time she needed with her daughter. "We could have an exchange of knowledge. How about for one month during the day you teach me everything I need to know to work in a neurosurgeon's practice and at night I'll teach you everything I know about raising a little girl?"

"That seems fair to me. Of course the first thing you'll need to teach me is how to choose a day care for my sister. I think I've already proved that I don't know what I'm doing as far as that is concerned," William noted.

"Then that's where we'll start. We'll go through a list of day cares together and pick the best one for Avery," Hannah said. Was she really going to do this? "You need to know that I haven't ever done anything like this. The only child I really have experience with is my own."

"You've done a great job with her and you're a single parent. That's the kind of help I need. I need to learn how to do this all on my own." William leaned against the island, the stress he'd showed earlier gone.

"Just so you know, I'm definitely not Mary Poppins. Don't expect me to break out in song or to dance a jig." She demonstrated a two-step she'd learned as a child in tap dancing class.

William laughed and she was struck once more by the difference in him here in his home compared to how he was at the hospital. "I'm not sure about that. I think you've got a shot at it."

"That's because you haven't heard me sing," Hannah said. Thank goodness her parents hadn't seen the point of voice lessons.

"Want to shake on it?" he said, holding his hand out to her.

The voice of her mother telling her to slow down and to make sure someone wasn't taking advantage of her made Hannah hesitate a moment. He was certainly quick to agree. She couldn't help but feel that she was falling in with his wishes a little too easily. Memories of living with her parents and their constant manipulation had her holding back and second-guessing herself. Was there anything for William to gain besides the care of his sister?

If there was, Hannah couldn't see it. She'd made sure they had an agreement that benefitted both of them and she believed his intentions were pure. She had to quit being so suspicious of everyone. This was a deal that put the two of them on equal standing. And it was a good thing, too. It had only taken a moment for his little sister to wrap her fingers around Hannah's heart. She wouldn't have been able to walk away without making sure the child was cared for properly.

"Unless Lindsey has a problem with it, I think we can make it work." She stretched her hand out and felt the warmth of his fingers as they slid through hers then folded around her hand. Their palms sealed the agreement, but still her hand lingered inside his a moment longer than necessary. Pulling back, she slid her hand against her jeans-clad thigh to ease the disturbing tingle from William's touch. How had a simple sign of an agreement turned into such an intimate touch? This new William, the relaxed, more easy-going William, seemed dangerous. She started to tell him that she had changed her mind, that this might not be a good idea, but realized she couldn't do that without admitting how much his touch had affected her.

"The movie's over. Can we go home now?" Lindsey asked as she came into the kitchen.

"What?" Hannah queried, still rattled by her body's response to William's touch.

"Lindsey, we were just about to come get you. I thought you and your mom might like to see my video gaming room," William said.

Hannah watched as her daughter's eyes widened and knew that everything was already settled. There was no way her daughter would turn down staying at William's place now. It looked like the next month would be an adventure for them all.

By the time they walked into William's house, each carrying a box, Hannah was having serious second thoughts. It had been harder than she had anticipated to lock down her apartment for the next month. While it was in no way as grand as William's home, she had worked hard to reach a financial position that could afford them a nice place to live. For Hannah, it was a true testament that she could make anything she believed in happen. Even Lindsey had been a little down when they'd left their apartment, but by the time they'd arrived at William's home, her daughter's natural good mood had returned.

With Avery down for a nap and Lindsey off to unpack, Hannah went to put away her own things. Opening one of the double doors to the room where she would stay, she was taken aback by its size. She could fit half of her whole apartment into the one room. She walked to the wall of windows and opened the blinds to a view of the large lake for which the neighborhood had been named. It was a beautiful sight; the rolling, manicured lawn ending at a small pier that stretched across the shore. She could envision a picnic table spread with sandwiches and drinks. A yard set up for playing a game of croquet. And a family enjoying the nice spring day.

"Momma, come see what I've done to my room," Lindsey called from down the hall.

Turning, she found William leaning against the doorframe. "Will it do?" he asked.

"It's perfect, though maybe a touch too big. But I love the view," she said.

"I know. It was the lake that sold the house." He moved across the room to join her at the window.

"But isn't the house a little big for just you?" Hannah asked. "Though it will be the perfect place to raise a family."

A shadow crossed his face as he looked away from her. She could almost feel the chill from the icy stare he shot through the window.

"Maybe it is a bit large, but I knew it was perfect when I bought it. It had everything I'd ever wanted, including this view. As far as the wife and two point five kids, that isn't in my future. A family is the last thing I planned for," he said before looking back at her.

"Why?" she asked. "Isn't that what everyone wants?"

"A wife and kids?" William scoffed. "It seems that what people want isn't always what they get. My father believed in that dream so much that he ended up having had four wives before he died. Maybe the fourth one was 'the one,' as they say. I hope so. But stepmom one and two were a nightmare that I would never want to repeat."

"I'm sorry to hear that. And I hope Avery's mom was the one, too." Hannah quickly turned her eyes toward the lake as a chill ran up her back. She'd been surprised at the bitterness in William's voice when he'd talked about his father and his father's wives, but she'd noticed that he hadn't mentioned his own mother. What part had she played in William's decision not to have a family?

But she had also detected sincerity in his tone and knew he believed what he'd said. The fact was he did have a family now, whether he accepted it or not. For all practical purposes, he was Avery's father as well as her brother. And Hannah had no doubt that someday he would add to that family. He just hadn't met the person he couldn't live without. It was the same for her, so she had no problem understanding where he was coming from.

As he turned and walked out of the room, she continued to stare at the lake. No matter what William might say, she was certain he had to feel a bit lonely when he walked around such a big house. The thought even made her a bit sad until she remembered that he wouldn't be alone any longer.

There was nothing like the laughter of a child to warm up a home, she thought, smiling to herself as she headed down the hall to Lindsey's room. William had said he wanted to learn everything he needed to know to take care of Avery. The first thing she would have to teach him was what it meant to be part of a family.

* * *

William took the steps down to the basement two at a time. The realization that he had said too much to Hannah had hit him the moment he'd seen the surprise in her eyes. If she only knew just how dysfunctional his family life had been while growing up, maybe she would understand that another family was the last thing he wanted. Yes, he had a sister now that he was responsible for, but that didn't mean he was going to fall for the whole happily-ever-after thing.

As always, dealing with other people's expectations for him to be the all-American family man stirred the demon inside him. Too often people assumed that because he was a single man he just hadn't met the right person yet. Women he barely knew tried to fix him up with their daughters or nieces. Coworkers hinted at other coworkers who would be happy to be involved with him. Even his patients seemed to find his single status anomalous, as if his marital state had anything to do with his talent in the operating room.

William had been given advice from more than one elderly man who had been married for decades. No one knew that he'd had all the family life he could handle with not one but three different stepmothers. He'd had enough family drama to last anyone a life time, and he had no intention of repeating his father's mistakes. For some reason, the man had never learned to live by himself. Well, he was not his father. William didn't need a woman in his life to make him happy. The whole reason for Hannah being there was so that he could learn to be an independent caregiver. His father could have saved himself a lot of heartache if he had only taken the time to learn that himself.

William walked into the bathroom where he kept a set of clothes for working out. In minutes, he was changed and in the workout room, pumping bars loaded with his maximum lift weight. He felt the irritation fade as he strained his body to its limit. He paced himself as he moved through the machines one at a time. His mind quieted with each repetition, and with the calm came the knowledge that he'd let old wounds push him into saying more than he should have to Hannah.

Why did everything feel so raw right now? The bandages he'd so carefully applied over the years were fraying, coming loose. With the death of his father, feelings and emotions he had held at bay for years were now surfacing. The arrival of Avery on his doorstep had not helped things, either, having disrupted the organized life on which he depended.

William had an orderly existence that he had been happy with for years. Now, things were changing, which was something he always had problems with. His life had transformed so much between one stepmother and the next that he cherished the comfort of the life he had made for himself. And now he was letting two more people into his life. Hannah and Lindsey. He knew Hannah was curious about him. He was curious about her, too. But expecting her to understand him was just too much to ask.

Excited to start her first day in William's office, Hannah was up early. After making sure that Lindsey was awake and getting ready for school, she'd helped William pack a bag for Avery, carefully going over every item that was needed. Though a little rusty at baby care, she'd quickly remembered the basics.

"Why do you count the diapers in the bag?" William asked as he scrambled an egg for Avery's breakfast.

True to his word, William had sat with her to go through the different day-care services with available openings in their infant/toddler rooms. She'd helped him weigh each of the day cares' pros and cons, and he'd picked a favorite that offered smaller rooms and a convenient location.

Of course, when she had explained that each child moved up to the next level of care according to their development, William had been certain that Avery would be advanced before any of the other children. That's when she'd noted the necessity of potty training. Pointing out that he had a little time until he would have to worry about it, he chose to put the lesson off. She didn't mention that by that time she wouldn't be around to help. There were just some things he would have to learn on his own.

"If you know how many you put into the bag every day, you can tell how many times the day care is changing her," Hannah said as she settled Avery into the high chair.

"Shouldn't they do that without me checking on them?" William asked as he cooled the egg then cut it into smaller pieces that Avery could pick up with her fingers.

"I don't think there will be a problem, but it doesn't

hurt to keep any eye on it yourself. Also, it's good to visit the day care at times when they aren't expecting you." Hannah tied a bib around Avery's neck, adding, "You've got this, so I'm going to check on Lindsey and finish getting ready."

After dropping Lindsey off at school, they'd arrived at the day care with a few minutes to spare and neither of them seemed to be in a hurry to go inside. Hannah couldn't help but worry about the little girl.

What if Avery thought they were leaving her just like her mother and father had the day they'd left her and never come back? Yes, children were very resilient, but the little girl had lost her mother and her father. Her world had been torn apart. She didn't have any way of knowing it wouldn't happen again. But then, did any of them?

Hannah's own daughter had lived one day at a time for years, and even now there was always the chance of her heart going into rejection. They both lived with that hanging over their heads, though they also chose not to let the fear ruin the life that they had now.

"You don't have to go in if you don't want to." William said as he opened his door.

"No, I want to go, too." Though she knew she should let him do it himself, she needed to see that Avery would be okay for herself.

Unable to wait any longer, she got out of the car and took Avery out of her car seat. Together, she and William walked into the daycare. You'd think the two of them were going to a firing squad by the way the two of them were acting.

She squeezed the wriggly little girl in a tight hug then handed her to William. "Avery, I have to go to work with William now, but we'll be back as soon as we can."

William took his sister and walked over to the teacher. After speaking a few minutes, he gave her a piece of paper and crossed the room to where the other children were playing.

With one more hug and a kiss on the Avery's soft, plump cheeks, he sat his sister on the rug with the other children. Rising, he stepped up to Hannah's side and they both watched as Avery immediately crawled to a toy train and began rolling it across the floor.

"It will get easier," Hannah said aloud, for both of them. She'd done this before with Lindsey, but she didn't remember it being so hard...though she was sure it must have been.

"She seems to be doing fine, though I don't really like the way that child—" William motioned to a curly headed little boy "—is eyeing her."

Hannah looked at the boy. He did seem to be sizing Avery up. "They'll be fine. It's her first day, so the other children aren't used to her. I bet by the time we get to the office she'll have made some new friends. Come on, big brother. We're going to be late for work."

William hesitated a moment before he followed her out of the day care. "It seems strange leaving her here by herself."

"I know, but it will be okay. What was on the note you gave to the teacher?" Hannah asked.

"I gave her the number to the Operating Room and the Emergency Room in case they can't get me on my cell," William said as they got into the car.

"That was a good idea. I didn't think about you not being available. We did put down my number as a secondary number, but there might be someone else you'll want to change it to after I move back to my apartment," she said as he pulled out of the parking space and headed for the office.

"I'll need someone for emergencies for after-day care hours and, of course, I'll need someone for nights when I'm on call," William said. "Thanks for covering that while you're at the house."

"It's fine. And it will all work out. I've still got some contacts with people who helped with Lindsey. We'll find someone to help out on those nights."

"This single parent thing is a lot more complicated than I thought," he said as they turned into the office parking lot.

"It is, but if I could handle it, I know you can, too. Now, let's get inside, where you can start teaching me all the things I need to know to be the best nurse practitioner the neuro field has ever seen," Hannah said as she opened the door. Excitement began to race through her. This was one more step that would take her closer to her goal and she was ready to take it.

CHAPTER FOUR

HANNAH DECIDED THAT she would be glad when her orientation was over. She and William had agreed over dinner the night before that it would be a good idea for her to just orient herself to the running of his office before she started seeing patients with him.

Of course, he hadn't warned her about Nurse Marion. She had to hand it to the woman. She ran a tight ship. As soon as patients checked in at the front desk, they were taken for weight checks and vital signs measurements. Any changes since their last visit were recorded, as were medication updates. But that didn't mean Marion had to treat Hannah like she was a brand-new nurse on her first day of orientation.

Hannah knew how to interview a patient and she was more than competent at taking a patient's vitals. It didn't seem to matter that Hannah had been responsible for the care of some of the neuro patients in the hospital. Nurse Marion, as she liked to be called, was going to make sure Hannah's orientation was very thorough.

It was easy to see there was a bit of hero worship going on when it came to William and, if the woman were twenty years younger, Hannah suspected Marion would be crushing on her employer. Regardless, when William gave Marion an order, nothing could sway her from her duty.

Hannah thought she might pull her hair out before it was even lunch time.

"Marion, can I see Hannah for just a minute?" William asked, standing in the open doorway to his office.

"Certainly, Dr. Cooper," Marion said. "I'll go prep the next patient."

Hannah watched the woman head to the waiting room before saying, "Thanks for the rescue."

"You looked like you needed it. Marion can be a bit much, but she keeps this office running," William said before turning back to his office.

"She thinks a lot of you," Hannah replied as she followed him.

"She was the first employee I hired when I opened the practice. She's very dedicated." William took a seat behind his desk. "I checked on Avery and her teacher said she was doing fine."

"I told you she'd be okay. I'll call a little later to see how she's doing. That way it won't look like you don't trust them," Hannah told him as she looked at her watch. Though working with Marion had been trying, at least the time was passing quickly.

"Good, and thank you. I'll drop her off tomorrow by myself." William sighed. "None of this is going to be easy, is it?"

"Not really. It's always harder than you think it's

going to be," Hannah said, "but you'll get the hang of it. What did I tell you was the first rule of parenting?"

"Don't let them see fear? I think it might be too late," William joked, smiling at her. "Knowing that you are looking out for Avery so I don't make any major mistakes means a lot, but I also know you have a child of your own and your courses. If it becomes too much, just let me know. Angela's at the house two days a week, so at least that's taken care of—"

The door to his office flew open. "I need you in the waiting room," Marion said before turning and running back to the front of the office.

Hannah and William rushed out behind her.

Hannah immediately recognized the young man on the floor. Zach had been in a car accident several months earlier and she had been his neuro nurse. Kneeling at his side, she noted that his eyes were open but not blinking, his muscles taut as violent spasms racked his body. Resting her hand on his chest as best she could, Hannah checked his breathing while William examined the bleeding cut on his head.

Remembering where she had seen the dressing tray, Hannah ran to the supply room and returned with some four-by-four gauze pads and wrap.

"Call 9-1-1 for an ambulance. Tell them he's having a grand mal seizure and I want him taken to the ER," William instructed Marion in that calm voice that Hannah had always admired.

She felt Zach's body go limp beneath her hand and was relieved to see his chest rise with a deep breath.

"Will he be okay?" a voice asked.

Turning her head, Hannah saw Zach's wife, Sheri, standing behind her, eyes full of tears.

Hannah left the young man's side as Marion made the call and William rechecked his vitals. She knew how scary it was to watch a loved one suffer while their life was in danger. All you could do was stand on the sidelines and wait.

"Yes, he's going to be okay. He had a tonic-clonic seizure, what they call a grand mal. He could be out for a while now that it's over, but his breathing is good. See how his color is all pink? That's a good sign," Hannah reassured her as she took the woman's shaking hands. "Has he done this before?"

"No, nothing like this. He's had those small ones like he had in the hospital, but he's been taking his medication just like the doctor ordered," Sheri said, absently rubbing her small baby bump. She looked up at Hannah. "What if I had been at home alone? What would I have done?"

"You'd do just what we did—call 9-1-1," Hannah said, turning to look at William as he came up behind her.

The door opened to the waiting room and the few people in the waiting room stepped aside as two EMTs pushed a stretcher into the room.

"I've already called and talked to the doctor in the ER that will be taking care of Zach," he told Sheri. "They're going to take him to CT as soon as he gets there. I'll be in to see you and Zach as soon as the results are back." At her nod, William stepped away to talk to the EMTs.

For the next hour, Hannah and Marion worked hard to get the last of the patients seen before lunch so that William could leave to check on Zach. She couldn't hide her excitement when William invited her to accompany him. This was what she had looked forward to—being able to see the patient from the perspective of the doctor.

"Avery's teacher says she's doing great, by the way," Hannah said as she climbed into William's car. "There was apparently a tussle between her and a little boy when he tried to take a toy from her, but no blood was shed and Avery maintained her control of the fire truck. So, it's all good."

"Blood? Is she okay?" William asked with that deer-in-the-headlights look she had come to expect from him whenever they talked about his little sister. He was so scared he was going to do the wrong thing. He was like a new dad, only he'd missed the newborn stage that would've helped prepare him for what was ahead.

"I was joking. It was just two toddlers wanting the same toy," she said.

"Maybe I should go back to my original plan and call the agency to have someone come into the house." He maneuvered the car onto the road.

"Let's try this first. I really think it could be good for her to be around other kids her age. There were times when Lindsey had to have home care because of her medical condition. It was hard for her to watch all the kids out playing and not be able to join them. Which reminds me of something I wanted to ask you," she noted as they neared the hospital. "Does Avery have a pediatrician here in Houston?"

"Yes, I had Shelley take her to Dr. Anderson in the pediatric clinic. One of my father's lawyers had her pediatrician in Dallas email her records over. And yes, I know I should have been the one to take her," he said as he pulled into the staff parking lot at the hospital.

"We'll go together the first time. And it's fine if you need help sometimes. Just because you're going to be a single dad, doesn't mean you can't have some help from your friends." Hannah felt her heart squeeze. Hopefully, she would be one of those friends.

William was glad to see that Zach was awake when they walked into his room. The CT results had come back and, fortunately, there had been no damage as a result of him hitting his head on the office floor during the seizure.

"Hey, Doc," Zach said when he spotted them. "Hannah? It's nice to see you. Are you working in the ER today?"

"No, I've taken some time off so I can concentrate on school," Hannah said as they approached his bedside, "and Dr. Cooper is helping me get my clinical hours in neuro surgery. I was at the office today when you had your seizure."

"You're looking better than when we last saw you," William noted as he examined the sutures on the side of Zach's head. "How are you feeling?"

"I'm a little freaked out and very tired, to be honest," Zach admitted, reaching for Sheri's hand. "We both are."

"Did the CT show anything? He fell pretty hard. I

tried to grab him," Sheri said, her voice breaking on a sob.

"It's not your fault, honey. There's no way you could have kept me from hitting the floor," Zach said then raised her hand to his lips for a kiss. "Besides, you have more than just me to worry about right now."

William looked away from the young couple. He'd never been one for public displays of affection. He heard someone sigh and looked over at Hannah, whose eyes were brimming with tears.

He leaned closer to her. "Do I need to get you a hankie?" he whispered, surprised to hear the tease come out of his own mouth.

"Even you have to admit that they're a sweet couple. They're going to make great parents," she said softly before sighing again.

William straightened and cleared his throat. "There's no change on the CT from the last one you had, but I want to admit you at least for one night. I'm going to adjust your dose of anti-seizure meds and hopefully that will take care of the problem. If not, we'll look at changing the medication to see if that helps. Right now, I want you to take it easy for the day and I'll—" he looked over at Hannah "—*we'll* be in to see you later."

They left the couple arguing about whether Sheri would spend the night at the hospital. William helped Hannah transcribed a note for Zach's chart and explained the admissions orders.

He wasn't surprised at how quickly Hannah caught on. She was smart and already familiar with the hospital's computer system. What did surprise him was how many of the ER nurses stopped to talk to her.

"Did you ever work in this ER?" he asked after another nurse stopped by.

"Worked here? No. Spent a lot of time here? Oh, yes. Before Lindsey received her new heart, she was in and out of the hospital so much that we both knew all the nurses."

"It must have been hard being a single parent of a child as sick as Lindsey," he said. He hadn't lasted three days with a soon-to-be toddler and that was with Shelley's help. He couldn't imagine what it had been like for Hannah all on her own.

He'd wanted to ask her several times about Lindsey's father, but as someone who wasn't comfortable with people querying his own private life, he didn't think it fair to ask questions about hers. Still, from what he had seen, Hannah had handled everything life had thrown at her and her daughter by herself. He just hoped he could do half as well with Avery.

CHAPTER FIVE

HANNAH FROZE, STUNNED by the sight in front of her. She needed a fan, a glass of water—anything that would cool her heated body and quickly.

Standing in the middle of the staircase that led into the basement, she had the perfect view of flexing muscles and a hard, bare chest that any man would be proud of. How had she not known what this man had been hiding under his lab coat?

Her breath caught as she watched William lift the heavy weighted bar over his head, giving her a view of sweat-drenched abs and a small line of hair that led to a pair of low-waisted gym shorts. She knew she couldn't just stand there and ogle the man, but her legs refused to continue down the stairs. And she certainly wasn't going to leave now. Her poor neglected body wouldn't have let her anyhow. It hadn't been this close to an undressed man, not intimately at least, in more than… was it four or was it five years? And she had never seen one like this.

A shudder ran through her as hot need settled in her lower abdomen and the parts of her body that she'd ignored for too long protested. Could a woman orgasm just by looking at a man? If it was possible, this would be the man that could make it happen.

The loud clang of metal brought her back to her senses just in time to see the man she was openly lusting after run a towel over tight, damp abs before moving to some type of leg machine that had him on his back. He started pumping strong thighs up then down.

Hannah realized she couldn't just stand there. At some point he would look over and see her, and there was no way she'd be able to hide the reaction that had taken control of her. She had two choices: sneak back up the stairs or walk down and face the temptation.

Who was she kidding? There was no way she was strong enough to leave now. She just had to make sure William didn't notice how the sight of all him hot and sweaty affected her.

She pushed back against all those long-ignored hormones fighting to free themselves. She could do this. She'd been without a man for a long time and survived. She'd just ignore him. It would be easy. All she had to do was to pretend he was naked…wait, what? No. God no, that was what you did if you were nervous giving a speech, not lusting after a man. It was hopeless. She needed to leave.

"Are you coming down or are you going to run away?" William quipped as he walked toward her.

She would have probably run if it hadn't been for the taunt in his voice. And was that a smile on his lips? In all the years she'd worked with him, she couldn't remember seeing Dr. Cooper smile like that. But this wasn't Dr. Cooper. This was William, and she had an uneasy feeling that this man was a lot more dangerous than the Ice Prince of the OR.

"I didn't want to disturb you." She forced the words out over parched lips. She really did need that glass of cold water. She remembered the monitor in her hand. "And you forgot this."

"Sorry. I haven't gotten used to needing a monitor yet. And you're not disturbing me. There's enough equipment here for two," he said before running the towel down the length of his body.

Hannah closed her eyes and bit down on her poor lip to keep a moan from escaping. Surely he didn't mean that the way it had come out. It had to be her sex-fogged mind that had turned his words into innuendo. She had to leave before she did something that would embarrass both of them. Hannah looked down at the baby monitor clenched between her hands. Water, she needed water.

She cleared her throat. "I'm going to run back up to the kitchen and get a bottle of water," she said and turned, fighting the urge to run.

"There's plenty in the fridge over in the corner. Hold on, I'll get you one," he said.

It was no use. The man was determined to torment her. It was okay. She deserved it. She should have run the moment she'd seen him. Instead, she'd stood there like a hormonal teenager.

Hannah walked down the stairs, reaching for the bottle of water he held out to her as she passed him. Twisting off the cap, she upended the bottle and drained half of it before pausing. She put the lid back on and then, straightening her back and holding her head high, walked to a stationary bike and sat the baby monitor and bottle of water down beside it. A few miles on the bike should be enough to cool her traitorous body down.

Four miles later, she was feeling much better. The bicycle faced a glass door that lead to the backyard and she'd forced herself to keep her eyes trained there. Behind her, bars and weights rattled and clinked together, but she refused to look over at the man who used them. By the fifth mile, the embarrassment was gone. Why was she feeling guilty of something? Okay, maybe she was guilty of a little innocent gawking. But if the tables had been turned, she was certain he would have done the same thing. Right?

And wouldn't it be fun to turn those tables on him? She waited for the voice inside her head to tell her not to do it. Apparently, her mother had been shocked speechless. It was a good thing, too, because Hannah had no intention of listening to her voice of reason.

William couldn't keep his eyes off the woman that had showed up in his home gym. Dressed in a tight exercise tee and shorts and sitting on the bike in front of him, he was tortured by every twist of her hips as she pedaled her way into dreams he had no business dreaming.

He'd taken her into his home and office, but he could not let her any closer. He had very precise conditions for the women he spent time with, and the first one they clearly understood was that there would be no happily-ever-after with him. He'd always been up front about that, and had otherwise provided them with all the things that he could give them. Yet Hannah was not the type of woman who would accept expensive jewelry or exotic trips instead of love and a future. He had neither of those things to give.

Dropping the weight in his hand, he reached for a towel at the same time Hannah stopped pedaling.

Good. Maybe now she'll leave.

He shouldn't have teased her, but when he'd turned to see her standing there, a look in her eyes that invited him to take everything he wanted from her, he'd had to change the mood. He knew he'd embarrassed her, and had assumed she'd run. It wasn't until she'd marched down the stairs and mounted the bike that he'd realized his mistake.

A deep moan echoed across the room and he felt his groin tighten with the sound. Oh, he'd definitely made a mistake in teasing her. She stretched her arms up and arched her back, shaking out golden hair that hung down her back in thick waves. Thoughts of knotting his hand through those waves and baring her neck for his lips were enough to have him turning away from her and looking for his bottle of water.

He let the cold fluid run down his throat and then splashed some across his face. When he opened his eyes, he saw that Hannah had moved to the chest press. He watched as she propped one long leg on the seat and ran the towel up and down from ankle to thigh. She then repeated the process on the other leg before looking over at him.

"I'm sorry, did you want to use this?" she asked.

She wasn't playing fair and she knew it. He waited

until she sat back on the bench and raised her arms to grab the handles before he pounced.

Hannah let go of the grin she had been hiding. She would have to be blind not to see that William had been just as affected by her as she had been by him.

Yeah, stud, let's see how you like it.

She felt the heat of his breath on her neck before she heard him.

"You're playing a very dangerous game, Hannah. You might want to make sure you understand the rules before you go any further."

She closed her eyes as his whispered words shivered down her spine. Her breath caught when she opened them. He was gone.

She waited until she heard his footsteps on the stairs before turning around. Her body trembled with a need she had never felt before her breathing was ragged and irregular. What had he meant? Games? Rules? The only thing that was clear was that he didn't play fair. She had only thought to get some of her pride back after being caught staring at him.

No, that wasn't true. She had wanted to see how he would respond to her. And he was right. She had no idea what the rules were for playing *games* with a man like William. But she was a quick learner when it came to something she was interested in. And she was finding herself more and more interested in this new Dr. Cooper. Besides, right now, they were just doing some innocent flirting. Lots of people flirted without things going any further. And if things did go further? Well, she'd worry about that later. What she needed was a cold shower, which had nothing to do with her workout.

William plowed through the long line of patients scheduled for the day. Unable to sleep the night before, he'd prowled the banks of the lake until early morning. He'd thought to scare Hannah off when he'd approached her with his words of warning in the gym. He'd wanted her to understand that she was playing way out of her league. Only, that wasn't what had happened. From the moment he'd caught her standing on those stairs with those deep blue eyes trained on him, he'd known that he was the one in trouble.

"Room three is ready," Hannah said from the open doorway to his office. "It's Mr. McGrew. He's here for his post-op visit after his lumbar fusion. I went ahead and reviewed his range of motion. His pain scale is down and he's very happy with the results."

It was the most she had said to him since the night before. Even so, she still wouldn't look him in the eye. Was she embarrassed? Did he owe her an apology? They should probably talk about it. Women liked to talk about things. But how could they talk about it when he wasn't even sure what "it" was? All he knew was that he couldn't forget how Hannah had looked when she'd turned the tables on him. He'd taken two cold showers and still been up most of the night.

"Hannah, we need to talk." His phone dinged with the ringtone that notified him of a trauma in the ER. Reading the text message, he pushed back from his desk.

"Tell Marion to take care of the office. There's a

trauma in the ER we need to go see," he said as he reached for his hospital lab jacket, already feeling his blood boil at the description of the patient's injuries and the ER doc's message that he was suspicious of the husband having caused them.

Domestic abuse. It never made sense. Why did men feel the need to mistreat the very women they'd promised to take care of? To love and to cherish? You didn't abuse someone you cherished. 'Til death do us part? In sickness and health? He'd learned from his father that those vows were just pretty words for a crowd of guests. By the time his father had wed his fourth wife, he'd proved that his vows meant nothing.

He had only been nine when his mother had fallen down the stairs and received a traumatic brain injury which had resulted in her spending the rest of her life in a nursing home. By the time he was ten, his father had divorced William's mother or wife number two and he was only a teen by the time wife number three had come into the picture. He couldn't help but presume that it had only been death that had stopped his father at wife number four.

A pang of sympathy slipped through the thick armor he had in place at the thought of the little girl he had been entrusted with. His half sister would never know either of her parents. He knew Avery would miss her mother just as he had missed his when his mother was taken away from him.

The ride to the hospital was quiet. He'd given Hannah his phone to access the portal that contained the hospital's patient records as much to get her up to date on the patient as to keep her occupied while he dealt with his own demons. These types of injuries always brought out the worst in him.

They stopped at the ER desk to review the CT of the patient's head. From the ER doctor's description and the test results, it was easy to see the woman had a hairline skull fracture and possible concussion. She'd recover this time. It was the circumstances of the injury, however, that most concerned them. Next time she might not be so lucky.

"Let me go in first," Hannah said. "It might be easier for her to talk to another woman."

"Okay, see what you can get her to admit to. So far, she's claiming she tripped and fell. Maybe she'll relax around you," William said.

"It's worth a try. Good luck," the ER doc said before he picked up a chart and headed off to see another patient.

While Hannah went to see the patient, William took a seat at the desk and searched the patient's records. He wasn't surprised to read that there had been more than one visit to the ER in the last six months with an injury that was always put down to some type of accident. On one visit, she'd claimed to have tripped over a basket of laundry. On another, a rug had caused the fall that had led to a sprained wrist and busted chin. Each time the staff at the hospital had tried to get her to admit that she had been abused, but the woman had always denied it, leaving their hands tied. She was just another example of misplaced love.

William heard the shouting and shot to his feet. He could hear Hannah's voice and that of an unknown male.

He found her standing outside a trauma room doorway, her body ridged and her head thrown back as she looked up at a large man who was over six feet tall. Was this the abusive husband? The guy raised his voice at Hannah. "That's my wife in there. You have no right to keep me away from her," he snarled, giving Hannah a nasty stare.

William stepped between the two of them as the man attempted to push past her.

"Hannah, go into the room. I'm sure this man understands that our patient needs some privacy while we examine her," William said, his tone cold yet calm even though he wanted to punch the man in the face.

Hannah's hand slid out to the man's arm and she pulled him aside as two hospital security officers approached.

Stepping in front of him, she lowered her voice. "I understand that you are upset, Mr. Jones, but we are just trying to do our job. Now, these two officers are going to find you a nice seat in the waiting room where you can wait till someone tells you that you can come back. If you choose to continue arguing with us, these officers will call the police and have you removed from the hospital. It's your choice," Hannah said.

The man settled down and the two officers escorted him from the ER with warnings of calling the police if he caused any more trouble.

"Now, if you'll let me do my job, I'll introduce you to Jeannine Jones," she said to William as she turned toward the trauma room. He followed her inside without saying a word.

What had he done? He'd only wanted to protect Hannah. To keep the man who he believed had beat his wife away from her.

A small woman was perched on the side of a stretcher. Dressed in a silk blouse and dress pants, she ran trembling fingers along the string of pearls at her neck. Her arm had been splinted, Velcro strips holding it in place. Her pale skin highlighted the long row of black stitches above her eye. Purpling bruises marred her forehead, contrasting with dullness of the blue eyes that stared up at him. All medical evidence suggested Jeannine Jones had been physically battered. In his mind, whoever had abused her deserved to be locked up.

"It's nice to meet you," William said, dragging his thoughts away from things he could not change. "I'm Dr. Cooper. I'm the neurosurgeon on duty today. Can you tell me what happened?"

"I've told everyone that it was an accident. I just tripped. I'm clumsy, that's all." The woman's eyes begged him to believe her. What must her home life be like? he wondered, unable to even imagine the fear she might be living with day by day.

"I know it's frustrating, but it helps us in our neuro assessment," Hannah said, stepping closer to the stretcher. "Just like how we keep asking if you know your name and date of birth. With the injury to your head, we need to make sure your mental status doesn't become altered as that could be a sign of a much bigger problem." She took the woman's hand and held it comfortingly in her own.

"But I feel fine," Jeannine insisted, pulling her hand back. "I don't know why Tabitha called that ambulance. It was such a small cut."

"Is Tabitha a friend?" William asked. If anyone needed a friend, it was this woman.

"She lives next door. She comes over for tea sometimes when Calvin is at work. Calvin thinks she's a busybody, but she's really a very nice girl."

A nice girl who had taken on the duty of guardian angel to a woman who'd apparently been abused for too long, it seemed.

"Head wounds bleed a lot. It probably scared her to see the blood, and she did the right thing. You needed the stitches to close the gash above your eye," Hannah said. "Maybe we could call Tabitha and you could stay with her until you feel better?"

"No, I need to go home. My husband needs me there," Jeannine said, panic coming back into her voice. Panic and fear.

There was no way William was letting this woman go home today.

"Actually, I've reviewed the CT and there's a good probability that you have a concussion. I need you to stay overnight so we can make sure that you're okay. I know Tabitha would want you to stay," William said as he looked to Hannah.

"Wouldn't she feel better knowing you were doing what the doctor asked?" Hannah picked up his cue. "How about I call her so I can let her know you're doing okay? She's probably worried about you. If you give me the number, I can call her for you," Hannah said as she pulled her phone from her pocket.

William stepped out of the room to let Hannah work her magic as he knew she could. Jeannine wasn't ready to admit that she was being abused. Hopefully, her friend Tabitha would find a way to help the woman.

Within a few minutes, Hannah stepped out of the room.

"Did she agree to stay?" he asked as they made their way through the emergency department. "Was her friend helpful?"

"Jeannine has agreed to spend the night. Her nurse is going to take a guard with her when she goes to tell her husband in case he tries to cause trouble." Hannah added, "Her friend was out, so I gave Jeannine my cell number in case she needs anything."

"I don't understand how people let themselves get into this type of situation. It doesn't make sense. How can someone who says they love you hurt you like that? And how can you love someone who would do something like that to you?" William said. "Don't they see that that person is just using their love against them?"

"I wish I had the answer," Hannah admitted. "I'm sure love means different things to different people, but I know that what Calvin Jones feels for his wife can't be real love. Jeannine knows it, too. She kept saying how embarrassed she was, and I don't think she meant the injuries. I think she sees herself as weak and that's what she's embarrassed about."

"Then why doesn't she leave?" William asked as

he opened the door that would lead them back to the parking lot.

"She probably doesn't feel like she can leave. It's scary being out on your own, William. They have no children and, if her husband is like most abusers, he's cut her off from her friends and family. I'm going to call the social worker on the neuro floor when we get back to the office to see if she can help."

Hannah opened the door to the car. "Maybe this time Jeannine'll reach out for help."

"I hope you're right," William said as he settled in behind the wheel and started the engine. "Because I have a feeling that the next time her husband decides to beat on her it might be too late."

CHAPTER SIX

STANDING AT THE kitchen window, Hannah watched William as he snapped his fishing line in the air above him before laying it precisely in the same spot over and over. He'd been out there for more than half an hour and she hadn't seen him pull in a single fish.

She was supposed to be studying while William and the kids played outside, but she had stopped for a moment to check on them and now she was unable to step away. The repetition of the movement was mesmerizing as he brought the line out of the water again and again, making it dance in the air above him before casting out once more. It was a beautiful sight and she was only watching for the elegance of the movements. It had absolutely nothing to do with the way William's body swayed with each cast, his muscles tensing as he whipped the line back then relaxing as he let it sink into the water. Nope, it had nothing at all to do with William.

Refusing to waste the precious time she had to herself, Hannah moved back to the table and settled down to study. She had no time to be gazing out the window. She had an assignment due before the weekend.

Only, being out of sight did not take the vision of William from her mind. Both the cool, calm and collected man who ruled the operating room and the man standing alone on the bank of the lake were fascinating. The more Hannah saw of him, the more questions she had. And it wasn't just the physical attraction she felt for William that had him constantly in her thoughts. The man was such a mystery that she felt the need to find out what had made him that way. How could he go from cold to hot so fast?

The sexual awareness between the two of them seemed to be increasing every day. At some point, one of them would make a move. When it happened, would they be risking their new friendship for something that could easily burn itself out? Would it be worth it? She remembered how William had looked just moments earlier. How his smile made the muscles in her stomach clinch and her breath catch. How the boyish grin he'd given her the night before while they'd bathed Avery had set her heart to racing. Would she have the strength to walk away from that man? No, she definitely would not.

"Mom, have you seen my video headset?" Lindsey asked as she rushed through the back door. "William says he'll play with me after he gets Avery to sleep since I've already gotten my homework done."

"I don't think I've seen it. Are you sure you brought it?" Hannah asked as she shut the textbook. She'd been reading the same paragraph over and over and still couldn't remember the information.

"Maybe it's in the stuff that I left in that black box

by my desk," Lindsey said. "I get to choose the game so I have the advantage."

Hannah shook her head as Lindsey ran down the hall to their rooms. It seemed that every couple of days Hannah had to make a trip to their apartment to retrieve something one of them had forgotten.

Deciding she might as well take a break, Hannah put together some drinks and took them out to the backyard. Setting the tray on the picnic table, she reached into the playpen where Avery was playing. The wiggly girl clapped her hands then wrapped them around Hannah's neck.

Hannah's heart squeezed. The child was quickly working her way into Hannah's heart, right along with her brother. If she wasn't careful, Hannah would have her heart broken by both of them when she had to leave. Something she wasn't sure she could survive. Unfortunately, her heart didn't seem to understand the danger.

The lake was calm, the water lapping against the bank in a slow, steady rhythm that had always soothed him. Only, today, it did nothing to calm the anger he felt toward a man he didn't even know. Inside, he knew there was nothing more at the moment he could do in a case like Jeannine's, but that didn't make him feel any better.

William couldn't shake the picture of Jeannine Jones sitting in the emergency trauma room all battered and broken. How many times had she awoken from a beating and wondered where her life had gone wrong? How many times had she regretted that she'd ever met her husband?

He looked back toward the house, relieved to see that

Hannah had moved away from the window. He'd known she'd been watching him. He'd seen that window a hundred times from the banks of the lake, had looked out of it himself hundreds more, but never had it looked so right to see Hannah standing there. It made him think of things that could not be. Not for a man with his family's history of mistakes. William had sworn to his own father that he would never make the same mistakes his father had repeated over and over.

Still, the sight of Hannah in his kitchen window had seemed so right at that moment. She wasn't just the nurse or the student or the friend who was there to help him, though she was all of those things. She was the woman he had discovered that night in the gym, the one still giving him restless nights.

But what did she see when she looked at him? Was it the renowned surgeon or the wealthy bachelor? Avery's half brother? The doctor she worked with? Or did she see the man who had almost lost himself to the need she'd made him feel that night in the gym? A need that tugged at him as she crossed the yard to him now.

"I thought you might need something to drink," she said, holding out a glass of what looked like lemonade. Taking the glass, he slowly sipped the tart yet sweet juice and then smiled at Avery as Hannah transferred her from one arm to the other. He was using the time to collect his thoughts from the dangerous ground where they had wandered.

"Thanks. I wanted to apologize for the way I acted today. I should have known that you could take care of yourself," he said, knowing he couldn't promise he wouldn't do the same thing again.

"I can take care of myself, William. I've been doing it for years. Calvin Jones isn't the first irate family member I've had to handle and he won't be the last. I'd already sent one of the techs to get the officers."

"I know you can handle it. I just lost it for a few minutes. All I could think about was how he had hurt his wife, someone he was supposed to care about. I figured he'd have no problem hurting you. But I should have known you were prepared," he conceded. "And you did a great job with Jeannine, too. I checked on her before I came outside and the nurse said she was resting well."

"Thank you, William," Hannah said, looking out over the lake. "I'm glad she's doing well."

"There's something else I want to talk to you about…" William he rested his glass on the grass. "I got a call from one of my father's lawyers and it seems there are a lot of papers in my father's office I need to personally go through and decide what to do with. So I'm going to have to make a visit to my father's house this weekend." He began taking his casting rod apart. "I don't expect you to come with me. I know you have a lot of studying to do right now."

"And miss you experiencing a road trip with Avery? Never. Besides, I think it's a good idea to take her back to her home."

Her words startled him. "What?" he asked, his hand stilling above his tackle box.

"I realized, talking to Lindsey just now, how much stuff we left behind that we probably should have brought with us," Hannah said. "There are probably things at your father's place that Avery is attached to. It's kind of like me moving Lindsey in here. I let her make the decision about the most important items to her—what she couldn't live without, sentimental items—and those are the things she packed to bring here."

"Avery's not even one year old. There can't be much that she's attached to at her age," he quipped softly. Sentimental? A pre-toddler?

"And what about photos? Someday she'll want to see pictures of herself as a baby. She also needs pictures of her parents. Those are things she'll cherish when she gets older. Things that can't be replaced. Things she'll guard for the rest of her life."

He thought of the small box he'd hidden in the attic all those years ago. Was it still there? It had held nothing of any real value, only memories of the childhood he had lost. Memories of a mother who had been taken away from him. Like Avery's mother had been taken away from her. He and his baby sister had too much in common.

"I don't know what the plans are for your father's house, but this is too important to leave up to the staff that might not know what to keep for Avery," Hannah said, her chin rising as if readying for a fight. Did she think he wouldn't take her concerns serious?

William trusted that Hannah knew more about what his sister needed than he did. "Okay, I'll make arrangements and see if Avery's nanny can meet us there this weekend. I don't know if she's taken another job, but

I'm sure she'll want to help if she's able to. Will that work for you?" he asked, glancing once more at the lake whose calm waves had always given him the peace he needed in his life.

Just the thought of returning to his childhood home caused his stomach to churn. With the way his life was changing, he had a feeling it would be many years until his life was peaceful again.

The fact that that thought didn't bother him as much as it had before Avery, Hannah and Lindsey had moved in with him scared him most of all.

Accompanying William on his rounds through the neurosurgery intensive care unit was one of Hannah's favorite things to do. Not only did she get to see all her friends and coworkers, she got to see the patients from a different perspective.

"Can you dictate the consult note?" William asked as they exited an elderly patient's room. The man had suffered a subdural hematoma after a fall and was being closely observed because of the anticoagulants he had been taking.

"Sure," she said as William approached the ICU doctor on staff for the day. The fact that he trusted her skills enough to take on the task made her smile as she took a seat at the nurses' station to type up her notes.

"So, what's it like to work with Dr. Frosty?" one of her coworkers said as she slid her chair over till it bumped Hannah's.

Kitty had a bit of a mouth on her, but Hannah knew she was meticulous in the care of her patients. She was also a friend who could always be counted on in a pinch. Should Hannah mention her current arrangement with William? It wasn't like they were keeping it a secret.

"Hush. He'll hear you," Hannah said, looking over to where William stood with the other doctor. "And it's great."

"You two certainly looked close," one of the respiratory techs said as she joined them.

"He's as great at teaching as he is at surgery. I couldn't have asked for a better preceptor." Hannah really wasn't sure what to tell them about William. He was a man who valued his privacy and she respected that.

Making a point to appear caught up in studying the patient's chart, she was glad when there were no more awkward questions. Eventually someone would see them together outside of work and the rumors would start. When that happened, she'd deal with it, but talking about William behind his back was not something she was going to do.

After completing their morning rounds, Hannah and William took the elevator to the parking garage. As the doors shut, she relaxed for a second. From patient rounds to surgery and then follow-up appointments, there just didn't seem enough hours in the day.

"Dr. Frosty, huh?" he asked as he leaned against the side of the elevator.

Hannah wished she could go through the elevator floor. Her face burned with embarrassment. Had Kitty's words hurt him?

"She didn't mean anything by it," Hannah said. What

would he say if she told him she thought of him more as Dr. Hottie than Dr. Frosty after that night in the gym? They'd both chosen to pretend that nothing had happened that night, but she knew neither of them had forgotten it.

His lips quirked into a half smile. "I guess it's better than Bill."

"Or Billy? I just can't see you as a Billy. Though, like Lindsey says, Billy the Brain Surgeon has a good ring to it." Hannah laughed at his look of horror. She was finding out that teasing the always-so-serious doctor was a lot of fun. He was always so good-natured when Lindsey gibed him. It made him seem so much more human.

Her thoughts suddenly took an unprofessional turn as she took in the way he looked right then, his body relaxed, his whole attention on her, which always sent shivers running along her spine. But he had no way of knowing that.

"Did you manage to get in touch with Jeannine?" he asked as he looked away. She'd caught that look of frustration before he'd turned his head and had no problem understanding it. Finding out the abused woman had left with her husband before they'd made rounds, her self-discharged had been upsetting for both of them.

"I've tried to call, but I just keep getting sent to her voice mail," Hannah said, taking out her phone and checking once again.

William's phone dinged. The ringtone was one she had come to know meant an emergency. He checked it before moving to the elevator buttons and punching in the ground floor.

"'Motor vehicle accident victim with head injury,'" he read aloud. "'Positive for loss of consciousness. Twenty-nine-year-old male. No seat belt. In CT now.'"

The doors opened and they both headed for Radiology, only to learn the patient had been sent back to the emergency ward.

"I want to go talk to the radiologist. I'll meet you in the trauma room," William said to Hannah.

"Okay." Hannah reversed her course. She'd never worked in the ER, but she'd made many trips to the pediatric side of the unit in the past. She had a lot of respect for the staff who worked there. It took a special person to deal with everything that walked through the doors.

The trauma room was crowded with medical staffers. The first thing she noticed was a nurse starting the rapid transfusion pump. That was a bad sign. The young man was bleeding from somewhere, which would make an emergent surgery even more complicated if he also had a head injury.

As someone from the lab exited the room, she entered. Standing at the head of the bed, she saw the man yank his arm away as one of the nurses tried to insert a large bore IV catheter into his arm. Taking out her pen light, Hannah checked his eyes. While a bit sluggish, they did react to the light. Noting the oval shape of one of his pupils, however, Hannah anticipated a major problem. The intracranial pressure in his head was building.

"What was his GCS?" she asked the nurse who was

busy recording the patient's vitals. The Glasgow Coma Scale would give them a clearer understanding of the man's consciousness level. Anything within the range of three to eight, Hannah knew, meant the patient was comatose.

"It was a twelve on scene but just dropped to eight," he said, never taking his eyes off the monitors that displayed the patient's vital signs. "He needs to go to surgery now. It's up to those two as to who gets to take him first."

Hannah looked over to see that William had entered the room along with the trauma surgeon, Dr. Weeks.

"What did the CT show?" she asked as William joined her at the patient's bedside.

"He has a large subdural hematoma. The OR team is on its way now to take him for an exploratory. If Dr. Weeks can get the internal bleeding stopped and the patient makes it through the surgery, we'll go in and evacuate it," William said as he conducted his own assessment of the patient, checking his pupil response and then examining the head laceration.

"Is he stable enough for two surgeries?" Hannah asked, feeling helpless as she watched the patient deteriorate before her eyes. More than once as a nurse, she had wished for the surgical skills that would allow her to take a patient to the operating room herself instead of having to wait for the surgeon on call to show up.

"We don't have a choice. He needs a crani to decrease his intracranial pressure or he won't have a chance. We'll just have to hope that Dr. Weeks finds the bleeding and fixes it fast." William stepped away from the young man's bedside. "I'm going to go talk to his family."

Hannah looked up as one of the monitors beeped an alarm.

"What's the holdup? This guy needs surgery now," Dr. Weeks said as the OR team charged into the room. "Let's go before he codes."

Hannah followed the team out of the room and joined William in the hallway to accompany him to meet with the family. Having never been in a critical care waiting room before, she knew it usually meant a patient was near death.

The room was full of people, all in some form of grief. Everyone stopped when she and William entered, and Hannah could feel the weight of their stares. Their eyes said they were expecting the worse, their expressions revealed they were all full of hope. How did William handle this kind of responsibility?

"I'm Dr. Cooper," William announced. "I'm the neurosurgeon called in to see Kyle. I was told his wife was here."

The group seemed to part as a woman not quite Hannah's age stepped forward. "I'm his wife and this is Kyle's mother and father." The young woman indicated the older couple beside her. "Is he…?" Her voice broke on the words.

"He's headed to the OR right now. As I'm sure Dr. Weeks told you, Kyle's condition is critical."

Hannah listened as William clarified some of the details of Kyle's surgery to decrease the cranial pressure. He used words the family would understand, explaining that the accumulation of blood was pushing on Kyle's brain and could cause permanent damage. She felt she had learned as much by listening to him than she had ever learned in one of those dry nursing school lectures halls. By the time he had received their consent to proceed with the neurosurgery, his phone was alerting him to a message.

"Dr. Weeks has located the source of the bleed," he told Kyle's family after reading the message. "As he suspected, it was the spleen. He's removing it now... I'm going to get ready. I'll have an OR nurse keep you up to date on our progress. I don't expect to be in surgery for very long," William added before he and Hannah headed out the door.

"Let me know when you finish. I'm going to hang out in the employee lounge," she told him once they arrived at the door that led to the OR.

"I thought you'd want to come in with me," he said, swiping his ID badge to pass through the door.

"Really? You'll let me in the operating room with you?" she said. There had been a holdup with her paperwork from school and she hadn't yet been given hospital clearance to attend his surgeries.

"I got special permission from the medical chief for you to observe only. Come on, I'll show you where to change."

By the time Hannah was directed to an area off to William's side, where she wouldn't be in the surgical field but would still have a good view, she was starting experiencing some serious jitters. The smell of Betadine and blood mingled in the air as the surgical team prepared. She made herself concentrate on the way the technician draped Kyle's head for the procedure, her stomach continually rolling in protest. What if she couldn't take watching? Performing brain surgery had been her dream for years but she'd never actually been present for one.

Then William's soothing voice enveloped her as he explained each confident incision, the sound of soft classical music filling the room. Some surgeons liked hard rock in their ORs, others liked soft jazz. Hannah should have known he would go for Tchaikovsky.

Soon she had forgotten her fears and was totally caught up in the procedure as the blood that had accumulated underneath the skull was evacuated.

The anesthesiologist called out that the patient's blood pressure was dropping, but William's hands never faltered. His voice was always calm and steady, and it was easy to see why they called him the Ice Prince of the OR. He was able to separate himself from every emotion while he had a scalpel in his hand.

Hannah remembered wondering which of William's personas was the real one. She hadn't understood the nickname then. She'd needed to see him here, now, to fully appreciate where the ability to withdraw from everything happening around him gave him the power to save lives. Only, the real world wasn't like this sterile room. To really live, he had to open himself up to others instead of shutting them out.

And who was she to say anything about someone shutting others out? After everything she had been through with Lindsey's dad, and then her parents turning their backs on her, she'd shut herself in as much the same way as William had. Her fear of losing her daughter had taken control of every aspect of her life. She'd devoted herself to taking the best care of Lindsey. Yes, she'd made friends with other mothers and coworkers, but she hadn't let anyone inside her and Lindsey's world. Just as William hadn't let anyone inside his world until now.

Maybe it's time for me to make some changes in my life, too.

Hannah eyed the monitors and was relieved to see that the patient's blood pressure was starting to rise. The anesthesiologist called out the new reading.

As William prepared to close the incision, he explained that they would store the section of skull that had been removed until he could confidently replace it once Kyle's vitals and crania had time to restore themselves. Most assuredly, before the patient was sent to a rehab facility.

"Thank you," William said to the operating staff as he stepped back from the table. He then turned to Hannah. "Well, what do you think? Do you still want to specialize in neurosurgery?"

"Yes," she said as she replayed the operation over in her on head. She had no doubts now. She was meant to be in a neurosurgeon's practice. "This is definitely what I want to do."

CHAPTER SEVEN

WILLIAM STOPPED AT the bottom step of the house that
had haunted his childhood. While his classmates had
moaned about being sent off to boarding school, he had
gladly left this place. Would things have been different if his father had sold the house after the accident?
Would he have been different without the reminder
every day of his mother's accident?

"This is where you grew up?" Lindsey asked from
beside him.

"Yes," he answered without explaining that he had
spent as much time away from the place as possible.
Hannah's daughter had been raised in a home filled with
love. He couldn't expect her to understand that his up-
bringing had been very different than hers.

"It would have been a cool place to play hide-and-
seek when you were little. I bet you could hide for hours
here," Lindsey said as she continued up the steps.

He'd spent most of his time hiding in his room or in
the attic, but he didn't have many memories of anyone
actually seeking him. As far as his stepmothers had
been concerned, if he was out of sight, everything was

fine. It was only when he'd showed up during one of their social functions that he'd become a problem. No one had been interested in the awkward child happier to be reading a book than talking with strangers.

The trip to Dallas had not been without challenges. While Lindsey had done her best to entertain Avery, the little girl had refused to be satisfied. She'd finally fussed herself to sleep. And that was why Hannah had insisted that they pack a bag to spend the night. She had known the trip there and back in one day would be more than any of them could handle.

He'd wanted to drive back to Houston that night, but he could now see that Hannah had known what she was talking about. A night trip would have been miserable for everyone. It was another lesson learned.

Lindsey had told him he should get a minivan with a DVD setup, but he drew the line at driving a "mommy van." That was not happening.

"It's a monstrosity that my father built to declare himself the king of Dallas real estate," he said as they climbed the steps to the front door. "'Real estate is all about perception,' he would say. 'No one wants to hire an unsuccessful agent.'"

"Are you okay?" Hannah asked, as she shifted Avery in her arms and reached for his hand.

Her touch was warm and comforting. Surprising himself, he closed his hand over hers. A strange calm came over him. Not like the calm that he demanded of himself in the OR, but a peaceful feeling that he wasn't alone. That there was someone to care enough to go through this with him. Was this friendship? Or was this something more? He should release Hannah's hand and step away, but at that moment he didn't know if he had the strength to go through the doors without her.

For the first time it really sank in that his father was gone. That he would never be there to greet William again. The weight of that knowledge slammed into him unexpectedly as he walked, hand in hand with Hannah, into the foyer where he had last seen the man.

He remembered taking a real good look at his father then—had acknowledged their similarities in height and coloring, and noted that his father's age had begun to show despite his fight to hold on to his youth.

His father had insisted that William come to meet his new wife. She'd turned out to be only a younger version of wife number three, whom he'd divorced a few years prior. William had made the effort; as always, hoping that he'd see some sign that his father had changed. There'd been no change. His newest stepmother had been surprisingly pleasant, though. An interior decorator before their marriage, she'd shared with him some of the changes she had planned for the house. But her time had run out too soon.

"Oh, there you are!" Ms. Adams, Avery's former nanny, called out as she rushed to Hannah's side and took Avery into her arms. "I've missed this one so much, but it's so nice to see that she's doing so well. And of course she belongs in Houston with her big brother, though I'm sure she's made a change or two in your life by now."

"This is Hannah. She's helping me and Avery with the transition," William said as he let go of Hannah's hand and immediately missed its warmth. "She would like to go through Avery's and her mother's things to see if there is anything we need to keep while I go through some of my father's paperwork.

"Would you also show her through the house, Mrs. Adams? I'll join you as soon as I'm finished," he added before leaving the women.

His father's lawyers had felt it necessary that he personally review some of the documents left in his father's private study. William had no idea what he was going to find, but would rather be buried in his father's paperwork than dealing with all the memories that he wasn't ready to face.

Hannah watched as William headed to a side door and disappeared.

If William's father had really wanted to impress, this was definitely the house for it. How in the world would Avery's mother have kept up with a toddler in a house this size? And, as far as she could see, there was nothing at all that looked child friendly,

She moved farther into the house, looking for anything that would tell her about the people who had lived there. She was hoping there would be something to explain William's outlook toward the house. Somehow, she knew that his whole attitude about family was tied to the childhood he had spent here.

After taking in the sitting room at the front of the house—Lindsey asking Mrs. Adams where they hid the television—they moved to a formal living room and dining room. Marble, wood, and crystal filled every room. Definitely impressive, but cold and impersonal, too. While Hannah was sure the rooms had been designed to impress, she struggled to grasp a sense of the people, the family, that had lived here not that long ago.

It wasn't until the former nanny finally took them upstairs to Avery's room that Hannah could see the small touches that made a place feel lived in. Before Ms. Adams could put her down, Avery was squealing for a ride on the toy train mounted on a set of rails that circled the room.

Lindsey helped her onto the seat and began to push her around the track while Avery laughed at the train sounds she was making. The way those two had bonded was amazing. Lindsey had never asked for a sibling— somehow the child had known that their family would always be just the two of them.

A door stood open to a room done in pastel pinks and greens, the carpet as white as snow. "Was this Avery's parents' room?" Hannah asked as she stepped inside. A silver hairbrush lay on a dressing table that held bottles and jars with names of expensive products she had only seen advertised in elite fashion magazines.

"This was Mrs. Cooper's room. Mr. Cooper's room is down the hall," Mrs. Adams said. "Mrs. Cooper said her husband was a light sleeper and she was concerned that a baby would disturb him so she had this room decorated before Miss Avery was born."

Hannah could tell that the woman had more to say about her employee-employer relationship, but for now Hannah wanted to make her own observations. If there was something in this house that would explain why

William was so withdrawn from other people, she didn't think she would find it in this room.

But there was something Ms. Adams could help her with.

"I was wondering if you knew where Avery's mother would have kept any photographs of Avery. You know, hospital photos, or her first time crawling? I know when she's older, she will want those. Also, anything special that you think we should keep for her. A favorite toy or book?" Hannah asked as she turned to the woman. "And anything of her mother's that she might appreciate later." She fingered the silver hairbrush. Had Avery's mother once used it to brush the child's dark curls?

"I helped the staff from the lawyers' office collect Mrs. Cooper's jewelry. They assured me it would be kept safe until Avery was old enough to keep it herself."

Mrs. Adams turned back to where Lindsey and Avery were playing in the room next door. "They only asked for the things they could put a dollar value to since they were cataloging those items." She took a hesitant breath. "No one seemed to really care about the little girl who had been left behind without her parents. I was so glad when the lawyers asked me to take her to her brother. She needed someone who wasn't looking at the dollar signs, it seemed to me."

The older woman smiled at Hannah before continuing. "I guess it took some time for the lawyers to find her parents' most recent will. But I had heard about Mr. Cooper's son being a doctor and all, and it made sense that the Coopers would want the child with her brother. The staff that had been here awhile spoke well of him, so it seemed to me that was where the child belonged. I wish you could have seen his eyes when I handed him little Avery."

Hannah stared at the woman with admiration. She was a lot feistier than her gray hair pulled back in a sedate knot at the back of her head and her feet clad in a pair of comfortable-looking sneakers made her appear. The woman was opinionated and certainly not afraid to tell you exactly what she thought.

"But I can tell he's doing better now," Mrs. Adams stated. "I knew from what I had heard of him that he wouldn't turn his back on his responsibilities. I'm so glad he found someone to help him with Avery."

"I'm just a friend, a coworker. We work together at the hospital," Hannah found herself telling the woman. It wasn't as if she needed to explain the arrangement to her.

A squeal came from the other room and they both rushed in to see Lindsey blowing raspberries against Avery's tummy, the child bubbling over with laughter.

"I'm so glad you are there for them." Mrs. Adams grinned at the children rolling on the floor. "Avery needed a real home and it looks like she's found one."

Hannah couldn't bring herself to tell Mrs. Adams that the family arrangement she was imagining for the little girl was just temporary.

It was becoming harder for her to believe that what she was feeling for both Avery and William wasn't real. Even Lindsey was forming a close connection with both Avery and William. The four of them fit too well together and she needed to remember that she was only there for a short time.

Soon, very soon, William wouldn't need her anymore and it would be time for her and Lindsey to move on. They'd moved on before. They could do it again.

Why hadn't she listened to William earlier when he'd told her it would be best for them to drive back to Houston than to spend the night in his father's house? She'd heard something in his voice at the time, but had chosen to ignore it.

Instead, she'd truly believed that having the night in her old home would be good for Avery. She'd also thought it would give her time to observe what items seemed most significant to the little girl. And that was why she now found herself trying to fall asleep in a dead woman's bed—where Hannah knew she didn't belong.

She'd been glad that William hadn't reminded her of his desire not to stay overnight. She'd even been surprised when he'd suggested ordering pizza and eating it in the small game room on the second floor where he had unearthed an old gaming system for him and Lindsey to play.

For a couple of hours, they had relaxed. Hannah playing on the floor with Avery while the other two screamed taunts of revenge at one another. It wasn't until after she had said good-night to William and seen Lindsey to the guest room, that the eerie feeling that she didn't belong in the room next to Avery's nursery had begun to haunt her.

It wasn't only the thought of Avery's mother spending her last night alive here, though it seemed sad that the woman had this big, beautiful room and still slept alone. It was the whole house. What had the late Mrs. Cooper seen when William's father had brought her here for the first time? Had she been impressed with all that wood and marble? Or had she found it cold and lifeless, like Hannah had? She couldn't imagine how William must have felt growing up in such a place. Or could she? Was the very nature of the mansion part of the explanation for William's aloofness?

Hannah punched the pillow and turned onto her side. She had no right judging the people who had lived here, but she couldn't help but compare this place to the home William had made. In some ways his house had seemed cold when she'd first entered it, but as she'd added small items and changed the grouping of some of the furniture, she had soon seen the possibilities in the house and it was quickly becoming a home for the four of them.

It's only temporary, she reminded herself.

She heard the screech of metal against metal and froze. Surely it was her imagination? There were only the four of them in this wing of the house, so who would be up moving around at this time? The sound of a board squeaking had her up and at Avery's bedside in less than a minute. The child was safe in her crib and sound asleep. She took a moment to brush soft wisps of hair from Avery's face then headed to the door that opened into the hallway.

Had Lindsey woken and been disoriented as to where she was? Or, more likely, had her daughter decided to do some exploring on her own while the adults slept?

Stepping up to the guest room door, Hannah cracked it open. Her daughter was stretched out in sleep as if she didn't have a care in the world, something that always made Hannah smile. Like every transplant recipient family, they knew that their lives could change at any moment, but Hannah didn't allow either one of them to spend time worrying about what the future could hold. They'd face that together when the time came.

Having assured herself that both Avery and Lindsey were where they should be, she headed along the hall to the room William had chosen for the night and stopped. What was she thinking? She couldn't just barge into the man's room! But even knowing the girls were safe wasn't enough. She needed to make sure that William was okay, too.

Rounding the corner, she saw that his bedroom door was open. Seeing his empty bed—a sight that had her body humming with dangerous excitement—she considered what to do next. It only made sense that the sounds she had heard were William's. The man had the right to prowl the halls of his father's home at night if he wanted to. But still, there would be no going to sleep for her until she could assure herself that he was okay. Had he been feeling the same out-of-sorts sensations she had? Just being in this house had to be hard so soon after the loss of his father. Of course, it could be that William wanted to be alone with his thoughts, but it seemed to her that he had been alone too much already in his life.

Her mind made up, Hannah headed for the stairs. She would check on William then leave him alone if he wished. She just needed to see him and, no matter what other parts of her body seemed to think, she was just checking to make sure he didn't need anything.

Like a friendly hug? she asked herself.

The kitchen was empty, but the light over the back stairway was on. She wasn't sure where it led, but she was certain she'd find William there.

Opening the fridge, she pulled out some milk and then checked the cabinets for the makings of hot cocoa. The warm, sweet beverage had always worked to calm her nerves, which was something she could use now as she contemplated following William up those stairs.

CHAPTER EIGHT

WILLIAM STOOD AMONG the boxes and furniture relegated to the attic when their usefulness ended. Somewhere in here, there was a box of his mother's belongings. Things his father had ordered removed from their bedroom when it had been determined that his wife would never be returning. But that wasn't what William was after.

He'd been through that box many times as a child missing his mother. Anything he'd thought needed to be preserved, he had removed and snuck back to the box he'd kept under his bed. The box that he had later hidden in the attic when he'd left for college. The box he had all but forgotten about until he'd planned this trip to gather some of Avery's mother's belongings.

He should have thought of that himself. The few things he'd had of his mother's had been priceless as he'd grown up and time had started to erase his memories. He didn't want that for Avery. He'd make sure that she always had access to her mother's belongings. William wouldn't be like his father and hide everything away. He'd even taken the picture he'd found in the office of their father holding Avery as an infant. He planned to place it on the fireplace mantel in his home.

Going over his father's accounts today, he had made the decision to sell the house and put all the proceeds into a trust fund for Avery that his father had already set up.

He only wanted one thing from this house and he needed to find it before they left in the morning. This would be his final trip to his father's ostentatious estate. He would leave everything else for the lawyers to handle.

"Here you are," Hannah said, her head peaking over the railing of the attic stairs.

He turned and watched as she stepped onto the landing, holding two cups. He enjoyed the sight of her tousled blond waves and the thin nightshirt that hugged her curves.

"What are you doing here?" he asked as he took one of the cups and a big step back from her.

"I heard something in the hall and saw that your bed was empty. I wanted to make sure you were okay," Hannah said.

"You checked my bed?" he asked, amused when a light pink blush stained her cheeks.

"I checked on Avery and Lindsey first," she said, looking around the large space. "I know it's your house, but everything I've learned from watching horror movies with Lindsey tells me that coming up into the attic at night is not a good move."

"But you came anyhow?" he asked, setting down his cup.

"My parents always said my curiosity would get me in trouble someday." She gave him a smile then turned to lift a sheet off the old desk that had been in storage since he'd been a little boy.

Did she not realize that he was the trouble her parents had warned her about?

"Are you looking for something particular?" she asked.

He'd come to the attic to be alone with his memories, but now he wanted to share those memories with Hannah. He wanted to let her see the lonely boy that had grown up to be the man he was today. The man whose coworkers referred to him as Dr. Frosty. Was it weak to want Hannah to understand him? Did he care if it was? He found himself wanting to share more and more with her every day. He'd waited for the fear of rejection to come, but it hadn't. He trusted Hannah, something he'd once thought impossible.

"That desk was my mother's," he said, shuffling boxes in the far corner of the room where he'd hidden his most prized possessions.

"It's lovely. You must miss her," she said, her voice coming from directly behind him.

He'd known she'd ask questions; her curiosity was something he enjoyed. He'd seen it in her interest in everything about their work, about Avery, about everyone and everything. Someone else might call her snoopy, but he had come to understand that it was just her desire to learn. To know those around her.

Moving a large box marked "Christmas," he paused

then said, "I do. It's not something I speak of very often, though."

He indicated a low bench under the eaves of the attic where a window looked out against the dark sky. "Let's sit over there," he said, picking up a small black box with the words "Private Letters" painted along the side in dark red paint.

William waited for Hannah to begin with her questions, but they didn't come. Taking a seat beside her on the bench, he looked out across a yard that held a lifetime of memories for him. Only, for his mother. it had been a very short lifetime.

"I was nine when Bennie, a man who worked for my father's business, came to get me from school. I had been expecting my mother as she was usually the one who picked me up. I didn't think much of it until I realized Bennie wasn't driving me home. He tried to explain to me that there had been an accident. My mother had fallen and hit her head and was very sick, but the only thing I understood was that my mother was in the hospital."

William would never forget the first time he had seen his mother in the hospital bed, tubes and monitors surrounding her. He'd not understood why she wouldn't wake up when he'd called her name. Day after day, he had gone to see the woman lying in that bed, her head wrapped in dressings. And day after day, he'd become angrier and angrier with her for not waking. For not coming back to him.

"It wasn't until later, after my father explained that my mother would be going to a place that could take better care of her than the hospital, that I realized she was never coming home." He took a deep breath.

"I'm sorry. That must have been terrible," Hannah sympathized.

"Yes. She suffered a traumatic brain injury when she fell and, despite all the specialists my father sent to see her, there was never any hope of recovery." He paused. "She passed away five years ago."

"That's why you went into neurosurgery," she said.

"I used to tell her every time I saw her that someday I'd be a doctor and I'd make her well. If I had known then what I know now, I would have made my father let her go when they first put her on a ventilator," he said.

"Thank you for sharing that with me. I know it can't be easy for you to come here with the memories of your mother and now your father."

"We weren't that close, my father and I. I think that maybe we were just too much alike in some ways. We were always bumping heads over something—most of the time it wasn't even anything important. Something happened when we lost my mother and we just never could work things out between us. I won't let things be like that for me and Avery. I won't let that history be repeated," he said as he opened the top of the black box and pulled out a handmade card.

"What's that?" she asked, leaning over. "Oh, a Mother's Day card. I have a box of them that Lindsey's made for me."

"It was the last one I made for my mother," he said then set it aside. She didn't need to know how angry his father had become when William had insisted on taking the card to his mother. It was the same day his father had rasped through gritted teeth that his mother would never be able to read the card. Would never be able to come home again.

Hannah reached into the box and brought out a signed baseball. "Astros?"

"Rangers. My father's company sponsored a family fun night when I was eleven," William said.

He let her examine the strange collection that had come from his childhood. An old picture of Elle Campbell from the eighth-grade dance. A rock from a riverbed he'd collected on the trip he had taken with his grandparents to the mountains of Tennessee.

Hannah held up an empty perfume bottle. It had been his mother's, one of the few things he had taken from the boxed items the staff had put it the attic. Over the years, the fragrance had evaporated until only the empty bottle remained. Just as his hope that his mother would return for him had dried up as the weeks and months had stretched into years.

"I had forgotten about these things until you mentioned gathering things for Avery," he said, gently taking the bottle from her and holding it to the light of the bulb hanging above them. "You were right, Hannah. There are things of her mother's that Avery will treasure when she gets older. You always seem to know the right thing to do."

"Me? I wish," she said and then hesitated.

He waited and watched as she bit down on her lower lip. A warm heat spread through him, part desire and part something else…something he refused to acknowledge.

"I've made a lot of mistakes," she finally said. "Done the wrong thing. Said the wrong thing. They've taught me some hard lessons."

"Was one of those mistakes Lindsey's father?" he asked, his curiosity getting the better of him.

"Best mistake I ever made," Hannah breathed. "It gave me Lindsey. She's a blessing, not a mistake. It was her father who was the mistake."

"I didn't mean Lindsey," he said. The funny girl who kept him on his toes was delightful.

"I know you didn't. But yes, in other ways, my relationship with Lindsey's father was a mistake."

"I take it he's not involved with Lindsey?" he asked. Did the man know what he was missing? Any man would be proud to be the girl's father.

"No. He had plans for his life that didn't include me or a baby. By the time I figured out that I was just a rebound relationship for him, he'd gotten back with his high school sweetheart."

"It's his loss, you know," William said as he put his cherished items back inside the box. "And I'm not just talking about Lindsey."

"Thank you," Hannah said. "I know it would have been easier if I'd had help, but it wasn't meant to be. Me and Lindsey—we were meant to be."

"Your parents couldn't help?" he asked. He knew from conversations he'd overheard between Hannah and her daughter that things were very tense between Hannah and her parents.

"That's a story for another time… It's going to be

a long car ride back to Houston tomorrow. We'd both better get some sleep."

Putting the lid back on the box, he stood, stashed it under one arm, and reached out a hand to help Hannah up from the bench.

For a mere second, they stood together, hands linked, bodies all but touching, breaths mingling.

William felt more aroused then he had ever felt in his life but he took a step back. This couldn't happen. Not here in this house. Not now. Because as much as he had tried to warn Hannah against him, deep inside he knew that no matter the risk, someday soon he would not be able to walk away from the hunger in her eyes.

"I'm not the man you think I am, Hannah." He tensed when she stepped closer to him, fought his body's arousal.

Resting her hands against his chest, she lifted her lips to his in a soft caress.

"You're not the man you think you are, either," she said before turning away, leaving him wondering what was it that she saw in him given all the baggage he carried with him.

CHAPTER NINE

LEAVING THE OPERATING ROOM, Hannah all but danced. She had passed the test required by the hospital to allow her to assist William in the OR and she couldn't wait to get back to the office to tell him. Her phone vibrated in the back pocket of her scrub pants and she pulled it out to see a text from William asking how it was going.

Done and passed! she typed. Her phone rang immediately.

"Meet me in the emergency room," William said, his words clipped, cold. She knew the tone only too well now. There was a critical patient who was not doing well.

"I'll head there now," she said as a bit of the adrenaline from her excitement drained from her.

While she understood why William internalized his feelings during surgery and when dealing with a patient that needed emergency care, she wondered how healthy it was for him to hold it all inside. It seemed that underneath all that control lay the root of whatever it was that made him think he needed to go through his life alone.

She'd only recently realized that even all of his hobbies were solitary. Had he spent so much time alone in the house his father had built that he didn't know how to live life any other way? Of course, his life was changing now with Avery. Whether within his comfort zone or not, he would be joining the rest of the world.

She spotted William's tall frame and brown hair above a group standing outside one of the trauma rooms and joined them. She also spotted a couple of officers, which sent shivers through her. Their presence meant that the patient was likely either a crime victim or a suspect.

"Excuse me," she said as she pushed past an X-ray technician leaving the crowded space.

Then she saw her.

Her arm still wrapped in the Velcro splint she'd been wearing the last time Hannah had seen her, there was now an ugly scar above her eye, the greenish hue of old bruises standing out against her pale face.

Jeannine Jones had been intubated and a respiratory tech was quickly setting up the ventilator. Grabbing a pair of gloves from the dispenser, Hannah made it to the side of Jeannine's bed. She carefully pushed the woman's hair back from the side of her face to assess her swollen, bloody eye.

"Orbital fracture?" she asked as William joined her.

"No, thank God. The blow knocked her back and she hit her head against a fireplace hearth. CT shows a cranial fracture with a subdural hematoma that I'll have to fix in the OR once she's stabilized."

He showed no emotion to the outside world, but Hannah knew him now and he didn't have to raise his voice for her to see how angry he was that they hadn't been able to save this woman. Did he look at her lying so lifelessly and see the body of his mother? she wondered.

"Where's her husband?" Hannah asked the officer taking information from the emergency doctor.

"He's in custody. The neighbor called us when she heard him shouting at her. We found Mrs. Jones on the floor, him passed out drunk beside her," the officer said.

The monitor beeped as Jeannine's heart rate climbed.

"Are you going to be okay assisting?" William asked Hannah. There was no censure in his words, no judgment if she refused. Hadn't that been just what she had been doing to him earlier? Judging him by his emotional reactions?

There was emotion in the man. He wasn't the Ice Prince everyone saw in the OR. She'd seen him laughing as he'd played on the floor with his sister just last night. It was easy to see the love he felt for Avery. And he was working hard to be the parent he needed to be for her.

Hannah looked down at Jeannine, whom she had only met once but had worried about often, imagining her being mistreated by her husband. This was what she'd always dreamed of doing. Though her part was only to follow William's directions, it was still close enough to make her heart race. She wiped her gloved palms against her pants. She had to take this step now to prove herself. Not just to William, but to herself.

"If you take her to surgery, I'm going with you." she said. "Was there anything else we could have done to help her?"

"I don't know. I spoke to the neuro social worker who met with her the last time she was here. Staff had tried to talk Jeannine out of leaving with Calvin, but she wouldn't listen. In the end, our hands were tied. Not that it makes me feel any better," William said as he left the room. "I'll have you paged if we're going to the OR."

While Hannah waited to hear if they would be taking Jeannine to the OR, she made a trip to the cafeteria. The last thing she needed was to be weak in the OR and embarrass herself.

"Hannah?" a soft voice inquired.

She turned to find a beautiful, dark-haired woman standing behind her—with a baby bump she couldn't mistake. "Sarah, you're pregnant!"

"I know. And thank you for not adding *again*."

"You look beautiful. I can't believe I didn't know," Hannah said—and meant it.

With Lindsey carpooling to her riding lessons, Hannah hadn't seen Sarah in weeks. She made a mental note to herself that once her studying was done, she would take some time to see her friends. She'd missed Sarah. The nurse practitioner who had played such a big part in Lindsey and Hannah's lives by advocating for the transplant was beautiful both inside and out. Even after Lindsey's surgery, she had been there to advise Hannah throughout nursing school.

"Lindsey tells me you've almost finished with your practitioner classes," Sarah said, following Hannah to the cashier. They each took their turn swiping their payment and found a table where they could catch up.

"I'm so close right now. I've got my preceptor hours with Dr. Cooper and I've learned so much," Hannah said.

"According to Lindsey, there's more than learning going on between you and William Cooper. I hear you've moved in together."

Oh, no. What had Lindsey been telling people?

"It's not like it sounds. I mean…yes, Lindsey and I are living with him. But it's only a temporary arrangement. He just needed some…help and it works out better if we live together." Hannah tried to clarify, saying, "It's more like an exchange of information."

"Maybe you need to start from the beginning," Sarah said as she sat her coffee cup down, "because somehow I have a feeling this is going to get complicated."

Hannah did as she asked, telling Sarah how William had come to have custody of his baby sister and had needed some guidance on the day-to-day care of a soon-to-be toddler. She explained that she had been given a chance to work with the neurosurgeon and also get her educational hours in while having evenings off with Avery and Lindsey.

"I have to say I'm a little disappointed," Sarah said as she pushed her tray away.

"I don't understand," Hannah replied. She thought a lot of the woman who had made such a difference in her daughter's life. Without Sarah's advocating so hard for Lindsey's transplant, it might not ever have happened. Sarah's example had been what had helped Hannah make the decision to go to nursing school. She would never want to disappoint her.

"I was hoping that maybe you'd finally taken some time for yourself. Some time for romance, Hannah. And I can't imagine anyone being more perfect for you than William."

"You know that's not what I want. My biggest responsibility is to Lindsey right now. The last thing I need is a man in my life," Hannah scoffed.

"You have noticed that William's a man, haven't you? And he is in your life, right? From what Lindsey says, y'all are getting along great," Sarah said.

Hannah hated to admit that Sarah was right. There was no doubt that William was a man—she was more aware of that than she should be. And Lindsey was right, too. Somehow the four of them living together worked.

It surprised her, now that she thought about it, but they had both been two single people living alone—except for Lindsey, of course—and they'd been happy with their lifestyles. If someone had asked if she would be agreeable to living with someone else, Hannah would have said no. She was too used to living independently to deal with someone else in her space and she was pretty sure William felt the same way.

But the two of them had worked through all those awkward problems that came with sharing a home. And, for the most part, things were working well. They had each made concessions and were happy with the current arrangement.

No, she admitted, she was more than happy with what the two of them shared now. But what about William? Was she just a means to an end for him? He'd made it more than plain that he'd liked his life before Avery had come to live with him. But he had made so many changes since then. He was really working hard to be the best substitute parent for Avery that he could be. But it wasn't all about Avery.

The hours they spent together at night after the kids had gone to bed had become one of her favorite times of the day. They shared experiences with each other, talking not only about the job and the kids, but about themselves. He told her about things he had seen that he thought would be of interest to her. She told him about something she had read that might interest him. Things had begun to change between the two of them. They'd become friends...and maybe even more.

"Hannah?" Sarah asked.

Hannah realized her friend was staring at her as if she had lost her mind. She also realized there was a good possibility that she had lost not only her mind but also her heart.

"So, I was right. There is more than you're telling me," Sarah said, briefly covering Hannah's left hand with hers. "Look, I've known William for a while now, and he's a good man."

"You have?" Hannah asked. For someone who said he wanted to be left on his own, he did seem to know a lot of people.

"I have. He's a big donor for our therapy program at the ranch. He covers the cost of all the safety equipment we use, including all the helmets we give each student," Sarah told her. "I've also heard he donates a lot of money to the children's oncology department.

And everyone knows what a good surgeon he is and how good he is with his patients.

"It's not something he wants attention for," Sarah attested. "That's not why he does it. He cares about people. I just don't think he's had that many people in his life who have cared about him. Which brings us back to you..." Sarah paused. "Hannah, I know you pretty well, too. You can't help but get involved with people—your patients, your classmates—you care for everyone. Sometimes that can put you at a disadvantage. I don't want to see you get hurt."

"I know I'm out of my league with William," Hannah said, giving up on getting the soup down and pushing her tray aside.

"No. From what you've told me, I'd say he's out of your league. I've seen the women he dates. They all look like the dolls we use to play with as kids—beautiful to look at but only fluff cotton inside. Not one of them would have done what you've done for him. You have to be scaring the life out of him, and I think that's a good thing. Emotions are messy and sometimes uncontrollable, which is not something William's had a lot of experience with."

Sarah was seeing romance, Hannah thought to herself, when, in reality, what William and Hannah had was a good friendship. And that was all it could ever be.

Her phone pinged with a message from William. They were going to the OR. With a hug and a thank you to Sarah, she headed off to get ready, pushing thoughts of what Sarah had said out of her mind.

* * *

William's hand was steady as he made the first cut, his mind fighting the doubts he still had about Jeannine Jones's outcome. Still, if she was going to have a chance at any quality of life, he knew he had to do whatever he could.

He took the procedure one precise step at a time, Hannah beside him, anticipating his needs for irrigation and suction. By the time he'd elevated the cranial bone and noted the blood flow increase, they had fallen into a natural complementary rhythm.

"Her blood pressure is dropping and her heart rate is up," the anesthesiologist announced. "Do we have any more trauma blood?"

"Cautery," William said to the OR tech, his hand out for the instrument. "Hannah, can you adjust the light?" He took care of the bleeders, concentrating on each detail as he ignored the others working around him.

"How's she doing?" he asked the anesthesiologist.

"Hypotensive, but starting to level off," she answered.

He evacuated a large clot and cauterized another section before preparing to close, repairing tears as he went. It was slow and tedious work but it had to be done.

"Heart rate one-fifty. Blood pressure beginning to drop again," the anesthesiologist informed him.

"Almost finished," William said as he began the work of reconstructing bone fragments. "I just need a few more minutes."

"Hang on, Jeannine," he heard Hannah say when the anesthesiologist called out for more blood. "Just hang on."

CHAPTER TEN

WILLIAM STARED BLANKLY at the computer screen in front of him. He'd made the excuse of wanting to catch up on some charting when he had sent Hannah home earlier. That had been hours ago. Since then, he'd haunted the recovery room to check on Jeannine Jones's blood pressure and consulted with a couple of new patients.

Back in the Neuro Critical Care Unit, just staring into space, it wouldn't take a psych doctor to tell him he had a problem. In fact, he could probably write a whole book on his emotional defects. Mommy issues. Daddy issues. He could see all of them in himself.

Until now, William had never minded his limitations. He had come to see that his shortcomings had helped make him the doctor he was today. The fact that he could isolate himself from everything around him while operating, including any feelings he might have for his charge, afforded him an innate ability to concentrate all his skills on his patient.

But that did not explain why he was sitting vigil for a patient he had only met once. Except, perhaps, for those mommy issues. Issues that made him fear that by saving Jeannine' life, he might be sentencing her to the fate of his own mother. If he saved Jeannine's life but she spent her last years comatose, he would have failed her. She had been a prisoner in her home with her husband; he couldn't bear to think of her as a prisoner in her own body.

"Hey, Dr. Cooper, how's it going?" asked one of the more seasoned nurses working the NCCU.

"Hey, Tom. You taking care of Mrs. Jones tonight?" William asked, turning his eyes from the computer screen. He'd reviewed every note that had been made on Jeannine's visits to the hospital and he couldn't find anything that might have changed the outcome. There was a paper trail a mile long detailing the escalation of her husband's violence, but the woman had denied it every time, leaving their hands tied.

"Yeah, I got her. Why don't you go on home? I'll call if something changes," Tom said, taking the seat next to William. "It's wrong what her husband did to her. So wrong. In my way of thinking, he can't be much of a man if he beats on his wife. The woman doesn't weigh a hundred pounds and she's barely over five feet tall."

"Yeah, I agree with you. It seems that love has struck again," William said, hearing the bitterness in his voice but not caring.

"That ain't love. We both know that. Love can make you do a lot of crazy things, but beating up on the person you love? No, that's nothing like love."

Changing the subject, Tom said, "Hey, I saw Hannah at the grocery store with Lindsey and the cute little girl she said was your half sister. That's crazy, man, right?"

"Yes, it's been pretty crazy." William looked down at his watch. Avery would be asleep by now. If someone had told him a month ago that he'd be upset because he'd missed reading a bedtime story to an eleventh-month-old, he would have thought them crazy. Now, he spent all day looking forward to getting home in time to put Avery to bed and to make sure Lindsey didn't need his help with her homework. And then, finally, when the house was nice and quiet, to enjoying a glass of wine with Hannah as they caught up with each other's day.

"I know I've never seen Hannah so happy and, after everything she's been through with her own little girl, it's nice. It's real nice. Now that is love for you," the RN said. One of the monitors beside them began to beep. "Gotta check that," Tom said, "but like I said, you go on home. I'll call if anything changes on Mrs. Jones."

Was Tom saying that Hannah was in love? No. He'd been talking about her love for Lindsey. Anyone who saw the two of them together knew that Hannah loved her daughter.

Rubbing his eyes, William stood and stretched. He knew that Tom was right, like always. He needed to go home and get some sleep. If he was lucky, he'd get in six hours before Avery woke and he had to start his day again.

Hannah filled her wineglass then settled on the couch where she was trying to finish a paper on community healthcare before the weekend. They had planned a party for Avery's first birthday, along with a trip to the zoo, and she didn't want to have to worry about home-work then.

Unfortunately, she couldn't concentrate on the words she needed to finish it. It had only taken one evening without William being there for her to realize how much she missed him. No matter how much she had denied her feelings to Sarah and to herself, what Hannah felt for William was stronger than any friendship she had ever had before. Was it love? How would she know? The one time she had thought she was in love had been a mistake.

If she could just forget the feel of William against her back that night in the gym and the touch of his lips when she'd kissed him in the attic. He'd been right when he'd said she didn't know the rules to playing games with men. The only game she knew was how to play it safe. She had learned the hard way not to trust other people.

Only, something had changed that night in the attic. He had trusted her with his childhood memories. She'd seen the hurt little boy whose life had been torn apart when his mother had been taken away from him. Having her still alive for all those years, but not with him, had probably made things even worse for the young boy; he'd always hoped that she would return to him.

But those were the emotions of a child. Somewhere along the way to adulthood, William had decided to leave behind all his childhood attachments. Did he see himself as weak because of the hurt and pain he'd felt at losing his mother? Or had it been his father's exam-ple—packing up William's mother's belongings and relegating them to the cold, dark attic, as if boxing away all the love and pain meant it no longer existed?

Hannah had no right to judge William's father too harshly. She had never met the man and she knew things weren't always as they seemed.

As a child, she'd thought she would always be able to trust her parents' love. Then she'd grown up and realized that their love was dependent on her following what they thought was best for her life, instead of supporting her when she had needed them the most.

Even now, she refused to depend on anyone else. She'd separated herself from anyone wanting control over her and had devoted her life to her daughter. She'd only allowed herself to be surrounded by those she knew couldn't hurt her. She'd locked away her heart just as William had, and she hadn't even realized it. Until now. Because it wasn't just his body and his friendship that she wanted. She wanted it all. But that wasn't in either of their plans.

She stood, sloshing her wine onto the floor. Setting the glass on a side table, she grabbed a rag from the bar, wiped up the spill then deposited the rag in the sink. Unable to sit still another minute, she walked over to the window and stared out at the reflection of the moon against the backyard.

"Hannah?" She heard the voice behind her and turned. William's face seemed drained of color, his eyes heavy from lack of sleep.

"How's Jeannine?" Hannah asked as she moved to him. She wanted to open her arms and have him step into them. She wanted to take away the pain she knew he still carried from his childhood. She wanted to be able to fix whatever it was that was broken inside him. She wanted to make him feel all the emotions that locked inside him.

"There's no change. They'll call if they need me. You should be sleeping," he said as he removed his jacket and undid his tie before running his hand through his hair. Never had he looked more human, more approachable, than at that moment.

Hannah pushed his hands away from the top button of the shirt he had been fighting to open.

"What are you doing?" he asked, his voice a low growl that vibrated against her hands and sent her blood racing.

How could she explain the loneliness she had felt sitting there waiting for him? How missing him tonight had become a pain in her chest? How could she explain what she was feeling when she didn't understand it herself? Could he feel how much she needed him right then? How much she wanted him to take her in his arms and hold her close? Could she make him as desperate for her touch as she was for his? She opened one button and then the next before resting her hands against his chest to support legs that had suddenly gone weak.

"Talk to me, Hannah," William said, his body tensing beneath her hands.

"Tell me what you're feeling right now," she said, moving her hands higher to rest on his shoulders.

"You don't want to play games with me," he said as his arms came around her.

"I thought you liked to play games. Do you want

me to go first?" She shifted until their bodies pressed together and she could feel him hard against her abdomen. She released the breath she had been holding as she'd waited for him to push her away. Stretching her body against his till her hand tangled in his hair, Hannah cradled him against her pelvis.

"I want you to tell me exactly how much of that wine bottle you've drunk," he said. While he made no advances, neither did he pull away from her.

"I've only had half a glass. I'm not drunk, William." Looking into his eyes, she could see that he doubted her words. "Do I need to walk a straight line to prove it?"

She realized what he was doing, but it wouldn't work. He could think of as many explanations for her behavior as he wanted, it still wouldn't change the fact that he was responding to her.

"Hannah, I don't want to hurt you," William said, though she noticed he still didn't move away. He wanted her, he just wasn't happy about it.

"The only thing I want right now is you, William, nothing else. If this isn't what you want then that's okay, but don't walk away because of some misguided fear that I don't know what I'm doing."

Hannah knew exactly what she was doing and she refused to regret one minute of it. All she wanted was for him to feel the same desperate desire that had overtaken her the minute she'd touched him. The same ache that flooded her senses with a need she had ignored for too long. But first, she needed to hear him say it, because she didn't want to spend the night with the man she knew had taken many others to his bed. She wanted the man who had stood in the attic and told her his deepest secrets. The man she had fallen a little bit in love with that very night.

She moved against him. He stiffened, his body rigid with a control she was determined to break. Pulling his head to hers until his lips were just a breath away from hers, she whispered, "Tell me what you feel right now, William. Tell me what it is you feel when I touch you. Tell me what you need."

"You," he said as she brushed her chest against him, her nipples hardening into tight peaks against the cotton of her shirt. "I need you."

William released the hold he'd kept for so long and reached for what he wanted most. His lips crushed hers and his tongue fought for entrance. She wanted to know what he was feeling? He felt like he would explode if he didn't get inside her. He was hard and thick, and he fit perfectly against the soft curve of her belly. She wanted to know what he needed? By the time the night was up she'd know the feel of him against her, inside her, surrounding her, until this need that had eaten at him for weeks was erased. She thought she could play games with the cold bastard he was and not get burned? He knew better. She'd hate him when she realized that this was all the emotion he was capable of, that this was all he could give her, but it was too late for either of them to turn back now.

Hannah moaned against his mouth as he ground himself against her. Then she nipped at his tongue and he pulled back. "The kids," she said as she started on his shirt buttons, yelping as he flipped her over his shoulder and headed to his bedroom.

He pushed the door open without putting her down then he let her fall against the mattress. He couldn't help but smile when she laughed at his caveman antics before pulling him to her. He found himself laughing with her as they discarded the clothing that separated them.

Then he was inside her with one thrust. Their hands searched and their legs tangled. She moaned into his mouth and he felt pleasure vibrate through him. The strength of her innocent abandonment tore at something deep inside him. Something William fought to hold back from her, but she wouldn't let him. Wrapping her legs around his hips, Hannah took him deeper until he let go and gave her everything he had. She covered his face with kisses, muffling a scream as her body took all of him and he lost himself inside her.

As William drifted off to sleep in her arms, he realized that Hannah had been the one surrounding him for all this time.

CHAPTER ELEVEN

HANNAH WAITED AT the entrance to the zoo while Lindsey entertained herself and Avery by pushing the stroller back and forth. William had left that morning before she'd awakened, leaving only a text message that he would meet them by noon.

Before leaving the house this morning, she had called to check on Jeannine Jones. Her nurse had informed her that Dr. Cooper had already been in to see her and there had been no changes overnight.

A part of Hannah felt vulnerable after the night they had spent together. She didn't regret it. She'd never forget it. But in the early morning, she had realized that either last night would be the end of the relationship they had shared or it would make it stronger now that they had acknowledged their mutual attraction. Either way, things were going to change and William had already said that he didn't like change.

A silver sedan, top lowered, swept around the corner and pulled into a parking spot. Hannah let out a breath. She'd planned the day carefully so that Avery and William's first trip to the zoo would be a great experience.

"Hey," he said as he jogged up to them.

"Hey," she said, the heat of a blush climbing up her face. She had known this was going to be awkward. She had expected it. What surprised her, though, was the sharp flash of desire that struck her midsection and made her catch her breath. It was a need inside her that had her standing dumbstruck in its intensity. She had never felt anything like it before. For a second, Hannah understood William's desire to keep everyone at bay. This man could break her in two. Her brain warned her to protect her heart while her heart told her it was already too late.

"Mom? Will? Hello, you two?" Lindsey said, pushing the stroller between Hannah and William. "Y'all can stare at each other later. Me and Avery are ready to see some lions," Lindsey roared at Avery, sending the toddler off into giggles.

"Okay, then. Let's go," William said as he broke the connection that had ensnared them both. To her surprise, he took her hand in his.

"Lindsey, slow down," she said, catching up with the two.

Once inside, they meandered the paths, Lindsey leading the way.

"She knows her way around here pretty well, doesn't she," William observed.

"There wasn't a lot we could do together before she had her transplant. Most things were either too strenuous or too expensive. So we spent a lot of time visiting the zoo," she said.

"You don't talk a lot about it. Her heart transplant,"

he said as they paused to watch the pale pink flamingos flap their wings.

"The transplant was the easy part. It was the waiting for the transplant that was hard. The time she spent in the critical care unit of the hospital, knowing that time was running out and there was nothing I could do to help? That was the hard part, the part I know I might have to relive someday. That's why we don't talk about it. You learn to take each day as it comes when you don't know how many you have left."

"You're a strong woman, Hannah," William said admiringly as they left the flamingo exhibit to follow the kids down the next path.

They both watched as Lindsey made faces at the lemurs, Avery clapping her hands at the monkeys jumping from tree to tree. Instead of things being awkward between the two of them, Hannah and William fell into the comfort of a friendship that, while new, seemed much older. It was as if they had known one another for years, but were still learning a lot about each other.

"Have you heard anything from Avery's great-aunt?" she asked.

"I got an email from her saying she'd be in town in the next two weeks. I'm kind of nervous about it, too. I spoke with one of my father's estate lawyers. It seems that being Alison, Avery's mother's next of kin, she could take me to court for custody. It doesn't mean she would get it, but I don't want to take that chance."

There had been a time when Hannah had worried that the woman would show up. That she'd push the point that William was not prepared to care for a child

Avery's age. But not any longer. William had worked hard, with a dedication that had been surprising. He could not be any more involved in Avery's care than if he had been her real father. She understood why the possibility of losing Avery worried him.

They tried to catch up with Lindsey as she sped away with Avery. "Lindsey, slow down."

"I'm fine, Mom," her daughter said, a big helping of preteen exasperation thrown in.

"She's in such a hurry to experience everything, as though she could make up for all those years she missed, that sometimes she does overdo it," Hannah told William.

"How about we let Avery out of the stroller for a while?" she asked Lindsey when they finally caught up. Bending to unbuckle the toddler, she added, "She needs her diaper changed, and that way you can go explore on your own. Do you have your phone?"

"Of course." Lindsey pulled it from her pocket and showed it to both adults.

"How about you meet us back at the small cat exhibit? Thirty minutes?" Hannah asked as she checked Avery and found her bottom dry.

"Okay! But I want to be there when Avery sees the big cats. She's going to love the lions." Lindsey rushed off, leaving the stroller with them.

"You don't think the lions will give her bad dreams or anything, do you?" William asked Hannah.

"She'll be fine. Bend down," she said as she lifted Avery and placed her on William's shoulders.

"Is she okay up there?" William stood frozen in

place, his hands gripping the toddler's chubby legs. "She won't fall?" he asked as Avery laughed and rocked back and forth as if sitting on the glittery pink rocking horse they'd brought back from Dallas.

"Just hold on to her legs and she'll be fine."

They walked through the exhibits with first Hannah and then William reading the information out loud on each animal. By the time they made it to the giraffes, William had relaxed and both he and Avery were laughing as the long tongue of one of the giraffes lapped at the food pellets he held out in one hand. Hannah quickly pulled her phone and took a picture. She'd have it printed later and take it into William's office for his desk.

"Do you want to talk about it?" William asked as he yanked a sanitary wipe from Avery's bag and reached up to clean her small, chubby hands.

There was only one thing he could be talking about. Did she? So far, today had been wonderful, and Hannah didn't want to risk ruining it.

But wasn't that exactly what had happened with Lindsey's father? She'd avoided all conversations with him about their relationship because, deep down, she'd known she cared more for him than he cared for her. And now she had the same feeling again. William had made it clear that he had no plans to enter into a permanent relationship with anyone. That had changed somewhat with his custody of Avery, but that didn't mean anything else had changed.

This thing between the two of them was so new. Hannah didn't even know whether she wanted anything more than what they had right now. Couldn't they just enjoy the time they had together? No expectations. No worries. Just the two of them getting to know each other.

The beat of her heart slowed to a comfortable level. She was not repeating old mistakes, she told herself. Instead, she was opening herself up to new possibilities and hoping that William would follow her wherever it led them. Was that too much to ask?

"I'm not sure what it is we need to talk about. We're both adults who find each other attractive. Why can't that be enough for now?" she asked, her heart beginning to race as she waited for his answer.

He finished with Avery's hands and then set Avery down between the two of them so that each could take a hand as the toddler wobbled on her inexperienced legs.

"So, still friends?" he asked as they started back down the path.

"Yes," Hannah answered, letting go of the ball of stress she'd held inside her all day. "Still friends."

As promised, they met Lindsey at the small cat exhibit and William settled Avery in the stroller so that Lindsey could push her to see the big cats.

By the time they'd talked Lindsey into leaving, Avery was tired and cranky.

As they exited the zoo, passing other families headed inside, Hannah couldn't help but note the contrast between those families and her group: a single parent, a fatherless child, an orphaned toddler and her big brother. They were a motley crew, but somehow they fit together perfectly.

* * *

William's home had been a nice quiet place when he he'd left it to make morning rounds. His morning had been quite peaceful; he'd worked his way through his patients just the way he liked to.

And then he'd come home to a horror that no man should have to face. His driveway was filled with cars. Cars. On a Sunday. In his driveway. Of course, he'd known that there was to be a birthday party. He and Hannah had picked out the design of the cake at the bakery the week before. Hannah had volunteered to take charge of the invitations and, naïvely, he had thought that meant half a dozen of Hannah's friends would attend with their kids. This was not half a dozen. There were at least a dozen cars here.

Leaving the safety of his silver sedan, he followed the sounds of voices around to the back of the house where pure mayhem seemed to reign. There were children everywhere, some chasing others, some playing on blankets laid out on the grass, and a couple older ones that surrounded Lindsey, one of which was a boy. Had Hannah known that Lindsey was inviting a boy? What were the guidelines for that? Was it one of those things determined by age? Thank goodness, he had a long time till he had to worry about that with Avery.

"Hey, Dr. Cooper. Nice house and a very cute kid," said a nurse he recognized as Kelly from the neuro unit.

"Have you seen, Hannah?" he asked.

"She just went into the house. She'll be right out." He turned to see a dark-haired beauty with a small round belly. She was holding toddler on one hip.

"Sarah. It's nice to see you," he said as he looked around. "Is David with you?"

"He's over there," Sarah said, pointing to a small group of men gathered at the bank of the lake. "I think they're plotting an escape. You can tell my husband that I've got my eye on him. Any attempt to flee before the cake comes out will be a breach of contract."

"Flee?" he asked. If there was any type of escape, he was going to be part of it.

"I accompany him to all those fussy functions you doctors are required to attend and he shows up at all the children functions with me— Davey, you get out of that tree right this minute!" she said before heading off toward a group of children.

William looked to the house and saw that Hannah had come back out. She carried Avery much as Sarah had held her little one, one hip cocked to the side as she balanced a large platter of food in her other hand. But the two women couldn't have been any more different in looks with Sarah's dark waves and Hannah's blond curls.

As he walked toward her, his eyes followed the line of Hannah's curves until they rested on her flat stomach. He knew the story of how Sarah had lost both her husband and her son in a motor vehicle accident. The loss had been devastating and he couldn't imagine that it had been an easy decision for her to have more children. Would Hannah ever want more children? She'd been through so much with Lindsey. Would she be willing to take a chance at having another child?

He watched as Hannah handed the large platter to an older woman. Mrs. Adams?

"I thought we were doing something small for her first birthday," he said as an aside to Hannah after thanking Avery's former nanny for coming.

"You were the one who wanted the blow-up bouncy house. Who did you think was going to bounce in it if we didn't invite some other children? All Avery can do is crawl in there," Hannah said.

"She's the birthday girl. Of course she can bounce in it," William said as he reached for Avery. "Come on, Avery. Let's go try out that house."

"Don't get her dress dirty. We need to get her picture taken with the cake," Hannah called after him.

After waiting their turn, William climbed up into the air-filled house and held the toddler's hands. "Okay, you jump up and down," he said, raising her by her arms then letting her feet touch the bottom.

Avery seemed interested in everything but the bouncy house he'd insisted on renting.

"You know she's too little for that, don't cha, Dr. Cooper. Her legs aren't ready," a young boy said as he stuck his head into the opening. "You should have gotten a pony. Everybody likes to ride a pony, no matter how little they are."

"I think you may be right, Davey." William smiled at Sarah's son as he crawled out of the house with Avery. "Next time I'll get a pony."

He quickly made the basic introductions of Avery to the people he knew from work, then joined the group of men by the lake. They were talking baseball and politics, subjects he found a lot safer than the ones he'd heard the women discussing earlier. Avery held on to his neck as they watched Hannah and Sarah lead groups of children through games he knew Avery wasn't old enough to play.

"So there you are," Hannah said as she approached the group and reached out for Avery. "It's time to cut the cake and we can't do it without her."

William claimed the responsibility for taking pictures of Avery as everyone sang the birthday song and he had to admit that his sister was adorable as she stuffed a piece of rainbow-colored cake into her mouth with both hands. Before he knew what was happening, however, he was organizing various groups for pictures.

"Where's Lindsey?" he asked after snapping a picture of Hannah bent over Avery as she tried to blow out her birthday candles. It would be the perfect picture to use as the new wallpaper on his phone.

"She's with her friends inside. I think," Hannah added as they started to cut the large cake into smaller pieces to hand out to each child.

"There's a boy here," he said to Hannah.

"There're lots of boys here. Avery's too young to want an all-girls party," Hannah laughed.

"No, I mean there's a boy here that's Lindsey's age," William said. "And what's an all-girls party? What am I supposed to do with that?"

"Yes, I know there's a boy here with Lindsey's friends, and you don't need to worry about any all-girls parties for a few years yet."

Both Hannah and William helped Avery open her

presents and then, finally, it was all done. As quickly as the presents had been opened, the wrappings were collected, along with the empty cups and leftover food. Everyone pitched in to clean the picnic tables, which apparently had been brought in by various guests. By the time he'd helped load the last table into the back of a truck and thanked Mrs. Adams's son for bringing her, his peaceful yard had been returned to normal.

He picked up a stray can that had been thrown into the fire pit and took a seat in the chair he'd dragged to the edge of the lake the night he had moved into the house. He'd known that the house was too big when he'd bought it, but somehow it had called to him. Something had told him that he belonged there and he had trusted his instincts enough to buy it. He'd immediately taken up fly fishing and though he enjoyed the sport, he'd still felt like something was missing.

Looking out over the lake, William tried to remember a time when he had enjoyed himself that much in his own backyard. Yes, he and the other men had groaned each time one of the women had come to ask for their help. But he'd also seen how the other fathers had kept an eye on their children when, on the surface, it had looked like they were ignoring everything that was going on. He'd kept his own eye on the boy who had followed Lindsey around the yard.

He stood, walked down to the pier and gazed into the water. His life was changing and he didn't feel as if he had any control over it. But he was becoming more confident in his role as Avery's guardian now. He still had a lot to learn and he knew he'd make mistakes along the way, but the panic he had felt those first few days when he'd been alone with Avery was long gone.

"Hey," Hannah said as she joined him on the pier. "Enjoying the quiet now that everyone's gone?"

"Yeah, that was some party," he said. "Can you tell me again why a child too young to retain any memories of their first birthday needs a party?"

"It wasn't that bad. She might not remember the party, but she'll have the pictures to show her how many people care for her. She definitely had a great time, too. I barely got her bathed and dressed before she fell asleep."

"Thanks for doing that," he said. "I guess I've been out here longer than I thought. And thanks for your help with the party. Those pictures will be just as important to me later on as they will be to her."

He thought of the picture he had on his phone. Would Avery ever see it? Would she even know who Hannah was by the time she looked back at those pictures?

"It's sad, isn't it? That she had to spend her first birthday without her parents. It should have been her mother putting her to bed tonight," Hannah said. She shivered as a cool spring breeze blew across the lake.

William pulled her in front of him and wrapped his arms around her as she settled back against his chest to share the warmth of his body as they looked out over the lake. Catching a glimpse of their reflection in the water, he was taken aback. There was something different about him when Hannah was beside him. It was the way his body relaxed into hers. She had some magic way of bringing the peace to his life that he had always sought. But would it last? Or, like his father, would he soon be bored and looking for someone else to entertain him? He told himself that he wasn't like his father, but inside he feared he might be. He'd spent his life in superficial relationships with women.

"I keep wondering why Avery's mother and my father wanted me to be the one to take care of her if something happened to them. I guess I'll never know," he said as he took Hannah's hand and led her back to the house.

"Maybe the thought of the two of you alone wasn't something they wanted. Maybe they knew that they could count on you to take care of your sister," Hannah said.

"I don't know. It doesn't really matter. I can't change the past."

"But maybe just accepting the possibility that your father might not have been as heartless as you thought he was will be enough for you to let go of the pain you felt as a child. None of us can really know what another person thinks or feels. Maybe just putting to rest those old feelings you still have will help," Hannah suggested, squeezing his hand. "Because it's never too late to forgive someone, is it?"

For the first time in a long time, William felt a spark of hope. He'd never thought he'd be able to forgive his father for divorcing his mother and bringing another woman in to raise him, but maybe it was time to let all of those old feelings go. It was time he moved on with his life and, if it meant forgiving his father, then he was ready to do it. He couldn't hold on to the anger he had felt for so many years while he raised his father's daughter. It wouldn't be fair to let Avery bear the brunt of his negative emotions for a man she would never know. He could unintentionally warp her feelings for her father and that wasn't something William could do to her. If he wanted to raise Avery, he needed to forgive their father.

CHAPTER TWELVE

HANNAH ENTERED THE house to find Lindsey standing with her backpack over her shoulder and her best friend at her side. Suspicious grins on each of their faces set Hannah's mother radar on high alert.

"Jessica's mom is coming to pick us up. She says it's okay if I spend the night there. And I can ride the bus to school with Jessica in the morning. Can I? Please?" Lindsey asked.

"Did you pack all your medications?" Hannah asked.

"Of course, Mom." Lindsey pulled out a bag of medication and shook it as if to show her mother that the bottles weren't empty.

Her daughter had sarcasm down to an art form.

"Is that boy going to be there?" William asked as he followed her inside.

"What boy? You mean Jason?" Lindsey exchanged looks with Jessica before rolling her eyes. "No. And he's just a friend. Of course, sometimes friends become... you know, other things."

"What other things?" William queried.

A horn honked outside and both girls sped out the

door. Hannah knew they were up to something. Fortunately, she also knew Jessica's mother well enough to feel confident they would be closely monitored for the night.

"She's too young to know about 'other things,'" William muttered from behind her, making her smile.

It wasn't until Hannah looked across the room that she realized what her adorable, scheming daughter and her friend had been doing while they'd been outside.

A small table had been moved into the center of the room, a vase with flowers she recognized from William's front garden holding center stage. The table had been set for two and there was a note propped against the vase.

"What's this?" William asked as they stood staring at the misplaced furniture.

"I think my daughter is trying to move us on to 'other things,'" Hannah said, laughing when she caught the grin on William's face. "I'm not sure my daughter's idea of 'other things' is the same as yours, though."

"I certainly hope not," he said, picking up the note. "According to this, our supper will be delivered at eight, but it doesn't give any details on what that might be."

"The only thing my daughter can afford on her allowance is pizza, I'm afraid."

Lindsey was such a special child and she was so lucky to be her mom.

Hannah thought of the little girl sleeping down the hall. Already, Avery had showed herself to be a resilient child, settling in comfortably with three strangers. She was silly and happy, but also stubborn. She was so cute in the way that all children her age were with her chubby cheeks and bright eyes, but Hannah could already see that Avery would be a beauty like her mother. William would have his hands full when his sister hit her teens. She'd love to be around to see it, but at this point in her life, Hannah wasn't even sure she'd be in Houston for much longer. But that wasn't something she was going to dwell on tonight.

With Avery down and Lindsey gone, she and William could have this one night to themselves. They had so little time left before she moved back home. She would not let tonight be ruined by things she could do nothing about.

"I'm going to go change. The smell of frosting is starting to get to me," Hannah said as she looked down at her shirt where smears of cake had dried.

"We have a little time before dinner," William said, checking his watch.

She wondered if she should tell him about the clump of frosting on his own shirt. No, let him see it for himself, she thought. Maybe the next time he saw a birthday cake he would think of today and the messy frosting from his little sister's first birthday. And maybe he'd remember her, too.

They parted at the top of the stairs, each headed to their own room.

Hannah quickly went through her closet, sorting through her mommy clothes and work clothes. She wanted William to see her as a woman tonight instead of as a coworker or babysitter. A strong woman that he could count on—something she knew he hadn't had since his mother was taken from him. But she also wanted him to see her as desirable. She wanted William to think of tonight as a date. A first date—the date that always determined whether there would be another.

Reaching to the back corner of the closet, she felt the soft cotton of her favorite floral sundress whose color almost matched the blue of her eyes. It was a little worn, but it would be perfect for tonight.

Glancing at her bedside clock, she rushed to the bathroom. She had just enough time to shower and apply makeup.

When she returned to the main floor, she noticed that the lights had been dimmed. Yet through the soft glow of candles strategically placed in the great room, she could see William sitting in a chair that had been turned to face her. Had he been sitting there just waiting for her? Her heart stuttered when he stood. Dressed in dark slacks and a buttoned chambray shirt, his hair still damp and brushed back from his face, he appeared even more dangerous than normal.

She stepped toward him until they both stopped just inches from touching. A delicious tingle flowed through Hannah's body as his eyes skimmed over her then settled on her lips. The air between them seemed to spark with a magnetic force that held the two of them in place. Her breasts felt heavy and the muscles at her core contracted, making her breath catch. She wanted to kiss him but they both seemed to know that that would be a mistake. One kiss would never be enough. They had the whole night together. There was no reason to rush things. Not tonight.

The doorbell rang, startling them out of the sensuous trance.

"I'll get it." William stepped away and went to the front door.

Hannah poured herself a glass of wine from the bottle he had opened and took a big sip. Her body trembled with a need she had never felt for any other man. How long had they been standing there? It was as if they could be intimate without even touching. Just the warmth of his gaze was enough to set her body on fire.

"I feel bad that Lindsey paid for our dinner," William said as he set the cardboard box on the table set for just the two of them.

"Why? You've been so great helping her with her homework while I've been busy with my own studies. By the way, she made an A on that history paper you helped her with," Hannah said as she took her seat, opened the box and breathed in the smell of crusty bread and tomato sauce rich with herbs. The only thing she could remember eating today was a piece of Avery's overly sweet birthday cake. She took two pieces of the pizza without even considering the calories. Hopefully, she'd burn it off later tonight.

"She's a smart kid," he said, taking his seat.

"She's had a lot of catching up to do after so much time in hospital. Lindsey missed so much school while she was sick that she's had to have tutoring for the last two summers. But she's finally catching up with her classmates," Hannah said.

As they ate, she told him about the particular heart defect Lindsey had been born with and the number of surgeries and complications she'd overcome. When they'd finished their meal, neither one seemed ready to rush the time they had together.

"You've done a great job with her," William said. "Your parents have to see that."

How could she explain her parents to him when she didn't even understand them herself?

"When Lindsey was born with a heart defect, my parents felt that it would be best if I let someone older, with more support, raise her," she said. *Not that they'd ever offered to help.* Then again, that had never been the plan.

Hannah's stomach twisted as she was reminded of the secret she'd hidden away. William wouldn't consider her such a wonderful mother if he knew—

But keeping the truth from him didn't seem right. She wanted him to know the real her, warts and all. Would he look at her differently when he learned the truth? There was only one way to find out.

"Lindsey doesn't know this…but the plan was never for me to keep her," Hannah told him. This was this one terrible truth that had haunted her as her child had lain sick and at times close to death. Who would have been there beside her child if she had let her parents have their way?

Hannah took a large swallow of wine before continuing. "When I came home from college and told my parents that I was pregnant and the father did not want to be involved, they arranged for a couple in their church to adopt the baby. A private adoption…

"I shouldn't have been surprised. They'd always controlled my life and I'd never been given the freedom that my friends had. My parents didn't see it as any different from deciding what college I would attend."

She paused as if to take a calming breath. "When I found out about the adoption arrangements, I was angry. I pushed back as hard as I could, but eventually they convinced me that the best thing for my child was for me to give her parents who could provide for her.

"I'm not trying to put all the blame on them," she quickly added. "I had the final decision on what I would do. I knew I had nothing to offer a child. I was the one who had been willing to give my daughter up. I was the one who would have signed the papers to give my daughter away."

"You were young, Hannah. Your parents made some good points," William said.

"I know, and sometimes I can convince myself of that. But when Lindsey was born with a heart defect and the family that was supposed to adopt her backed out, I knew I couldn't give my baby up.

"My parents refused to understand why I insisted on keeping her. That's when I realized that what they really wanted was for us all to pretend that Lindsey had never happened. They wanted me to leave her at the hospital, where she would have gone into foster care if another couple couldn't have been found by the adoption agency. I refused, and they wouldn't support my decision. Hannah took a sip from her wineglass. "It's only been in the last year that they've showed any sign of wanting to be a part of our lives."

It still hurt to admit that her parents had abandoned

not only their granddaughter, but also their own child. It had taken years for Hannah to come to terms with the fact that her parents had controlled her whole life up until the moment she had walked out with Lindsey. Part of her had thought they would come after her, that they would change their minds, but they were too proud for that. They would never admit that they had made a mistake.

The two of them sat in silence for a moment. Some of the candles had burned down, leaving the room in almost total darkness.

She had told him everything now.

"I've never regretted the decision I made to keep my daughter, William, even though there were times I wasn't sure how we were going to make it. I wouldn't have been able to live with myself if I had walked away and left her in that hospital. Just like I know you wouldn't have been able to live with yourself if you had turned your back on Avery."

"Hannah, you are one special lady," William said.

"And you are one special man."

"I'm not—" he said, stopping when she put a finger to his lips.

"To me, you are. And that's all that matters tonight."

William nipped at her finger and she drew it back and placed it in her mouth. His eyes blazed with heat as candlelight flickered across them. He held his hand out for hers and she gave it to him, mesmerized as he raised it to his lips and kissed each fingertip.

This was the man no one else knew. Right now, he was *her* William. Tomorrow he'd step back into the shoes of the William others knew as the ice-cold neurosurgeon. But that was tomorrow. Tonight, he was all hers.

They stood and she stepped into his arms as he reached for her. The first time they had made love, they had both been desperate. This time, she wanted to take her time as she loved him with her body. She would give him the tenderness of her lips, the warmth of her breasts, and the sweet completeness of their joining. They'd made no promises to each other. Tonight would be special, and they both knew it. She would make sure that he would never forget this night.

Hannah kissed him lightly on the lips before pulling away and taking his hand.

"My room," she said as they got to the top of the stairs. For some reason, the choice mattered to her. Home advantage? Maybe, she thought as she shut the door behind them so they wouldn't disturb Avery.

As the door clicked softly into place, strong arms surrounded her. She turned into them as William pulled her close. His lips met hers as he held her tightly against him. She could feel every inch of his hard body. Wrapping her arms around his neck, Hannah ran her hands into his hair and gave over her mouth to him. His tongue tangled with hers and her body shuddered. She'd thought she could control this need they had for each other. She'd been wrong.

"Too many clothes," he said, his lips leaving hers and his hands reaching behind her for the zipper of her dress.

"Yes," she said as she pulled back and began to work the buttons of his shirt.

Hannah felt the cool air against her skin as her dress landed at her feet. She pulled the shirt loose from his pants and ran her hands up the strong chest she had not been able to forget since that first night in the gym.

William's clothes quickly followed hers to the floor as they touched and tasted, each taking the time to explore. He moaned when she grazed his nipple with her teeth. He returned the torment as he cupped her breasts and tortured each nipple with his tongue.

He lifted her into his arms and lay her on the bed before returning to his pants to retrieve something from his wallet.

When he was back beside her, Hannah opened herself to him and welcomed him into her. She sighed with contentment as he covered her body with his. Never had she felt so complete, so whole. Reaching up, she pulled his head down and looked into eyes that spoke of something she knew he wasn't prepared to confess.

Did he see that same desperate emotion in her eyes? What if she said the words she knew he didn't want to hear? Would it push him away? Did he know he filled not only her body but also her heart? She had to take the chance. She had to tell him.

"William, I—" His lips crushed hers, taking the words she would give him away.

All thought left her. He moved inside her, but not with the slow, gentle loving he'd showed her before. Gone was that gentle lover, replaced by a man who demanded that she give him total possession of her body.

He drove himself into her with a desperate need she answered with her own.

Arching into him, Hannah wrapped her legs around his hips, pulling him closer as her body began to tremble. Holding back nothing, she screamed as the force of the climax took over. Still, William thrust inside her, claiming her body as he took everything she had to give until he joined her in completion.

CHAPTER THIRTEEN

SOMEONE HAD HOLD of his face. Groaning, William turned his head away only to have two small hands turn it back. So that was how the game was played. He turned his head the other way and Avery giggled then turned it back toward her. He wiggled his mouth back and forth and the giggling increased as the toddler patted his cheeks. Opening his eyes, he was greeted with deep brown ones that were all but plastered to his face.

"Good morning, Avery. And how did you manage to get in here?" he asked. He'd been so busy trying to catch up in his role as Avery's substitute parent that he hadn't thought about what having a young child in the house would mean for his sex life. He couldn't imagine any of the women he had dated being happy about his new role. If there was one thing he'd learned from his father's experiences, it was that women did not like to share a man's attention with anyone else.

"She woke up in the night and I just let her sleep with us," Hannah called out from the open bathroom door.

"Probably too much partying last night," William joked as he moved Avery over to the other side of the bed while he sat up and rearranged the comforter. "I'm sorry I didn't hear her."

He didn't make it a practice to wake up in a women's bed and the few times he had, it had been extremely awkward for both him and the woman. Somehow, this morning didn't feel that way. It was just another day for the two of them to juggle childcare and work. And that was Hannah's doing. She always seemed to know what he needed from her.

He'd sworn he'd keep her out of his life, but somehow she'd found a way inside the walls he'd constructed to keep others out. She now knew more about him than any other person. Having someone know all your secrets was somehow liberating. And that definitely surprised him. He'd always been afraid to share that much of himself with anyone.

"Too much sugar," Hannah said before he heard the hair dryer turn on.

William remembered the first three nights Avery had been with him. They had both been miserable, neither getting much sleep. The giggling child who was now playing with a stuffed toy was much more appealing than the one who'd cried continuously every time he had tried to get her to go to sleep in the small cot her nanny had dropped off with her. He'd ordered a crib as soon as the store had opened the next day. It hadn't helped.

It had only been when Hannah had moved in that the situation had improved. She'd had the answer to every problem...and now she had shared hers with him. He wasn't the same man he had been then. With Hannah's help, he'd learned to take care of Avery as well as any other father could.

"It was her birthday. Of course she had too much sugar," he said as Hannah stepped into the room. She'd already dressed in scrubs for her day in the office yet she looked just as beautiful as she had last night when they'd dressed up for dinner. He found her beauty a soft gentle thing that tugged at his heart as well as his body—

His mind came to a screeching halt. Was he somehow romanticizing this thing between them? Just because he was more comfortable around her than he'd ever been around another person didn't mean there was a future for them. That wasn't the plan.

The plan had never included becoming lovers, either.

"She hasn't woken in the middle of the night in weeks, so I wouldn't worry about it." Hannah reached down and picked Avery up. "I'll feed her this morning while you get ready. I would have woken you earlier, but I knew your first appointment this morning wasn't till nine, so you should have time to do your rounds before you come to the office."

He looked over at the clock on the bedside table as Hannah left the room. He had no idea where this thing between them was going. He'd been honest with her concerning the future he had seen for himself before Avery had come into his life. Now the thought of the empty life he'd planned seemed to be losing some of its appeal.

Last night they had found a passion he had never experienced before. One that had driven Hannah to almost whisper those three words that had always sent him running. Words she would have regretted once her body had been satisfied and her mind had cleared. Words she wouldn't have been able to take back once she'd said them. Words that hurt when they weren't returned.

He'd refused to hear them, choosing instead to protect her from the pain she would have felt this morning. If one person could understand why he didn't believe in the love all the romantics talked about, it was Hannah. She knew he had no belief in the happily-ever-after love his father had promised not one, but four different brides. William might be able to forgive his father for moving on with his life after his mother's accident, but that didn't mean he could change what he had seen and experienced in the name of love.

William picked his pants up from the floor where he had dropped them and headed for the shower. Maybe the best thing was for them both to ignore what was happening between them. If he was lucky, his day would be a busy one with no time to think about the night before, because there was a part of him that couldn't help but wonder what might have happened if he'd been brave enough to let Hannah say those three little words. And that was a thought that scared him to death.

"Hannah!" Mrs. Nabors called out as Marion walked her and her daughter along the hall to an examination room.

"Mrs. Nabors, how are you doing?" Hannah inquired, giving the woman a hug. "You look great."

"The rehab has really helped," Lisa, her daughter, said.

"I can take them," Hannah told Marion. While still not singing her praises, the older nurse had stopped hounding Hannah about everything she did.

"So you're not working at the hospital anymore?" Lisa asked as Hannah settled them into the room.

"I've taken some time off to complete my remaining clinical hours for my bachelor's degree. That's why I'm working here with Dr. Cooper," Hannah said as she applied the blood pressure cuff to Mrs. Nabors's arm.

"Well, you're working for one of the best," the older woman said. "And he's such a nice young man—"

A door slammed down the hall and she heard Marion cry out. Had she fallen?

"I'll be right back," Hannah said before rushing out of the room.

Expecting to see the nurse on the floor, she dashed around the corner of the hall and stopped. Marion was leaning back against the wall opposite a man Hannah recognized as Jeannine Jones's husband. She glanced at Marion. "Did he hurt you?"

Marion shook her head, though Hannah could see that she was cradling her arm.

"What is it you want, Mr. Jones?" Hannah asked. His wife had been moved out of the critical care department only the day before with strict orders that he was not to visit once they had learned he'd been released on bond. Surely, the staff had not let him in to see her.

"I want to see the doctor that's told those nurses I couldn't see my wife. And I want to see him now!"

William had been on a call for a consult with another doctor earlier, but she knew he'd be out at any minute.

In the mood that Calvin Jones was in, there was no telling what he would do. She needed to notify the security officers that minded the entrance of the office complex without letting him know what she was doing.

"Dr. Cooper is over at the hospital making rounds. I'll call him and let him know you want to talk to him. I'm sure there's been some mistake," Hannah said as she took her phone out of her pocket and dialed the building's security number.

The phone was answered on the second ring. "Hey Dr. Cooper, Jeannine Jones's husband is here in the office and wants to talk to you." She listened as a man told her she had the wrong number. "I understand you're busy, Dr. Cooper, but Mr. Jones is very upset about his wife refusing to go home with him. Thank you, I'll let him know you'll be right here."

She hit the end call button and prayed that the security officer she'd talked to had understood that she needed help.

"The doctor will be here in just a few minutes. I'll show you to a room where you can wait for him," Hannah said. She needed to get Mr. Jones out of the hall and away from Marion.

"I'm not going anywhere till I see that doctor. He had no business talking to my wife when I wasn't there. Thinks just because he's got some degree that he knows what's best for everyone. I'll make sure he keeps his nose out of our business from now on," Jones said. "And you! You're that nurse who wouldn't let me into the room to see my wife that day in the ER. You called those guards on me. You're just as bad as he is."

Calvin Jones pushed past Marion and headed for Hannah. He thought he could intimidate her just as he had his poor wife. She wouldn't give him the satisfaction. She was tired of dealing with this bully. He'd beaten his wife until she was scared to tell the truth about the horror of her marriage. He preyed on the weak, but that wasn't who Hannah was anymore. She would stand up to this man just as she had stood up to her parents the day she had refused to leave the hospital without her daughter.

"Mr. Jones, I was only doing my job. Just like Dr. Cooper is doing his job to protect his patient. It would be best if you left right now before you do something that's going to cause more trouble for you. It's my understanding that there is a restraining order that states you aren't allowed to see your wife," Hannah said calmly as the man approached her.

She yelled as he grabbed hold of her hair and pulled her up to her toes. "Lady, if you know what's good for you, you'll stay away from my wife. And I'm not going anywhere until I see the doctor."

"Let her go. Now!" Hannah heard William give the order from behind her. "If you have a problem with me, we can discuss it like men."

Hannah's head slammed into the wall as Calvin Jones pushed her away and stalked toward William. Marion reached her before she hit the floor then held her back as she fought to go after him.

She saw the ice-cold determination in William's eyes. "I'm going to give you one opportunity to walk out of the office," he said calmly, as if talking to someone about the weather. "I'm not a violent man, but I'm twenty years younger than you and I'm willing to take my chances."

The man snarled a comment that Hannah couldn't hear before two officers pushed through into the office. Hannah tried to yell out as she saw Jeannine's husband lunge at William. And then it all disappeared into black.

Hannah opened her eyes slowly and realized someone was holding her down. Staring up at the white-tiled ceiling of an exam room, she tried to recall how she had gotten there. The pounding of her head brought back the memory of hitting something. The wall. She'd hit the wall before Jeannine's husband had attacked William. "William," she said as she tried to sit up before falling back to the table as the room began to spin.

"It's okay. I'm right here," William said from beside her.

Turning her head slowly, Hannah reached out for him. "You're okay," she said as he took her hand. She put her other hand on his face and turned it side to side. There was no damage.

"I thought I saw him hit you," she said, closing her eyes again. The lights were too bright.

"I'm fine. The man is all brute and no style," he said. "How are you feeling?"

"My head is killing me, but besides that, I think I'm okay." Her roiling stomach felt as if she had just gotten off a carnival ride, but she knew it was because of the pain in her head.

"The cops are talking to Marion and there's an ambulance on its way to take you to the ER," William said.

"I just need something for this headache," she said, turning toward him. The room spun once more.

"You know as well as I do that you need to get checked out. They'll get a CT just to make sure you're okay." The door opened and two emergency medical technicians came in with a stretcher. "Now, be nice and don't give these young men any trouble," William told.

William stood beside the CT technician and watched as the screens changed from one view to the next. He'd confirm his findings with the radiologist, but it appeared that Hannah had not received any type of brain or cranial injury.

When he'd seen Jeannine's husband throw her against that wall, he had experienced an anger that he had never known before. Part of him even wished he'd had a chance to punch the man. He'd given his statement to the police officers who had arrived with the ambulance crew and had promised to call them when Hannah was up to talking, but it wasn't enough.

William wanted to know that Calvin Jones was going to spend some time in a cell for what he'd done to Hannah today. He wanted to know the man wouldn't be able to come after Hannah—or his wife—again. Unfortunately, the officers hadn't been able to reassure him.

Marion had given her report to the police before she'd been sent off to get her arm x-rayed. From what his office nurse had said, it seemed that Hannah had been trying to keep Calvin Jones from knowing that he was in the office. She'd tried to protect him; something he couldn't remember anyone else ever doing in his life. She'd taken on a man as strong as an ox for him. He would never forget that and he'd never forget the fear he'd felt when she'd lost consciousness.

William's mind had immediately imagined the worst, fearing that Hannah had sustained the same type of injury his mother had. What would he have done had she been critically injured? He'd been the neuro trauma doctor on call, but he would never have trusted himself to operate on her. Because no matter how much he could compartmentalize his emotions while he was in the operating room, there was no way he could have done that if Hannah had been his patient.

He took one more look at the CT before leaving the room. Thank goodness, it wasn't anything he had to worry about now. He was going to find the ER doctor and get the paperwork started to take Hannah home.

CHAPTER FOURTEEN

"Sit down, Momma," Lindsey said for the hundredth time as Hannah stood then quickly sank back down on the couch. It had been two days since she'd been attacked and still her daughter and William wouldn't let her do anything.

William had canceled his office visits today and had arranged for a colleague to make the rounds on his surgical patients. He didn't know it yet, but Hannah was going to assist him in the scheduled surgeries tomorrow. The ER doctor had cleared her to return to work and she wasn't about to miss a chance to be inside the OR.

With her headache now gone, there really wasn't any reason she couldn't get back to normal. Not that she was protesting their protectiveness. It felt nice to know that she had someone to take care of her for a change. With her down for the count, William had been glad to take over care of Lindsey. He'd even taken care of her carpool duties for the day.

"Will, what temperature does it say that the oven needs to be on?" Lindsey asked, pulling out a large round pan.

"Four fifty," he said as Avery's hands stretched out to touch the dough he had been meticulously rolling.

Reaching into a bowl, he picked out a slice of a sweet bell pepper and gave it to her to chew on. After one taste, Avery threw it to the floor. "Apparently she's not a fan of peppers."

"Try the pepperoni," Hannah said as she took in the mess the kitchen was becoming. For a man who was meticulous in the operating room, he was a disaster in the kitchen.

William put Avery in the high chair and handed her a slice of pepperoni. "Sit here for just a minute while I get the pizza in the oven."

"Ill, Ill," the little girl called when he crossed to the other side of the island.

"Ill?" he asked as he carefully took the dough from a wooden board and placed it on a round baking tray. "That's a new one."

"She's trying to say 'Will,' you dork," Lindsey said.

"Lindsey, don't call William a dork. It's not polite." Hannah had a hard time keeping the smile off her face.

"Forget about it, Lindsey. I can't have my sister going around calling me 'Ill.' What kind of name is that for a doctor?" William joked.

"It's better than Billy," Lindsey quipped as they began layering the meat and veggies they'd managed to agree on.

"Not by much," William said. "We'll have to work on that vocabulary of yours, little sister."

"Ill," Avery said, reaching for him again.

"Let me get the pie in the oven, then you can get

down," he said to Avery then turned to Hannah. "Isn't it time for her to start walking? She's been pulling up on things for a while now. Maybe I should check with the pediatrician…"

The doorbell rang and Lindsey bolted for it. "I'll get it," she called back to them.

"It's a little late for a delivery driver," William said, putting the pizza in the oven and setting the timer. "Maybe I should go see who it is."

"I'll go," Hannah said as she started to stand. She was starting to feel a little guilty. She really did feel better.

She looked over at the kitchen counter covered in flour. *Perhaps one more day of rest won't hurt.*

An odd feeling settled in his stomach. "Stay with Avery. I'll be right back," William said to Hannah.

There was no good reason for someone to be at the door at this time of night. There was only one person he had been expecting at his home. The text he had received from his father's lawyer earlier in the week had been sent to prepare him, but he had chosen to ignore it. With Hannah injured, he hadn't wanted to deal with anything that would upset her. And, he had to admit— even if it was just to himself—this was likely going to upset them all.

"Will, this woman says she's here to see Avery," Lindsey said when he entered the hallway, her arms crossed at her chest. He had seen that look on her mother's face often enough to know it always meant trouble. "Is she that aunt I heard you and Momma talking about—the one who thinks you can't take care of Avery?"

"Ms. Crane?" he asked the woman standing in the open doorway. His heart rate sped up as the woman nodded. Why was she here?

"Lindsey," Will said as he placed his arm around her shoulders, "this is Avery's great-aunt."

"I'm sorry it's so late, but I only just managed to make it to town and I couldn't wait to see Alison's little girl," the woman said as Lindsey slipped from under his arm and bolted to the great room.

She was dressed in tasteful but sensible clothes, reminding William of Avery's former nanny, Mrs. Adams. Though much older than his stepmother, he could see the resemblance.

"Please come in." William stepped back, welcoming her into his home.

He looked to the high chair where Avery had been just minutes before and found it empty.

"This is Hannah, Lindsey's mother." He introduced her as she joined them. "Hannah, this is Avery's great-aunt—" The oven timer went off. "Let me get that."

Hannah led the woman into the great room. "Please, have a seat," she said, surprising him with the control she seemed to have of her emotions. If the woman's arrival had upset her, Hannah sure wasn't showing it. "You must be tired. William says you raised Avery's mother. This must be so hard for you."

"Yes. I'm still in a bit of a shock, I'm afraid. Alison was so young. I didn't find out till the ship I was on made port, and by then I had missed the funeral. Of course, I wish I had been there for Avery. It's like history repeating itself. Though, Alison was much older when we lost her parents."

Ms. Crane looked around the room where toys covered the rug and a basket of clean clothes sat in a corner waiting to be folded and put away. By the look in her eyes, she was not impressed. What did the woman expect when she showed up unannounced?

William pushed a bowl to the side and set the hot pizza pan on the counter. Yes, the kitchen was a mess, too, but he wasn't going to apologize for it. "We're having homemade pizza for dinner if you would like to join us."

"That sounds nice, but I'm afraid I can't. Spicy food before bed just doesn't agree with me." She stood. "And as you said, it is getting late. I just wanted to spend a minute or two with the child."

"When was the last time you saw Avery?" Hannah asked, walking around to the side of the kitchen where he stood. She poked him in the side. He ignored her. He knew Alison's aunt was there to check him out, to judge how well he was caring for Avery. It wasn't like he could throw her out. He needed to show her that Avery was well and happy.

"The last time I visited Dallas was right after she was born. She was such a cute little thing. Alison was so proud of her," Ms. Crane said.

"She's a beautiful little girl and she's just crazy about her big brother," Hannah said.

"I'm sure she is, dear, but I'm also sure you can understand my concern for my Alison's only child. My niece would expect me to make sure that her daughter was being taken care of properly," she said. "There's only the two of us left in the family now that Alison is gone."

William looked at the woman and realized that, like him, she was all alone, except for Avery. He didn't have to imagine how lonely she might feel. He knew. He'd felt that way himself, though he'd convinced himself that he liked his life that way.

"Avery has already been put down for the night, but we'd love to have you over for dinner tomorrow night, if that would work for you?" Hannah said, turning on her Texas charm. She was up to something, but William wasn't sure exactly what.

The woman hesitated for a moment then nodded. "Tomorrow night would be lovely. It will give us a chance to talk about our plans for Avery."

After agreeing on a time for dinner the next night, William showed her out then waited until the car turned out of the driveway.

When he returned to the kitchen, he found Hannah surveying the room.

"You need to rest," he said, though he knew he was wasting his breath.

"We don't have time to rest. It would have been best if I'd invited her the night after, but I don't think we could have put her off that long," Hannah said as she started loading the dishwasher.

"She seems like a nice woman," he said.

"A nice woman that wants to talk about plans to take your sister away," Hannah retorted.

"You make it sound like we're going to war."

"What is more important than fighting for your child?" Hannah asked. "Go upstairs and get Lindsey and Avery. We have a dinner to prepare for. By the time she leaves tomorrow night, you'll have Avery's great-aunt singing your praises and putting your name in for father of the year."

"How about we just settle on convincing her that Avery is being properly taken care of?" William suggested as he left the room. Because if Avery's great-aunt really cared about her, it wouldn't matter if the floor was cluttered with toys or what the state of his kitchen was. The only thing that would really matter was that Avery was healthy and happy. Hopefully, the woman was smart enough to understand that.

"Lindsey, please open the door," William said as he knocked for the second time.

"Is that woman gone?" she asked, unlocking the door to let him in.

Avery was sitting on the floor playing with a stuffed unicorn he recognized as one of Lindsey's. Chewing on the stuffed animal's horn, his sister giggled up at him.

"She's not really going to try to take Avery away, is she?" Lindsey asked as she joined Avery on the floor.

He sat next to her and crossed his long legs. "No one is going to take Avery anywhere," he said and prayed that it was true. His lawyer had assured him that he had a strong case for keeping custody of his sister, unless Avery's great-aunt could show that the child was in danger or neglected, which certainly wasn't the case.

"Look, your momma has invited Ms. Crane over for

supper tomorrow night. She'll come and see how great Avery is doing and then she'll leave," William said. "But in the meantime, we need to go help your mother get things together for tomorrow night. Okay?"

"Okay. Let's go, Avery," Lindsey said to the little girl as William rose with her in his arms. "We'll show that great-aunt of yours just how great a dad William is, even though it's kind of weird that he's your brother, too."

William looked down at the young girl and laughed. Like daughter, like mother. The two of them had fought together since the day Lindsey was born. First to stay together and then just for Lindsey to stay alive. He couldn't think of any two people he'd rather have on his side.

CHAPTER FIFTEEN

THE TABLE WAS SET. The kids were bathed and dressed appropriately. There was not one piece of laundry in sight. The battlefield was ready for whatever Ms. Crane threw at them and still Hannah felt she wasn't ready. This was so important. They couldn't mess this up.

She looked over to where Avery stood holding on to the couch as she slowly made her way across to the lone toy on the far cushion. William had protested when Hannah had moved all the toys out of the room. He'd felt that Avery's aunt needed to see the real environment that they had made for Avery. But she had seen the way the woman had looked at the disarray of the great room the night before.

"How old was Alison when she went to live with her aunt?" Hannah asked him, once again straightening one of the placemats. Should she have gone with the white linen she had found in the dining room cabinet, or were the dark blue ones they usually used okay? It had seemed a bit much to bring out all the white linen for the cozy family meal they were about to host.

"Nine? Ten? I'm not sure. But I know that Alison

lived with her for many years. Why?" William asked as he knotted his tie.

"Did her aunt have any children of her own?" Hannah she straightened another place setting.

"I don't think so. If she did, the lawyers didn't say anything about them when I asked for information on Alison's family. As far as I know, it was only the two of them after the death of Alison's parents. Is that important?" he queried.

"It just seemed to me that she looked awfully shocked at the mess in the room last night. If she'd ever raised a toddler, she'd have known to expect the mess, wouldn't she?" Hannah began checking the silverware for water spots.

"I can tell you that I had no idea that such a small child could create such a mess, let alone how much garbage," William said. "You might not realize it, but I've always been a bit of a neat freak."

She rolled her eyes and he laughed. He might have relaxed his standards on housekeeping in the house now that Avery was there, but he hadn't changed one bit at work.

The doorbell rang.

"It's showtime," Hannah said as they heard Lindsey holler that she would get the door.

William picked Avery up and started toward the door, but Hannah held him back. "Let her do it. She knows how important tonight is for you. She'll behave."

"We are so happy that you could join us tonight," she heard her daughter say in her most adult-sounding voice as she came into the great room, Ms. Crane at her side.

"It was lovely to be invited. You have a very charming daughter, Hannah. You must be very proud of her. Most young people today have no manners," Ms. Crane said.

"Thank you. I am very proud of my daughter," Hannah said. Not that the young girl dressed in a soft pink shirt and black skirt, resembled the daughter she was used to. "And I'm sure you know this little girl."

Ms. Crane reached out to take Avery and Hannah reluctantly released her. She knew they had to make a point of welcoming Avery's great-aunt, but the mere act of handing over the little girl put Hannah's mother instincts on high alert. She tamped down her need to protect Avery.

Dressed in a butter-yellow sundress, her hair combed into soft, dark curls, the child looked like an angel. "Oh, you poor child. I know you must miss your mommy so much," her great-aunt said as tears appeared in her eyes. "I'm sorry," she said to William and Hannah. "It's still so hard for me to accept that Alison is gone. She was so young."

"It's okay," William responded. "We understand."

"Of course. It's a loss for both of us," she said to William. There was nothing as powerful as grief to forge a bond between two people.

Avery studied the woman holding her with dark, curious eyes. Was there something about her that reminded Avery of her mother? Suddenly she held her two chubby hands out. "Ill," she said, reaching for William.

"It's okay, baby girl. This is your momma's aunt," William soothed as he patted Avery's back. "Ms. Crane, if you wouldn't mind, would you put Avery in her high chair? I'm just going to help get the food on the table."

While not as enjoyable or relaxed a meal as he'd come to expect with Lindsey's persistent questions and Avery's boisterous laughter, William felt confident they were making an impression Ms. Crane—or "Maria" as she had asked them to call her. While they'd danced around the subject of Avery's future during the meal, she'd asked questions about William's practice and how the little girl had settled into her childcare.

"And how about you, Hannah? I take it that you've worked with other children, besides your daughter, of course?" The woman gave Lindsey a smile. "I'm sure William checked your references before you were hired."

Realizing the misunderstanding, William answered before Hannah. "I'm sorry, Maria. I think there's a bit of a misunderstanding. Hannah's not a nanny."

"I'm a nurse, Maria. I'm actually finishing my classes for my nurse practitioner's license this month," Hannah said.

"I'm sorry. I didn't realize that the two of you were involved. I just assumed that William would have to have someone living here to help with Avery," Maria said.

"Hannah's a good friend who agreed to help me till I could get comfortable with taking care of Avery and balancing it with my work. She's been a great teacher. I don't know what I would have done without her," William said. He'd never said words that were any truer.

"Well, that was so nice of you, Hannah," Maria said as she turned to her. "And what an exciting time for you. What are your plans, dear?"

"I'm not sure yet. My goal is to work with one of the neurology practices in town," Hannah told her. "I've been so busy with my course that I haven't had time to start putting in any applications, though."

"Well, I do hope things work out for you, and I so appreciate the care you've given Avery. I'm sure William will miss your help," Maria said. "I have to admit that, after last night, I had my doubts. But still, William, it has to have been hard having Avery to look after while still maintaining your practice. Are you sure that this is what you want? You're a young man. You need to think about starting a family of your own. Won't Avery be a problem? Not every woman wants to take on another woman's child."

The anger he felt every time someone tried to pressure him into a future they insisted he needed rose again. "I think we're talking about two different things, Maria. My care for my baby sister is the most important thing in my life. I can provide everything Avery needs on my own. We don't need anyone else. Yes, my life has changed. So has Avery's. But we're going to make it."

The table went quiet. Even Avery stopped her jabbering for a moment.

He heard a giggle and looked over just in time to see Avery throw one of the carrots on her plate at Lindsey. "Avery, we don't throw our food," he said calmly.

Rising to take his sister out of her high chair, he announced, "I'm going to take her upstairs. If you'll excuse me, I'll get her ready for bed. It's well past her bedtime and she'll be fussy in the morning if she doesn't get enough sleep. I'll bring her down in a few minutes to say good-night."

"May I be excused, too?" Lindsey asked her mother. "I need to get back to my homework."

Hannah nodded then sat back and looked at Maria. "You have to understand," she began, "how hard William has worked to make a place in his life for Avery. When I first came here, he was a mess. But he was determined to do right by Avery. You'll never find a man as dedicated to a child as he is to his sister. I believe that Avery is good for him, and he is definitely good for her. I can't say I understand your loss, but don't let your sorrow over losing Alison get confused with what is best for Avery."

"But I miss Alison so much," the older woman said, her voice quivering with emotion. "I just want to make sure that her daughter is taken care of properly. She's all I have left."

Hannah took Maria's hand in hers. "You don't need to worry. I promise you, there's not another person in this world who wants that more than William. She's safe with him, Maria. She's all he has, too. And he'll always protect her. With his life, if it should come to that."

Hannah quietly stood and began clearing the table, surprised when Maria asked if she could help.

The woman barely spoke while they worked.

"I didn't mean to imply that William wasn't capable of taking care of Avery," she finally said as she helped load the dishwasher. "I realize times have changed and there are a lot of single men that are responsible for their children. It's just that, from what my niece said, I didn't think William would be one of those men."

"What did Alison say that made you think that?" Hannah asked. She felt her temper begin to flair. William's stepmother had barely known him.

"It wasn't that she said anything bad. It's just that I inquired about him when I came down to see Avery and Alison told me she'd hardly even met him. She said that he seemed to prefer his life by himself…

"I thought that when I arrived in town I would find someone glad to give over the responsibility of my great-niece. Instead, I find a man who has embraced his new life," Maria said. "While I admit I'm a bit sad that I won't be taking Avery home with me, I'm glad they're doing well together. I would never want to cause them any trouble."

Hannah felt the knots she'd had in her stomach all night relax. He'd done it! Maria wouldn't be giving William any problems as far as Avery's custody was concerned.

"Well, we're ready for bedtime now. I thought you might want to say good-night to her before you left," William said as he came up behind them. The smile on his face made it clear he had heard Maria's words.

"You are such a precious child," the woman told Avery as she hugged the toddler to her. As if to comfort the woman, Avery patted her back with one chubby little hand.

"It's okay, little one. You're in good hands," Maria

said then looked at William. "I would like to come see her whenever I can get here to visit."

"You're always welcome," William assured her as he took Avery back into his arms. "She'll need you to tell her about her mother when she gets older."

Assured of her welcome the next time she was in town, William and Avery showed Maria out while Hannah headed upstairs to check on Lindsey.

Mingled in with the happiness she felt for William and Avery was the knowledge that they wouldn't need her anymore. William was ready to go it on his own now. Hannah just needed to find the strength to leave him. Her job here was done.

William laid a sleeping Avery down then sat on the chair beside her bed and looked around the room. It was hard for him to remember how the place had looked before it had become Avery's nursery. Had it only been a few months since Mrs. Adams had pushed the little girl into his arms then driven away? His life had changed so much since then. First with the arrival of Avery and then with Hannah and Lindsey. His quiet, orderly sanctuary had quickly turned into a loud, disorderly home. And the surprising thing was, he'd loved every minute of it.

He saw that Lindsey's light was still on as he left Avery's room and knocked on her door. "May I come in?"

"Sure," Lindsey said. She was sitting cross-legged on her bed with books and clothes piled around her.

"Having trouble sleeping?" he asked from the doorway.

"Did you mean it when you said you didn't need anyone besides Avery?" the little girl asked.

Was that really what he had said? He'd wanted Maria to know that he could take care of Avery. He hadn't meant to make Lindsey feel as if she didn't matter to him. If anything, having Hannah and Lindsey in the house had made him see that he did need other people. But he could tell by the sadness in her eyes, eyes so like her mother's, that he had hurt her. "I didn't mean that I don't care about you and your mother. I just meant that I could take care of Avery on my own."

"So you don't need me and Momma to help with Avery anymore? That means it's time for us to leave," Lindsey said, her whole attention on him as he crossed the room.

"What's this?" he asked as he picked up a large album from the bed. Opening it, he saw pictures of houses cut from magazines and papers. Flipping through, he could see where the first pictures had been of small cottages that had been gradually advanced to pictures of full-size houses.

"That's our wish book—mine and Momma's. We've had it as long as I can remember. When we see a picture of a house we like, we put it in the album. Momma says that soon we'll be able to have a house of our own, just like one of these," she said as she turned the page to a nice brick house with a fenced-in yard. "Then she says I can have a dog."

William could see how much this meant to both Lindsey and her mother. Hannah had worked hard to make it as a single mother. She had a dream of providing a home for her daughter. A dream from the album that spoke of many nights combing through magazines looking for that special place for the two of them and she had almost reached that point in her career when it would be possible. Lindsey was right. There wasn't any reason for them to stay now. He'd asked Hannah to teach him how to take care of his sister and she had. That had been the agreement. He couldn't hold her here any longer.

CHAPTER SIXTEEN

IT HAD BEEN a week since they had moved out and William didn't know how much more of this quiet house he could take. He'd marked off each day on the calendar Hannah had insisted they hang on the refrigerator. Each day he'd missed them a little bit more until now there was a physical pain in his chest.

He went through the motions at work, his office seeming empty now that Hannah had also completed her time with him. Each afternoon he came home with Avery and did his best to keep his mood as upbeat as possible for his sister. Each night he tossed in his bed and wished that Hannah was beside him.

Where was that peace he had felt when his house had been quiet and orderly? He'd been happy with his life before.

He'd made it clear to Hannah from the beginning that he wasn't one of those men who believed he had to have a woman in his life to complete him. But that had been before he'd realized what a lonely existence his life was without Hannah and Lindsey. He'd been stubborn and had needed to prove to himself that he didn't need someone to help him with Avery. He'd had to prove that he wasn't like his father, that he didn't always need a woman just to exist.

"We're going to be okay," he told his little sister while trying to convince himself that it was true. "Let's get your toys out and play."

He reached into the toy box that he and Hannah had moved from the nursery into the great room and pulled out a stuffed unicorn. Lindsey must have left it. What if she was looking for it? Maybe he should call Hannah to let her know it was here. Or better still, maybe he should drop it off tomorrow on his way home from work.

"You're pitiful," he said to himself. He held the unicorn out for his sister to take and was surprised when Avery let go of the chair she had been holding on to and took a step toward him. He held his breath. Her little mouth was closed tight and her eyes were fixed on him as she took another step.

"You're doing it, baby girl."

Avery smiled at him, clapped her hands together then fell back on her diaper-padded bottom. Her lips quivered and her eyes filled with tears.

"It's okay. You are amazing." William reached out and took her into his arms. He was so lucky that he had been there for this. He sobered. Hannah should have been there with him. He looked down at Avery. "Is there any chance you're up for an encore?"

Someone knocked on her door and Hannah pushed her computer to the side. Ever since she and Lindsey had returned to their apartment, her neighbors had been stopping by to see them. She had been glad to catch up with each of them, but wasn't up to making small talk right now. She had felt empty ever since she and Lindsey had packed up their car at William's and headed home. It was if she had left some part of herself behind, and she was pretty sure that it was her heart.

"William?" she said before she stepped back so that he and Avery could enter. She immediately took Avery into her arms, she had missed the little girl so much.

"You won't believe what happened. She took two steps," William said, dropping the diaper bag on the living room floor.

"Really? She was so close before I left." And by leaving when she had, she had missed it.

"Watch." William took Avery out of her arms, stood her against the couch and then held out his hands to her. The toddler stared at him, dropped to the floor and crawled to the two of them.

Hannah started to laugh at the crestfallen look on his face. "She's not a trick puppy dog. She's going to walk when she's ready. Besides, she has a truckload of your Cooper stubbornness in her."

The joy left William's eyes and his voice turned somber. "Have you ever thought that there was something that you didn't like, but when you finally tried it, you found it wasn't so bad, after all? Maybe even more than that. Maybe you found out that you really couldn't live without it?"

"Like broccoli?" Hannah asked. She wasn't sure where this conversation was going, but she didn't care. Just having him to talk to was enough.

"Yeah, like broccoli. It looks all green and strange before you taste it, then you put some cheese sauce on it—because who doesn't like cheese sauce?—and you find out it's really quite good." William turned away from her then turned back around. "I'm not very good at all of this emotional stuff. I'm going to mess up."

Hannah held her breath. He was talking in terms of the future. "We all mess up, William. It's part of life."

"I've spent most of my life convincing myself that I didn't need anyone else in my life. I thought I was being strong taking on the world by myself. But now I know I was just too scared to take a chance on someone caring about me," William said.

For a moment, Hannah was confused. While he thought he was describing himself, he could have been describing her just, as well. She had left him because she had been too scared that he would turn away from her if she told him how she felt.

"When I told Maria that I didn't need anyone else, I was lying," he said as he moved closer and brushed his fingers down her face. "I do need you, Hannah. I need both you and Lindsey."

Hannah froze in place. She'd prepared herself to never feel his touch again and now he was offering her so much more. She had to make a decision. She could put herself out there with William and risk getting hurt. Or she could let fear keep her from what she wanted the most.

"I love—"

"No—" he sealed her lips with his before raising his head to look her in the eyes "—I want to say it first. I love you, Hannah. I love you with every beat of my heart."

"And that family you swore you'd never want? You seemed pretty adamant that family life wasn't for you," she said.

"What did I know? I'm just a simple brain surgeon who found out that, sometimes, if you're lucky, some unexpected miracle comes along that changes your whole life."

He brushed his lips against hers again. "That's what you are to me. You are my unexpected family."

EPILOGUE

HANNAH PUSHED THE side door from the garage open and placed the stack of books on the kitchen counter. The house was quiet and some of the excitement she had felt on her drive home disappeared. She'd known that William had planned to take Lindsey to her riding lesson with Sarah after work, but when she had called to tell him her good news, she'd hoped that he would cancel Lindsey's lesson so they all could celebrate together tonight.

Taking a bottle out of the refrigerator, she'd started to head upstairs to change when she heard a giggle she would recognize anywhere. It was coming from the door that led outside. Stepping through it, she was stunned to see the group of people gathered in their backyard.

"What are you doing?" Hannah asked as she rubbed the small, round bump of her abdomen and watched Avery chase Lindsey across the yard.

"We're having a celebration, of course," William said, turning the steaks he was cooking on the grill.

"You did all this for me?" she asked, stunned he'd

pulled this together so quickly. It had only been this morning that she'd gotten the call that she had been accepted into Houston University's medical school program.

Suddenly, she was surrounded by her friends—some from work and others from her college classes—all wanting to congratulate her. She couldn't ever remember having a party planned just for her. Except for her wedding reception, of course.

"So, William tells me the plan is for you two to have a joint practice," Sarah said when the others had moved on to where William was passing out the steaks. "I'm not going to lie. It takes a lot to coordinate your work life with your family life when you're in the healthcare field, but I know you can do it."

"William's been very supportive. And Lindsey, too, of course. She can't wait to take care of a little brother. With those two behind me, I know it will all work out," Hannah told Sarah as they joined the others at the picnic table. As her friend went to join David, Hannah stopped to look across the backyard.

"What are you thinking?" William asked as he came up behind her and pulled her back against him.

"Just that I was right. This home was definitely meant for a family," she said, leaning into him and thinking about the man who had sworn he hadn't needed anyone in his life.

He had changed so much since that day.

They had both changed as they'd learned to trust each other, that depending on one another didn't make them weak. It made them stronger.

"No, this home wasn't meant for a family." William he rested his hands over their growing child. "It was meant for ours."

* * * * *

MILLS & BOON

Coming next month

THE VET'S UNEXPECTED HERO
Traci Douglass

Lucy looked up at Jackson. "He's trained to be a therapy dog. He knows better than to jump up on people like that."

"Really. It's okay. I'm used to it. Like I said, some people find me irresistible." Jackson gave her a charmingly crooked, wry smile she felt all the way to her toes.

Oh boy. Not good. Not good at all.

Lucy needed something, anything, to distract herself from her unwanted awareness of this man. "Fine. Whatever. Good for you if people find you irresistible. I don't. I mean, there's nothing wrong with you, but—"

He crossed his arms, his smile widening as she babbled away like an idiot.

Her cheeks felt hotter than Hades now, and the more he teased her, the more frazzled she got.

Jackson studied her, his expression serious.

Flustered, Lucy forgot to be nervous and just laughed, easing some of her inner tension. She shrugged and stared down at her toes.

"Well, it was nice to meet you, Lucy Miller," he said, clasping his hands atop the table. Nice hands. Long, tapered fingers, well-kept nails. Strong hands. Capable hands. He was a paramedic, after all. He saved people. A small spark of warmth burst inside her. He'd certainly saved her just now, from dying from terminal embarrassment. "I wish I'd known earlier you were going to be here. I'd have brought a copy of the required binder with the emergency response team plan for you. I don't have a spare with me now, but if you give me your address, I'm happy to run one by your place on Big Pine Key tomorrow. It's my day off."

"Oh…uh…" Sitting beside him in the conference room was disturbing enough to her equilibrium. The thought of him at her compound had her quaking in her tennis shoes. "That's okay. Give it to Stacy and she can bring it to me. Or I can swing by the hospital and pick it up." She pulled a clean sheet of paper from her legal pad and picked up her red pen. "Just tell me what time would be best."

Jackson frowned. "It's really no problem, and it would be more convenient for me to drop it off. I'll be in your area anyway. Unless there's some reason you don't want me there?"

An awkward silence fell between them as they studied each other.

She couldn't help wondering what it might feel like to slide her fingers through his short black hair, learning its texture and temperament. The fluorescent overhead lights gleamed off his high cheekbones and there was a hint of dark stubble on his firm jaw. His lips were full and firm, with a slight tip to the outer corners that gave him a perpetual smirk, like everything amused him.

"Don't worry, I won't overstay my welcome. Promise. I'll Google your address," he said at last. Jackson stood and picked up his papers but didn't hold out his hand this time. The smile was there again though, still charming, too. "See you tomorrow, Lucy Miller."

Continue reading
THE VET'S UNEXPECTED HERO
Traci Douglass

Available next month
www.millsandboon.co.uk

COMING SOON!

We really hope you enjoyed reading this book.
If you're looking for more romance, be sure to
head to the shops when new books are
available on

Thursday 27th May

To see which titles are coming soon, please visit

millsandboon.co.uk/nextmonth

LET'S TALK
Romance

For exclusive extracts, competitions and special offers, find us online:

f facebook.com/millsandboon

🐦 @MillsandBoon

📷 @MillsandBoonUK

Get in touch on 01413 063232

For all the latest titles coming soon, visit
millsandboon.co.uk/nextmonth

MILLS & BOON

THE HEART OF ROMANCE

A ROMANCE FOR EVERY READER

MODERN

Prepare to be swept off your feet by sophisticated, sexy and seductive heroes, in some of the world's most glamourous and romantic locations, where power and passion collide.

HISTORICAL

Escape with historical heroes from time gone by. Whether your passion is for wicked Regency Rakes, muscled Vikings or rugged Highlanders, awa the romance of the past.

MEDICAL

Set your pulse racing with dedicated, delectable doctors in the high-pressure world of medicine, where emotions run high and passion, comfort a love are the best medicine.

True Love

Celebrate true love with tender stories of heartfelt romance, from the rush of falling in love to the joy a new baby can bring, and a focus on th emotional heart of a relationship.

Desire

Indulge in secrets and scandal, intense drama and plenty of sizzling hot action with powerful and passionate heroes who have it all: wealth, status good looks…everything but the right woman.

HEROES

Experience all the excitement of a gripping thriller, with an intense romance at its heart. Resourceful, true-to-life women and strong, fearless m face danger and desire - a killer combination!

To see which titles are coming soon, please visit

millsandboon.co.uk/nextmonth